cursed

BENEDICT JACKA

ACE BOOKS, NEW YORK

THE BERKLEY PUBLISHING GROUP
Published by the Penguin Group
Penguin Group (USA) Inc.
375 Hudson Street, New York, New York 10014, USA

Penguin Group (Canada), 90 Eglinton Avenue East, Suite 700, Toronto, Ontario M4P 2Y3, Canada
(a division of Pearson Penguin Canada Inc.) • Penguin Books Ltd., 80 Strand, London WC2R 0RL,
England • Penguin Group Ireland, 25 St. Stephen's Green, Dublin 2, Ireland (a division of Penguin
Books Ltd.) • Penguin Group (Australia), 250 Camberwell Road, Camberwell, Victoria 3124, Australia
(a division of Pearson Australia Group Pty. Ltd.) • Penguin Books India Pvt. Ltd., 11 Community
Centre, Panchsheel Park, New Delhi—110 017, India • Penguin Group (NZ), 67 Apollo Drive,
Rosedale, Auckland 0632, New Zealand (a division of Pearson New Zealand Ltd.) • Penguin Books
(South Africa) (Pty.) Ltd., 24 Sturdee Avenue, Rosebank, Johannesburg 2196, South Africa

Penguin Books Ltd., Registered Offices: 80 Strand, London WC2R 0RL, England

This is a work of fiction. Names, characters, places, and incidents either are the product of the author's
imagination or are used fictitiously, and any resemblance to actual persons, living or dead, business
establishments, events, or locales is entirely coincidental. The publisher does not have any control over
and does not assume any responsibility for author or third-party websites or their content.

CURSED

An Ace Book / published by arrangement with the author

PUBLISHING HISTORY
Ace mass-market edition / June 2012

Copyright © 2012 by Benedict Jacka.
Excerpt from *Taken* by Benedict Jacka copyright © 2012 by Benedict Jacka.
Cover photographs: Tower Bridge © Paul Knight / Trevillion;
sparkler © Patrycja Mueller / Shutterstock.
Cover design by Judith Lagerman.
Interior text design by Laura K. Corless.

ISBN: 978-1-937007-59-1

ACE
Ace Books are published by The Berkley Publishing Group,
a division of Penguin Group (USA) Inc.,
375 Hudson Street, New York, New York 10014.
ACE and the "A" design are trademarks of Penguin Group (USA) Inc.

PRINTED IN THE UNITED STATES OF AMERICA

10 9 8 7 6 5 4 3 2 1

cursed

chapter 1

The old factory was the kind of place you only find in the very worst parts of big cities. Its bricks had once been red, but years of grime and pollution had darkened them to a brownish-grey. The outer wall was topped with ragged coils of razor wire. The wire was rusted and full of holes that hadn't been repaired in years, as if the owners had decided that they couldn't keep the burglars out but might at least be able to give them tetanus on the way in.

The rest of the dead-end street was dark, empty-looking buildings and shops hiding behind steel security gratings. The gratings were covered in graffiti and it was hard to tell whether the businesses locked behind them were still open or whether they'd been abandoned too. The only shop that looked in good shape carried the triple-sphere sign of a pawnbroker's. Behind the shops and factory was the sort of council estate where the muggers use broken bottles because they can't afford knives.

It was only eleven o'clock and the rest of London was filled with the sounds of the city, but on the street nothing moved. The road was empty except for parked cars. Half of them were missing wheels, windows, or both, and none would have looked out of place in a junkyard—except for the minivan parked at the top of the street. Its polished black paint melted into the shadows, with the orange glow from the streetlights picking out the silver hubcaps and lights along with the Mercedes symbol mounted on the grill. I rolled my eyes when I saw it. My senses told me there was no immediate danger but I stayed in the shadows of the alley and scanned the street for another minute before walking out towards the van.

Most of the streetlights were broken and the ones still working were patchy. I walked the street's length cloaked in darkness, with only the occasional circle of orange piercing the gloom. Looking over my shoulder I could see the pillars of light of the Canary Wharf skyscrapers, visible over the rooftops. We were close to the river, even if I couldn't see it, and as I walked I heard the mournful sound of a boat's horn echoing off the water. Ragged clouds covered most of the sky, their cover blending with the glow of the streetlights to hide the stars.

As I reached the van one of the front windows slid down, and the street was quiet enough that I could hear the purr of the motor. I stopped by the door and looked at the man sitting inside. "Could you possibly have made it any more obvious?"

My name is Alex Verus. I'm a mage, a diviner. In mage terms I'm unaligned, which means I'm not affiliated with the Council (the main Light power block) but don't count myself as a Dark mage either. Although I'm not part of the Council I do freelance jobs for them, like this one. The man in the passenger seat to whom I was talking was my contact with the Council, a mage named Talisid, and he gave me a patient nod. "Verus."

"Good to see you." I looked the van up and down. "Seriously, a Mercedes? Did you get it waxed, too?"

"If you're concerned about stealth," Talisid said, "perhaps we shouldn't be talking in the open?"

Talisid is a man in his forties, shorter than average, with greying hair receding from a balding head. He always seems to be wearing the same understated business suit, but with a sort of steadiness that suggests he might be more than meets the eye. I'd met him in the spring, at a ball in Canary Wharf where he'd offered me a job. Things didn't exactly go to plan, but Talisid had held up his end of the bargain, and when he'd asked for my help tonight I'd agreed. I stepped back and watched as the passengers piled out of the van. Talisid was first and following him was a tall, thin man with a long face like a greyhound, who gave me a nod. His name was Ilmarin, an air mage. I didn't recognise the next three but I hadn't expected to; their guns marked them as Council security.

"Still planning to take the lead?" Talisid asked me quietly as the security team went through their preparations, checking rifles and headsets.

"That's what I'm here for."

"It's also what *they're* here for," Talisid pointed out. "It's their line of work."

I almost smiled. When Talisid had called me yesterday and given me the briefing, he'd assumed I'd be staying at the tail end of the formation, maybe all the way back in the van. He was offering me another chance to back out. But there was another message in there too, which wasn't so funny: the security men were expendable and I wasn't. "I'm not going to be much use from a hundred yards back," I said. "I'll give you all the warning you need, but I need a good view."

Talisid held up a hand in surrender. "All right. You'll be on point with Garrick. We'll move on your signal."

The man Talisid had nodded towards was the one who'd been in the driver's seat, now standing a little apart from the others. He was tall, with short sandy hair and an athlete's build, strong and fast. He was wearing black body armour with a high-tech look, along with dark combat fatigues, black gloves and boots, and a webbing belt that held a handgun, a machine pistol, a knife, and half a dozen metal cylinders that looked suspiciously like grenades. A second pistol rested in an ankle holster, and he carried a weapon in a sling that looked like a cross between a submachine gun and an assault rifle. He watched me with calm blue eyes as I walked up. "Garrick?" I asked.

Garrick nodded and spoke in a deep voice. "What's the layout?"

"I'll tell you once we get inside."

"Going with Talisid?"

"With you."

Garrick raised an eyebrow and looked me up and down. I was wearing combat trousers, black sneakers, a belt with a few things hooked into it, and a light fleece. If Garrick looked like something out of a military thriller, I looked like an amateur camper. "I'm flattered," Garrick said, "but you're not my type."

"I'm your recon," I said.

"That's nice," Garrick said. "You can do it from the van."

"I'm not going to be in the van."

"This is a combat mission," Garrick said patiently. "We don't have time to babysit."

A lot of people think diviners are useless in a fight. All in all it helps me more than it hurts me, but it's still a bit of a nuisance when you want to be taken seriously. "I'll be the one doing the babysitting," I said. "Those guns won't do much good if this thing takes your head off from behind."

I expected Garrick to get annoyed but he only gave me a look of mild inquiry. "What are you going to do? Punch it?"

"I'm going to tell you exactly where it is and what it's doing," I said. "If you can't figure out a way to beat this thing with that going for you, then you can back off and let us handle it."

Garrick studied me a moment longer, then shrugged. "Your funeral." He turned to the other men. "Let's move."

. . . .

The inside of the factory was pitch-black. The power had been turned off a long time ago and the lights that hadn't been smashed or lost their bulbs were dark. Corridors were cluttered with old machinery and pieces of junk that had been piled up and left to decay, forcing us to pick a winding path through the obstacles and making it difficult to get a clear line of sight. The air smelt of dust and rusted metal.

The creature we were hunting was called a barghest: a shapeshifter that can take the form of either a human or a great wolflike dog. They've got preternatural speed and strength, and they're difficult to detect with normal or magical senses. Or so the stories say; I've never met one. But all the sources agreed that the creatures killed with claws and teeth, making these sort of dark, cramped quarters the absolute worst place to fight one. There were too many possible hiding places, too many ways the creature could lie in wait to attack from behind.

Of course, that was the reason Talisid had brought me along.

To my eyes, the factory existed on two levels. There was the present, a world of darkness and shadow, broken only by the torches in my hand and on Garrick's rifle, looming obstacles blocking our path and the threat of danger around every corner. But overlaid upon that was a second world, a branching web of lines of glowing white light, the web branching over and over again through four dimensions, multiplying into thousands and millions of thinning wisps, every one a possible future. The futures of the corridor and the objects within it were fixed and solid, while my and Garrick's futures were a constantly shifting web, flickering and twisting with every moment.

Looking through the futures I saw my possible actions,

and their consequences. I saw myself stepping on the loose piece of scrap metal in front of me, saw myself tripping and falling, and corrected my movements to avoid it. As I did, the future in which I fell thinned to nothingness, never to exist, and the futures of me stepping around it brightened in its place. By seeing the future, I decided; as I decided, the future changed, and new futures replaced those never to happen. To anyone watching, it looks like pure fluke; every step in the right place, every hazard avoided without seeming to notice. But the obstacles were just a detail. Most of my attention was on the near and middle future, watching for the flurry of movement and weapons fire that would signal an attack. As long as I was paying attention, nothing in this factory could surprise us; long before anything got into position for an ambush, I could see it and give warning.

This was why Talisid had wanted me along. Just by being here, I could bring the chances of things going seriously wrong down to almost zero. Knowledge can't win a battle, but it's one hell of a force multiplier.

Something caught my attention as we passed through a doorway, and I signalled for Garrick to stop. He gave me a look but held up his hand and I heard the main body of the group halt behind us. I crouched and brushed a hand across the dusty floor, feeling the chill of the concrete.

"What is it?" Garrick said at last.

"Someone forced this door," I said, keeping my voice quiet. "Not long ago either."

"Could have been the barghest."

I held up a broken link of chain. The outside was rusted but the edge where it had been broken glinted in Garrick's torch. "Not unless our barghest uses bolt cutters."

Garrick raised an eyebrow and we moved on. I didn't mention the second thing that had been out of place: The rest of the chain had been taken away.

We moved deeper into the factory. Garrick and I were

on point with two of the security men ten paces behind. Talisid and Ilmarin walked in the centre of the formation, the last of the Council security bringing up the rear. When I sensed that the barghest was near, I was to withdraw and let the mages and soldiers move up into a combat formation, ready to take it by surprise. At least, that was the plan.

Things weren't going to plan. By now I should have sensed where and how the fight was going to start. Looking forward into the future, I could see us searching every room of the factory, yet there wasn't any sign of combat. In fact, I couldn't see *any* future in which *any* of us got into combat. I could feel the men behind us growing tense; they knew something was wrong. The only one who seemed unconcerned was Garrick, radiating relaxed confidence. Had Talisid's information been wrong? He'd been certain this was the place . . .

Around the next corner was a bigger room with a high ceiling and again I signalled for the others to stop. I closed my eyes and concentrated. Searching for combat wasn't working. Instead I started following the paths of our group through the timeline, looking to see what we would find. Something in the next chamber would occupy everyone's attention, and I looked more closely to see what it was . . .

And suddenly I knew why there wasn't going to be any fighting tonight. I straightened with a noise of disgust and called back to Talisid, no longer making any effort to keep my voice down. "It's a bust."

There was a pause, then I heard Talisid answer. "What's wrong?"

"We came here for nothing," I said. "Somebody beat us to it." I walked around the corner and out onto the factory floor.

Most of the machinery on the floor looked to have been removed or cannibalised for parts long ago, but a few pieces were still rusting in the gloom, piles of rubbish in between. My torch cast only a weak glow in the darkness, the beam of light disappearing up into the wide-open ceiling, and my footsteps echoed in the silence as I picked my way through broken boards and half-full plastic bags. The smell of dust and old metal was stronger here, this time with something underneath it that made my nose twitch.

The barghest was lying in the centre of the room, and it was dead. With its life gone, it looked like a grey-brown dog, big but not unnaturally so. It was lying on its side, eyes closed, with no blood or visible wounds. There was no smell of decay; it obviously hadn't been there long.

The others moved up into the room, following me. Garrick came up to my side. Although his weapon was lowered, his eyes kept moving, checking the corners and upper levels of the room. Only once he'd swept the area did he look down at the body. "Doesn't look like much."

"Not any more it's not."

The next two security men reached us, followed by Talisid and Ilmarin, and we formed a circle around the creature. They made a lot more noise than Garrick, as if they didn't know where to place their feet. "Well," Talisid said at last.

"It's dead?" Ilmarin asked me.

"It's not getting up any time in the next few years," I said. "Yeah, it's dead."

"Correct me if I'm wrong," Garrick said, "but I thought the mission was to kill this thing."

"Looks like someone else had the same idea."

"Can't find any wounds," Ilmarin said. Air mages are great at sensing movement but not so good with objects. "Verus, any idea what killed it?"

I'd been looking through the futures of me searching the body of this thing, watching myself rolling it over and running my hands through its fur. All I'd found was that it was heavy and smelt bad. Actually, I didn't need my magic to notice that it smelt bad. "No wounds, no blood. Looks like it just dropped dead."

"Death magic?"

"Maybe. Anything from the living family could do it."

Talisid had been studying the body; now he looked at me. "Is there any danger in splitting up?"

I looked through the futures for a few seconds, then shook my head. "This place is a graveyard. The only way anyone's going to get hurt is if they fall off the catwalks."

Talisid nodded and turned to the others. "Spread out and search in pairs. Look for anything unusual." Although he didn't raise his voice, there was a note of command that assumed he would be obeyed. "Check in every ten minutes and we'll meet back here in an hour."

ıııııııı

Somehow or other I ended up with Garrick. We worked our way through the factory's ground floor, searching methodically.

The bodies of the barghest's victims were in a side room off from the factory floor. There were seven, in varying states of decay. I didn't look too closely.

"Had an appetite," Garrick remarked once we'd left the room and called it in.

"That's why we came," I said. I was trying not to think about the corpses.

"Really?" Garrick looked mildly interested. "My contract was to make sure it was dead."

"Looks like someone did your job for you."

Garrick shrugged. "I get paid the same either way." He gave me a glance. "So how far into the future can you see?"

"Depends."

"On what?"

I returned Garrick's gaze. "On who's asking."

Garrick looked back at me, then gave a very slight smile. It made me think of an amused wolf.

I went back to the factory floor and found Talisid. "The bodies are in the second room off the back corridor. Nothing else worth checking."

Talisid nodded. "I've called in the cleanup crew. You may as well take off."

I looked at the barghest's body, still undisturbed amidst the rubble. "Sorry I couldn't help more."

Talisid shrugged. "The problem's been dealt with."

"Even though we didn't do anything?"

"Does it matter?" Talisid said. "There'll be no more killings and we took no losses." He smiled slightly. "I'd call this good enough."

I sighed. "I guess you're right. Did you find anything else?"

Talisid's smile faded into a frown. "Yes. Scorch marks on the walls and signs of weapons fire. Several places."

I looked at Talisid. "A battle?"

"It seems that way."

I nodded at the barghest. "But that thing wasn't burnt or shot."

"Not as far as we can tell."

"So what happened here?"

Talisid surveyed the dark room, sweeping his gaze over the rusting factory floor. With everyone else gone the place looked like it had been abandoned for a hundred years, and once we left there would be no trace of our visit but for footprints. This was no place for living people, not anymore. "We'll probably never know," Talisid said at last, and gave me a nod. "Good night, Verus."

〰〰〰〰〰

I left the factory, passed Talisid's new Mercedes, and turned right at the corner of the street. I walked half a block, turned back towards the river again, then slipped down an alleyway next to a dark, squarish building. A fire escape took me up to the roof.

Stepping onto the roof felt like coming out of the woods. The Thames was just a stone's throw away, the vastness of the river winding past like an enormous serpent, forming a huge meander around the Isle of Dogs. Surrounded by the Thames were the skyscrapers of Canary Wharf, reaching up into the night, shining from a thousand points, the white double strobe of the central tower flashing regularly once a second. The lights of the skyscrapers reflected off the black water, forming a second set of towers that seemed to reach down into the darkness. Off to the west I could see the lights of Whitehall and the West End and the landmarks of central London. I could still hear the sounds of the city, but this close to the Thames it was almost drowned out by the rhythmic *shhhh* of the water, the waves lapping against the banks as the water continued its steady flow out to sea. The air carried the scent of the river, not pure, but not unpleasant either.

"It's me," I said into the darkness.

There was a moment's pause, and then a girl stepped out from the shadow of the building. She was a touch below medium height, with wavy brown hair held up in two bunches, and had a careful, deliberate way of moving, always looking where she was going. Her age would have been hard to guess—she looked perhaps twenty-one, but there was a distance in her manner that didn't match her youth. Her name was Luna Mancuso and she was my apprentice.

"It's cold," Luna said with a shiver. She was dressed warmly, in a green pullover and faded jeans, but it was September and there was a chill breeze blowing off the water.

"There's a warmer spot down in the alley."

Luna followed me quickly, leaving her corner perch. The roof of the building had a clear view down onto the factory, which was why I'd picked it. If anything had gone wrong, I'd told her to get out. "Did you get a count?"

"You went in with six others. That was it."

"Did you see anyone else?"

"No. Was there?"

"No."

The alleyway bent through an S shape at the bottom of the fire escape, leaving a corner sheltered from the wind, obscured by machinery and old boxes. It was the kind of place that would make most people afraid of being mugged, but one of the fringe benefits of being a mage is that you don't have to worry much about that kind of thing. A pair of hot-water pipes ran vertically into the concrete, raising the temperature a few degrees, and I let Luna huddle against them, keeping my distance. There was space for me, but that would mean coming within arm's reach of Luna. "What was I watching for?" Luna asked.

"No idea," I said. "You don't bring backup for the things you know about. You bring backup for the things you *don't* know about."

Luna was silent for a moment, rubbing her hands together next to the heating pipes. "I could have watched a lot better if I'd been closer."

"Luna . . ."

"I *know* I can't go inside," Luna said. "Not that close. But can't I meet them?"

"It's dangerous."

"You said the barghest was inside the factory."

"I meant the mages."

That made Luna look up in surprise. "I thought you were working with them?"

"Today?" I said. "Yes. Tomorrow?" I shrugged.

"Seriously?"

I sighed. "Luna, if an order went out tomorrow to bring the two of us in, those guys would be first in line to do it. I might not be on the Council's hit list anymore but that doesn't mean they *like* me. I don't think they're out to get me. But if it ever became in their interests to get rid of me, I doubt they'd think twice. And every bit of information they have on you makes you an easier target."

Luna was silent. I hoped she was listening because

I wasn't exaggerating. Tonight I'd worked with Garrick and Ilmarin and the security men, and we'd done a good, professional job. But if one of those same men tried to threaten or kidnap or even kill me, a week or a month or a year from now, it really wouldn't surprise me much. "What about Talisid?" Luna said at last.

"He doesn't know everything that you can do, and the more time you spend with him, the harder it'll be to keep that secret."

"I don't *care* about keeping everything a secret. What's the point in staying safe if I can't *do* anything?"

I could hear the frustration in Luna's voice and was about to reply but stopped. I could have told her she needed to be patient. I could have told her mage society was a dangerous place, and that sometimes the best thing was to stay away from it. I could have told her that her position as my apprentice wouldn't do much to protect her if things went wrong.

All of those things would have been true, but they wouldn't have helped. Luna is an adept, not a mage. An adept is like a mage with a much narrower focus; they can use magic, but only in a very specific way. In Luna's case it's chance magic, altering the flow of probability. Chance magic can only affect things that are sufficiently random. It can't win you a chess match or make money appear out of thin air, because there's nothing for the magic to work on. But it can send a breeze a different way, make someone slip a fraction, cause something to break at a certain point: countless tiny changes that can make the difference between success and failure, danger and safety, life and death. It's not flashy, but it can be powerful.

Unfortunately for Luna, her magic isn't a gift; it was laid upon her as a curse, passed down through the generations all the way from one of her ancestors in Sicily. The curse twists bad luck away from Luna and onto everyone nearby. For Luna, it's like she has a charmed life. She doesn't get sick, she doesn't have accidents, and any bit of random ill

fortune will always hit someone else. You're probably thinking that doesn't sound like much of a curse, and you'd be
right . . . except that all that bad luck gets intensified and
redirected to everyone nearby. To my mage's sight Luna's
curse looks like a cloud of silvery mist, flowing from Luna's
skin to surround her in a protective cloud. To anyone who
comes too close, that mist is poison. Passing within arm's
reach is dangerous, and a touch can be fatal. There's no way
to defend against it, because there's no way to know what
it'll do—it might be a scraped knee, it might be a heart
attack, and you'll never know until it happens. Luna knows,
every minute of every day, that simply by being near anybody she's making their life worse, and that the best thing
she can do for them is to stay as far away as possible.

It adds up to a pretty horrible form of isolation, where
every time the bearer lets herself get close to another living
thing, something terrible happens. From what I've learnt,
most victims go insane or kill themselves within a few years.
Luna grew up with it. She survived . . . but not by much.
Luna told me once that the reason she started the search that
eventually led her to me was because she realised that if she
didn't, there was going to come a day where she simply
didn't care enough to stay alive anymore.

And what all that meant was that warning Luna of the
dangers of the mage world wasn't going to work. Not
because she didn't understand the danger, but because she'd
quite coldbloodedly decided a long time ago that any amount
of danger was better than the life she'd had. "All right," I
said at last. "Next time, you can come along."

Luna blinked and looked at me. She didn't smile but she
seemed to *lift* somehow, as if she'd grown a couple of inches.
With my mage's sight, I felt the mist around her ripple and
recede slightly. I turned and started walking back towards
the main road, and Luna followed at a safe distance.

Somehow, as of a little while ago, Luna's started to learn

to control her curse. I still don't know exactly how she managed it, partly because I don't really understand how her curse works in the first place and partly because it happened in the middle of a rather eventful few days during which I was trying to keep myself from being killed, possessed, or recruited. Since then Luna's been training to master it, under what guidance I can give her. "Next session is Sunday morning," I said. "Make sure you're at Arachne's for ten."

Luna nodded. We'd reached the railings where Luna had locked her bike—she can't take public transport without killing whoever sits next to her, so a bike is about the only way she can get around. Luckily no one had tried to steal it. I watched as Luna unlocked it, but instead of getting on, she hesitated. "Um . . ."

"What's up?"

"You're at the shop tomorrow, right?"

I nodded. "Coming in?"

"Yes. Well . . . Could I bring someone?"

I blinked at that. "Who?"

"A friend."

I almost said *but you don't have any friends*. Even I'm not usually that clumsy, which should tell you how surprised I was. Luna's company is lethal to anyone who doesn't know to stay clear. How did . . . ?

It must have shown on my face, because Luna ducked her head with an expression that didn't look happy. "I know," she said at the pavement. "I won't go near him. I just . . . he was interested. In your shop. He wanted to see."

I looked at Luna; she didn't meet my eyes. Again I wanted to warn her and again I held back. God knows I don't need to remind Luna of how bad her curse is. But if she was just setting herself up for something worse . . .

"What's his name?" I said at last.

Luna looked up with a quick flash of gratitude. "Martin."

I nodded. "I'll be in all day. Drop by whenever you like."

"Thanks!" Luna climbed onto her bicycle. "Bye!"

I watched Luna as she cycled out of sight, checking quickly through the futures to make sure she'd be safe. Her curse protects her from accidents but not from things done on purpose; it wouldn't stop a gang from deciding to pick on her, though it'd mess them up pretty badly if they were stupid enough to go through with it. But that wouldn't be much consolation to Luna, so I watched until I was satisfied she'd make it out of Deptford safely before turning to leave myself.

I'd been planning to go home to bed but instead found myself taking the trains past Camden to Hampstead Heath. Once there, I got out and walked, passing Parliament Hill and carrying on, heading deeper into the Heath. Within a few minutes the lights and sounds of the city had been left far behind, and I was alone in the vastness and silence of the park.

Not many people go into Hampstead Heath by night. Partly it's because of crime, but there's something else as well, something more primal: the ancient fear of the woods. The Heath is the wildest of London's parks. During the day it's easy not to notice, but at night, when the rolling hills blot out the lights of the city to leave the park in utter darkness, when the branches and undergrowth rustle and whisper in the silence, when the forest itself seems to be watching and waiting . . .

Most people would admit it's scary. But not many would admit why. Deep down, in the corners of their minds, the reason people don't go into dark forests at night isn't because they're afraid there might be *people*. It's because they're afraid there might be *things*.

And it doesn't help that they just so happen to be absolutely right.

The little earthen ravine was tucked away behind a ridge, concealed by the lay of the land and by thick bushes and trees. None of the footpaths came near and even during the daylight hours it was deserted. But for the distant sounds of the city, I could have been alone in the world. I found the overhanging oak, then felt around its roots embedded into the bank until I found the right one and pressed two fingers into it in a certain way. "Arachne?" I said into the darkness. "It's Alex."

There was a moment's pause before a clear female voice spoke out of nowhere. If you listened closely you might hear a faint clicking rustle under the words, but only if you knew it was there. "Oh, hello, Alex. I wasn't expecting you. Come right in."

With a rumble the roots unwove themselves, earth trickling away as the bank gaped wide to reveal a tunnel, sloping gently down. I stepped inside and the hillside closed up behind me, sealing me into the earth.

ı ı ı ı ı ı ı ı ı

Although it doesn't look it, Arachne's lair is one of the best-protected places in London. Tracking spells can't find the lair or anyone inside, and gate magic can't transport in or out. The only way to get in is for Arachne to open the door. An elemental mage could probably smash his way in but by the time he did Arachne would have more than enough time to prepare some surprises. It's not as unlikely as you might think, either. While Arachne doesn't get many visitors, mages know she exists—and generally mages and creatures like Arachne don't get on too well.

Arachne is a ten-foot-tall spider, her body covered with dark hair highlighted in cobalt blue. Eight thick legs hold her body well off the ground, and eight jet-black eyes look out from over a pair of mandibles that do little to conceal her fangs. She'd weigh somewhere near half a ton, but for all her bulk she can move with the speed and grace of a predator. She looks like a living nightmare and a glance would be enough to make most people run screaming.

She was also on a sofa sewing a dress, which made her

a bit less intimidating. Not that I was paying attention anyway. Arachne looks like a horror out of darkness, but you don't last long in the mage world if you put too much stock in appearances, and I don't even notice her looks anymore unless someone points them out. "You're up late," I said.

"So are you," Arachne said. The dress was some sort of green one-piece thing that shimmered slightly and she was working on it with all four front limbs at once, moving in a blur of motion. Arachne's legs are covered with hairs, becoming gradually finer and finer the farther down you go, and she can use the tips better than I can use my fingers. I've always suspected she uses magic in her weaving, but there's no way to tell; for creatures like Arachne, everything they do is tied in with their magic one way or another. "Something wrong?"

Arachne's main chamber is so covered in brilliant-coloured clothing that it's hard to see the stone. There are sofas and tables scattered around and every one of them is draped with dresses, coats, skirts, jumpers, shirts, scarves, shawls, tops, gloves, belts—you name it. They're red, blue, green, yellow, and every colour in between, and the whole room looks like a clothes shop with so much stock there's no room for customers. "No," I said.

Arachne rubbed her mandibles together with a clicking, rustling sound. "Hm. Just move that pile over there. No, the other one."

I did as Arachne said, shifting a double handful of jackets over to a nearby table before settling down on the sofa with a sigh. It was pretty comfortable. "Sewed any good clothes lately?"

"All the clothes I make are good."

"Yeah, I was just making conversation."

"You're terrible at making conversation. Why don't you tell me why you're really here?"

I sat on the sofa in silence for a few moments, listening to the quick *ftt-ftt-ftt* of Arachne's sewing. I wasn't thinking about what to say; I was trying to work up the courage to say it.

I've known Arachne for ten years. For me that's a long time; for her, not so much. When I first met Arachne I was still apprentice to the Dark mage Richard Drakh. She didn't trust me at first, and with hindsight I can't really blame her. But if it hadn't been for her I doubt I'd have survived, and over the years she's become probably my closest friend, funny as it sounds. "Do you think I'm doing the right thing teaching Luna?"

"What an odd question." Arachne didn't look up from her work. "You're hardly going to turn her out on her own."

"Of course not. It's . . ." I hesitated. "Am I teaching her *right*? She's still pushing to get involved with other mages. I thought she'd ease off on that. I mean, she gets to meet people at the shop."

"Not very often, from what you tell me."

"She can't afford to do it very often. With her curse . . ."

"Is that the real reason?"

I sighed and let my shoulders slump. "No. It's that I don't want her around other mages more than I can help it." Even as I said it, I knew it was true, and it shocked me a little. The whole reason Luna had come to me in the first place was out of a hope that she could become part of the mage world. And yet I'd been trying to avoid it . . .

Arachne only nodded. "And she can tell. And you feel guilty for keeping her away."

"I'd feel *more* guilty if I got her into trouble." I looked up at Arachne. "I still don't think she understands how dangerous mage politics can be. I was out tonight on a hunting mission. But tomorrow or next week or next year those same men might be my enemies. And if she'd been there . . ."

Arachne didn't answer. "You think I'm trying too hard to protect her," I said at last.

"I think what you're really afraid of is that you'll introduce her to something that'll get her hurt or killed."

I sometimes wonder whether Arachne can weave more than threads; whether she can see the connections between people, as well. She can seem to pay no attention, and yet strike right to the mark. "I've done it before," I said.

"Yes," Arachne said. "But it was her choice too." She set down the dress and turned her eight eyes on me. "Alex, the trouble with you is that you've spent so long on your own you've forgotten how to live with someone else. The only way she'll learn these things is by experience."

"Yeah, well, I guess she's getting that one way or another. She's bringing some guy to the shop tomorrow."

"Jealous?"

"No," I said automatically.

Arachne just went back to her sewing. She doesn't have any eyebrows to raise, but somehow she conveyed exactly what she thought of that.

I sat grumpily for a minute before remembering the other reason I'd come. "Oh. Something weird happened tonight." I put Luna out of my mind and leant forward. "Talisid tracked down the barghest in Deptford, and he called me in to help. I met up with his team outside the lair, and we made it all the way in. But here's the thing: it was dead. Someone had taken it out before we got there."

"Strange." Arachne picked up the dress she was working on in her front two legs and examined it, turning it around. It was turning into a narrow, vaguely Chinese-looking gown that reflected the light and sent it back with a pale green shimmer. She put the dress down at a different angle and returned to work. "Have you any idea who it was?"

I frowned. "No. And it's a bit odd. I mean, sure, that creature was preying on people, but it's not as if most mages would care. Not enough to risk a fight anyway. I mean, barghests have a pretty scary reputation. Why would anyone go after one when they could just wait and have the Council take care of it?"

"Was it an escapee?"

I nodded. "Yeah, Talisid and I were wondering that. If it was some mage's fault that the thing was there, then it makes sense they'd want to clean it up quietly. But we couldn't find any trace that it used to be someone's property. Besides, if they really wanted to keep it quiet, they would have gated away the body—oh. And another thing. There were signs of a battle at the lair—fire and ice magic—but no freeze or scorch marks on the barghest."

"What killed it, then?"

"Nothing. At least, nothing I could see."

The *ftt-ftt-ftt* stopped. I looked up to see that Arachne was watching me, her needles still. "Elaborate."

"Um . . ." I tried to think of what to say. "It was just . . . dead. Wolf form. No marks. I thought it might have been death magic but . . ."

Arachne didn't answer. "Arachne?" I asked.

Arachne seemed to twitch, then returned to her sewing, the *ftt-ftt* starting up again. "I see."

"Something wrong?"

"Perhaps." Arachne paused. "If you could establish the cause of death, I would appreciate knowing."

I hesitated a second before nodding. "Okay. I'll see what I can dig up."

Arachne went back to her work. She didn't say anything further, and I didn't ask. "How many of them do you think there are?" I said after a pause.

"Of which?"

"Magical creatures like that barghest. Living here in our world."

"Few. Fewer each year." Arachne continued to work, but there was something a little distant about her voice. "So many have been killed or enslaved. The survivors have hidden themselves in remote places or in other worlds. Perhaps what you saw today was the body of the last barghest."

An hour later, walking back home through the darkness of the Heath, I found my thoughts going back to Arachne's words. I'm so comfortable with Arachne that I forget other mages think of creatures like her as aliens at best and monsters at worst. This was the first time I'd gone on this sort of hunt, and I'd had a good reason—but that didn't change the fact that the creature I'd been intending to kill was basically not that different from Arachne.

For the first time I wondered exactly how long magical creatures would still be around. As far back as mage histories go, they've always been there, but for a long time the number's been decreasing, mostly because of expeditions like the one I'd been on today. Usually it's only the dangerous ones that mages go after . . . but not always, and *dangerous* is pretty subjective. Now that I thought about it, the only magical creatures I'd seen over the past few months had been either working with mages or under their control. I hadn't come across one in the wild for a long time. If things kept going the way they had been, then the only creatures left would be property, powerful enough to hide themselves, or dead. It would mean no more killings like the ones the barghest had been responsible for . . . but it would mean none of the gentler or more wondrous creatures, either.

I wasn't sure how much I liked the idea, and I wasn't so sure any more that I'd done the right thing by agreeing to help Talisid. I headed home to sleep and to see what the next day would bring.

chapter 2

I t was a new day and it was raining.

My shop's tucked away down a little side street in Camden, only a minute's walk from the canal. The rail and road bridges that interlock the area make it tricky to find, but plenty of tourists still filter through. The sign above my door says *Arcana Emporium*, along with a description of the contents that's technical enough to stop most people immediately thinking *magic shop*. A notice on the door lists my opening times as ten A.M. to five P.M. Mondays to Saturdays, and every now and again it's actually right.

As far as I know, I'm the only mage in England who runs a shop. Most mages think it makes me eccentric or just plain stupid, and to be fair they've got a point. Money isn't a big concern to most mages. Sure, they need it, but it isn't the primary medium of exchange the way it is to regular folk, for the simple reason that most mages who know what they're doing and are willing to put in the work can leverage their power into as much money as they're realistically likely to need. They aren't all millionaires, not by a long shot, but they don't generally have to worry about paying the rent either. So as a rule you can't buy anything really valuable from a mage with cash, because cash isn't scarce enough for them to value it.

The real currency of the magical economy is favours. Mages are specialists: A typical mage is great at one thing and poor to useless at everything else. If he's faced with a problem that requires a different type of magic from the kind he can use, he can't do anything about it—but he probably knows someone who can. And that mage might need someone *else's* help a bit further down the line, and so on. Established mages have whole networks of friends and contacts to call on, and let me tell you, mages take those favours *seriously.* Failing to pay your debts in mage society is bad. We're talking "sold to Dark mages as a slave" levels of bad. Of course it still happens if the guy in question thinks he can get away with it, but it's rarely a good idea in the long term and at the higher levels a surprising number of things run on simple promises. They might not be as good as gold, but they can buy you a hell of a lot more. That was the basis on which I'd been working for Talisid last night. He hadn't offered payment, and I hadn't asked, but all of it was done on the understanding that the next time I asked him for help he'd give it to me, no questions asked.

Or maybe not. But life would be very boring if it was too predictable.

Anyway, to get back on topic, what this means is that anyone with enough magical items to set up a shop is generally powerful enough that they don't have any reason to sell said items in the first place. They also tend to be leery (for good reason) of putting large stocks of highly valuable items in an easily accessible place. Or maybe they just think serving customers is beneath them. Who knows.

There's a certain band of items, though, that you can

make a business out of selling—the stuff that's just useful enough to be worth keeping but not powerful enough that a mage would bother to trade a service for, like old or weakened focuses, or the kind of one-shots that don't do anything dramatic. Then there are rare components, which don't do anything useful on their own but are really inconvenient to run short of right in the middle of a ritual. And finally there are things that aren't magical at all, like crystal balls and tarot decks and herbs. They're pretty much useless for anything except window dressing, but they're good camouflage.

Put all of that together and you've got the contents of my shop. There's a roped-off area in the back-right corner next to the door to the hall that contains the genuine magical items, or at least the weaker ones. Two shelf stands hold a collection of nonprecious and semiprecious stones, as well as figurines and materials, and a rack holds herbs, powders, and various types of incense that together make the whole shop smell vaguely like a herbalist's. Staffs, rods, and blades of various types take up another corner, and you can get a good view out onto the street through a wide window, which was currently streaked with water from the steadily falling rain.

And lastly, you get the customers.

My clientele used to be strictly small fry. A tiny fraction who knew what they were doing, a slightly larger fraction who sort of knew what they were doing, and a whole lot whose knowledge of magic would fit on a Post-it note. After the business five months ago, things changed. My shop suddenly got popular, and adepts, apprentices, and even mages started coming along.

Trouble is, along with the influx of knowledgeable people, I've also picked up a whole lot of idiots. On a Saturday like today, I'm lucky if one customer in five knows enough to be trusted. The rest . . .

. . . well.

। । । । । । । । ।

"Hi, I'm looking for some gaff coins?"

　　"You want the Magic Box, other side of Camden. Here's one of their cards."

"Oh. Which tricks have you got?"

"None of them. You've got the wrong shop."

"So what do you sell?"

". . ."

"Wait, this is supposed to be a *real* magic shop?"

". . ."

"Oh my God, you're serious! Ha-ha-ha!"

". . ."

"Ha-ha . . . oh man, this is awesome. Okay, okay, I'm going."

। । । । । । । । ।

"Um . . ." (giggling)

　　"Can I help you?"

"We're looking for—" (more giggling)

". . ."

"Have you got, um . . ."

"Take your time."

". . . a wand?" (chorus of giggling from all three)

"No. And my name's not Harry and I didn't go to Hogwarts."

(yet more giggling)

"Um . . . hee hee . . . what about . . ."

". . ."

"Do you know how to find any vampires? Like, the really hot ones?"

। । । । । । । । ।

"I want a refund for this spell."

　　"Which spell?"

"This one."

"Hmm . . . 'A Spell to Make You Win the Lottery.' I'm going to go out on a limb and say it didn't work."

"I want my money back."

"Your money, right. How much did you pay?"

"Fourteen ninety-nine."

"Uh-huh. How much would you expect to get from a lottery win?"

"At least a million."

". . ."

". . ?"

"And you don't see a problem with this."

"What?"

"Okay. The first problem is that you've got a product here with a sale value of fifteen pounds—"

"Fourteen ninety-nine."

"Fourteen ninety-nine, sorry, which is supposed to win you over a million. Now, stop and think how that would work."

"I don't care. I want a refund."

"Right. The second problem would be I never sold you this spell."

"I bought it from this shop."

"That would be quite impressive, given that I don't sell spells."

"I know my rights. If you don't give me a refund I'll sue you."

"If your understanding of the legal system is on par with your grasp of economics, I don't think I've got much to worry about."

"Oh, is that right? I'm going to call the police! I can get this shop closed down, I think you'll find!"

(stomp stomp stomp SLAM)

". . ."

"Um, hello? Excuse me?"

"Yes?"

"Uh, could I get one of those spells to win the lottery?"

| | | | | | | | | |

"Hi!"
      "You again?"
"Yeah, I decided I didn't want to go all the way across Camden. So what tricks do you sell?"
"We don't sell tricks."
"Okay, okay. So what 'magic' do you sell?"
"Could you not make a hand gesture in the air when you do that?"
"Sure. Whatcha got?"
"Just what you see."
"Okay, okay."

| | | | | | | | | |

"Um, hi."
      "Hey. What do you need?"
"I heard you can . . . uh . . . find out things?"
"Who told you that?"
"Uh . . . it was . . . can you find out something for me?"
"Not likely."
"But I need to know! It's really important!"
"Fine. What is it?"
"I . . . I need to know if my girlfriend's cheating on me."
"Probably."
"What! Why?"
"Because if you're asking that question, the answer's probably yes."

| | | | | | | | | |

"So is there any way to use magic to talk with people who've . . . passed on?"
"Passed on?"
"I mean, died."
"No."
"But all those psychics say—"

"Psychics make their living telling people what they want to hear. Magic can't let you talk to someone once they're gone, and as far as I know neither can anything else."

"So . . . there's no way they can send a message?"

"No."

"Nothing at all? Once someone's dead, that's it?"

"Yes."

"And they couldn't tell anyone how they died, right?"

"No, they—wait. Why do you want to know this again?"

"Um, no reason."

" . . ."

" . . ."

"That death spell won't work."

"Wh-what? I-I wasn't . . ."

" . . ."

"Could—"

"No, I'm not going to teach you how to do it."

. . . .

"Hey, man."

"Oh, for the love of God. *Why* are you still *here*?"

"Look, I'm just curious. Now, I know you don't sell tricks over the counter—"

"We. Don't. Sell. Tricks."

"Hey, what are you so angry for? I'm just asking."

"I'm going to go through this one last time. This is a shop. There are things on the shelves. You want to buy the things on the shelves, bring the things on the shelves to the counter."

"C'mon, I'm not that stupid. I've seen loads of guys coming up. You must have some good stuff, right? I mean, for people in the know?"

"And you want to know the secret?"

"Yeah."

"Okay. It's a secret."

"Fine, I get it. I'm going."

"..."
"Oh, one more thing—"

....

After noon edged into evening. It had been raining all day, but as evening drew near, the clouds became thicker and the rain heavier. By five o'clock the light was dim, the window was translucent with running water, and the raindrops were drumming so hard on the pavement outside that I could feel the vibration through the legs of my chair.

The weather had finally driven the customers away and only one was left, a guy in his twenties. He circled the shop a couple of times before drifting over to the counter. I didn't lift my eyes from my paperback. He cleared his throat.

"Can I help you?"

"Oh, hi. Yeah, I was wondering if I could ask you something."

"I don't sell spells."

"... Okay."

I turned a page. "I don't sell spells, and I don't sell tricks. I don't carry illusions or marked cards or weighted coins. I can not sell you an endless purse or help you win the lottery. I can't make that girl you've got your eye on fall in love with you, and I wouldn't do it even if I could. I don't have a psychic hotline to your dead relatives, I don't know if you're going to be successful in your career, and I don't know when you're going to get married. I can't get you into Hogwarts or any other kind of magic school, and if you even mention those stupid sparkly vampires I will do something unpleasant to you."

"... Ookay?"

"Good. Now that's settled, what do you need?"

"You're Alex Verus, right?"

"That's me."

"Hi, good to meet you." A hand appeared above my book. "Martin."

I looked up and got my first good view of Martin. He was twenty-four or twenty-five, slim, with small blue eyes and dark blond hair that was spiky from gel and swept in a fashionable style from left to right. I guessed most women would have found him good-looking. He was wearing a button-down shirt and trousers, with a coat slung over one shoulder, and moved with a sort of casual confidence that made me think of money.

I disliked him on sight. I probably would have disliked him anyway, but the haircut made it a lot easier. I said, "Hey," and reached out to shake his hand.

In the fraction of a second before our hands touched, I focused on Martin with my mage's sight. The technique isn't really sight—it's a whole other sense, separate from the five—but for whatever reason sight seems to be the way all mages interpret it. It lets you perceive magic directly rather than just the vague feelings a sensitive or adept gets, all the wisps and auras and strands that make up the currents in the world around you. Most are so faint you have to strain to see them but anything really powerful, like a mage's spell, is dazzling. If you're good—and I'm very good—you can pick out what the spell does, how long it's been there, and even the nature of whoever cast it. I didn't need any skill to recognise the silvery mist around Martin though. It was Luna's curse, and it meant he'd been close to her. The mist was only a thin layer swirling gently around his skin. Despite all the time I've spent around Luna I've rarely seen her curse in action, and I wasn't sure how long it would have taken for Martin to pick this much up. I didn't think it was enough to put him in serious danger, but it might be.

My hand clasped on Martin's and the moment was gone. I couldn't feel the silver mist over Martin's skin but I could see it. It didn't spread from him to me; that's not the way the curse works. "Great to finally meet up," Martin said as he shook my hand. "Luna's told me a lot about you."

"She's not supposed to."

"Not—Oh, ha-ha! Yeah, I see what you mean. Don't worry, I won't spread it around."

I had my doubts about that. "Looking for something?"

"Yeah, I really wanted to have a look at some focuses and one-shots. They're over there behind the rope, right? Mind if I have a root through?"

"You don't want to mess with those things unless you know what you're doing."

"It's fine, I know the score. Besides, you can tell me what they do, right?"

I really wanted to say no. But the aura on Martin confirmed he was the guy Luna had been talking about and I didn't have a good reason to tell him to get lost. Reluctantly, I walked over as Martin unhooked the rope and started looking through the contents of the shelves, asking me questions all the while.

In between answering Martin's questions, I asked a few of my own. According to Martin, he'd grown up here in London, moved away for university, then moved back to get a place of his own. He was a musician and played in a band. He was vague on the details of exactly how he'd learnt about the magical world. He'd just picked things up, he said. He'd been trying to break into mage society but was finding it difficult. He'd met Luna through a mutual friend. She'd mentioned my shop to him and he'd wanted to learn more.

I learnt other things about Martin too, not so much from what he said as how he said it. He had charm, knew how to be funny, and knew how to flatter. He was clever, though maybe not as clever as he thought. Although he didn't come out and say it, he knew I was a mage. He knew the basics of how magic worked but couldn't use it himself—he was only a sensitive. That was the only point at which his smile slipped a little. It was only for a second, but enough to make me wonder if it was a sore spot. Maybe he'd just made friends with Luna to take advantage of her connection to me.

And maybe I was just being jealous. I didn't like Martin,

but if I was being honest with myself I had to admit I didn't have a good reason for it. He was pleasant, charming, and probably the only new friend Luna had made in months.

Which also put him in danger, as the silver mist hanging off him proved. I'd have to find out from Luna how much she'd told him. As if I didn't have enough to remember already. "So would any of the focuses work for me?" Martin was asking.

"Probably not. They're for helping with a spell or a type of magic you have trouble with. They don't let you cast from scratch." I nodded at the twisted wand of rowan in his hands. "That's a defensive focus. If you could put together a protective spell and if you put in the work to attune yourself to the wand, it might help, but on its own it's just a stick."

"How do you attune it?"

"Trial and error. You have to figure out how the thing interacts and adapt your own way of doing things to match it. Sometimes it's impossible and there's no way to know without trying."

"Can't you just make it do what you want?"

I shook my head. "Doesn't work that way."

"Okay, what about something that worked on its own?"

I raised my eyebrows. "You're talking about imbued items."

"That's how they work, right? Anyone can use them?"

"Not . . . exactly. Imbued items choose their bearers. They decide when to use their powers, not you." I thought of an ivory wand beyond a sealed door and pushed the memory away.

"But I'd be able to use one?"

"If you ever got one, yeah. And no, before you ask, I don't have any here." Which was true, if by *here* you meant *on these shelves*. I had several upstairs, which I was most definitely not telling Martin about. Imbued items are priceless, and mages will quite literally kill for them.

Martin was quiet, no doubt dreaming of an imbued item

of his own. If he'd known more, he might not have been so eager. Imbued items have minds of their own and the stronger their power, the stronger their will. The most powerful imbued items can reduce their bearers to little more than puppets. Oh, it looks like the bearer's in charge—but somehow, everything they do ends up being what the item wanted.

I scanned through the futures, looking to see when Luna was going to turn up. Her arrival had been vague all through the day but as I looked I saw that she was due to knock on the door any minute. I was glad. The rain hadn't let up and the glass of the shop window still ran with water.

And then I felt something snap and change. I jerked my head around, looking for danger. The shop was quiet and Martin was holding a white and blue lacquered tube in his hand. The silver mist of Luna's curse was gone. "What's this?"

I stood dead still. The two of us were alone in the shop, and the only sound was the steady patter of rain. Martin looked at me. "Hey, Alex? What's this one?"

I spoke quietly. "I wouldn't take that if I were you."

Martin frowned and looked down at the tube. It was ten inches long and two inches wide, its ends rounded, made out of what looked at first glance like lacquered wood. The tube was white, with raised engravings of blue flowers twining about its length. A braided cord hung from one end. "Why not?"

I didn't answer. Martin started to return the tube to the shelf and stopped. He stared at me. "Wait. This is one of those, isn't it? An imbued item?"

I stayed silent, and Martin's eyes went wide. "Thought you said you didn't have any?"

"It's not mine."

"So why'd you put it on the shelf?"

I looked at Martin and spoke quietly. "I didn't."

Martin didn't seem to hear. He held up the tube to the light, turning it around. When nothing happened he shook it gently, and there was a faint *katta-katta* sound. "There's something inside."

"Yes."

"How much is it?"

I took a deep breath. "Martin, listen very closely. I don't know you and you don't know me, but you have to believe me when I tell you that if you take that thing away with you, you will regret it for the rest of your life."

For an instant Martin hesitated and I saw the choices branching before him. Then his eyes narrowed and the choice was gone. "Imbued items choose their wielder, don't they?"

I sighed. I could see the futures laid out ahead of us and in every one of them, Martin was going to leave my shop with that item. "Yeah," I said with an effort.

Outside, hurrying footsteps blended with the rain and the door opened with a rush of sound and a cold wind. Luna ducked inside, trying to fit through the door while folding a big golf umbrella, water running everywhere. "Sorry I'm so late! Ugh, it's awful out there." After three failed tries she managed to get the umbrella folded up, then she pushed the door shut and the shop was quiet again except for the drip of water from her clothes. "The weather was so bad my bike . . ." Luna finished propping the umbrella in the corner and finally noticed something was wrong. She looked from me to Martin. "Hello?"

Martin and I hadn't taken our eyes off each other. "Martin, I need to talk to Luna," I said. "Could you wait here for five minutes, please?"

There was a beat, then Martin nodded. "Sure."

I turned to Luna, who was still looking between both of us, trying to figure out what was going on. "In the back."

ı ı ı ı ı ı ı ı ı

The door at the back of my shop leads into a small, dark hallway. What little space it has is mostly filled with the stairs up to my second-floor flat. There's one side door leading into a back room where I store stuff that isn't important enough to secure properly, and I led Luna inside and shut the door behind her. "You have to get away from Martin."

"What?" Luna stared at me. "Why?"

"Because he's done something very stupid and you don't want to be around to get caught in the results."

"How—? I don't understand."

"You remember the little white and blue lacquered tube I showed you three months ago in the safe room? The one I told you to never ever touch?"

"Yes . . . Wait. It was that? You gave him that?"

"I didn't give him anything."

"Then why didn't you tell him not to take it?"

"You think I'd be telling you this if he'd listened?"

I turned away from Luna and walked to the corner. There was a single window of frosted glass high on the wall and I stared up at it. "What does it do?" Luna asked from behind me.

"It's called a monkey's paw," I said without turning around. "It grants wishes."

"Wishes? You mean . . . anything?"

"Pretty close. It's the most powerful item I've got."

"Is there some kind of catch?"

"Of *course* there's a catch. You don't get anything like that for free. Trying to use that thing is *really* bad news."

"How? I mean, do the wishes have a price or something?"

"I don't *know*, Luna, because no one who's ever tried using the damn thing has been around afterwards to answer questions." I turned to face her. "I want you to keep your distance from Martin as long as he's got it."

Luna paused. There were drops of water clinging to her hair and the sleeves and ankles of her clothes were still wet. "Wait. You just said that nobody's . . ."

I was silent, and Luna went still. "You're waiting for something to happen to him."

"I'll do what I can to make him give it up," I said. "But as long as he has it, he's a threat."

"Until when? Until he's dead?"

"Luna . . ."

"Why do I have to stay away?"

"Because he's dangerous."

"I don't care if he's dangerous." I could see Luna was starting to get angry. "You said you weren't going to keep me away anymore!"

"There's nothing you can do to make it better and a lot of ways you could make it worse," I said harshly. "He had your curse on him when he came today."

As soon as I said it, I knew I shouldn't have. Luna stared at me, then I saw understanding dawn in her eyes. "You think it's my fault."

"It doesn't matter anymore." I wished I hadn't brought it up now but there was no use going back. "But it's sure as hell not going to help if you stay nearby. The best thing you can do is keep your distance."

"If this thing's so bad why can't I just talk to him?"

I sighed. "Because taking the monkey's paw wasn't the only stupid thing Martin did."

"What?"

"He's not waiting for us to finish. He walked out into the street thirty seconds ago."

Luna looked in the direction of the shop, then back at me. "Why didn't you tell me?" she said quietly, and now for the first time I knew she was really angry.

I stood my ground, meeting her gaze. "Because if Martin were the kind of person who'd listen to warnings, the monkey's paw wouldn't have picked him in the first place."

Luna stared at me for a second longer, then in two quick steps was at the door. "Luna!" I said. "Wait!"

"Maybe you don't care about him," Luna said. "But I do." She pulled the door open.

I started towards Luna, wanting to hold her back—and

stopped. To my eyes, the silver mist of her curse glowed around her, filling her space and the doorway. One more step forward and it would be me that mist would be touching. "Luna, you don't understand how bad this thing is. As long as Martin's carrying it, he's a danger to everyone around him."

Luna looked back at me. Her blue eyes were cold and when she spoke, her voice was too. "Like me?" The door slammed and she was gone.

I moved to follow her, then stopped. I heard the sound of running feet, cut off by the bang of the shop door. Luna had run out into the rain after Martin. Looking through the futures I could see the exact point at which she'd catch him up. I could track them down and find them.

And all it would do was make things worse. If I went after Martin he'd think I was trying to chase him, and if I went after Luna it would lead to a worse fight. I wanted to run after them, or do something, and all I could do was stand there. I smacked a hand into the door, hard, and swore, then stood there and listened to the rain beating against my window.

I was angry and upset. I wanted to go after Luna. Instead I went upstairs to the small living room in my flat, hung up the heavy bag that I keep in the corner, and started beating on it. The bag shook and I felt the vibrations run down the beams and through the floorboards of the house. While I kept punching, I scanned through the futures, waiting to see if Luna would come back. She didn't.

After forty-five minutes I knew Luna wouldn't be coming back that night. I abandoned the bag and went for a shower to wash the sweat from my body. I washed my hair, towelled myself dry, and dressed in a clean shirt and a pair of jeans. Once I'd done that I checked again to see if the future had changed. Nothing.

Now I'd burnt through the worst of my frustration I could think clearly again. Unwillingly, I had to admit that it had been stupid to tell Luna to stay away from Martin. If I'd thought about it I'd have realised that telling her not to go near one of her only friends was a bad idea. I haven't had many fights with Luna, and this was the angriest I'd seen her in a long time.

The sun had set and the sky outside my window was darkening from grey to black. The rain had died away to a steady drizzle, forming a fine mist in the air that was visible only in the yellow glows cast by the streetlights. There were lights in the houses and blocks of flats beyond the canal—many lights; few people were out in weather like this. As the evening turned into night and the weather began to dry, the streets would begin to fill once again. I paced back and forth across my small room and thought about the monkey's paw.

I don't keep records, but I remembered the day I'd acquired the thing very clearly. One winter evening three years ago, an old man came into my shop and asked if I would be interested in an imbued item. There would be no charge; he just wanted to pass it on to a good home. He explained that it could grant any five wishes its owner desired and I could use it however I saw fit.

I refused. I told the old man that wish-granting items usually came with some sort of horrible price, and you never got something for nothing. If he was offering it for free, it was a pretty safe bet it wasn't something I wanted to have.

The old man agreed that the wishes came at a high price. He asked if I would be willing to simply keep hold of the item and give or sell it on.

I refused again. If the thing was that dangerous, I wasn't going to be responsible for handing it over to anyone else. The old man smiled and left.

The next day, the monkey's paw was sitting on the shelves in my shop next to the focuses. I put on a pair of gloves, picked the thing up, and placed it in my safe room upstairs. Three months, six months, nine months went by and I forgot about it.

Then one day a woman picked the monkey's paw off my shelves, out of a spot I would have sworn was empty. She wanted to buy it. I said no and closed the door firmly behind her. When I checked that evening the monkey's paw was gone. I found out the woman's name and learnt that the monkey's paw was in her possession.

She committed suicide a week later. The monkey's paw was back on the shelves the same evening. I put it back in the safe room and left it there.

A year later, someone else picked up the monkey's paw in the exact same way. This time I didn't try to stop the man from taking it. I agreed to give it to him on the condition that he promised never to use it. He gave me his promise and left, happy.

The man came back to my shop one last time, on a Saturday evening just before I closed up for the night. I remembered his shifty eyes, the tension in his movements, his insistence that everything was fine. Under pressure he admitted he'd been using the paw. According to him he'd made four wishes. There had been problems. He wouldn't go into details but he wanted to know if there was some way to make a wish do exactly what you wanted.

I never saw him again. By the next day he had disappeared, and no one ever found out where he'd gone. But while cleaning the shop that Sunday night, I saw the monkey's paw had returned.

And now Luna was alone with the thing's next owner. Just the thought of that made my skin crawl. I thought of ringing her, but what would I say? To stay away from him? Yeah, that had worked so well last time . . .

I wondered whether Luna's curse would be enough to keep her safe. The luck-twisting effect of the curse is a powerful protection but it has its limits, and I didn't know how it would interact with the monkey's paw. The only bit of reassurance I had was that judging from the last two times, the monkey's paw wouldn't do anything straightaway. Luna was supposed to be meeting me tomorrow to train at Arachne's. I couldn't tell for sure whether she'd show up but I didn't think anything terrible would happen before then. Maybe she'd have calmed down enough to listen to me. And maybe I wouldn't screw things up so badly next time.

With that decided, I felt a bit better. I went and fixed myself some dinner, then washed up and returned to my room. As I did, I turned my attention to the immediate future and saw that someone would be wanting to get into my shop. It was well past closing time but most mages don't like to go shopping during business hours. It's not common for them to show up after dark but it's not rare, either, and it's happened enough that I've installed a bell by the front door.

The bell rang just as I finished tying my shoes. I pulled on a jumper and walked down the stairs, flicking on the light as I reentered the shop. The place always feels a little eerie after dark; row after row of silent shelves, watching and waiting. I could see the outline of somebody through the shop window, half hidden by the door.

I opened the door and the most beautiful woman I'd ever seen stumbled in, gasping and wide-eyed. "Please, I need your help! There's something trying to kill me!"

My precognition screamed. I took one look at what had set it off, grabbed the woman, and yanked her back, pulling her with me into the middle of the shop. An instant later, the shop window exploded in a shower of glass as something came flying through, landing with a slam on the spot the woman and I had been standing in just a second ago. Without pause the creature pulled itself to its feet and lunged straight for us.

Some days are just better spent in bed.

｜｜｜｜｜｜｜｜｜

I shoved the woman out of the creature's path and let the momentum push me back so the thing went between us. The move would have been a lot more graceful if I hadn't hit the herb rack on the way, almost tripping over. The woman stumbled and fell, and the creature was on top of her before she could recover. It dropped to its knees, its hands reaching for her throat.

The creature looked human, but wasn't. It had two arms, two legs, a head and a body, but there was something about it that was just *wrong*. Before it could get a grip on the woman's neck, I took a step and swung a roundhouse kick into its ribs.

I'm not a real hand-to-hand expert but I've done a fair bit of training in the past, and a swinging kick against a low target carries an awful lot of force. The impact flipped the thing over and sent it rolling to slam against the shelves. The shelves swayed and crystal balls and statuettes rained down on the thing with a crash. I pulled the woman to her feet and hustled her towards the door to the hall. "Get out! Go!"

The creature stood up. Now that I got a good look at it, I saw it had the face of a nondescript man in his thirties with brown hair, brown eyes, and a bland expression. The eyes were locked on me now, and as I looked into the future I saw that its movements were solid lines of light, changing to match my decisions but without choice or variation. A construct. The woman and I backed to the door and the construct followed.

My counter is an L shape set against the wall. As the woman opened the door I moved into the dead-end space, reaching for what was under the counter. I'm not so paranoid as to carry weapons in my own home, but I'm just paranoid enough to stash them where I can reach them quickly. I knew without looking that the construct would follow me, and as it came around the counter I straightened up with the gun in both hands, thumbed off the safety, sighted at a range of less than two feet, and shot the thing in the middle of the chest.

My gun's a M1911, a single-action semiautomatic. It had

been a while since I'd fired the thing and I'd forgotten how damn loud it was. The crash echoed around the shop and made me flinch, and the construct jerked. As a general rule anything worth shooting is worth shooting twice, so I brought the gun down and shot the construct again.

The construct jerked a second time, then closed in. In the instant before it reached me, I had just enough time to realise two things: first, the shots had done absolutely nothing, and second, I was backed into a corner with nowhere to run. A moment later, the construct had its hands around my neck.

By construct standards, the thing was weak. Unfortunately, weak by construct standards is still freakishly strong for a human. The thing's fingers locked around my throat like iron, crushing my windpipe and cutting off the flow of blood to my brain, and in panic I dropped the gun and grabbed at its hands, trying and failing to pull them away. The construct stared at me, its eyes empty and bland as it methodically choked me to death. My vision was just about to grey out when I remembered my training. I put my hands together under my chin knuckle to knuckle, fingers down and slightly hooked, then jerked my arms apart in a single explosive motion.

The leverage was enough to break the construct's grip. Its hands flew apart, air flew back into my lungs, and before the construct could recover I kneed it in the groin with the strength of panic and slammed both palms into its chest. The knee to the groin did nothing but the palm strike sent it stumbling backwards. Its legs caught on the rope to the magic item section and it went over, its head slamming into the floor with a *crack*. It started to get up immediately.

I staggered through the door into the hallway, gasping for breath. The woman was there, looking at me with wide eyes, and I gestured and rasped, "Up!" The woman turned and ran up the stairs, I followed, and as I scrambled upwards I heard the construct come through the door right behind us.

Constructs are made things, a physical body animated by magical energy. The most powerful ones use the bound spirit of an elemental, but even the weakest can be deadly because they're so persistent. They don't feel pain, they don't get tired, and they can't be bought off or bargained or negotiated with. Once a construct's been given an order, it'll follow it to its own destruction, and it's not harmless until it's completely destroyed. I'd been fighting for less than a minute but already I was gasping for breath, my limbs heavy and tired. The construct hadn't even slowed down.

The woman raced up the stairs with me right behind her. The construct reached through the banisters, grasping for my ankle, and missed. The extra few seconds were enough for me to reach the landing. The woman was there and looking from side to side. I rushed past her into my living room. "Hold the door!"

The woman hesitated. She was small, frail-looking, with long dark hair. "I can't—"

I slammed the door behind her just as the construct appeared at the top of the stairs. "Learn!"

The moment's breather had given me time to get my brain working. Weapons weren't going to hurt this thing—the only way to physically destroy it would be to literally tear it to pieces. But I'd picked up an item a long time ago designed specifically for this. Now where had I put it?

My bedroom's just through the living room, separated from it by a connecting door. I pulled open a desk drawer and started rifling through. There was a thump as the construct hit the living room door and out of the corner of my eye I saw the woman recoil, then throw herself desperately against the door and slam it closed again. I rummaged through the drawer: knives, tassels, jewellery boxes, marbles, figurines, carved stones, bags of powder, vials, clear plastic boxes filled with everything from dried flowers to Russian dolls. Wrong drawer. I yanked open the next one. Counterspell ingredients, no. Gate stones, no. Notebooks, no. Wands—

"It's coming through!" the woman shouted from the living room, her voice high and panicked.

"Hold it a second," I told her. Fetishes, no. Crystal holders—wrong kind. I moved on to the next drawer.

"I can't!"

There. Beneath a sheaf of handwritten papers was a needle-thin stiletto made of gleaming silver. I snatched it up and moved back into the living room. The construct had stopped hitting the door and was simply pushing. The woman was being slid back as the door was forced steadily open, the carpet scuffing up beneath her heels. "Let go!"

The woman jumped back almost as soon as I spoke and the door flew open. I'd been watching the futures and I knew exactly how the construct would come through the doorway, its hands up, grasping blindly. I let the door breeze past my face, saw a flash of the construct's emotionless eyes as it came in at me, then I ducked and the thing's hands swept over my head. The construct ran straight onto the stiletto, the blade piercing its stomach.

The construct's eyes seemed to flash. Sea-green energy wreathed its body, pouring out into the air, soaking down through the floor, then the energy cut out and the eyes went dead. It was over in an instant. The construct dropped to the floor like a puppet with its strings cut.

And everything was quiet.

I stood still, feeling my heart pounding in my chest. The construct lay motionless and a scan of the futures confirmed that it wouldn't be getting up. I kept looking, searching for other threats.

"Is it dead?" the woman asked at last.

I opened the window and stuck my head out, looking down into the street. I could see movement at the far end near the corner, but no one was approaching. I scanned through the futures, checking to see if police were coming. The fight had been noisy, and there had been shots fired, but I couldn't find any trace of a future in which police cars arrived. I gave a silent thank-you to the rain and to the fact that most Londoners don't know what gunshots sound like.

"What *was* that thing?" The woman's voice was shaky. "How did—?"

I held up a hand. "Wait here. Don't touch anything."

The shop downstairs was a mess. Shattered glass and merchandise were scattered across the floor and a cold wind was blowing away the smell of gunsmoke. I checked to see if either of the bullets had gone through the construct and into the wall behind (they hadn't), then got some plastic sheeting from the stockroom and tacked it over the broken window. It didn't do anything to keep the cold out, but it blocked line of sight. With that done, I locked the door and hid the gun. The adrenaline rush of the battle had worn off, and I knew that if I did what my body was telling me and sat down, I'd go to pieces. Experience has taught me that the best way to get through postbattle shakes is to walk them off, so I went back upstairs.

The woman was sitting on my sofa with her knees together and her hands clasped, shivering slightly. She didn't try to speak as I knelt over the construct and gave it a quick search. I came up empty, as expected; mages don't send construct assassins out with identification. The wounds hadn't bled or oozed. Most constructs are basically a big energy battery with a simple guidance program and this seemed to be one of the more basic types, an outer shape wrapped around a jellylike storage material. At a glance it looked similar to the ones I'd seen made at Richard's mansion: a short-range design, without the intelligence or stamina to operate for long on its own. That suggested whoever had sent it was close by. The stiletto had been a one-shot designed to disperse a construct's energy pattern. It had worked perfectly. I'd have to get another.

I was avoiding looking at the woman. I sat on the chair facing her and met her gaze.

It's hard to describe just what made her so incredibly

beautiful. She had near-black hair, long and slightly wavy, falling down her back and framing a diamond-shaped face with slightly tanned skin and dark eyes. She was small, only a little over five feet, but with such perfect proportions that you wouldn't realise it unless you stood right over her. She wore dark clothes that looked so simple that they had to be very expensive, and a single ring on her right hand. Somehow, though, neither her clothes nor her features seemed to matter—they were the adornments of a painting or a picture, not the real thing. What made her so captivating was something else, not so easily named: the way she moved, the glance of her eyes, the manner and sound and form. All I wanted to do was sit and gape. If I'd let myself fall into her eyes, I think an army of constructs could have battered down the door and I wouldn't have noticed.

"What's your name?" I said. I'd meant to say *Who are you?* but found myself changing my mind at the last second.

"Meredith." She leant forward a little. "Thank you so much. You saved my life." Her dark eyes shone with a hint of tears. "Without you I wouldn't have had a chance."

I felt my face burn and wanted to look away. A less polite but more vocal part of me spoke up with several suggestions as to how she could show how grateful she was. "Don't worry about it. Where did that thing come from?"

Meredith shivered. "I don't know! I was just—" She covered her face with her hands and started to cry.

Somehow I found myself on the sofa next to her, my arm around her shoulders, speaking quiet reassurances. Meredith hung onto my sleeve and kept crying. Gradually her tears ran dry and eventually she excused herself and vanished into the bathroom. She was gone for ten minutes and when she reappeared she looked a bit more composed. "I'm sorry, I didn't mean to go to pieces. I'm not usually like this."

"It's okay, you just had a shock. I did a lot worse my first time." Was that true? I couldn't remember. "Feeling better?"

Meredith nodded. "Yes, thanks. I must look terrible."

"Really, you don't."

Meredith returned to the sofa, sitting down naturally next to me. "I'm sorry for all this. I didn't mean for this to happen. I was trying to find your shop and then that . . . that thing started chasing me."

I glanced over at the construct's body, still lying on the floor. Meredith followed my gaze. "I've never seen one before. I heard stories but—"

"It's an assassin," I said. "Programmed to go after you. It only attacked me when I got in its way."

Meredith shivered. "It's horrible. There . . . won't be any more?"

I shook my head, and Meredith sighed in relief. "Do you know who sent it?" I asked.

"I don't know their names. I was so afraid they'd come after me. I heard it and I just wanted to find you and—"

"Why me?"

Meredith looked up in surprise. "But you're famous. Everybody knows about you. You fought all those Dark mages in that battle in the British Museum. And you can see the future."

"Um . . ." That took me aback. I'm definitely a lot better known since that business with the fateweaver but it was the first time I'd heard the word *famous*. "And you thought I could help you?"

Meredith clutched my arm. "Please don't send me away! I don't know if they'll try again. I know it's a lot to ask but can't I stay here? Just for tonight?" Wide dark eyes looked up at me pleadingly.

I'm not sure I could have said no even if I'd wanted to.

                    ı ı ı ı ı ı ı ı ı

And that was how, an hour later, I found myself lying on my bed with Meredith on the sofa in the next room, about ten feet away. The house was quiet but for the sounds of the city. I could hear the shouts and calls from the restaurants one street over and the hum of traffic from the main hub of Camden Town.

I found myself listening for what Meredith was doing. I couldn't quite hear her breathing and I wondered if she'd moved. Maybe I should have offered her the bed. No, that wouldn't have been smart. All of my items were here. But still . . .

I shook my head sharply in frustration. What was wrong with me? I'd even found myself wondering if she might come through into my room—

No. *Stop being stupid and think.* Who was she? She obviously wasn't a normal. An adept or a mage? It was the kind of thing I would normally have asked but for some reason I hadn't. In fact, I hadn't taken any of my normal precautions.

It's rare for there to be a woman sleeping over in my flat. Like, once-in-a-blue-moon rare. I could say it's because I'm a diviner and it would be sort of true—being able to know another person's secrets doesn't do wonders for a relationship. I could also say it's because I suck at romance and that's definitely got something to do with it—I've never been good at knowing what to say to women and my lifestyle hasn't given me much chance to improve. I could say it's because I used to be an outcast from both mage factions and that sure didn't help.

But if I'm being honest the biggest reason is that I have serious issues with trusting people. Since I was young, every time I've put my trust in another person and depended on them, it's ended badly. Sometimes very badly. I first learnt magic as a Dark apprentice in a society where everyone was a predator and giving away the wrong piece of information could get you hurt or killed. Things got worse before they got better and by the time I got to relative safety it was burnt into me to treat everyone as a potential enemy. I don't like it—it's not natural to me—but it's an ingrained habit and it's saved my life at least once. Even if I don't have any reason to be suspicious of someone, or even if I'm actually *trying* to be trusting, there's a part of me that stays on guard, always alert.

So I didn't fall asleep. I dozed, but that wary animal instinct stayed alert, listening for movement from the living room. And when Meredith's phone gave a muted buzz, I was awake instantly. I heard the sound of her picking up and the murmur of her voice, then her footsteps crossing the room and the creak of the door.

I swung my legs off the bed and moved to the connecting door, my bare feet silent on the carpet. The living room was empty and I could see the blanket lying ruffled on the sofa. The door to the landing was open and I could hear the sound of Meredith's voice from below.

I crossed the living room and slipped through, the planks of the landing cool under my feet. Through the banisters, I saw a flicker of movement: Meredith was below, in the hall, her head down, speaking into her phone. ". . . have much choice!" Her voice was pitched low and she sounded scared and angry. "You said they wouldn't come after me!"

The other person replied, an inaudible buzz. Whatever they said, it didn't make Meredith any happier. "Don't give me that! Did you know this was going to happen?"

". . ."

"No! This wasn't the deal."

". . ."

"Don't you dare."

". . ."

"What, be your bait?" Meredith gave a shaky laugh. "You wish."

". . ."

"No shit I'm angry! If I hadn't come here I'd be dead right—"

". . ."

"Oh, now it's *my* fault?" Meredith paced up and down the hall, only barely keeping her voice down. "Screw you!"

". . ."

"Go to hell. Why am I even talking to you?"

". . ."

"Yeah well, I'm a lot safer here than with you."

The voice on the other end started to answer again but Meredith cut it off halfway through. "You're gonna have to do better than that." She hung up and switched off the phone.

I withdrew silently back across the living room, pulled the door to behind me, and lay down on my bed. A minute later I heard footsteps on the stairs, followed by the sound of the door to the landing being softly shut. A moment later the sofa's springs creaked and there was the rustle of blankets followed by a soft sigh.

I lay awake, listening, but nothing further came. It was a long time before I fell asleep.

chapter 3

I woke to the sun on my face. Rays were streaming through my bedroom window, lighting up the drab room in yellow and white. Outside the window I could hear the chatter and bustle of the city. The storm had passed and the sky was blue with white cloud.

From the living room and kitchen, I could hear the bustle of movement. Meredith was making breakfast. I rose quietly and slipped into my jeans and shoes, then moved out onto the landing. The smell of something frying drifted from under the door to the kitchen and I heard the clink of plates. I opened the door out onto the balcony and stepped outside, shivering slightly in the cold, and the sounds from the kitchen cut off as I shut the door behind me. I climbed the ladder set into the wall and stepped off onto the roof.

It was a beautiful morning. Puffy white clouds were scattered across a clear sky and the sounds of the city washed up all around me, carried upon fresh, cold air. Puddles of water were scattered on the flat roof, left over from last night's storm, but the sun had been up long enough for most of the damp to dry. A breeze was blowing, cool and brisk, sending ripples racing across the water. Chimneys and TV aerials rose up all around, and a little farther away were road and rail bridges as well as the square shapes of blocks of flats. The morning sunlight was clear and crisp, outlining every brick and stone in sharp-edged shadow. It was London: dense, ancient, and my home.

I took out my phone and dialled Talisid's number. In case you're wondering why I was climbing onto the roof to make a phone call, it's because I didn't want to be overheard.

It's a perfectly reasonable thing to do. Stop looking at me like that.

Talisid answered when I'd expected. "Morning, Verus."

"How did things go on Friday?"

"Routine. As far as the Council's concerned, the matter's closed."

"Did you figure out what killed the barghest?"

"No need. Now that it's dead, no one has any reason to spend the time."

"Is the body in storage?"

"Destroyed."

"Oh."

"Did you want it examined?"

"I'd been hoping it would be." I couldn't honestly say it was unexpected but it was a bit disappointing all the same.

"I could always give you the autopsy report."

". . . Wait, what?"

I heard Talisid chuckle. "Glad to see you're not entirely immune to being surprised."

"I thought you just said there wasn't any need?"

"There wasn't. I had the corpse analysed anyway."

"Why?"

"Because you were curious."

"And you thought you'd satisfy my curiosity?"

"No, I decided if you were curious, it was probably worth looking into. Consider it a compliment."

I snorted. "All right, Sun Tzu. What did you find?"

There was the rustle of paper in the background. "Physically, the barghest was completely undamaged apart from minor bruises and lacerations. As far as nonmagical analysis can show, the creature was in perfect health."

"Apart from being dead?"

"Apart from being dead. Magical scans also negative. Fatal life or death magic usually leaves distinctive evidence in the cellular structure, and the same goes for mind and charm magic in the brain. There was no evidence that living family magic had caused the creature's death."

I frowned. "So that means . . . what? It wasn't killed by injury *or* by magic?"

"Not quite. There was no spell residue but there was something missing. The creature's natural residual aura was only a fraction as strong as it should have been. Something drained the energy right out of the thing. The examiner thinks that was the cause of death, and I agree. Barghests are magical creatures. Take away their magic, no more barghest."

"Huh." I stood thinking. "That's not a normal way to kill something, is it?"

"It's not. What's your interest in this?"

"Favour for a friend. Do you want me to copy you in if I find anything?"

"Please. Was there anything else?"

"Yeah. Know anything about a woman called Meredith?"

"Meredith . . . Dark, petite, late twenties to early thirties? Could cause a traffic accident walking down the street?"

"That's the one."

"Unaligned mage. Affiliated with several different Council mages over the years, but she's always stayed independent. Probably got a few connections in the Dark camp as well, though nothing's been proven. She dabbled in politics for a while and used to be a regular on the social circuit, but she got too close to that business with Dagon last year and had her fingers burnt rather badly. Haven't seen her at the balls since then."

I paced slowly up and down. "What type of mage?"

"Enchantress. Not too powerful but very skilled. Could twist men around her little finger."

I stopped moving.

"Verus? You there?"

I was silent for a few seconds. "Yeah," I said at last.

"Is there a problem?"

"No," I said. "No problem. Any connections?"

"No master, no apprentices. Her name's been linked with plenty of other mages, but the relationships never seem to last. They're usually active in Council politics and always men. You can guess what the rumour mill has to say about that, but the truth is no one knows very much about her."

I stood quietly on the roof. "Thanks for the help," I said eventually.

"No problem. I take it you weren't asking from academic interest."

"No."

Talisid sounded amused. "Well, consider yourself forewarned. You'll have to tell me how it goes."

"Assuming I'm around to tell you. I'll be in touch about the barghest."

"Good to hear. Until then." Talisid hung up.

I lowered the phone and stared down at it. The cool wind blew over me, ruffling my hair and chilling my bare arms, and I shivered.

Enchantresses use charm magic, also known as emotion magic. Men who can use it are called enchanters, but they're rarer and it's always seen as one of the stereotypically female branches. They can't affect thoughts and concepts in the way a mind mage can, but they're masters of feeling and emotion. In terms of raw power they're on the low end of the magical scale but they have one distinctive ability: their magic is incredibly hard to detect. It's almost impossible to tell when an enchantress is using her magic and when she's not. The whole distinction between magical and normal is much more fuzzy for enchantresses than it is for other mages; magic for them is as natural as talking and just as easy, and they're sometimes not aware they're using it at all.

Mages tend to be wary of enchantresses, almost as much as they are of diviners. Our emotions are one of the most basic parts of what we are. The idea that someone can *make* you like or love or hate, and that there's no way to know when they're doing it . . . well, most people find it disturbing.

Including me. As soon as Talisid had said the word *enchantress*, I'd had a jolt. Right now I was running back through my memories from last night. Had I been under Meredith's spell? Was that why I'd let her in and helped her so readily? I'd hardly even asked her any questions. A subtle urge to trust, to protect . . .

Or maybe it was what I would have done anyway. This is why charm magic's such a headache. It *could* have been magic. Or it could have been because Meredith had needed my help and asked me for it, or because if I hadn't acted she would have been killed right there on my shop floor, or because she was really hot and I'm single.

I shook my head and started climbing back down to the balcony. It was time to ask Meredith some questions.

· · · · · · · · · ·

The smell of frying bacon greeted me as I walked into the living room. The table was set, and Meredith was working at the kitchen unit. She looked different in the morning sunlight, but just as lovely. She turned at the sound of the opening door. "Oh, you're up! I'll be done in just a minute."

"Okay," I said, but didn't sit down. Instead I walked over to see bacon sizzling in the frying pan, along with some mushrooms.

"Was it okay to use your kitchen?" Meredith asked. "I didn't want to wake you."

"No, that's fine. Uh . . . where did you find all this?" My kitchen isn't exactly what you'd call well stocked.

"Oh, I went out and got a couple of things. You don't mind? I made some for you too."

"Thanks." My breakfast usually doesn't get any more advanced than cereal. This smelt really good.

"Great!" Meredith took out a couple of mugs. "Tea or coffee? I didn't know which you prefer so I made both."

"Tea would be great." I'm used to being alone in the mornings. Looking around at the warm kitchen and the smell of cooking food, it occurred to me that this was really nice. Much better than eating on my own and—

Suddenly I shook my head. What was I *doing*? I'd come in resolved to get some answers out of Meredith yet as soon as she'd started talking to me I'd forgotten all about it. "Look," I said. "Don't take this the wrong way. But I think it's about time you explained what's going on."

Meredith was turned away from me so that I couldn't see her face. She didn't react visibly. "What do you mean?"

"I think you've got a pretty good idea."

Meredith paused a second, then turned and looked at me with those big dark eyes. "What do you want to know?"

"Let's start with the basics. Who sent that thing after you and why were you coming to my shop last night?"

Meredith hesitated. "It's . . . Do you mind if we sit down?"

I sat. Meredith moved things from the counter to the table. I waited, knowing she was going to speak eventually. "I don't know their names," she said at last.

"How did you meet them?"

"I didn't! I've never met them."

"All right," I said. "Why don't you start from the beginning? How did you get involved in this?"

Meredith leant against the counter, her hands wrapped
around her arms. She was staring off into the corner and
seemed to have forgotten about both me and the food. "It
was . . ." She hesitated. "It was Belthas."

"Who's Belthas?"

"A Light mage. With the Council."

I didn't recognise the name, but that wasn't surprising. I
know the names of the Junior and Senior Council and a few
of the heavy hitters but I'm not well connected enough to
know everyone the way Talisid does. "Same cabal?"

Meredith shook her head. "No. He came to me and
wanted my help with something. We're not partners or
anything . . . Oh, you know."

I nodded. A lot of business amongst mages gets done in
these kinds of loose arrangements. Sometimes they last,
sometimes they go their separate ways once the job's done,
and occasionally they fall apart right in the middle of what
they're supposed to be doing (doesn't happen often, but when
it does it's usually spectacular). Once you start to pick up a
reputation, it's pretty common for mages to approach you
with offers like this. Sometimes it's genuine and sometimes
it's a con, and it can be tricky to tell which is which. "What
did he want?"

Meredith hesitated again. "I'm not sure—"

"Come on, Meredith," I said. "You want my help, this is
part of the deal."

Meredith looked at me for a second, then turned back to
the stove. She switched off the heating ring and the kettle
and started putting out the food. I waited, knowing she was
making up her mind about what to say.

"Belthas told me about a group of Dark mages," Meredith
said without looking up. "They were supposed to have gotten
their hands on some sort of ritual, something powerful. He
wanted to stop them."

"What kind of ritual?"

"I don't know. He just told me that he wanted me to find out where they were." Meredith set the plates down on the table with a clink. "I found they were in London and where they were going to be. Belthas and his men went to meet with them to make a deal. Something went wrong. There was a fight. After that, the Dark mages started hunting me. They knew I'd been talking to Belthas."

"Why did you come here?"

"I was scared," Meredith said quietly. "The other people at the meeting got hurt really badly. Belthas wasn't answering and . . . and I came to you. You've done this sort of stuff before, haven't you? With that thing that happened at the British Museum?"

I picked up my knife and fork and took a bite, chewed, and swallowed. "Don't believe everything you hear."

"But everyone says—"

I cut across without raising my voice. "And if it *were* true, it would be covered by Council secrecy and I wouldn't be allowed to talk about it."

"So . . . you *did* do all that?"

I looked at Meredith silently. After a few seconds she dropped her eyes.

"Meredith, don't get the wrong idea," I said. "I'm a diviner. I find things out. I don't get into fights if I can help it. If you want a bodyguard, you're in the wrong place."

Meredith looked down at the floor. "I haven't anywhere else to go," she said. "There isn't anyone who'll help me, not without . . ." She trailed off, staring at the wooden floor, looking very small and vulnerable.

I suddenly felt a wave of sympathy for Meredith, wanted to help and protect her. I fought it off; I didn't trust my feelings at the moment. "So you want my help," I said.

Meredith nodded, without raising her eyes.

Damn it. The sensible thing would be to tell Meredith that I was sorry but it wasn't my problem and turn her out.

I didn't want to get into a fight with a bunch of Dark mages and I didn't know how much I could trust Meredith or what her real intentions were. I still had the feeling she wasn't telling me everything.

But I was pretty sure she was telling the truth about being scared. That construct had been no joke. If I hadn't been there it would have killed her. And when it came right down to it, I hate turning someone away who's come to me for help. It's not that I'm especially selfless or anything, but I know what it's like to be alone and hunted and afraid. I've seen the expression on people's faces as they decide not to get involved, the look in their eyes as they shut you out, and I hate it. Maybe when it comes down to it, that's all that matters.

"All right," I said. Meredith's eyes lit up in relief and I raised a hand in warning. "Two conditions. I'm not fighting your battles for you. I'll do what I can but I'm going to avoid trouble as much as possible. Second, you tell me everything. If I find out you're keeping anything back, you're out. Understand?"

Meredith nodded instantly. "Yes. Thank you. If there's anything I can do—"

Her eyes were *really* distracting. "You can owe me a favour. I think the first thing is to talk with Belthas. I'd like to know what got these Dark mages so upset."

"I can try and get through by phone. He's got a business address in the City."

I nodded. "Get in touch and set up a meeting as soon as you can." I glanced at my watch; it was almost ten o'clock. "Right now I've got somewhere to be."

⁙⁙⁙⁙⁙

Meredith wasn't completely happy about being separated from me, but once I'd promised she wouldn't be in danger for a few hours she reluctantly agreed to wait. Settling her down and explaining what she should do took longer than I'd expected and by the time I'd finished I didn't have time to make it to the Heath on foot.

I went back up to my roof. Camden had woken up and the air was filled with noise and the rumble of traffic. This time I hopped across to the roof next to mine and kept walking until I was amidst the chimney stacks and ventilators of the block of flats a few buildings down. I use this roof when I don't want anyone watching or when I'm feeling especially paranoid, both of which happen more often than they probably ought to. I took out a small glass rod from my pocket—a focus—and wove a thread of magic through it, whispering. "Starbreeze. Traveller, watcher, listener, queen of cloud and sky. I call—"

Something flipped my hair into my eyes and I cut off, turning around with a sigh. "Heard it before, huh?"

Starbreeze is invisible to sight and to most other senses too. It's not that she conceals herself, it's just that she's made of air, and she looks exactly like what air looks like. To my mage's sight, though, she looks like a woman drawn in blurry lines of blue-white, ever-shifting. She changes her looks daily but there's something in her face that's always the same, something ageless. Starbreeze is an elemental, and she's immortal and eternal, fast as the wind and as powerful as the sun.

She's also got the memory of a goldfish. It's like her mind's got a storage limit, and for every new thing that comes in, one old thing goes out. Sometimes I think her immortality and her ditziness are connected: she can never age because she can never change. But she's saved my life at least once and I care about her a lot, though I'd never tell her so.

Today Starbreeze looked like a woman in a flowing dress with long hair falling to her ankles. She whipped around me in a tight corkscrew. "Where've you been?"

"I've been dealing with monsters and assassins and trying to persuade someone not to . . . You know what, if I explained it you'd forget halfway through."

"Forget what?" Starbreeze said brightly.

"Never mind. Can you take me to Arachne's lair?"

Starbreeze came to an abrupt halt, upside down with her head eye level with me, her hair hanging down to the floor. "Present first."

"Here you go." I took a small silver piece of jewellery out of my pocket, a stylised dolphin designed as a brooch. I keep a stack of them in a drawer. "I just—"

"Ooh!" Starbreeze snatched the dolphin out of my hands and whirled up into the air, tossing the brooch around in delight. "Starbreeze!" I yelled.

Starbreeze halted, looking down at me from twenty feet up. "Hmm?"

"Can you take me to Arachne's lair?"

Starbreeze's face cleared. "Oh right." Before I could blink she'd darted down, turned my body into air, and whisked me up into the sky.

I love flying with Starbreeze. When I was younger I used to wish I could fly but being carried by an air elemental is better. Starbreeze transforms the bodies of whoever she's carrying into air, then mixes them with her own form, carrying them along with her. It means you can go as fast as she can, and Starbreeze is *fast*.

The city shrank underneath me as Starbreeze rocketed upwards, the buildings and roads becoming a winding grid. London looks sprawled and confusing from above, the twisting, irregular roads making it hard to pick out where you are. I could see the winding shape of the Thames to the south, and the green spaces of Regent's Park and the Heath ahead and to the left. Starbreeze could have gotten me to Arachne's lair in ten seconds flat but she was obviously enjoying herself far too much to hurry. She kept climbing until we were on the level of the clouds then started soaring between them, twining her way between the fluffy masses like they were some kind of gigantic obstacle course. Looking down at London spread out below me, I could see the shadows of the clouds dotted across the city, the sun and darkness alternating almost like a chessboard. I was supposed to be at Arachne's lair, but really, I didn't mind that much. I relaxed, letting the scenery scroll beneath me.

There was a flat-topped cloud the size of an aircraft carrier drifting over Crouch End. Starbreeze swung towards it, soared vertically up its bumpy sides, then levelled off over the top, her wake brushing the cloud's surface as she cruised over it. "Oh!" she said suddenly. "Someone's asking about you."

"Asking about me?" I said. My voice sounds weird when I'm in air form; a sort of buzzy whisper, though Starbreeze seems to understand it easily enough. "Who?"

Starbreeze brought us up onto a tower reaching up out of the top of the cloud. It gave a panoramic view of London, the city stretching away in all directions. "You!" Starbreeze said. "Cirrus told me a nightwing told him a man asked the nightwing."

"About me?"

"Mm-hm." Starbreeze frowned. "Wait, the nightwing told me. Maybe a man told Cirrus." Her frown cleared. "Where are we going?"

"Just a second. What were they asking about me?"

"Who?"

"The men talking to Cirrus."

"No, to the nightwing."

"And they were talking about me?"

"They were?"

I sighed. "Let's go to Arachne's lair."

"Okay!" Starbreeze whirled me up, did a somersault, and dived straight down into the cloud. There was a second of icy chill as near-freezing vapour rushed past us, then we were diving towards the Heath at what felt like a thousand miles an hour. I had one lightning-fast glimpse of rushing grass, people, and flashing trees, then Starbreeze turned me solid again, dropped me in the ravine, and darted off before I could even say good-bye.

I checked that no one was watching, found the right spot in the oak roots, waited for Arachne to recognise my voice, and entered the tunnel, my mind focused on what Starbreeze had just told me. Starbreeze hears everything and she probably learns as much of what happens in the mage world as the highest members of the Council—it's just that she forgets it as fast as she learns it. But the fragment she'd repeated was enough to worry me.

I'm not ranked amongst the movers and shakers of magical society, and all in all, I like it that way. I've found my life is much easier if no one thinks I'm important enough to mess with. Having someone asking about me was disturbing. When mages take a sudden interest in a guy it usually means one of two things: they're considering an alliance, or they're planning to get rid of him.

ı ı ı ı ı ı ı ı ı

Luna was waiting for me in Arachne's living room, twirling a ribbon between her fingers. Arachne was perched over a table to one side, sewing away at something and apparently paying no attention at all. I felt awkward talking to Luna and it seemed she felt awkward too; I think both of us kind of wanted to apologise but didn't want to raise the subject. It was a relief to focus on training.

Mages normally take an apprentice who specialises in the same type of magic that they do. The branches of magic are *very* different; trying to teach a type of magic you can't use is a lot like trying to teach an instrument you can't play. But sometimes you just have to live with it, especially if you happen to be landed with one of the more uncommon kinds: If some kid's just discovered a talent for shapechanging, it's not exactly practical to wait five or ten years for one of the handful of master shifters to free up his schedule to teach him. In Luna's case, I wasn't sure if there even *was* a mage with her exact talent, and she wasn't a true mage either, meaning it was me or nobody.

Unfortunately, I was just as new to the master business as Luna was to being an apprentice, and the teaching methods I'd tried out over the last five months had been kind of hit-and-miss. Most had been ineffective, a few had turned out promising, and two or three had led to really spectacular disasters. But while sweeping up the mess from the last one, it had occurred to me that there might be a way of making use of how Luna's curse worked on objects. Her curse affects inanimate things as well as living ones; it's just that it's a lot weaker against dead material. But as we'd found out the hard way, the more vulnerable an item was to random chance, the more easily the curse seemed able to destroy it. After a bit of research, I tracked down the most unreliable and fragile brand of lightbulb on the market and bought a case of them.

Which was why Luna was standing in the middle of Arachne's living room with a lamp in either hand. We'd cleared a section of the room of fabric and furniture, and the brilliant white light cast a rainbow of colour from the clothes hanging all around, the fluorescent bulbs making a faint, persistent buzz. "Do I have to do this?" Luna asked.

"The better you learn to control your curse, the less likely you'll hit someone you don't want to."

"I get *that* part. Why do I have to *dance*?"

Luna was perched with her weight on her right foot, the left foot resting lightly with the leg straight, her right-hand lamp held at chest level in front of her and the other down by her side. This was her third session on Latin—the last two weeks had been ballroom—and it had taken me a good hour to get her stance right. It's a lot harder to correct someone's posture when you can't touch them.

To my mage's sight, the silver mist of Luna's curse swirled around her like a malevolent cloud. At her hands, though, the mist was reduced to a thin layer. The two lamps had a few strands of mist clinging to them, but not many. Luna was holding her curse back, keeping it from reaching the items in her hands. The bulbs were fragile and I'd learnt from experience that a single brush from her curse at full power was enough to burn them out. "Again," I said. "From the top."

Luna rolled her eyes but did as I said. I'd been teaching her a routine, and as I watched she ran through each move in the sequence. The silver mist flickered and swirled, but it stayed clear of her hands and the lamps shone steady and bright. "Good," I said once she'd stopped. "Now start doing basics and I'll give you instructions."

Luna settled into the basic rhythm, soft-soled shoes quiet on the stone floor. "Wouldn't it be more useful if I learnt martial arts or something?" she asked after a while.

"No."

"Why not?"

It was something I'd already thought about and decided against. Given the kind of situations I tend to get into, it would be a useful skill for Luna to know . . . except she'd be far more likely to end up hurting a friend than an enemy, and quite honestly, her curse is lethal enough already. "What you practice, you use without thinking. The last thing I want is to teach you to hit someone by reflex. Flares."

Luna hesitated an instant, then stepped into left and right stretches, one arm holding a lamp low, the other lifted high to the ceiling. "I can't even dance."

"New Yorks," I said. Luna obeyed reluctantly, turning on the spot in place of the backwards step. "I know dance, so you get to dance. Be grateful it's Latin and not Morris dancing."

"Might as well be," Luna said under her breath.

Ballroom dancing was one of the odder skills I picked up as apprentice to Richard. Light and Dark mages are quite traditional at the upper levels and a proper apprentice is supposed to be able to fight a duel, dance a waltz, and know which fork to eat dinner with afterwards. "Fan and hockey stick."

Luna hesitated again, trying to remember the complex figure, and this time the silver mist around her hands pressed outward. For just a second the lights flickered, then she stepped into the move and they steadied. She finished with a basic and started the next. "See? It's not—"

"Alemanas."

This time Luna managed without any hesitation. "Outer balance helps with inner balance," I said. "Your routine again."

Luna stopped talking for a few minutes as she worked through the pattern. The first time she got it wrong, but her concentration didn't waver and the lights shone steady. The second time was perfect. "Good," I said. "Now backwards."

"Oh come on!"

"And keep doing it till I tell you to stop."

Luna rolled her eyes again. I noticed, though, that even when she was struggling over the transitions, the silver aura around her didn't flicker. I'd started to suspect over the past week that Luna's control over her curse was tied more to her emotions than her thoughts: There didn't seem to be any connection between the difficulty of what she was doing and how likely it was that she'd slip. "There," Luna said after she'd done the reverse sequence three times in a row.

"Not bad. Now freestyle. Basic rhythm, any moves you like."

"How much longer are we going to stick with this?" Luna said as she stepped smoothly into the figures. Her technique was still pretty bad, but she was moving with more grace. Luna's never done much sport but she's not naturally clumsy and she was learning fast.

"Until you can dance with someone without killing them."

Luna stumbled, and the silver mist around her flared. The lights buzzed and flickered but she recovered control just in time, clawing the mist away from where it had been reaching for the lights. For a few seconds she stayed on basic steps, recovering her equilibrium. "That's not easy," she said at last, her voice quiet.

"Didn't say it was. But if you can dance body to body with someone without letting your curse touch them, that's when you'll be ready."

Luna returned to her routine, though with a little more caution in her steps than before. "How long?"

"However long it takes."

"It'll take forever." Luna's curse flickered, but only slightly.

I smiled slightly. "There's a story that Napoleon once told his advisors he wanted to plant trees by the sides of every road in France, so that his soldiers could march in the shade. His advisors said, 'But sir, that will take twenty years!' And Napoleon said, 'Yes, so we must start at once!' "

Luna was silent.

"You see, if something is going to take a long time—"

"I get it."

"How did things go last night with Martin?"

The silver mist around Luna surged. There was a blue-white flash and a ringing sound, and both bulbs blew out.

Luna rounded on me, glaring, and with my mage's sight, I saw tendrils of silver mist reaching towards me. They were ten feet away, five, and I tensed . . . then the tendrils halted and slowly pulled back, thinning as they withdrew. Only once they had merged back into the aura around her did Luna speak. "That wasn't fair."

"Wasn't meant to be," I said quietly. I didn't think Luna understood what she had just nearly done. But she understood what the lights burning out meant.

"It doesn't even—" Luna started to say in frustration, then caught herself. She turned and walked to the corner, unscrewing the bulbs from the lights, and dropped them into the bin. There was a clinking sound as they joined the pile.

I waited for Luna to cross the room and come back, giving things time to settle. "We're done for the day," I said. "I need to speak with Arachne. Wait outside and I'll catch you up."

Luna obeyed silently. I watched her go with a frown, then turned to see that Arachne had stopped work. Her eight eyes studied me, unreadable. "Okay, so that could have gone better."

Arachne didn't answer and I looked at her. "What's wrong?"

"I see why you were unsure about training her."

I winced. "That bad?"

"She isn't acting like your apprentice. And you're not acting like her master." Arachne crossed the cavern and settled down with her front legs brushing my sides, her head and fangs looming over me. "But that's a matter for the two of you. What did you learn?"

I hesitated, then put Luna out of my mind. "A friend of mine had the barghest's corpse looked at. He's not a hundred percent sure but best guess is that the thing was killed from having its magic drained out of it."

Arachne went still.

I waited but she didn't speak. "Arachne?" I said after a moment.

"I . . . see." The clicking sound under Arachne's voice was stronger.

"All right." I put one of my hands on Arachne's front leg and looked up at her. "What's going on? Something's bothering you about this."

Arachne turned and started walking slowly across the room. I followed her closely, keeping pace by her side and skirting around sofas and chairs. "You're worried this thing might be coming after you, aren't you?" I said. Arachne didn't react and my eyes narrowed. "No, that's not it. You're worried *you* might die the same way."

Arachne's mandibles rustled. "You see clearly in such matters."

"You mean when it doesn't involve Luna?" I shrugged. "If you tell me what you know, I might be able to help."

Arachne halted at the north end of her chamber. Arachne's living room/workroom is huge and roughly circular. The south end is the exit out to the Heath, to the northwest are a few small changing booths, and to the east are some spare rooms in which Arachne keeps supplies and facilities for her few guests.

At the north end, though, just next to where we were standing, was a tunnel sloping down into darkness. It wasn't lit, but from what light was reflected, I could see that it led into a T junction, forking away and down. Arachne's never told me what she keeps down there and I've never asked. But from what I've seen, I've gotten the impression that the tunnels keep on going down . . . maybe a long way down. For all the time I've spent with Arachne, she keeps a lot of secrets, and there's enough space under the Heath for those tunnels to spread a very long way.

I had to resist the urge to poke my head in and look. It wouldn't be polite, but it would really satisfy my curiosity. "Do you know of the Transcendence movement?" Arachne asked.

I frowned. "Vaguely. They were that group of rationalist mages who thought magic was the next stage in human evolution. They were trying to find ways of boosting magical potential, turn everyone into a mage."

"And what happened?

I shrugged. "They never got anywhere. People decided it couldn't be done, they started losing members, and then the Gate Rune War kicked off and everyone had other stuff to worry about. Why?"

"Most of your account is true but there is one fact you leave out. There was a way to increase magical power and the Transcendents were well aware of it."

"What do you mean?"

"You know it as Harvesting."

I flinched. Harvesting is the act of ripping a mage's magic from his body and taking it for yourself. It's always fatal for the victim, often fatal for the harvester, and usually comes with a variety of horrible consequences. It's the blackest of black magic, even forbidden by Dark mages, and that should really tell you something. "Are you serious? There's a *reason* that ritual's banned. Besides, it doesn't make any sense—the Transcendents wanted to make more mages, and anyone with half a brain can tell you that if you go in for Harvesting, you end up with *fewer* mages."

"Yes," Arachne said. "They could not draw the magic from humans. So they drew it from magical creatures instead."

I stopped. I'd never thought of that. "What happened?"

"They were successful," Arachne said. "The recipients gained the power and strength of the creature they harvested. The process also drove them insane. After enough deaths, the project was abandoned."

I frowned. It was the first I'd heard of the story; thinking about it, though, it made sense. Mages have a few (not many) compunctions about killing other mages but treating non-human creatures as living battery packs would suit them just fine. And mages don't like to publish failure. If experiments go disastrously wrong, they usually cover it up. "What are you getting at?"

"There are rumours that a mage—perhaps more than one—has returned to the Transcendents' research. I did not know whether they were true." Arachne turned her eight opaque eyes on me. "It seems they were. I believe this will be our last meeting for some time."

I nodded, resigned. Arachne hasn't lived however many hundreds of years by being careless, and I've seen her do this before. When danger comes, she vanishes. I've never known where she goes but I suspect the answer's somewhere down in those tunnels. "Well, I'll tell you if anything happens."

"I will be contactable for another two or three days," Arachne said. "After that . . ." She gave an odd rippling motion that I've come to recognise as a shrug.

Walking up out of Arachne's lair, I wondered just how many times she had done this over her long life, and how it worked. I've never heard of any other creatures like Arachne—giant intelligent magical spiders aren't a known type in the way that, say, elementals are. I've wondered sometimes if Arachne is unique . . . but then where did she come from? Are there others of her kind, out there somewhere? Or was she once something else?

· · · · · · · · · ·

I watched the earthen bank rumble back into place, the roots writhing and retwining themselves to lock the door closed, and knew I wouldn't be going back there for a while. It made me a little sad. There aren't many places where I feel comfortable, and Arachne's lair is near the top of a very short list.

Luna was standing nearby. I started walking out of the ravine and she fell in by my side. With my mage's sight I could see that the silver mist around her was muted. "What were you about to say back there?"

The sun shone down out of a blue sky, white clouds drifting with a brisk east wind. It was September and there was a chill in the air, but even so there was a scattering of people around the park, most wearing greatcoats or ski jackets. "When?" Luna said.

"You were about to say that trying to control your magic doesn't matter." I looked at Luna. "What's up with you? I thought you wanted this."

Luna walked silently for a few seconds. She was wearing her green coat, and the wind whipped at its sleeves and ruffled her hair. We reached a path that would lead us southeast and turned onto it. "What if there's another way?" she said without looking up.

"What do you mean?"

Luna sighed quietly. "Look, I've been doing this for months, okay? And I *suck* at it. It's been half a year and I still can't get through a session without burning the lights out!"

"We always knew it was going to take time," I said. "Luna, mages spend *years* learning to control their powers. It's not just you."

"Yeah, well, they don't kill everyone around them when they make a mistake." Luna stared down at the path. "I *know* what it means when one of those lights burns out. I can't make it so that it never happens. What's the point if I only *sometimes* kill people? It's just as bad."

The path crested the ridge and sloped into a wide, open hillside. We were in the part of the Heath just north of the tumulus, where the rolling meadows descend gradually in a long stretch of grassland before flattening out into the woods and ponds at the park's edge. It's open to the sky and we could see for miles. People, alone and in twos and threes and with dogs, were scattered across the great meadow, strolling. On the other side of the ponds, the ground rose again into the huge shape of Highgate Hill, the roofs of houses and a single church poking up between the trees. The valley between gave the illusion that the hill was much closer than it was, almost as if you could reach out and touch it. In the distance East London stretched away, clear in the autumn sun.

Luna and I turned off the path and started down the meadow. Beyond the ponds at the bottom was the main road. "So what are you going to do?" I asked. "Give up?"

Luna walked quietly for a minute. "What if there was another way?" she said again. "Make it safe without all the work. Wouldn't that be better?"

I looked sharply at her. "Are you—?"

Something flickered on my precognition and I stopped talking. Precognition is a kind of mental discipline and pretty much any diviner who spends much time in dangerous situations learns it by necessity. All diviners have the ability to see the future but we can only look in one place at a time. So what we learn to do is to recognise the outlines of the most important events that'll affect us personally, things like sudden changes or danger, and then we train our awareness so as to always keep a vague eye on the immediate future, at the back of our mind. It's like peripheral vision: you can't see details, but you can sense if something's about to happen, enough to turn your head and took a closer look.

I took a closer look.

Somebody was about to shoot me through the head in exactly eight seconds.

"Luna," I said. I kept my voice calm, even as my heart sped up, dumping adrenaline into my system. "We're about to get shot at. On my mark, go right and take cover."

Luna stared at me. "Wait, what did—?"

From somewhere on Highgate Hill a rifle fired, and a supersonic bullet flew towards me.

chapter 4

Most mages don't use guns. Mages will tell you that gun-powder weapons are crude and inferior, and it's kind of true: While mages have whole libraries of spells and tricks, all a gun can do is kill people. What mages tend to overlook, though, is that guns are *really good* at killing people. If someone lines up a gun on the right spot and twitches their finger, you're dead, end of story. Oh, it may not look impressive compared to battle-magic—a fire mage could incinerate your body, a life mage could stop your heart with a touch, a water mage could disintegrate you into dust—but when you get right down to it, most of that is just overkill. Dead is dead.

In a face-to-face fight, spell generally beats gun. Spells are just so much more versatile; a mage can counter pretty much anything with a second's warning. If the mage doesn't *get* that second's warning, though . . . well, a shot in the back has been the death of an awful lot of mages. Once a bullet's gone through your heart, it doesn't matter much how tough you are.

If I'd been an elemental mage I would have died on that hill. But I'm not; I'm a diviner, and while I have no power to affect the physical world, one thing I can do really well is spot an ambush. I shouted "Go!" to Luna and jumped to the left. An instant later a sniper bullet went through the space my head had been occupying.

A supersonic bullet makes a really distinctive noise and once you've heard it you never forget it. First there's the high-pitched *crack* of the sound barrier breaking, then an instant later the pitch drops into an reverberating echo as the sound waves from the bullet's flight path wash over you. The noise makes your heart jump, but hearing a sniper bullet is a *good* thing. The bullet outruns the sound wave; if it's on target, it kills you before you ever hear the sound of the shot.

I broke into a sprint, racing down the slope at an angle. I couldn't spare the time to look back at Luna; all I could do was hope she'd listened. The grass swished under my feet, and looking into the future I could see another shot coming. The hillside was open and bare, and I wouldn't get to cover in time.

The sniper fired again and I went into a roll. Another *crack* lashed my ears as the bullet whipped over me, driving into the grass and earth. I came up without breaking stride and kept running. There was an old thick tree up ahead, on a low rise; if I could reach it I'd be safe. I could sense the sniper getting ready to fire again, and I'd had long enough to mark the delay on the shots. His bullets were taking about half a second to cross the space between us. Doesn't sound like much but in combat that's a long time. The next shot was aimed at my body, and just as he fired I braked, slowing enough that the shot *cracked* past a couple of feet in front of me. A final shot fell short as I dived behind the tree and hit the deck.

I lay flat, my heart hammering. The earth under the tree was covered with thin grass, twigs, and nut shells, and they pricked my hands as I held myself still. The sun was shining down and the echoes of the shots had faded into the sounds of the city. There was no way you could have told from looking that someone was trying to kill me.

I was about halfway down the slope of the meadow. The ponds and forests at the bottom of the hill were clearly visible but to reach them I'd have to cross more than a hundred yards of open grass. As I looked around, I saw to my amazement that there were still people walking. A couple were looking around to see what the noise was, and one woman with a dog was shading her eyes and watching me, but most of them didn't seem to realise anything was wrong.

I pushed myself to my knees, being careful to keep the trunk of the tree between me and the sniper, and looked around for Luna. I couldn't see her, which was good. Carefully I leant my head around the tree trunk. The sniper had to be firing from Highgate Hill. I could see the giant shape of the hill rising up half a mile away and I scanned it with my eyes, but it was useless. Trees, houses, buildings, a thousand places to hide, all of them with a straight line of sight across the valley to the open meadow I was stuck in the middle of—

My precognition warned me just in time and I jerked my head back. Half a second later there was a high harmonic *crack* as a bullet whipped through the space that had just a moment ago been occupied by my right eye. My would-be assassin was a very good shot.

That last bit of information was enough to make me sure that I did not want to make a run for it. The ground around the tree was rolling grassland for fifty yards in every direction and I had no intention of trying my luck. I hugged the tree and waited.

Ten seconds passed, twenty. How long would the assassin stay with his sights trained on the tree? He couldn't afford to wait forever; the more time he spent in his position the better the chance of being found. Thirty seconds. Forty. I looked into the future and saw that putting my head out wasn't going to attract another bullet. Maybe he'd gone? No, there was another attack coming, it was—

My eyes went wide. *He's going to shoot me with a WHAT?*

I scrambled to my feet, leapt around the tree, and threw myself flat. Just as I dropped, something with an exhaust glow flashed very fast over my line of vision, then hit the ground on the other side of the tree and exploded.

It made a hell of a noise. I was less than five yards from the thing and all I heard was a massive bang followed by a ringing sound. Concussion whacked at my legs and arms but the tree was thick and solid and the shrapnel embedded itself on the other side. Leaves and twigs showered down. I couldn't hear but I knew another sniper round was coming and I scrambled back around the other side of the tree again, getting out of sight before the sniper could manage to fire.

I lay still as the ringing in my ears began to fade. The ground was warm and there was a blackened patch of scorched earth and grass about fifteen feet away where the explosive had gone off. I scanned frantically through the futures, trying to see if another rocket was coming so that I'd be able to get out of the way in time. Nothing. The people who'd been watching were scurrying away. Londoners might not be much good at recognising gunshots but they aren't going to stick around when someone's firing a bloody rocket launcher.

Gradually, as my hearing returned, I realised I couldn't sense any more attacks. I poked my head out cautiously, ready to spring into movement. Nothing happened. The tree trunk was pockmarked with scars where bits of shrapnel had torn into the bark. I looked into the future to see what would happen if I left the cover of the tree and saw nothing. I double-checked and triple-checked, but the futures stretching out before me were free of weapons fire. The assassin was gone.

I pulled myself to my feet and started jogging uphill. I looked through the futures for the ones where I ran across Luna and adjusted my course to match. The adrenaline was still coursing through my system and I covered the first hundred yards at a good pace until the reaction hit me and I suddenly felt like I'd just run a marathon. I forced my legs to keep going until Luna peered out from behind a clump of trees ahead of me. As she saw me, relief flashed across her face and she said something I couldn't hear.

"What?" I shook my head. "Sorry. Ears. Don't stop."

I fell into the fastest walk I could manage and Luna hurried to keep up, torn between wanting to get close and having to keep away. "Are you okay?" she said more loudly, her voice anxious.

"I'm okay. Keep moving." I adjusted our course to avoid curious bystanders. People were heading for the site of the attack but we would be able to steer clear of them.

My hearing returned as we reached Parliament Hill, just in time to pick up the distant wail of sirens from behind us, first one and then several. We headed down the hill as the sirens grew louder, passing the athletics track on our left and heading southwest. Only once we'd crossed the railway bridge and left the Heath behind us did I start to relax. "What *was* that?" Luna said at last.

"That was somebody trying to kill me," I said, managing to keep my voice steady. "Congrats, you've just had your first assassination attempt."

"They were trying to shoot you?"

"Yes they were." I shivered at the thought of how close they'd come. Divination magic is great for avoiding danger but it also lets you see every possible fate in vivid detail. In the process of dodging those shots, I'd seen exactly what would have happened if I *hadn't* dodged them and I'd gotten to watch myself torn apart by high-velocity bullets over and over again. It's gruesome and it's one hell of a mental shock if you're not prepared for it. I stuffed my hands into my pockets to stop them from shaking. "He was firing from Highgate Hill, across the valley."

Luna hesitated. "Do we . . . ?"

I shook my head. "No point. He'll be miles away by now."

"Who—"

"Not a clue."

Luna fell silent and we headed west on foot towards Camden Town, taking the back streets instead of the main roads. As I walked, I started making a list of everyone in the mage world whom I'd opposed, fought with, or otherwise irritated. After I ran out of fingers to count on I decided to limit the number to people I'd pissed off relatively recently. Two names topped the list: Morden and Levistus.

Five months ago I got involved in a hunt for a Precursor relic, a powerful imbued item called a fateweaver. Levistus wanted me to bring him the fateweaver and (as I found out the hard way) didn't want any witnesses to his involvement. Morden wanted the fateweaver too, and by a funny coincidence *he* didn't want anyone left to point fingers either. For my part, I didn't particularly care who got the fateweaver but did have quite strong opinions on staying alive.

As you've probably guessed, neither Morden nor Levistus got what he wanted, and I'd been expecting them to do something about it ever since. There was no way to be sure which one to blame the sniper on but my instincts said Levistus; sending agents to kill from a distance was very much his style. But there was a snag. If Levistus had wanted me silenced, the time to do it would have been five months ago. It was possible he just held a grudge and I wasn't ruling that out, but as a motive for murder it felt a bit thin.

There was a more recent and more obvious person to blame: the Dark mage who'd sent that construct. If I hadn't been there last night, it would have killed Meredith. Maybe this assassination attempt had been intended to make sure that next time I wouldn't get in the way.

But whoever it was, it was clear I'd gotten into something a lot bigger than I was prepared for. I walked the rest of the way in silence, laying plans. Luna didn't break into my thoughts. It wasn't until I was almost home that something occurred to me to cheer me up. Despite the argument, Luna had obeyed me instantly when danger had arrived, and the relief in her eyes when she'd seen that I was uninjured had been real. It was enough to make me feel a little better as I unlocked the door to my shop.

Luna did a double take. "Uh . . . ?"

"Hm?"

Luna pointed and I turned to see the smashed window. "Oh, right. That was the *other* assassination attempt."

Luna stared at me.

I sighed. "I need to get it fixed. Go on, I'll catch up." Luna picked her way through the trashed shop, looking around at the damage, as I called the number of a glazier who I knew wouldn't ask any questions. It's not like it's the first time this sort of thing has happened. Once I'd made the arrangements I followed Luna upstairs, then walked into the living room and stopped.

Luna was next to the sink with the cupboard open, having just taken out a glass. Meredith was in front of the balcony with the doorknob in one hand and her mobile phone in the other. She'd obviously just stepped inside after having made a call. In between Luna and Meredith was the body of the construct. I hadn't done anything about the thing and it was still lying facedown where I'd left it. Meredith was staring at Luna. Luna was looking up and down between Meredith and the dead construct. Then, in perfect unison, both of them turned to look at me.

"Uh," I said brilliantly.

The silence stretched out and I tried to figure out what to say. Well, both of them were technically my guests.

"Okay, so. Introductions. Luna, this is Meredith, a mage. Meredith, this is Luna, my apprentice. Luna, this is Bob the Dead Construct. Bob, meet Luna. So now we all know each other."

Okay, so social graces aren't my strong point. Hey, you try to come up with a polite way of introducing an apprentice, a mage, and a dead body.

Meredith reacted first. "Oh, of course." She glanced at Luna. "You didn't tell me you had an apprentice, Alex."

"No, I—" Luna looked from the construct to Meredith to me.

I was about to explain but Meredith spoke, moving to my side. "It was a construct assassin sent last night to kill me. Alex"—she put her hand on my arm—"saved me." She smiled up at me.

My face went red. "No, that's—"

"Oh, I'm sorry." Meredith looked at Luna, contrite. "Do you usually stay here? I didn't realise I was taking up your space."

Luna stared at the two of us for a long moment before answering. "No." Her voice was toneless.

"That's good." Meredith smiled at her. "So, you're Alex's apprentice? Have you been studying long?"

Luna was still staring and I realised she wasn't looking at me but at Meredith's hand where it rested on my shoulder. I moved away, breaking the connection, and as I did, Luna's eyes flicked up to my face, then down. "No." She put the glass down. "I should go."

I stared. "Already?"

"I'm supposed to meet Martin." Luna moved towards the door. Her movements were sharp, jerky, without her usual control. My precognition flared and instinctively I moved out of her way, and a moment later Luna was through the door.

"Luna, wait!" I followed her out into the landing.

Luna was halfway down the stairs. She stopped as I spoke, and as she did I pulled myself up short. To my mage's sight, the silver mist was lashing around her, its range and strength far greater than normal, tendrils snaking through the air and soaking into the walls and floor. Another step and I'd be in deadly danger.

I stood my ground. "I need to talk to you. Martin as well. Ask him to come to the shop tomorrow morning."

"Why?" Luna's voice was flat but there was an edge to it I hadn't heard before.

"You wanted me to help, right? If he comes in, maybe I can do something about that item."

A beat, then Luna nodded. "Fine."

I hesitated. I wanted to say more, something to encourage her, about how she'd done well today. But before I could think how to say it, Luna started back down the stairs and her curse flared again in the instant before she vanished into the hall. I heard the door shut, followed a second later by the bang of her leaving by the front door.

I frowned. For a moment I tried to figure out everything that had just happened, then my thoughts vanished in a wave of exhaustion. I returned to the living room and made it to the sofa before my legs collapsed.

"Alex?" Meredith said in concern. "Are you all right?"

"I'm fine," I said without looking up. The reaction from my near-death experience on the Heath hadn't worn off yet, and for some reason I didn't want to talk to Meredith right now. I felt as though what had just happened was her fault, though I couldn't explain why.

"Well . . . I got in touch with Belthas."

For a moment I didn't know who Meredith was talking about. It was funny; while I was with Luna and Arachne, all the details with Meredith just didn't seem important. Then I remembered. "Belthas, right."

"He says he'd like to meet you. I could take you to him this afternoon?"

All I wanted to do was sit there. "Okay," I said with an effort. "Give me half an hour and we'll go."

Meredith hesitated an instant, then withdrew. I leant back on the sofa and closed my eyes. I needed to figure out who was trying to have me killed and why. I needed to find out more about Belthas and Meredith and what their goals were. And I needed to do something about Luna and Martin and the monkey's paw. But right now all I wanted was to sit and rest, and remember a simpler time.

· · · · · · · · · ·

I made my preparations and travelled with Meredith to Canary Wharf. According to Meredith, Belthas had an office in one of the skyscrapers. It's not as rare as you'd think: Mages like towers. They're a kind of status symbol in the magical world, even though no one seems able to explain exactly why. Some say it's a leftover from the old days where mages had to worry about actual armies laying siege to their homes and a tower gave you a tactical advantage. Others say it's from when mages went in for astronomy—a tower makes a better observation platform. Other explanations I've heard include a better view, attracting attention, reducing electromagnetic interference, impressing members of the opposite sex, a way to reduce the danger of vertical teleportation mishaps, and *my tower is bigger than yours*. My personal suspicion is that mages like to feel above everyone else, but I usually keep that to myself. Belthas's office was near the top floor of the second- or third-highest skyscraper in the cluster, which meant he was either powerful and successful, concerned about his reputation, or compensating for something, depending on your point of view. The ground floor was huge, with tall wood-panelled walls and a shining white floor. A doorman showed us through the security gates and we stepped into a lift that carried us upward.

The back of the lift was mirrored and as we ascended I used the mirror to study Meredith. She'd been quiet all the way, hardly saying a word, and I wondered if she was

thinking about the mage we were about to meet. I hadn't
forgotten about the conversation I'd overheard last night and
I wondered if it had been Belthas she'd been talking to.
Meredith had sounded as if she wasn't happy about their
deal.

There was a *ding* and the lift stopped on the thirty-eighth
floor. From what I could see, Belthas seemed to own about
half the floor space. There was a receptionist to greet us but
my attention was on the men with guns and body armour
standing against the wall watching us with alert eyes: Council security. We were shown into a room, and after a brief
wait, the receptionist put her head in with a smile. "Mr.
Belthas will see you now."

It's not the first time I've been to see an important mage
in Canary Wharf. The last time, it was at night in the middle
of a ball, I was shown in alone, and I very nearly never
walked out again. The mage I'd met had been Levistus and
it had been a near thing. I could still remember the sound-
proofed room, silent and empty.

Belthas's office was very different. It was set into the
corner of the tower and sunlight streamed in from two glass
walls, leaving bright patterns on the carpet and keeping the
air comfortably warm. Belthas rose from his desk as we
entered and walked around to shake my hand. "Verus. I'm
glad you could make it."

Belthas was tall, almost as tall as me. His hair was almost
entirely white and he looked like a very well-preserved fifty.
His features were difficult to place: His face looked English,
but a faint accent to his words made me think of Eastern
Europe. He had a pair of clear blue eyes and a ready smile,
and his manner as he greeted me was friendly, but there was
something in those eyes that made me cautious. You don't
get places in Council politics without playing the system
and somehow I had the feeling that Belthas was watching
me just as I was watching him. He went through the usual
formalities while I gave the usual replies. Belthas wasn't

acting as though he had anything to hide . . . but then the best manipulators don't.

"Well then," Belthas said once we were seated and I'd refused the offer of a drink. "What can I do for you?"

"How much has Meredith told you?"

Belthas frowned. "I haven't been fully filled in. I understand you came under attack?"

"That's one way to put it," I said dryly. "Someone sent a construct assassin after Meredith."

Belthas's eyebrows went up. "I see."

"Yes. I'd appreciate knowing why."

Belthas steepled his fingers, seeming to think. Meredith was sitting quietly to one side, but otherwise the three of us were alone in the office. "I can certainly understand why you'd be upset," Belthas said. "And I'm grateful for your assistance. However, as I'm sure you're aware, the details are not common knowledge."

"Belthas, please don't play games," I said. "I'm a diviner. If I wanted to find out I could, and you know it."

Belthas didn't react, which was revealing: If he'd really meant to keep it a secret he wouldn't have taken it so calmly. "Perhaps this would go more smoothly if you explained your goals."

"I don't have any," I said. "At least I didn't until that construct came through my front window last night. Now whoever sent it's got a reason to go after me too, and Meredith's asked me to help her. Whether I agree depends on you."

Belthas didn't answer straightaway. I could feel the tension in Meredith off to my right but I couldn't detect any danger. The futures branching before us were only conversation . . . for now. "I can understand why you'd feel that way," Belthas said at last. "Perhaps if I explained how this situation came about."

I nodded and Belthas leant back in his chair. "It begins

with a mage named Jadan. He was Dark, but not as hostile as some, and I had some small contact with him. As far as I was aware he was devoted to his research and rarely ventured from his sanctum. He died last month, but it appears that before his death he made a breakthrough. From what I've learnt, he was able to finally develop a genuinely practical method of drawing energy from magical creatures."

I went dead still. I don't think I showed anything on my face, but it was a near thing. Belthas was looking at me, waiting for a reaction. "Harvesting is banned under the Concord," I said at last.

"Harvesting of *humans*. The laws don't apply to magical beasts."

"And the side effects?"

"As I understand it, the subjects came out sane." Belthas regarded me. "However, as far as I know, the knowledge of how to perform the procedure is currently in the hands of only one group: a small cabal of Dark mages. They are, for obvious reasons, attempting to keep it secret."

"And you found out about it."

"Yes," Belthas said. "I met with them recently and attempted to come to an understanding. It was my hope that we could negotiate something in exchange for an agreement that the technique would not be used. Negotiations were . . . unsuccessful."

"And after that they decided to finish off your associates."

"It appears so." Belthas looked at me. "I hope you can see why I don't wish the information to become public. Jadan's technique has the potential to place a vast amount of power in the hands of this Dark cabal. This would not be to anyone's advantage. In addition, there are suggestions that the technique could be adapted to humans. If this were the case, I'm sure I don't need to remind you of the potential consequences."

"I get it," I said shortly. My head was still whirling as I put everything into place.

Belthas glanced at Meredith, then leant forward, placing his elbows on the table. "Then with that in mind, perhaps you would be interested in hearing my offer."

I knew what he was going to say. "Your offer?"

"A simple contract of service. At present Meredith and I are the only mages opposing this group, and to be frank, we could use some assistance. You've already proved your ability. I would like to hire you."

"To do what?"

"Find the Dark cabal. Stop them."

"I'm not a battle-mage."

"From what I understand, you've acquitted yourself quite well against opponents who are." Belthas raised an eyebrow. "I've read the reports of the fateweaver incident. The uncensored reports."

"Then you know I don't get into fights if I can avoid it," I said. "If you're looking for someone to kill these guys, I can't help you."

Belthas shook his head. "Force is not in issue. I have enough influence with the Council to deal with the cabal in any direct engagement. What I need is an investigator. Someone to find the Dark mages and discover what they know about Jadan's method. Once we know that, we can move in."

"*You* can move in," I said. Belthas nodded and I thought fast. "And in return?"

"As I said, I have some influence with the Council. I could assist you in any endeavours with them, should you require it. If not, I can promise future service. I would of course insist on paying for your time as well, if only on a token basis. Would ten thousand pounds a day be reasonable? In advance, of course."

I had to stop my eyebrows going up at that. Like I said before, mages don't value money all that much. But they still use it as a sense of scale: that much per day meant that the favours he was promising were significant. Of course, if this job would put me in the sights of a Dark cabal, they'd have to be.

"There are some things I'd like to know first," I said.

"Of course."

"Meredith was on her way to see me when she was attacked. Why?"

"We had already identified you as a potential ally," Belthas said. "I delayed approaching you in the hope that we could resolve the matter without spreading the information any more than was strictly necessary. It seems Meredith decided on her own initiative that the priorities had changed." He glanced at Meredith, who nodded after a second.

"What are you going to do with this technique if you get it?" I said.

"I would prefer knowledge of its existence suppressed if possible."

"And if it's not possible?"

Belthas frowned. "Then the task will be considerably more difficult. However, I see no way to avoid that risk."

I fell silent. Belthas waited patiently for my answer. Looking into the future, I could see that I wasn't in any danger: Belthas wasn't going to try to silence me or anything if I said no. The question was whether I wanted to.

If this technique of harvesting magical creatures really existed—and from what Belthas and Arachne had said, it seemed pretty damn likely—I wanted it destroyed. The idea of the magical creatures of our world being hunted down in a race for their life force made me feel sick. I didn't know if it could be done but I was going to try.

On the other hand, I wasn't sure how much I trusted Belthas. His explanation had been plausible and smooth but something still made me hesitate. I'm pretty good at telling when I'm being lied to; if I had to bet, I'd have said Belthas was telling me the truth but not the *whole* truth. Although his manner was friendly, I couldn't shake the feeling that underneath it was something calculating. He was keeping something back, maybe something important.

But for exactly that reason, I didn't want to refuse. If I walked away, I'd have no way of learning what Belthas was up to. I already knew I wasn't going to let this drop; it was a choice of investigating with him or without him. Then there was Meredith. I didn't like the idea of just cutting her loose and it was pretty clear the Dark mages weren't going to give up easily. I looked at Belthas. "You've got a deal. On one condition. I don't want anybody else to gain access to Jadan's research. If we get it, I want it destroyed."

"Agreed." Belthas smiled slightly. "Welcome aboard."

To my side, I felt Meredith relax slightly. "So what's your plan?"

"I'm working with my contacts in the Council to assemble a strike force. I need you to find out where the Dark cabal is operating from and how powerful they are."

"And once I do?"

"I will eliminate them." Belthas's words were matter-of-fact, with no sign of bragging, and I pricked up my ears.

The split between Light and Dark mages is thousands of years old. There have been wars in the past, but at present there's an uneasy peace governed by a set of rules called the Concord. Under the Concord, there's a truce between all mages, whether Light or Dark . . . in theory. In practice, all the rules really come down to just one: don't get caught. Open warfare is rare nowadays but violence isn't, and a lot of brief, brutal skirmishes take place in the shadows of mage society, away from witnesses. Dark mages tend to come off best in these fights. It's not that they're any more powerful than their Light counterparts—they're not—but they're meaner and a hell of a lot more experienced and there aren't many Light mages who'll willingly engage a Dark one. Conventional wisdom is to steer clear of them; sooner or later someone else will take them down, and it's a lot safer if that someone isn't you. But somehow, as I met

Belthas's steady gaze, I didn't get the feeling he was exaggerating.

"How much do you know about them?"

Belthas nodded. "As you say, that is the weak point. So far, the cabal have worked hard to keep their identities secret. I've only seen them once and they were masked. There were at least two, of which one was a fire mage, but the encounter was too brief for me to learn much of value."

"Any leads?"

"They would have had some connection to Jadan, but I do not know what. I suspect, to start with, the best avenue of investigation would be the location of the battle. I met with the Dark cabal last Thursday at—"

"—an old factory in Deptford, just south of the river," I finished.

Meredith started and Belthas raised his eyebrows. It was the first sign of surprise he'd shown. "You're well informed."

I just looked at him. I didn't explain how I knew. Bad for the mystique.

"Meredith." Belthas turned to her. "I think it would be best if you assisted Verus."

Meredith's eyes went wide. "What? No!"

"You have a problem with working together?"

"I don't want to get anywhere near these guys. It's too dangerous. I didn't sign up for this!"

"I believe you agreed to gather information." Belthas's voice was mild.

"Not like this. You—" Meredith hesitated, then started again. "You know what I agreed to. This isn't it."

I wondered exactly what Meredith *had* agreed to. The silence stretched out and Meredith shifted uncomfortably. "Well," Belthas said finally. "If you wish to distance yourself, I will not do anything to stop you. However, I cannot guarantee the same of our opponents."

Meredith frowned. I wondered what Belthas was getting at; it didn't sound like a veiled threat unless . . . oh.

"What do you mean?" Meredith said suspiciously, then suddenly she got it. "Wait! They're still after me!"

"Then it would seem to be in your best interests to stay with Verus, wouldn't you say?" Belthas said. He looked at me. "Assuming Verus has no objection."

After a moment, I shook my head. Meredith stared at Belthas. She wasn't happy and I could tell she wanted to say more; maybe my presence was stopping her. If nothing else, I was sure by now that Meredith and Belthas weren't close allies. Unless I missed my guess, Meredith was only still working for him because she couldn't see any other way out.

"Then it's agreed," Belthas said. "I'll see to the arrangements."

. . . .

I left Belthas's office an hour later. As promised, he'd given me a run-through of the other information he had as well as setting up payment into one of my bank accounts. I didn't have any worries about the money, but the information was another matter. I walked out into the waiting room at exactly the same time that a familiar blond-haired man strolled in the other door.

Garrick was wearing civilian clothes instead of the body armour and fatigues that I'd seen him in on Friday night but he was unmistakable; there was something about the lazy grace with which he moved that made me think of a predator. His eyes registered me without surprise. "Verus."

"Garrick," I said. I looked him up and down. "No guns?"

"Off duty."

"Working hard?"

Garrick smiled slightly. The two of us faced each other across the small reception room. The window to one side gave a spectacular view across London but neither of us paid it any attention. "Up to anything interesting?" I asked.

"Looking to hire me?"

"Depends who you're working for."

"Sorry. Confidential."

I looked at Garrick. He looked back at me. I'd been fired at just a few hours ago by someone involved in mage business who was a very good shot. There wasn't any proof that that someone had been Garrick . . . yet. "Funny coincidence you showing up here."

"Business."

"What *is* your business, by the way? You don't exactly act like Council security."

"Could say the same for you," Garrick tilted his head. "So you're working with Belthas?"

"Business," I said. Garrick's mouth twitched.

We stood looking at each other a moment longer. "Want some advice?" Garrick said suddenly.

"Why not?"

"Take a holiday."

I looked at Garrick with raised eyebrows. "I'm kind of busy."

"Didn't say you weren't." Garrick studied me. "But if I were you, I'd clear my desk and take a break. Maybe a month."

I started to answer, then paused. It sounded like a threat, and Garrick was the kind of guy you'd pick to deliver one. But as I looked at him, I got the odd feeling that he was giving me not a threat but a warning.

The door behind me opened and Meredith stepped out. She stopped as she saw Garrick. Garrick gave me a nod and walked past into Belthas's study. I gave him a last glance, then headed for the elevator. Meredith hurried to catch up. The security guards watched us impassively as we left and I wondered if I'd be seeing them again.

⁙⁙⁙⁙

As you'd guess from the name, Canary Wharf wasn't always a financial district. Only a few decades ago it was a dock, part of the vast wharf network running along both sides of the Thames in what used to be the greatest port in the world. Nowadays it's steel and glass, skyscrapers rising up past the Docklands Light Railway and mixing with cafés and shopping malls, but the layout is still that of the old Docklands. Channels are carved out of the mud, inlets flowing in from the Thames. It's gracefully landscaped and framed with stone but there's no hiding the huge bodies of water, enough to make the skyscrapers feel almost like islands. I walked along one of the old piers, watching the crowds thronging the plazas. The concrete was warm from the late-afternoon sun but the breeze off the water was cold.

Meredith was still with me. She seemed to have come out of herself since meeting Belthas and I could tell she was about to speak. There was a stone bench near the waterside, and I sat down on it. "Thank you," Meredith said.

"For what?"

"Agreeing to help." Meredith sat down next to me, close enough that our knees were touching. It might just have been the cold. "I know you didn't have to."

Meredith's dark eyes looked up at me but I avoided meeting them; I probably would have said yes to Belthas even without her, and I felt uncomfortable being thanked for it. "What about you? Why did you sign up with him?"

Meredith's gaze drifted down and she looked out over the water. "I'm not sure." Her voice was doubtful. I looked at her as she gazed away, watching her brush her long hair back as she stared over the Thames. "I mean, he offered the same things . . . favours, credit, you know. It's been so much harder since last year, since . . ." She seemed to realise what she was saying and looked back at me. "Do you think I should have said no?"

"I'm not sure." Meredith was right next to me, looking into my eyes, and it was *really* difficult to think straight. I forced myself to look away. "It's your choice to make."

Meredith sat quietly. "What should we do now?" she said at last.

"I can think of a couple of things," I said. I braced myself and turned to Meredith. "The question is what *you're* doing."

Meredith looked up at me in surprise. "What do you mean?"

"Look, Meredith, it's pretty obvious you're not too keen on the parts of this that involve people trying to kill you. And I can promise you it's not going to get any safer. Are you sure you want to stick around?"

"Belthas said—"

"I don't care what Belthas said. The investigation side of this is going to be dangerous. If you want to stay out of it, it might be best if we found you a place to stay out of trouble."

Meredith hesitated, and I felt the forks of a decision opening up before her. She was really thinking about this. Then the futures settled and she shook her head. "No."

"Are you—"

"I want to stay with you. And I won't be useless. I can help."

Now it was my turn to hesitate. But Meredith's answer had put me on the spot and it was likely I really would need the help. "All right," I said at last. "We could ask around to find out more about this cabal. But that was what you were doing when you got targeted, right?"

Meredith nodded. "Did you have any leads?" I asked.

"I'm not sure. I thought I was getting somewhere but . . ."

"But some of the people you were asking tipped off the people you were looking for."

Meredith looked at me in surprise. "How did you know?"

I shrugged. "Not hard to guess." Asking around about a mage is dangerous. Mages who aren't prepared for trouble tend not to live very long so one of the first priorities of most mages is to establish an early-warning network to spot potential threats, in the same way I'd been warned by Starbreeze. And anyone willing to sell you information about the mage you're looking for is just as likely to sell the information to them the instant you turn your back. "Anyway, it sounds like this cabal's gone into war mode. I don't think there's much point going fishing. Last thing we want is for them to jump us halfway through."

Meredith nodded with obvious relief. Apparently she hadn't been looking forward to that idea either. "So let's try Belthas's plan," I said. "Check out the factory."

"Right now?"

I shook my head. "Not yet. I need to make some calls."

ııııııııı

The classic thing to do in this situation would have been to go to the factory, magnifying glass in hand, and look for clues. There were several good reasons why I wasn't going to do that, the main one being I'd already tried it and it hadn't worked. I hadn't been able to find much on a search even *before* a bunch of mages and Council security spent several hours tromping around the place. Besides, why root around when someone's done it for you?

I called Talisid but came up dry. The investigation of the barghest and factory hadn't turned up anything else useful. In exchange, I relayed the information from Arachne. "Harvesting nonhumans?" Talisid said in surprise. "Really?"

"Do you know anything about it being tried?"

"God no." Talisid sounded revolted. "In every instance I know of, the harvester went violently insane. If that was what they killed the barghest with, I'm surprised we didn't find their bodies too."

"Why's it so lethal?" I kept my voice casual, as if from idle curiosity, though I didn't expect Talisid to believe it for a moment. "Harvesting works on humans, doesn't it?"

Talisid snorted. "If you can call that 'working.' It's like ripping out half someone's mind and injecting it into your own. Usually turns whoever did it into a deranged psychopath, though if they were willing to use Harvesting in the first place, most people probably wouldn't notice much difference."

It matched with what I'd heard. Magical power isn't something that can be given away; it's part of who you are. The only way to take a mage's power is to rip out most of him with it. I can't imagine what it would be like to try to merge that maimed fragment with your own self, and that's if what you were taking came from a human. Trying to assimilate something totally alien, like a barghest . . .

"So now what are you up to?" Talisid broke into my thoughts. "Trying to track down the mages who did it?"

"Yup," I said. "Anyone still searching the factory?"

"Empty."

"Okay."

"You didn't have anything to do with that business on Hampstead Heath, did you?"

"What would that be?"

"Someone tried to settle a disagreement with military-grade weapons." Talisid's voice was dry and I knew he had his suspicions. "Anything you want to tell me?"

"Yeah, but I shouldn't."

"Hm. Watch yourself."

Talisid broke the connection and I dialled another number, and this time I had more success. It took only a few minutes to tell the story and fix a time for the meeting. I dropped my phone into my pocket and went back to Meredith. "We're done."

Meredith looked up from her coffee. We were sitting in a Starbucks, the late afternoon sun slanting through the glass of the shop front. "Did you find the guy you were looking for?"

"He won't be here till tomorrow." My meeting with Luna and Martin wasn't until the morning either, meaning I had nothing immediate for the rest of the evening. "Want to get dinner?"

"Really?"

"Not much we can do for the rest of the day. Besides, we might as well relax while we've got the chance. There'll be trouble enough soon." Which was about to prove more prophetic than I would have liked.

There was a beat, then Meredith nodded, looking at me appraisingly. "I'd like that."

⋮⋮⋮⋮⋮⋮⋮⋮⋮

Meredith wanted to go back to her flat, having been away for more than a day, and I went with her. Apart from anything else, the Dark cabal might be planning to take another shot at her, and if they were, her home was the natural place to set an ambush.

Meredith's flat was in Kensington and Chelsea, a little west of Cadogan Square. It's expensive even by London standards and I don't go there much. As we turned into the street, I saw that it was lined with old white-pillared terraced houses. Once upon a time, sixty or seventy years ago, those would have been used by the gentry and their servants and families; these days they'd been converted into flats for rich professionals. Some things change, some stay the same. The sides of the road were tightly packed with lines of well-polished sedans and sports cars. I stopped on the patio of Meredith's house, my instincts warning me to check the area before going in. The sun had set during our journey and as I looked from west to east I could see the colour of the sky fading from a deep yellow sunset to midnight blue. There was a scattering of people but the street was quiet with the coming evening and nothing set off my alarms. I followed Meredith inside.

Meredith's flat was the top one of four, the stairs thickly carpeted. "I really need to change," Meredith said. "Could you wait a few minutes?"

If there was anything messy about her appearance, it was more than I could tell. "No hurry." Meredith disappeared into the bedroom. I knew what "a few minutes" meant in girl talk and settled down to wait. A moment later I heard a shower start up from somewhere past the bedroom and I added another quarter hour onto my guess.

Meredith's living room was decorated in pale green, with tables and chairs of light wood, and a carpet lined the floor. A bookcase stood by one wall—the shelves were less than half full and most of what was there seemed to be boxes or CDs. There was a TV and stereo system, both new looking, the remote controls on the table next to a bowl of dried flowers. Two soft-looking white sofas were piled with cushions and the wall held a piece of artwork made of curves of black metal. The room looked nice but somehow I didn't feel particularly comfortable. It was a room for receiving visitors, not a place where you could put your feet up and relax. I sat on the sofa and found it was as soft as it looked.

"Where are we going?" Meredith called. I could make out her voice clearly, which meant the bathroom door was probably open . . . and I stopped that line of thought before it went any further.

"It's a surprise," I called back. Actually I hadn't thought ahead that far. I tried to think of somewhere to take Meredith and came up blank. There are a lot of things I'm really good at but entertaining women isn't one of them.

"So what should I wear?" Meredith called over the sound of the shower.

"Meredith, I think you're going to look good whatever you wear."

Meredith laughed; she sounded pleased and for some reason that put me in a good mood. The sound of the shower stopped, replaced a moment later by the whirr of a hair dryer. I got up and wandered over to the bookshelves. There wasn't much there; it seemed Meredith was more into music than reading.

"Alex?"

I turned to see Meredith standing in the doorway wearing nothing but a small towel and a couple of hair clips. My brain kind of shorted out at that point and I didn't notice much else. Gradually I realised that she'd just asked me a question. "Sorry?"

"Which one do you like better?"

I managed to tear my eyes off Meredith long enough to see that she was holding up a couple of dresses on hangers in front of her. "That one," I said.

"Which, this?" Meredith let one of the dresses she'd been holding in front of herself fall to her side, giving a very interesting view for half a second before she draped the other one over the front of her body. "Do you think?"

"Yeah," I said. Honestly, I was having trouble even noticing what colour it was. Meredith was looking down at the fall of the dress, apparently completely absorbed, thin tanned arms bare all the way to her shoulder blades. "Go with that."

Meredith disappeared back into her bedroom and I let out my breath, only then realising that I'd been holding it. This was getting dangerous.

I still didn't know what to do about Meredith. I knew she'd been recruited by Belthas and I knew she had a very different set of priorities than he did. I was tempted to think of her as a partner . . . except for that nagging voice of paranoia wondering what her real motives were. Was Meredith staying close to me because she wanted to? Or because she'd been told to? Or for some other reason I couldn't guess?

As if that weren't enough, there was Meredith's ability to manipulate emotions. I still didn't have a clue just how much of what I felt towards her was my own feelings. She could be nudging me for her own ends . . . and then again she might not be, and the hell of it was I didn't have any idea how to find out. So I hesitated, and the longer I hesitated the more I found myself thinking about her. The sounds from the bedroom suddenly went quiet and I turned to see that Meredith had returned.

Even prepared, it was hard not to stare. Meredith had changed into a black dress trimmed with gold. A deep V-neck showed off her cleavage and the lines of the dress followed the curves of her body closely from the waist down to the knees. She'd somehow found the time to restyle her hair and it hung loose around her shoulders with a slight wave. "Well," I said at last. "I feel underdressed."

Meredith smiled and walked forward, running her hand down the lapel of my shirt. "I think you look nice."

"You're about the only one." Stupid thing to say.

Meredith didn't take her hand away and I found myself staring down into her eyes. Her touch was soft and I couldn't help thinking how nice it felt. It had been a really long time since I'd had a pretty woman do that. "Maybe we should . . ." I began, and tailed off.

"Mmm?" It was a wordless sound, rising inquisitively, and my heart beat faster. I looked down at Meredith and wondered what would happen if I were to—

The doorbell was loud, an electronic shrill, and it cut right through my head, making me jump. Meredith started as well and looked towards the door with annoyance. After only a few seconds it shrilled again, and Meredith sighed. "I'll get rid of them." She walked out into the hall. "Who's calling this late . . . ?"

I stared after her, standing and feeling out of place. Something was nagging at the back of my mind but my thoughts were moving slowly. Meredith picked up the receiver just as the bell shrilled again. "Hello?" she said over the sound of the bell.

Suddenly my head cleared and I saw what was about to happen. "Meredith!" I shouted. As Meredith turned in surprise I grabbed her around the waist, dragging her back into the living room as the handset clattered against the wall.

Just as I did so, a column of searing flame tore through the door. The hallway of Meredith's flat became an roaring inferno, red fires tinged with black. The walls crisped and ignited and the handset Meredith had been holding melted, the plastic liquefying and evaporating as the air heated to a furnace.

Then just as suddenly, the torrent of flame cut off. The

hallway was left burning fiercely, flames licking up the walls and reaching eagerly into the living room. Over the crackle of flames, I heard footsteps. Heavy boots kicked the burning remnants of the door aside and stepped into the flat.

chapter 5

It was a good ambush. Anybody caught by that blast would have been turned into a living torch, writhing and screaming in horrible pain for the few seconds it would have taken for the fire mage to finish them off (and yes, I saw that in more detail than I wanted to). The fight would have been over before it began, which was of course the point. There's a duelling code under mage law for resolving formal challenges. The code is impartial, requires mages to give their opponent fair warning, and is completely ignored by almost everyone. Any mage with the tiniest bit of sense knows that combat is dangerous and that the best way to survive it is to finish the battle as quickly as possible. If you're a diviner, like me, that means running away. For a fire mage, like the guy who'd just kicked down the door, it means killing your enemy with the first strike.

Of course, for the same reason, mages who are easily ambushed tend not to live very long. I'd pulled Meredith far enough back that the first blast had done nothing but dry our skin, but in only a couple of seconds the fire mage would be in view, and I dug through my pockets for something to hold him back.

But I'd underestimated Meredith. I hadn't expected her to be any use in a fight, and to be fair, she hadn't given me much reason to think otherwise: in the battle with the construct, the best that could be said was that she hadn't gotten in my way. But it hadn't occurred to me that the reason she'd been so scared was because she'd been facing something her magic couldn't touch. The fire mage was deadly and powerful but he was still human, and even caught by surprise, Meredith didn't waste more than a startled breath. She turned to face the door and my senses tingled as she sent *something* into the hallway.

Over the crackle of flames, I heard the sound of staggering footsteps as the mage fell back. He recovered fast, though, and I saw the attack coming in time to snap "Down!" and pull Meredith to the floor.

A beam of fire slashed through the doorway and sawed sideways through the wall, slicing through wood and plaster and sweeping the living room at waist height. I covered Meredith with one arm and tried to burrow into the carpet. A flash of terrible heat rolled over my back and I felt the hair on the back of my head crisp, then in an instant it was gone and I looked up just in time to see the beam cut through the shelves. The shelving and everything on it literally vaporised in the instant before the beam cut out, leaving the burning upper half of the shelves to crash to the floor.

The beam had left a neat one-foot gash in the wall and past the red-hot edges I could see the upper body of the fire mage silhouetted against the flames. He'd only have to bend his head slightly to see us too, so before he had the chance to realise that I pulled what looked like a marble from my pocket and hurled it. I've picked up a few unusual ways to use my divination magic over the years and one of them is a way of accurately throwing small objects. All in all it's probably one of my more useless skills, but it does occasionally come in handy. The projectile flew neatly through the centre of the gap, past the fire mage, and shattered against the opposite wall.

The object I'd thrown was a sphere of glass with a fingernail-sized bit of mist swirling inside it. The mage who makes them calls them condensers but I think of them more as instant cover. A cloud of fog rushed out, enveloping the hall, the flames, the fire mage, Meredith, and me, cutting out all vision beyond a few feet. The mist was totally harmless, but the fire mage fell back reflexively, probably wondering if the thing was mind-fog or poison or worse. I felt the surge of a protective spell as Meredith rolled over and sent another strike at her would-be killer, making him stagger again.

The fire mage seemed on the back foot but I didn't expect that to last, so I pulled Meredith to her feet and hurried back to the bedroom, my magic picking the path that my eyes couldn't see. As we made it through the doorway there was a roar and another red flash, but this time the blast didn't come near us and I slammed the door.

My heart was racing as though we'd fought a full-length battle, though looking back on it the whole thing couldn't have taken more than ten seconds. I dug through my pockets, vaguely taking in the look of Meredith's bedroom: fluffy pillows, dresses tossed carelessly on the bed, a big window. "Can you hold him off?"

Meredith shook her head. "He's too strong!"

The floor juddered and there was a *boom* from the other room. I pulled out a pair of gold discs and dropped them on either side of the door, saying a command word. There was a faint *thrum* as an invisible vertical barrier sprung up, barring the door and reaching almost to the edge of the room. Meredith looked at it in surprise. "What did you do?"

"Forcewall." It wouldn't last long but it would buy us time. I pulled the window open. Already the air inside the bedroom had heated to uncomfortable levels; hot air rushed out as cooler air was drawn in. I pulled out my glass rod, channelling a thread of magic through it. "Starbreeze." The focus tingled, carrying my words away into the night. "I need help. Please come here, and hurry!" Starbreeze could pull us out but there was no guarantee she'd arrive in time. "There's—"

We must have been speaking too loud. Meredith ducked as another searing beam slammed into the wall separating the bedroom and living room. It looked like fire but cut like a razor; I didn't want to know what it would do to living flesh. The beam sawed left to right and the wall melted into flames, but the force barrier behind it held. Through the red-hot gash I could see mist and smoke. The temperature shot up.

"Alex!" Meredith called, and I turned to catch something glittering as it flew towards me. It was cold against my palm. "Ice crystal!"

I pulled open the door to the bathroom. "Anything that'll get us out of here?"

Meredith shook her head. She was rummaging through a bag that had been under her bed and as I watched she slung it over her shoulder, hurrying past me to the bathroom. As she crossed the threshold the fire mage hit my forcewall with a wide-angle blast, setting what was left of the wall behind it alight.

The bathroom was tiled in green, with a spacious bath, and would have smelt nice but for the smoke. So far we'd survived by giving ground, but we were quickly running out of places to run, and as I stuck my head out the window my heart sank. The back of the building was a sheer wall, opening into a doughnut block of enclosed gardens, and we were on the fourth floor. "Tell me there's another way out."

Meredith shook her head with a cough. "Gate stone?"

"He'd rip the building apart before we got halfway."

The fire mage struck with another of those white-hot

beams and this time he'd obviously figured out about the forcewall. The beam carved upwards, reaching over the force barrier and slicing into the ceiling and the attic beyond. Burning fragments showered into the bedroom, landing on the carpet and the bed. The beam cut off and I leant around the corner and threw the ice crystal. A hundred possible trajectories flickered through my senses and I released the crystal as they merged with the target. The crystal arced through the air to drop through the gap the fire mage had opened up with his beam. "Now!" I called.

Meredith said a word in a harsh-sounding language, and on the other side of the force barrier, the ice crystal detonated. I ducked back into the bathroom. "How good are you at climbing?"

Meredith looked at the window and back at me with wide eyes. "Out *there*?"

"There are two ways out of here—out there or past him."

Meredith took a look over my shoulder and went pale. Forcewalls are great at holding off direct attacks but there were still plenty of ways for the heat to get in, and most of the flat was either on fire or getting that way. The living room was blazing and licks of flame were starting to spread around the bedroom, the dresses on the bed smouldering and catching alight as embers tumbled down from above. Even with the windows open, the air was growing thick with smoke, hot enough that it was getting hard to breathe. Smoke kills more people than flames; in a regular house fire you're in more danger from asphyxiation than you are from burning to death, though having a pyromaniac throwing magical napalm around changes those odds a bit. But if this went on much longer, it'd be a race to see which killed us first—the smoke, the fire, or the mage.

A patient attacker would have backed off at this point and let the smoke and flames do his work for him. Apparently the fire mage wasn't very patient because he chose this point to smash a curling blast of flame through the side wall and around the force barrier, igniting the whole far half of the bedroom. Meredith ducked back with a yelp as a wave of searing air rolled in. It was so hot I could barely stand to look through the doorway, but as I did my heart jumped. The part of the floor holding up the left disc was burning fiercely. The gold discs needed to stay steady to maintain the barrier; as soon as that patch burnt through, there'd be no more forcewall.

But it gave me an idea. If this fire mage was so impatient, maybe we could lure him in. "Got another ice crystal?"

Meredith placed it in my hand. This one was bigger, a blue-tinted gem of cold glass. "Last one."

I leant around the door frame, ducking my head against the scalding heat, and tossed the gem. It rolled to a stop a couple of feet behind the door. An instant later a piece of ceiling fell in with a crash, taking a patch of floor with it.

I felt the forcewall go down and the fire mage did too. I ducked back into the bathroom and slammed the door as a red light flashed and the wood of the door heated as the fire mage hosed down the bedroom. A second later, over the roar of flames, I heard the tread of footsteps. I waited until the fire mage was on top of the crystal, then signalled to Meredith.

The timing was perfect. The crystal exploded into a hundred tiny shards of jagged ice, throwing the fire mage from his feet and stunning him. "Come on!" I called to Meredith as I pulled the door open.

But as I looked out into the bedroom I realised with a chill that we'd left it too late. Everything in the bedroom was blazing. The bed was a bonfire, a wall of flame separated us from the living room, and the living room itself was an inferno. A wall of heat hit me, crisping the hairs on my arms, and choking smoke rolled over us, setting us ducking and coughing. I slammed the door again.

Meredith looked up me at with wide eyes. I tried desperately to think. Run through the flames—suicide. Stay here—suicide. Climb out—probable suicide. Probable suicide won. "Out the window."

Meredith stared. "I'll fall!"

"Falling beats burning."

Meredith took a step to the window, looked out at the sheer drop, and turned back, her face ashen. "It'll kill me!"

"Going out *might*. Staying here *will*. Pick!"

Meredith hesitated, then began to climb out, white-faced. There were enough handholds on the wall to make the climb just about possible for a expert mountaineer. Meredith wasn't one and neither was I. I looked into the future to try to gauge her chances . . .

. . . and saw to my disbelief that the fire mage was coming back for another go. The roar of the flames through the bathroom door drowned out almost everything else, but I could just hear the sound of embers going *crunch* under the soles of heavy boots. "Oh, come on!"

"Come where?" a cheerful voice said in my ear.

I spun and saw to my utter delight the shape of Starbreeze, hovering just outside the window. "Starbreeze! Get us out of here!"

Starbreeze pointed in interest at Meredith, hanging halfway out of the window. "Her too?"

"Yes!" Meredith shouted.

The bathroom door exploded inwards, filling the bathroom with a cone of burning splinters. It missed Meredith by a couple of feet and I had just enough time to dodge into the corner. "Starbreeze, go!" I shouted as the fire mage strode in.

He was a big man, as tall as me and much heavier, with muscles that bulged under his dark clothes. A dim orange glow flickered around him, so faint as to be almost invisible, flaring where the flames licked around his feet. A black mask covered his face but I knew who he was; I'd known as soon as he'd cast that first spell. As he saw me, Cinder stopped dead, staring.

An instant later Starbreeze had turned the both of us to air and whipped us out into the night. I had one lightning-fast image of Cinder diminishing behind us through the window, then we were out of view and climbing. Smoke was pouring from the house's top floor, flames glowing from the bedroom and attic, and as we rose higher I could see people emerging into the street to point and stare. Higher still and I spotted the flashing blue lights of the fire service, half a dozen streets away but closing in. As we kept rising I could see the yellow spark of the fire and the flickering blue of the engines becoming a cluster of points, then a faint glow, then a fuzz. And then there was nothing but the London sprawl.

The night view over the city was beautiful, a web of light against the dark patches of the parks and open spaces, but I wasn't in the mood to enjoy it. Now that we were out of danger, as weird as it might sound, I was angry. I'd saved Cinder's life and this was the thanks I got?

Cinder hadn't looked very dangerous the last time I'd seen him. He'd been bloodied and out cold after losing a duel with another Dark mage named Onyx. I'd let him go on the condition that he owed me one. Okay, I hadn't exactly been myself at the time, but I *had* been myself when I'd found him in a Precursor energy trap a few hours earlier and saved his life *again*. I hadn't expected gratitude, but I'd kind of hoped he'd at least stop trying to kill me.

I sighed. Apparently I'd been optimistic. It wasn't quite as stupid as it sounds. At the time I'd needed all the help I could get and having a couple more mages who weren't immediately hostile had done a lot to tip things in my favour. And, odd as it sounds, some Dark mages—not all, but some—do have a sense of honour. They'll kill you without a second thought but if you help them out they'll try to return the favour, if only to encourage other people to do the same in the future. I'd known Rachel was way too nuts to be depended on in that way but I'd hoped Cinder might be different.

Thinking of Rachel reminded me of something else. I spoke to Starbreeze, asking her to drop us off on my roof, and she did so cheerfully enough. I gave her something in thanks (she'd already forgotten what I was thanking her for) and watched her vanish into the night.

Meredith wasn't talking and started to shiver as I brought her down from the roof. I recognised the signs of shock and guided her into my bedroom. She lay down without complaint, and by the time I'd fetched her something to drink she was asleep. Lying on my bed, her hair spread across the quilt, she looked very small and fragile. I looked at her for a little while before spreading a blanket over her and going back into my living room.

For whatever reason, the usual postcombat shakes hadn't hit. Maybe it was because this time I'd had Starbreeze and Meredith instead of doing everything myself. Or maybe it was because it was the third bloody assassination attempt in twenty-four hours and I was getting desensitised. I turned my attention to Bob the Dead Construct, who was still lying on the carpet where I'd left him yesterday.

Now that I knew what to look for, I found it quickly. The construct wasn't just similar to the ones I'd seen made in Richard's mansion; it was identical. More than that, I recognised the style. The magic from the thing had faded but there was enough of a residue to identify the water magic of Rachel, otherwise known as Deleo, a Dark mage, dangerous, powerful, and close to insane. She was Cinder's partner, but I'd known her longer than he had. After all, we'd been apprenticed to the same master.

There had been four of us, back then: Rachel, Shireen, Tobruk, and me. In the mansion of Richard Drakh we worked together, studied together, lived together. But in the end, there was room for only one. Tobruk died. Shireen died. Rachel won . . . sort of. She got the power and status she'd always wanted, the position of Richard's Chosen. But I'm not sure it was worth the price she paid. When next I saw her, she called herself Deleo . . . and there was very little left of the girl I'd once known.

It was time to get rid of Bob. Constructs don't biodegrade but even the off chance that Rachel could track the residue was more risk than I was willing to take. First I had to get the construct through a gate stone portal (which was not what the things were designed for) and then I had to bury it at the other end. It took a long time. I don't have much experience disposing of bodies. I suppose it would be a bit worrying if I did.

I stepped back into my living room, letting the portal close behind me, and dropped onto the sofa, staring at the wall. For the first time I seriously considered taking Garrick's advice: drop everything, get out, and wait for the dust to settle. I didn't want to fight Rachel and Cinder. For one thing, they were stronger than me. Meredith and I had thrown everything we had at Cinder tonight and barely slowed him down. One on one, Cinder would take me apart, and Rachel would probably do it even faster.

But if I was being honest, the bigger reason was our history. Rachel and I had never been friends; we'd tolerated each other at best and hated each other at worst. I'd fled Richard once I finally understood what he was, while Rachel had given herself over wholly to his path. But twisted as she was, Rachel was one of the last links to my past—someone once told me that she was what I could have been and they were right. And as far as I knew Cinder was the only person she trusted. The more you know about someone, the harder it is to kill them. I didn't want to kill Rachel or Cinder, and if I got into a fight *without* being ready to kill them, there was a good chance *they'd* kill *me*.

But if I didn't do anything, I'd be leaving them free rein with creatures like Arachne.

I sighed and rubbed my eyes. I hate decisions like this. No matter what I did, bad stuff was going to happen. What I wanted was for Rachel and Cinder and Meredith and

Belthas to drop the whole thing and stop trying to kill each other (and stop catching me in the crossfire while they were at it). But I couldn't make them do that. The only choice left to me was whether to be involved. I studied my phone, thinking how easy it would be to send a message to Belthas telling him I wanted out.

The sound of the opening door brought my head up. Meredith was standing there, looking at me. "Hey." I came to my feet. "Feeling better?"

Meredith walked forward. Her bare feet were quiet on the carpet; she'd lost her heels somewhere in the fight. Her dress was dotted with tears and ash marks and her hair was tangled, although it didn't do anything to diminish her looks. "Are you okay?" I said. Somehow, the closer she got, the harder it became to do anything but look.

Meredith stopped next to me, looking into my eyes. She had to tilt her head to do it; she barely came to my shoulder. Her eyes were a deep brown and I started to lose myself in them. "Alex?" she said softly, and her voice seemed to come from all around me. "I don't want to be alone tonight."

I stood dead still for a second. A small voice at the back of my mind was trying to tell me something, but it was hard to listen. Then Meredith stood on tiptoe to kiss me and I stopped thinking about anything at all.

｜｜｜｜｜｜｜｜｜

I don't usually sleep well. I sleep even less well the closer I am to someone else. But I found some peace that night and when I woke I felt better than I had in days. I lay propped up on one elbow for a while, watching Meredith as she slept, until she stirred and opened her eyes to give me a smile. "Morning."

Over breakfast, Meredith and I talked about our plans for the day. "You're staying in your shop?" Meredith said in surprise.

"It's a workday."

"What about . . . ?"

"I'll close early," I said. "I need to check out the factory in the afternoon. You?"

"I'm meeting some people." Meredith brushed at the ash-stained dress with a resigned look. "And shopping. All my stuff was in my flat."

I hesitated. "You could stay here if . . ."

Meredith shook her head with a smile. "That's okay. I don't want to be too much trouble."

"Are you going to be okay on your own?" I'd made the mistake last night of thinking that there wouldn't be another assassination attempt so soon and I didn't want to be caught napping again.

"I don't know." Meredith looked worried. "How did they find us last night? I was sure they couldn't track me."

"They probably didn't," I said. "Just posted someone to watch your flat and waited for them to call in."

"Oh. Could you . . . ?"

"No problem."

丨丨丨丨丨丨丨丨丨

It didn't take me long to sweep the area for spies. My area of Camden isn't large and I know it like the back of my hand. Meredith left after a kiss. I watched her go, then returned to the shop in a good mood. My doubts about Meredith from last evening didn't seem to matter anymore. Although I was planning to stay in the shop all morning, I didn't feel like keeping it open for customers. Instead I flipped the sign to *CLOSED* and settled down at my desk to wait.

Most mages will think twice about attacking another mage's home. Not only is it messy, but mages tend to treat fortifying their house as a personal hobby. My shop had been raided five months ago, and since then I'd gone to some effort to set up a few surprises for intruders. I could probably give even Cinder a run for his money if he tried to break in, and for exactly that reason I didn't expect him to do

it—mages who make a habit of launching attacks on prepared targets tend not to live very long. But after last night
I wasn't in any mood to take chances, and I spent a couple
of hours exhaustively searching the futures for attacks. I
came up blank, which was moderately reassuring. At least
nothing was being planned right at the moment.

The glazier arrived while I was working and replaced
the window. Once he was finished the morning light was
pouring in again, making the shop much more cheerful.
Luna arrived ten minutes later, and to my surprise, Martin
was with her.

I'd included Martin in my invitation more for Luna's sake
than anything else; I hadn't seriously expected him to show
up. But he followed right behind Luna as she let herself in.
I raised my eyebrows and he had the grace to look embar-
rassed. "Martin," I said.

"Hey," Martin said. "Listen, I'm really sorry about Saturday. I was just kind of out of it. Didn't think about what I
was doing."

"Uh-huh."

"So, uh, how much do I owe you? I meant to pay for it,
it was . . ."

"Martin, did you listen to a word I said? You didn't pick
it. It picked you."

Martin hesitated. "Uh . . . okay. Sure."

"Look," Luna said. She'd been watching from one side
and now she sounded like she was choosing her words carefully. "We did listen. I told Martin why the thing was dangerous. We talked about it and we did some research too.
This thing's really famous."

"Eyewitness reports?" I asked. "Or stories?"

"Just stories. But they matched with what you said."

"I'm guessing they didn't have happy endings."

Luna nodded.

I looked at Martin. "But you decided to keep it anyway."

Martin looked confused. "Well, yeah."

"And you think this is a good idea because . . . ?"

"Look, we're not idiots, okay?" Luna said. "We talked it over."

I took a breath. "Okay," I said once I'd gotten myself under control. "What did you figure out?"

"The monkey's paw only takes things," Luna said. "It was in all the stories. It can't make anything new but it can take something away and give it to someone else."

I stopped. I'd never considered it but now that I thought about it, it made sense. "All right."

"And you told me imbued items have a purpose, right?" Luna said.

"Yes," I said slowly. "Okay. I see what you're getting at. But that doesn't change the fact that it's been bad news for everyone else."

"Only if you use it wrong," Martin broke in. "Look, all the characters in the stories are stupid. They wish for something that'll kill them. All you have to do is word it right and you can get anything you want! You'd have to be crazy to give it up."

Luna and I both looked at him. I looked at Luna. "It worked," she said defensively.

A nasty feeling went through me. "What?"

Luna didn't answer. "You used it," I said.

"Martin did."

"For what?" I asked Martin.

But it was Luna who answered. She rose from where she'd been sitting on the edge of the table and walked to Martin. Four steps brought her next to him, and she placed a hand on his shoulder.

My jaw dropped. "Wait!" I called, starting to move, then stopped. Looking at Luna with my mage's sight, I could see the silver mist of her curse being drawn off her in a steady flow. Instead of soaking into Martin, it was streaming into something in the pocket of his jeans . . . the monkey's paw.

Luna's curse wasn't gone, it was just as strong as ever . . . but instead of hovering around her it was being drawn in.

"It's okay," Martin said with a grin. He slipped an arm around Luna's waist with an easy familiarity. "Safe, see?"

I just stared with my mouth open. I knew I looked stupid, and I had the feeling both Martin and Luna were enjoying it, but I was trying to understand what I was seeing. Luna was touching Martin, yet instead of flowing into him, the mist was sliding along the surface of his skin, funnelling into the monkey's paw. I'd never seen this—wait, yes I had. Just once. It must be the same—

"It was Martin's first wish," Luna said, echoing my thoughts. "Protection from magic. We've been testing it and it works. It *works*. My curse can't hurt him!"

I kept staring, trying to make sense of it. I'd seen it once before. Arachne had woven a ribbon to counter Luna's curse, drawing it in and nullifying it. But it had lasted only a few hours before crumbling to dust and Arachne had admitted to me afterwards that it had taxed her to her limits. If what Luna was telling me was true, this thing could nullify *all* magic, not just Luna's, and do it indefinitely. There wasn't a mage alive who could match that.

I suddenly realised that both Martin and Luna were looking at me, Martin cocky, Luna expectant. "Taking," I said. "What the monkey's paw does."

Luna nodded eagerly. "That was what I thought. It's what it's made to do!"

In other words, Martin had just done in one evening what I'd failed to do in five months. "I guess that's good," I said after an awkward pause.

"Of course it's good! Aren't you happy?"

Luna was looking at me, her eyes bright. Martin still had his arm around her, but she seemed to have forgotten. I shifted uncomfortably. I knew how Luna wanted me to react and it wasn't what I was feeling. "I hope it works," I said at last.

"It *does* work! And if it can do this, think about what else it can do! Maybe it could take my curse away completely!"

Alarm bells went off in my head at that. But Martin shifted. "Come on, Lun." He pronounced it *loon*. "We said we weren't going to try that."

Luna flinched away from Martin, seeming to remember he was there, before stopping herself. "Listen, we were hoping you could help us," Martin said. "With figuring out how to use it. I mean, you know as much about this thing as anyone, right?"

"Maybe," I said slowly.

"Okay, so how many wishes do you get? Three?"

"The man I got it from said five," I said. I could see Luna listening attentively. "I know one man who used it four times. He disappeared right after."

"So five," Martin said.

"What happened to him?" Luna asked.

I shook my head. "I don't know. The last conversation we had, he was asking how to make the thing do what he wanted."

"So it was doing what he told it to, right?" Martin said. "He just wasn't wishing for the right things."

"Maybe," I said reluctantly.

"What about after all five?" Luna asked. "Once you've finished? Someone else can use it, right?"

"Yes—no! Luna, don't even think about it!"

Luna's expression didn't change; she'd obviously expected my reaction. "Those stories are just to stop people trying it, aren't they?" Martin said confidently. "They don't want anyone else getting something this good."

I looked at Martin in disbelief.

"I want to try it," Luna said quietly. "If there's any chance."

I took a deep breath. "I want to ask you something," I said once my voice was steady. "You're hoping if you use it in the right way, the monkey's paw will give you what you want, right?"

"Yeah," Martin said. Luna nodded.

"What does it get out of it?"

Both of them stared at me. "What do you mean?" Martin asked.

"It's what it's made to do, isn't it?" Luna said.

"If it were that easy, everybody would be using these things."

"Unless they didn't know how to use it right," Martin pointed out. "People are smarter now."

I restrained the urge to hit Martin over the head. "Look," I said. "You don't need my help to use the monkey's paw. It *wants* to be used. *Not* using it is what's hard."

Luna and Martin looked back at me, and I knew I hadn't convinced them. "I know it's dangerous," Luna said at last. "But it's the best chance I've got."

And that was that. There was some desultory conversation between me and Luna, but Martin's presence put a damper on it. "I've got some new work," I told Luna. "We're going to do some investigating. Want to come?"

"When?"

"About an hour. Same place as Friday. I could use some help."

Luna hesitated. ". . . I can't."

"You can't?"

"Martin and I were going to do some more research." Luna looked awkward. "Sorry."

I looked at Luna. She shifted uncomfortably. "You've been asking to come on these jobs for months."

"It's not that," Luna said. "It's just . . ." She looked at Martin.

"Yeah, you're right." Martin glanced at his watch. "We better go."

I looked between Luna and Martin. Luna avoided my eyes. "Okay, then," I said at last.

"So yeah, great talking," Martin said cheerfully, getting up. "Sorry again about the whole Saturday thing. Really appreciate you being so big about it."

I didn't answer, looking at Luna. "See you later," she said at last, and walked to the door. Martin held it open. As the door swung closed I saw him put his arm around her again. And then they were gone.

I sat there for a long time, staring out the window. There was an odd feeling inside me. It had been a long time since I'd felt it, and it took me a while to remember what it was. It was the feeling you get when a relationship that's been fraying finally breaks.

What do you call an apprentice who doesn't train and doesn't join their master on jobs?

You don't call them an apprentice at all.

I started to get angry. I'd known Luna for more than a year. In all that time I'd helped her whenever I could and hadn't asked for much in return. And now she was disappearing. I got up and started pacing up and down.

I might have kept doing that a long time, getting more and more pissed off, but a knock snapped me out of it. The help I'd been waiting for had arrived. I took a deep breath, cleared my head, and opened the door.

The boy standing on the doorstep was about average height, with glasses, untidy black hair, and scruffy clothes. He looked like a research assistant and the hand he stuck out was ink-stained. "Hey, Alex," he said with a grin. "Need some help?"

I found myself smiling back. "Hey Sonder." I stepped out into the street. "I'll tell you the story on the way."

chapter 6

We took the Tube to South London, changing at Bank. I've had an aversion to taxis ever since an incident with a fire mage five months back—it's a lot harder to ambush someone underground. The noise of the train is also handy when you don't want to be overheard.

I first met Sonder during the business with the fateweaver (the same day Cinder blew that taxi out from underneath me, in fact). Back then he was on probation, having just completed his journeyman tests. Although he was working for the Council, I found myself liking him, and to my surprise the feeling turned out to be mutual. After everything settled down he started dropping by, and kept dropping by even after my brief flurry of publicity faded. He'd helped me out several times since, usually without asking for any particular reward.

For that reason, I made sure he knew about the possible dangers on this one. "So it's Cinder and Deleo?" Sonder asked.

"Cinder definitely," I said. "Deleo almost definitely. I haven't seen her but it's a safe bet she's around."

"Any others?"

"Maybe. I'm hoping you can narrow it down."

Sonder nodded. "I was wondering what those two were up to."

It was a pretty calm reaction, but as I've learnt, there's more to Sonder than meets the eye. He looks like a history geek (which, to be fair, he is) but he's smart and surprisingly cool under pressure. The biggest reason I like him, though, is that he's honest. If you ask Sonder a question, his first reaction is to tell you the truth. That's pretty rare among mages.

"So is Luna coming?" Sonder asked.

Of course, his social skills could use some work. "No."

"Is she meeting us there?"

"She's not coming."

"Why not?"

I resisted the urge to tell Sonder to stop asking. It wasn't fair to take it out on him and he was Luna's friend too. "She's gotten involved with some idiot who's taken up the monkey's paw." I sketched out the story in a few short sentences.

"That's . . . really bad," Sonder said. His eyebrows had climbed up beneath his hair.

"Yeah."

"But she knows the thing's dangerous, right? You've told her?"

"Yes, Sonder, I told her."

Sonder fell silent. I could tell from his expression that he was worried. "Don't focus on it for now," I said. "I don't think there'll be anything dangerous waiting for us, but let's not get distracted."

Unfortunately, now that Sonder had made me start thinking about it again, I couldn't stop. The worst part was that even though I hated it, I could kind of see Luna's point. This was what she'd always wanted: a way to deal with her curse.

My training was slow, hard, and boring. The monkey's paw was fast, simple, and easy. It wasn't hard to see why she'd want it.

And there was the nagging worry underneath it all. What if I was wrong? What if the monkey's paw really *was* Luna's best chance of a normal life? I didn't like Martin, and when it came to magic he had the common sense of a gerbil, but the uncomfortable truth was that so far it was working. Maybe by luck or cleverness, he really *could* manage to get the monkey's paw to do what he wanted. It didn't make any sense that the monkey's paw should be a meal ticket . . . but life *doesn't* always make sense. Sometimes stuff happens that you couldn't have expected and you just have to deal with it.

And following up on that was an even nastier thought. Luna had come to me in the first place because she needed help with her curse. If Martin and the monkey's paw could cure that . . . then maybe she didn't have any reason to stay.

The factory didn't look any better by day. The sunlight did a little to reduce the general aura of creepiness but it also enhanced the view of the rubbish scattered around the yard and the rust on the barbed wire. The street outside was emptier than any healthy neighbourhood should be, and the couple of people I could see seemed to be trying to avoid being noticed. "There's nobody inside, right?" Sonder asked.

I did a scan, taking my time to do it thoroughly. In the futures before me, Sonder and I explored every room of the factory, branching at every turn. All that greeted us was empty darkness. "We're clear."

The Council search team hadn't bothered to lock the place behind them, which made it much simpler to get in this time. The midday sunlight faded into gloom before we'd gone five steps and the sounds from outside died almost as quickly. The walls seemed soundproof. "This place is really creepy," Sonder said under his breath, clicking on a torch.

I nodded. There really is such a thing as a good or bad aura when it comes to places, and the factory had a bad one—dark, rotting, and cold. It wouldn't do any harm on a visit but you wouldn't want to live here.

The journey into the factory was uneventful, beyond Sonder tripping a few times. "This is it," I told Sonder as the corridor opened out into the factory floor. There was still a space where the barghest's body had been, but not much else.

Sonder nodded. His eyes had that abstracted look that I knew meant he was concentrating. He pushed his glasses up as he looked around. "What am I looking for?"

"The battle," I said. "It—"

"Found it. Eighty-four hours ago . . . no, eighty-five. Thursday midnight."

Sonder's a time mage. It's one of the most difficult of all types of magic to learn; while elemental mages learn their craft in months or years, mastering time magic takes decades. Sonder doesn't know many tricks yet, but what he does, he does very well. "I need to know what happened here," I said. "Details of the battle, lead-up, conversations—anything you can find."

Sonder nodded. He still had that absent look and I knew he was seeing the past, not the present. He took a notebook from his pocket and began circling the room, pencil in hand, while I watched out of curiosity. I always find it interesting to see the way Sonder does things; the types of magic we use are so similar and yet so different. Then I shook it off and got back to work. Sonder was pretty much oblivious while he was doing this, which meant it was my job to watch out for him. Scanning ahead, I saw that nothing much was going to happen while we were in the room. Sonder would finish, we'd head out, and—

Fire, pain, darkness. My reflexes took over and I forced the vision away and I was back in the present again, staring at the blackened walls. What the hell? We'd been walking down the corridor by which we'd come in, then . . .

I looked again and understood. A bomb. Someone had booby-trapped our way out. In fact, they were doing it right now. There was another assassin, here in the factory, fewer than eighty feet away, and he was trying to kill us.

I snapped.

"Hey, Sonder," I said, not taking my eyes off the corridor. "Need to take care of something. Back in five."

Sonder didn't answer. I snapped off my torch and walked into the darkness.

⋮⋮⋮⋮⋮⋮⋮

The man was dressed in dark clothes and he was crouched halfway up the corridor. He'd placed his torch on a nearby box where it illuminated a splash of the hallway. In the white light, I could see a backpack leaning against the wall and a gun resting on the floor where it could be quickly snatched up. He wore a knitted cap.

The land mine was already almost hidden. The man had tucked it behind a heating pipe and he was busy covering it with pieces of rubbish. It looked like a metal cylinder about the size and shape of a coffee can. Looking into the future, I could see that when it was tripped, it would hurl a bomb into the air to burst at about waist height. The explosion would throw a spray of metal balls in all directions, ricocheting off the walls and turning the corridor into a death zone.

I stood quietly in the shadows at the end of the corridor, watching as the man finished setting the mine. He'd already placed the trigger mechanism. I didn't know whether it was a trip wire or some sort of beam but I knew that once he armed the mine, anything going down the corridor at a certain height would set it off.

I'm not all that proud of what I did next. All I have to say in my defence is that I had had enough. It was the fourth attack in two days and I was sick of it.

The man twisted the switch to arm the mine and there

was a click. I picked up a length of wood, then stepped out and threw it down the corridor.

It took the stick just over one second to complete its flight. It took the man a quarter second to catch the movement, a half second more to snatch up his gun and see what was happening. And by the time he realised that the stick was on course to fly through the trigger area of the mine—the same mine he was next to—it was far too late.

· · · · · · · · · ·

S onder was looking in my direction as I walked back into the room. "What was that?"

"What was what?"

"I thought I heard a bang."

"Rats."

"And something that sounded like a scream?"

"Big rats."

Sonder looked at me. "Sonder, trust me," I said. "You don't want to know." Violent death is a long way outside Sonder's comfort zone. The same does not apply to me, which is not really a good thing. "We should go."

Sonder's not great at taking hints but he got the message. The two of us took the back way out, my divination magic picking the way through the obstacles. I didn't know if the man I'd just killed had a partner and I didn't plan on sticking around to find out. We negotiated our way through the council estate, and ten minutes saw us out in the sunlight again, on the main road.

"So how much did you find?" I asked once I was satisfied no one was going to be coming after us.

"A lot," Sonder said, the distraction forgotten. "Want to know about the Dark mages first, or the ones fighting them?"

"The Dark mages."

"Well, it was Cinder," Sonder said as we turned onto another main road, heading towards a different Tube station.

"And Deleo, just like you said. They hid on that gantry, waited for the barghest to show up, then stunned it."

"Was there anyone else?"

"Just them."

That was a relief. Cinder and Deleo were bad enough, and I still had nightmares about the last guy they'd partnered with. "It was over really fast," Sonder said. "Then they went down and started working on the barghest."

"What were they doing?"

Sonder frowned. "I don't know. Some sort of ritual. They had a couple of focuses I've never seen before: like sort of dark purple metal spikes. But it took a long time. They kept stopping and starting."

"Timing requirements?"

Sonder shook his head. "I don't think so. I think they were . . . working it out as they went along? Like they weren't really sure what they were doing."

I hesitated. Something in that seemed off but I wasn't sure exactly what.

"That was when the others showed up," Sonder continued. "There was one mage and eight auxiliaries. I think the mage tried to talk to them. At least he said something, but Cinder and Deleo attacked him on sight. He was under a shroud so I couldn't see much."

"Huh," I said. Shrouds are highly specialised items designed to block surveillance magic, rare and expensive. "So I guess you couldn't see who it was."

"Actually, I did," Sonder said. I looked at him in surprise, and he shrugged. "It wasn't that good a shroud."

Sometimes I think Sonder doesn't realise how talented he is. "Belthas?"

"Belthas. I just got bits and pieces from there. The auxiliaries opened fire and so did Belthas, and they drove Cinder back. Cinder dropped one of those focuses—the purple things—and one of the men ran to grab it but Deleo disintegrated him." Sonder shivered slightly. "Literally. There was nothing left but dust. Cinder grabbed the focus and they fell back to the east doorway. Deleo held them off while Cinder opened a gate, and they got out."

I frowned. "Wait. You mean Belthas was the only other mage?"

Sonder nodded. "And he still forced them back. He's an ice mage and he's *really* good. I think he would have been a match for them on his own."

I remembered how calm Belthas had been at the prospect of facing the Dark cabal. If he was really that good, he had little to fear from anything short of an entire Dark kill team. It gave me another thing to think over as we turned into the station.

I spent the trip back quizzing Sonder about what else he'd learnt. There were no revelations but a few useful titbits. According to Sonder, the barghest had died either before the fight had started, or as a result of Cinder and Deleo getting interrupted midritual. Either way it was clear the ritual hadn't been a success: the barghest might have had its magic drained, but neither Cinder or Deleo had profited from it. While that was probably a good thing, what I really wanted was some way to track them down. "You're sure they didn't gate in?" I asked for the second time.

"I'm sure," Sonder said. "They walked in the same way we did." He hesitated. "I got a look at their exit gate. I might be able to track it . . ."

I shook my head. "It'll be a staging point." Smart mages never gate directly home; there's too much risk of being followed. Instead they jump to another location, usually somewhere desolate and empty, walk a short distance, then do the same thing again, maybe two or three times if they're being particularly careful. Experienced mages keep libraries of literally hundreds of staging points and it's all but impossible to track them. "Anything else about them?"

Sonder held up his notebook. "I think I found out Cinder's phone number. Would that help?"

I couldn't help smiling. "Probably not."

We'd come out of the Underground at Euston and were talking amidst the square concrete pillars of the bus station. The station was busy with the afternoon rush, people of all looks and ages crossing the plaza. "Thanks for coming today," I said. "Anything I can help out with?"

Sonder hesitated. "What are you going to do about Luna?"

I sighed, my brief good mood fading. The attack at the factory hadn't been fun but it was the kind of thing I knew how to deal with. This wasn't. "I don't know."

"But you're not going to leave her with this guy, right?"

"What am I supposed to *do*, Sonder?" There was an edge in my voice; Sonder was hitting too close to what I was thinking myself. "She wants this. If I push her, she'll just say no and I can't make her."

"But you're supposed to," Sonder said. "You're her master."

"Am I?" I leant against one of the pillars, staring out at the hurrying people. "Luna's not part of the mage world the way you are. She didn't grow up with the customs. I've been teaching her, but she never really agreed to be an apprentice. I'm not even sure she knows what it means."

"Well, she ought to."

"You really think that?"

"Yes. The master and apprentice system is important." Sonder looked at me earnestly. "Yes, it goes wrong sometimes, and the kind of things Dark mages do with their apprentices are pretty awful. But it's how mages learn—not just their magic, everything. It's what everything's built on."

I looked back at Sonder. He was serious, and for the first time I stopped and faced up to the question of how I really felt about Luna.

Partly I thought of her as a friend. I lead a fairly lonely

life and Luna's one of the few people I like and trust. Partly I thought of her as a sort of protégé. I'd been teaching her for months now and I wanted her to be able to make a life for herself in mage society. And partly I thought of her as something more.

But as I thought about it I realised that I'd been acting like a mixture of all three. I'd been trying to treat her as a friend and as an apprentice and as a potential girlfriend all at the same time, and it wasn't working. I remembered Arachne telling me that she wasn't acting like my apprentice and that I wasn't acting like her master, and I understood that Arachne had been right. I couldn't be both Luna's master and her friend, and I *definitely* couldn't be both her master and her lover. I was going to have to pick one of the three.

But no matter which, one thing I was sure of was that I wanted to keep Luna safe, and that meant the monkey's paw came first. "What do you think we should do?" I said.

"What if I went and talked to Luna?" Sonder said. "And I could find out some more about this Martin guy. He sounds dodgy."

I couldn't help smiling; I couldn't honestly see Luna paying Sonder any attention. But Sonder had surprised me before. "Can't hurt to try," I said. "But if that's what you're planning, do you think you could spend some time researching the monkey's paw first? How it works, what it wants—anything you can find. The more we know about this thing, the better."

Sonder nodded immediately. "I will. And, um, be careful."

"You too."

I got back to my flat and started trying to figure out how to find Cinder and Rachel. It took a long time.

A lot of people think divination magic can tell you anything you want to know, but it can't. What it can do is tell you the consequences of a possible action. If I want to know what's behind a door, that's easy. I look into the future in which I open the door. Cracking a password is easy too: I look into the futures in which I try every possible password and see which one works. If there are a lot of choices it might take a while, but sorting through even millions of passwords is easier than you'd think because all the possible futures except for one are so similar. In 999,999 futures the lock doesn't open; in the last one it does.

But once you start dealing with people instead of machines, it gets much, much harder. With people, all the possible futures are *different*. If I look into the futures of searching two different houses I see totally different things, and I have to look at each one individually to see if it's right. Cracking a password is like spotting one white marble in the middle of a million black marbles. Finding a person is like spotting one white marble in the middle of a million multicoloured marbles. One is a hell of a lot harder than the other.

That doesn't mean divination can't find people; it can. In fact, it's really good at finding people. If I know who I'm looking for and the rough area that they're in, I can pinpoint them in seconds. But I need a place to start. Otherwise, divination magic is just a slightly faster way of taking a wild guess.

I had three points of contact for Cinder and Rachel: the construct attack at my shop, the burning of Meredith's flat, and their battle with Belthas at the factory. Unfortunately, none of those were any use for finding them. They'd be operating out of a base and there was absolutely no reason that base had to be anywhere nearby. The fact that they'd used a short-range construct *did* suggest they were some-where in London, but that didn't narrow it down anywhere near enough. I didn't have anywhere to start looking.

Although . . . I frowned. *Maybe I did.*

I'd been to one of Cinder and Rachel's bases, five months

ago. It had been a brief and not very pleasant visit but I'd managed to identify the place: a disused warehouse in Battersea. It was deserted now of course; there was no way Rachel or Cinder would go back again. And there was no reason for them to have picked a similar place this time.

Except . . . I knew Rachel. And one thing I knew about Rachel was that she tended to do things the same way. It had always been Shireen who had been the original one, Shireen who had come up with the ideas. Rachel had liked to think of herself as unpredictable, a rebel, but the truth was she'd always been more conservative than she'd been willing to admit.

So I worked on the assumption that she'd do things the same way again. I took out a map of London and started making a list of warehouse districts and industrial parks within close distance of the city centre. Then I struck out all the ones that saw high traffic or were otherwise too busy for secrecy. That still left too many, so working on a hunch I limited it to places near water.

By the time Meredith returned, it was late afternoon. "Hey," I said without looking up as she walked in.

Meredith leant over next to me to look at the map. She'd replaced the ash-stained dress with a dark jumper and pair of jeans, and she smelt of some fragrance I couldn't place. "What are you doing?"

Meredith was giving me an odd feeling at the moment. When I was with her, looking at her, I couldn't stop thinking about how beautiful she was. But as soon as I spent any time thinking of something else, Meredith seemed . . . less important, somehow. So despite how close she was, I didn't meet her eyes, keeping my attention on the map. It wasn't that I didn't want her around or anything—I did. I liked having Meredith there, because . . .

. . . because . . .

. . . I couldn't think of anything. When I tried to think past Meredith's beauty and her magic to what kind of *person* she was, I came up blank. And that was odd, wasn't it? We'd spent enough time together, the last couple of days. But somehow all our conversations seemed to end up being about me or our work, rather than her.

For some reason, that bothered me. "Trying to find those Dark mages," I said.

Meredith pointed to the map. "What are those tags?"

"I think we should try searching there."

Meredith looked taken aback. "All of them?"

I looked up at Meredith. "Unless you've turned up any leads."

"No, but . . . Isn't there a better way?"

"Like?"

"Tracer spells?"

I shook my head. "These two aren't stupid. If it were that easy Belthas would have done it already." Cinder and Rachel had made use of those spells to track down prey before. They'd be ready and waiting for someone to try the same trick against them.

Meredith hesitated. "All right," she said at last. "If you think so."

⁞⁞⁞⁞⁞⁞⁞⁞⁞

Five hours later, the sun had set. It had turned into one of those clear, freezing autumn nights, where the stars are sharp and bright and your breath makes puffs of vapour in the air. We were huddled by the side of a long, deserted road, only a few parked cars breaking up the emptiness. To the south was the Thames, far wider and darker than it had been at Deptford, and from the north, over the rooftops, came the distant roar of aircraft. The air smelt of river and cold stone.

I was tired and cold and wanted to go home to bed. We'd been searching our way eastwards along the river as the light faded from the sky and the crowds of commuters poured out of the city and towards the suburbs. By the time we'd reached Silvertown, all but a few stragglers had been driven away by the deepening cold, and now the streets were deserted.

"Can we stop for the night?" Meredith asked. She was wrapped in a coat bigger than she was, hunched over with her arms engulfed by the muffler, but she was still shivering.

"Just three places left," I said.

Meredith sighed but fell in behind me as we started down the road. In truth, I didn't think we had much chance of finding anything. It had been a lonely, cold evening, walking though lonely, cold parts of London, looking through warehouse after warehouse with my magic, and it was looking like my hunch had been wrong. But we were here and we might as well finish the job. Besides, there was another reason, one that I didn't especially want to say out loud: Cinder and Rachel might be looking for us too and it's a lot harder to find someone who keeps moving.

Meredith stayed quiet for the length of the road, and as we reached the next industrial park she went smoothly into the routine, moving to the front gate to talk to the security guard at the checkpoint. The guard looked up from his desk with a *what do you want?* expression. It didn't last—he was smiling in seconds and had told Meredith everything she wanted to know within a minute.

"There's a maybe," Meredith told me after he'd waved her good-bye. "A couple renting a unit who might match." I nodded and the two of us walked past the guard unchallenged. He was staring after Meredith with his mouth slightly open and I don't think he even noticed I was there.

Ten minutes of scanning the park turned up nothing. I hadn't really expected much—the place didn't feel right, not deserted enough. But as we were finishing up, I caught a glimpse of an older pair of warehouses behind the back wall, cut off from the road. "I'll check there and we'll move on," I said. I had to speak loudly—we'd come in close to London City airport, and it was hard to talk over the roar of planes.

Meredith nodded with another shiver and we split up, Meredith heading back towards the exit while I went further into the maze of buildings.

The back warehouse was dark and windowless, and passing the outer fence, I found that the building itself was sealed. I couldn't pick up any magical wards, but that didn't prove anything: Cinder and Rachel weren't stupid enough to leave obvious defences. But there was something off about the place all the same, even if I couldn't put my finger on exactly what it was.

I took a look around. The warehouse was built right between the industrial park and another complex of buildings next to the airport. Apart from the way I'd come in, there didn't seem to be any other way out; trying to go in any other direction led me to a dead end. High walls limited vision, giving the place a cramped, uncomfortable feel, and the nearby airport made it hard to hear anything.

I decided to take a closer look. I circled the building and approached the door, reaching into my pocket for my picks and wrenches. Since diviners aren't as good in combat as elemental mages, we tend to pick up a bunch of less-than-reputable skills to make up for it. Lockpicking's easy when you can see into the future, and I'm pretty good at it.

As I examined the door, though, I frowned. The lock looked simple, but for some reason, looking into the future didn't reveal any way to open it. That was odd. I knelt by the door, feeling the cold of the concrete through my jeans, and studied the keyhole. There didn't seem to be anything unusual, but—

My precognition warned me just in time. I caught a glimpse of something coming, took a closer look, and jumped to my feet in a dead run. As I ran I pulled a grey cloak from my bag and swept it around my shoulders. I was up against the wall with the mist cloak wrapped around me within five seconds. A moment later, the far corner of one of the buildings went black.

People describe night as black, but it isn't; it's more like a patchwork grey. When something that's an actual, light-eating black appears, it stands out against the darkness like a black hole. The blackness formed a vertical oval, starting at ground level and reaching seven feet in height, then shimmered and began to lighten. The shadows of another place were briefly visible, then two people stepped through.

My mist cloak is an imbued item like the monkey's paw, and it's the only imbued item I really trust. Mist cloaks are designed for concealment, and inactive, they look like soft cloth, coloured a sort of neutral grey that your eyes slide over. When worn, though, their colours shift and change, fading into the background so subtly that if you're not watching it happen you'd never even notice. But mist cloaks conceal more than sight; they block magical senses completely. You can pick out someone in a mist cloak if the light's good and you know what to look for, but to magical detection, it's like someone in a mist cloak just isn't there.

Which was good because right now that was the only thing stopping the man up ahead from turning me into charcoal. Cinder is a fire mage, and as I learnt the hard way a long time ago, fire mages can see a man's body heat as easily as you or I can see light. Cinder swept the area from left to right as he emerged from the gate, waiting for the woman behind him to step through before ending the spell. The gate turned back into darkness and dissolved away to nothing.

Even though Rachel was only a silhouette in the darkness, I knew it was her. She was saying something to Cinder but just barely too far away for me to hear. The two of them walked towards the warehouse and I held perfectly still, straining my ears to hear their conversation.

"—not going to work," Rachel said.

Cinder said something in his low rumble that I didn't catch. Rachel shook her head. "Not enough time. We have to kill him."

The two of them stopped by the warehouse door. They

were maybe twenty feet away, and I tried to breathe quietly. Cinder seemed to be thinking. "Back off?" he said at last.

"No!" Rachel said angrily. "I'm not letting some Light mage chase us away. This is *ours*."

"Can't get what he knows if he's dead," Cinder pointed out.

"We don't need him. We can make it work." Rachel stared past Cinder. "All we need is enough time."

My skin crawled. I didn't know if it was coincidence, but Rachel was staring right at me. At some level I knew that in these shadows and with my mist cloak, I'd look like nothing but a patch of wall. But still . . .

Even through the darkness, we were close enough that I could see the dark smudge of the mask covering the top half of Rachel's face. "Which?" Cinder said.

"The enchantress," Rachel said, as if talking to herself. "Blind him . . . Yes. But only if . . ." She looked suddenly away from me back to Cinder. "Let's go."

Cinder gave a grunt and fished in his pocket for a key. There was a tiny flicker of light as he inserted and turned it with a click. The door swung open and Rachel marched in. "What about Verus?" Cinder said just as he swung the door shut behind them. It closed with a clang and I couldn't hear anything more.

I've never felt so relieved and yet so frustrated. I was glad to have a solid wall between me and those two—but just *one more* sentence and I'd have known what they were planning. I thought about getting closer to eavesdrop and actually seriously considered it for a few seconds, which should tell you how badly I wanted to hear it.

But common sense won. I slipped away into the shadows.

Five minutes later, I was two streets over and out of danger. My mist cloak was tucked back in my bag where it could be drawn out quickly if needed. I'd picked a place by a crossroads, hidden in the shadows of a doorway where I had clear lines of sight down two streets. The only light came from the phone in my hand.

On the small screen was a short message addressed to Belthas containing Cinder and Rachel's location. My thumb hovered over the Send button, then moved away. I kept staring at the message until the screen went dark.

All I had to do was press the button and I'd be done. Belthas would take over and deal with Cinder and Rachel. I wouldn't even have to get involved; I could back off and watch the fireworks.

So why was I hesitating?

The last time I'd gotten involved with Cinder and Rachel, they'd alternated between trying to recruit me and trying to kill me, as well as taking the odd shot at Luna. They'd been working with a third mage, Khazad, who *would* have killed me if I hadn't been quicker to do unto others. It wasn't as though we had fond memories.

And yet I probably couldn't have gotten out alive without them. It hadn't been due to any warm feelings on Rachel or Cinder's part, but by the end we'd at least gotten to the stage of talking to each other rather than shooting on sight. And I'd definitely saved their collective butts at least once, on condition that they'd owe me a favour.

Of course, Cinder's assassination attempt had pretty much put paid to that. But still I hesitated. Was I being sentimental because of our history? Stupid. Rachel would kill me without a second thought . . .

I saw Meredith coming a long way off. Once she'd reached visual range I stepped out of the shadows, letting her see me. "What happened?" Meredith said once she was close enough.

I looked at Meredith and shook my head. I tapped the screen of my phone and heard the quiet delivery sound. "I found them."

Meredith's eyes went wide. "Did they—"

"No."

"Are you going to—"

"Already called him."

Meredith looked around, then wrapped her coat tighter around her and stepped into the doorway. We waited in silence.

ı ı ı ı ı ı ı ı

Belthas didn't waste time. In less than half an hour I heard the growl of engines and looked up to see headlights at the end of the street. As they grew brighter I saw that they belonged to a van, black and unmarked, with two more following behind. The vans pulled in by the side of the road and the engines died. In the silence I heard the slam of doors.

A man walked towards me. I stayed leaning against the corner and didn't raise my head. The footsteps stopped a few feet away. "Verus," a familiar voice said.

I lifted my eyes. "Garrick."

Garrick was wearing the same body armour I'd seem him in three nights ago, along with enough guns to star in a production of *The Matrix*. Behind him a steady stream of armed men piled out of the vans. "So I guess this answers the question of who you're working for," I said.

"For now." Garrick holstered the same compact-looking assault rifle I'd seen him carry before. "What's the layout?"

"Warehouse, single storey. Two access routes, through the industrial park at the front or a back entrance. Internal map's here." I handed Garrick a paper I'd sketched while waiting. "No outside defences, didn't get a look at the interior."

"It's a start. Still want to take point?"

"I think I'll leave this one to you guys."

"And here I thought you had something to prove."

I just shrugged. When he saw he wasn't going to get a rise out of me, Garrick moved away.

Belthas had disembarked from the end of the convoy and was speaking to Meredith. I walked over and Belthas turned to face me. "Ah, Verus. Well done."

"Don't break out the champagne yet," I said. "They were in the warehouse half an hour ago. Can't guarantee they're still there."

"Nevertheless, your speed is impressive." Belthas looked like a ghost in the darkness, thin and pale. "Let's make sure it's not wasted."

Meredith was watching the men. I followed her gaze to see that Garrick had grouped them into a loose circle and was issuing orders. They had a dangerous look, more so than usual for Council security, but they weren't carrying any magic. "No other mages?"

Belthas raised an eyebrow. "Are you volunteering?"

"I'm not a battle-mage."

"Yes, you mentioned." Belthas smiled slightly. "If you'll excuse me." He walked towards Garrick and the men, who fell silent at his approach. He issued some quick orders and the men began to take out submachine guns, checking the weapons and loading ammunition. They'd stopped talking and the only sound was the clack of metal. There was a feeling of tension in the air.

I looked at Meredith. "I'm guessing you don't want to join in."

Meredith shook her head. "Is there somewhere safe?"

"Come with me."

⁙⁙⁙⁙⁙

The industrial park was big and—in theory—locked up. But between the two of us, it didn't take long to find a building with a good view and get inside.

By the time we reached the top floor, Belthas's men were moving into position. The building we were occupying over-looked the south and east sides of Cinder and Deleo's ware-house, and beneath us I could see dark shapes slipping from shadow to shadow, moving to encircle the warehouse. Although the building we were in was sealed, it wasn't heated and I shivered as I stood by the window and looked down into the darkness. In less than five minutes Rachel and Cinder were about to get one hell of a nasty surprise, and for once I wasn't going to be on the receiving end. It was an odd feeling.

I took out a small black headset, examined it briefly, then clicked a switch. A red light flashed and there was a brief hiss of static, quickly damped. Meredith looked at me in surprise. "Did Belthas give you a radio?"

"Not exactly." I clicked through the channels until I found the right one, typed a three-digit code, then settled down to wait.

A voice spoke through the radio link. "North entrance in sight."

Garrick's voice answered. "Hold position. Wait for the scan."

A hiss, silence, then Garrick again. "External clear. Move to breach."

"Moving."

"Look," Meredith said quietly, pointing. I followed her finger and saw shadows closing on the warehouse, converging on the doors.

The radio spoke again. "Alpha team at north entrance."

"Bravo team, south entrance."

"Setting charges."

A silence, then Garrick's voice. "Alpha team, charges ready. Bravo, what's your status?"

"This is Bravo, charges set."

"Copy that. All teams check in."

"Alpha team standing by."

"Bravo team standing by."

"Charlie team standing by."

Garrick spoke again. "Weapons free. We are weapons free." His voice was calm. "Breach on my mark. Five . . . four . . . three . . ."

Meredith was staring down at the shadows at the south end of the warehouse. I put my hand to her head and gently turned her face away. "Cover your eyes."

"Two . . . one . . . *mark!*"

I closed my eyes just as the charges detonated and saw the white flash even through my eyelids. The roar came a fraction of a second later, and I opened my eyes to see a cloud of dust swirling about what had been the south door. Shadowy figures moved through the opening, lights flickering, searching for targets.

The radio crackled. "South clear."

"Contact north!"

I heard the stammer of three-round bursts: *ratatat, ratatat*. An instant later sullen red light flickered from the windows and there was a piercing scream.

"Man down!"

"—hit, hit, we—"

More gunfire, followed by a flat *boom*. "Taking fire, taking fire!"

"Bravo, tossing flashbangs, fire in the hole!"

The warehouse lit up with white flashes and two deafening bangs. The wounded man continued to scream as Garrick's voice spoke over the radio. "Move up!"

Lights flashed again, blue flickering against red over the staccato of the gunfire. I could sense spells being thrown, full-strength battle-magic intended to cripple or kill. Voices spoke over the radio, shouting, giving orders, drowning each other out. There was a final roar and a blue flash, followed by an ominous silence.

"Cease fire, target is down, cease fire."

Garrick's voice. "Bravo, take the stairs. Alpha, secure our position."

"Bravo, moving up."

Through the walls, I felt the signature of a gate spell. "Movement!" someone called.

"Flash the room. Go, go, go!"

Another white flash and a bang, this one slightly muffled. More gunfire and the distant thump of something heavy. Then the gunfire stopped. The warehouse below was silent but for the distant patter of boots.

"Clear left."

"Clear right. First floor clear."

"Ground floor clear."

"Bravo, report." It was Garrick's voice.

"We got—" There was a burst of static. "—went in."

"Bravo, repeat."

"Negative, negative. We hit him, he fell through."

"Confirm status of Target Two."

"Evac'd. He's gone."

"Target One's breathing."

"Confirm that," Garrick said. "Lock the place down. Charlie team, you're on medic duty."

The radio traffic died away. The man who'd been wounded earlier started screaming less often, then went quiet. I realised I'd been holding my breath and let it out. Meredith was still tense and the two of us stayed there, watching and waiting.

⁜⁜⁜⁜⁜

Infantry combat doesn't end with a bang or fanfare. It draws out into a long, tense silence as the ones still holding the field search to make sure the enemy's gone. Only as the minutes tick by and the silence stretches out does the tension ease.

After fifteen minutes Belthas's men began to emerge, making a sweep of the immediate area. Once they began looting the warehouse, I knew the battle was over. The vans drove into the industrial area, parking near the warehouse with their back doors opened and turned towards it, and a steady stream of men moved back and forth.

The wounded were brought out first. I suspected it was public relations on Belthas's part rather than genuine concern for the men but it made sense either way. Two were still walking, while the third was on a stretcher. I could see burns down his left side but he wasn't moving.

Next came items. I couldn't make out any pattern in the things Belthas's men were taking from the warehouse and I suspected they were just grabbing anything that wasn't nailed down. There were clothes, weapons, and papers. One thing in particular caught my eye: a set of spikes about the length of my hand. Light reflected off them with a flicker of purple but before I could get a close look they were stowed away.

And finally they brought out Rachel. She was on a stretcher, pale and unconscious in the artificial light. Garrick and two other men were guarding her as the stretcher was wheeled out and lowered behind the van. Rachel's mask had been lost somewhere in the fighting and I could almost make out her features, her hair spread out like a fan on the pillow. I stood next to Meredith, looking down through the tall windows over the industrial park, watching the men bustling around Rachel's still form as she was lifted into the van. The doors shut behind her with a *clang*.

No one else came out. Rachel had been captured but Cinder had escaped. I considered asking Belthas what had happened but decided against it. They were a lot of men with guns down there, and now that Rachel and Cinder were gone, they didn't have any need to stay quiet. It wasn't that I *expected* Belthas to have me shot just to tie off a loose end; I just didn't see any reason to give him the opportunity. I caught a glimpse of Belthas getting into one of the vans next to Garrick and the three vans pulled out one after another. The growl of their engines grew louder as they passed our building, then softer, until they'd faded into silence.

ıııııııı

Meredith and I descended the building and left the industrial park by the front entrance. The security post was empty. We walked back to the station in silence.

Only when the glow of the railway station was in front of us did I speak. "Want to get some dinner?"

"I can't," Meredith said. "I need to sort out a new place to stay."

I hesitated. "You can use my flat if—"

"Thanks," Meredith said. "But I need to get some other things done as well."

"Okay."

There was the crunch of tyres on gravel and as I looked into the road I saw a taxi pulling up. The driver signalled through his window and Meredith waved at him before turning back to me. She gave me a quick hug, then pulled away. "Will you be okay getting back?"

"Uh, sure. What about—?"

"I'll be fine. Thank you for everything."

Meredith walked quickly to the taxi and slipped inside. It pulled away and I watched the red lights disappear into the distance. It turned a corner and vanished, and I was alone.

I took the train home. My flat was empty and I went to bed.

chapter 7

I woke up early next morning, heart racing and breath quick. Another nightmare. I don't get them as often now but when I do they're just as bad. The sounds of the London morning drifted through the window. My flat was quiet.

There was a message on my phone from Belthas, congratulating me on the successful completion of the mission. I skimmed it and hit Close. I didn't feel like talking to Belthas.

The next message was from Sonder; he'd started research on the monkey's paw but was having trouble finding all the books he needed. I closed that too and looked to see if there was anything from Meredith or Luna. There wasn't.

I reviewed and tested my home defences. I had breakfast, went over my stock of items, and laid out the most useful ones in case of another attack. Finally, at nine o'clock and with nothing else to do, I opened my shop.

The morning dragged. I enjoy running my shop most of the time but nothing makes work less fun than wishing you were somewhere else. The customers annoyed me more than they should have, and I kept glancing at my phone to see if I had a message from Meredith or Luna. Finally, at noon, I gave up, shooed out the last few stragglers, and flipped the sign to *CLOSED*.

I was restless. Something was bothering me and I didn't know what.

I didn't want to work but pushed myself to do it anyway. Sonder's message had included a list of books that were supposed to contain references to the monkey's paw so I put on my coat and went out into central London to look for them. I didn't expect it to be easy, and it wasn't—the books Sonder had listed were obscure as hell. But finding a book in a bookshop, even an obscure book, is a lot easier than finding a person in a city.

Two and a half hours and twelve bookstores later, I'd tracked down seven out of the nine books on Sonder's list and decided to call it a day. I went home to my desk upstairs and pulled the first volume from its parcel. It was old and smelt of dust. A third of the way through, I found what I was looking for.

. . . the First Age, where the monkey god was brought to battle by Morthalion the Destroyer. For three days and three nights they battled but the monkey god's claws could not pierce Morthalion's shield. Neither could Morthalion's death magic slay the god, for being divine, its spirit could not be parted from its body by mortal means.

Seeing this, on the fourth day Morthalion reached down and tore away a part of his own shadow, from which he formed himself a blade of darkness, slim as a leaf and sharper than the frost. Wielding it, he struck off the god's foot, then before the two could be reunited Morthalion burnt the foot in black fire until it crumbled to ash. Again and again Morthalion struck, cutting and burning feet, legs, arms, head, and finally body. At last only one part of the god remained: a single paw.

Morthalion could not destroy the paw and instead bound it up with a white thread, enspelling it so that all should forget the monkey god's name, and thus his power could never be restored. But the monkey god's spirit lived on within the paw, and survives to this day, filled with hate for the race that destroyed him.

The passage ended. I flipped to the end, but the monkey's paw wasn't mentioned again. I closed the book and picked up the next.

—of wish-granting items, little needs to be said. Their powers are generally overrated and greatly inferior to those of True Mages, who—

I rolled my eyes and tossed the book aside. The next one, titled *Encyclopaedia Arcana*, was thicker and the writing denser.

Wish magic, or desire magic, works quite differently. It magnifies the power of speech: Rather than the words being a trigger, it is the speaking of the wish itself that rewrites reality.

Stories abound of carelessly or ambiguously worded wishes causing disaster; these legends, unfortunately, have a firm basis in fact. While wish magic will not misinterpret or "twist" a wish, neither will it take into account context or intention, and phrasing is absolutely crucial. Clear, simple sentences are best; convoluted wording often results in too weak a "lens" for the magic to focus through, and vague wishes bring totally unpredictable results. Many mages blame such results upon malicious intelligence on the part of the granting power, but this is inaccurate. Wish magic is essentially neutral.

It grants only what is asked; nothing more and nothing less.

There is a qualification, however. Most sources of wish magic have individual prohibitions against wishing for a certain outcome, a common example being the taking of a life. Should the user attempt a forbidden wish, the magic will fail to take effect or rebound upon the wisher. There is usually no way of discovering such limitations except through trial and error, making such experimentation a highly dangerous process.

More than any other, wish magic is capable of creating extraordinarily powerful effects; however, experienced mages generally consider it more trouble than it is worth.

Books four and five didn't have anything new. The sixth was more interesting.

. . . imbued items capable of bestowing wishes, generally referred to as "monkey's paws" regardless of their actual form. Their magic works as an unspoken contract, granting the user between three and as many as seven wishes.

At first, the wishes will appear to work to the user's benefit. However, with each wish the monkey's paw gains a greater hold over its bearer and soon it will begin to twist the wishes, subtly at first, then more forcefully. In every case, the user is made to feel that the only way to escape his problems is to use the paw again; each wish leads to greater and greater calamity, until he is destroyed.

Although wholly evil, a monkey's paw is bound by rules. First and foremost, the monkey's paw cannot force a bearer to accept its contract. It can tempt or promise but the truly innocent are safe; at some level, the bearer must knowingly and willingly consent to the item's power. The monkey's paw must also follow the letter of a wish, if not the spirit. This has led many to believe that a clever wielder could make extended use of a monkey's paw by wording his wishes carefully, but such success is rare.

The final book was a slim volume that seemed handwritten rather than printed. Squinting, I realised it skipped from account to account, and I was in the middle of a paragraph before realising that it was what I was looking for. I went back to the beginning of the section and read it from start to finish.

The monkey's paw is one of the most ancient of all artifacts and the truth of its origin is unknown, though many have crafted lesser copies in an attempt to imitate its power.

The monkey's paw grants wishes with few if any limitations. Most believe that these wishes follow fixed and certain rules. This is false. The monkey's paw is sentient and free-willed. The paw, not its bearer, chooses whether and how to grant a wish. Any bearer who believes he controls it soon learns his mistake.

While inactive, the paw lies dormant. In these periods, the monkey's paw will often adopt a place, or a person, to remain with. This "host" seems to enjoy limited protection from the item; perhaps the monkey's paw prefers not to harm those who do not use its power, or perhaps it simply chooses not to bite the hand that feeds it. The reason, as with so much else concerning the item, is unknown. The monkey's paw is not in the habit of explaining itself and rarely leaves witnesses in its wake.

The section ended. I read it through twice more, then sat back in my chair. Something about that last one made me uneasy. *A host . . .*

I tried to figure out some way I could put the information in the books to use but came up blank. Bound or unbound, limited or unlimited, evil or neutral: Each book told a different story, and without knowing which was true they weren't much help. The one thing they all agreed on was that the monkey's paw was dangerous—and I'd known that already. I walked to my window and looked out over London.

The morning had been overcast but the clouds had vanished one by one and the sun was shining down out of a clear sky. Sunset was only a couple of hours away and the colour of the sunlight had changed to a rich yellow-gold, the chimneys and rooftops casting long shadows with the coming evening. The windows in the houses and flats were still illuminated by the sun but as dusk drew nearer I knew they would light up one by one, making squares of light in the darkness.

I was still restless. I'd tried to shrug it off all day and it hadn't worked, and I didn't know why. I'd done a job for Belthas and succeeded. Okay, I didn't know everything, but Rachel and Cinder had been stopped. I wasn't completely happy about the way things had ended, but I hadn't had much choice.

Was it about Luna and the monkey's paw? I thought about it and realised that wasn't it. Working on the monkey's paw wasn't making me feel any better; the problem was somewhere else. Something was wrong.

But what?

It was because I didn't understand. I'm like all diviners: I need to know things. I'd learnt bits and pieces but that wasn't enough. I had to know how they fit together. The assassination attempts, Belthas, Rachel and Cinder, Arachne . . .

Start at the beginning. Which part related to me the most?

The assassination attempts.

There had been four. The construct in my shop, the sniper on the Heath, Cinder burning Meredith's flat, and the bomb-maker in the factory.

Why did someone want me dead so badly?

The obvious explanation was because I'd stopped that first attack on Meredith. I'd prevented Rachel and Cinder from killing her so they'd turned their attention to me. The sniper and the bomb-maker had tried to kill me, and Cinder had tried to kill both of us. I remembered that last glimpse I'd had of Cinder, staring at me as Starbreeze snatched me and Meredith out of the window.

I frowned. *Staring at me . . .* There was something nagging at me. What was it?

It was the method. It didn't fit. The construct and fire had been brute-force magical attacks. The sniper and the bomb-maker had used modern technology, precise and deadly.

And now that I thought about it, I'd never seen Rachel or Cinder use guns. Like most mages, they rely on magic for pretty much everything. If they wanted me dead, they'd either send a construct or do their own dirty work.

But that was stretching things. It made sense that the same group would be behind all the attacks. I knew Rachel and Cinder had been trying to get me killed . . .

. . . didn't I?

Again I remembered how Cinder had looked when he'd seen me in Meredith's flat, the way he'd stopped to stare. Except . . .

. . . if he'd been trying to kill me, why had he stopped?

I knew how fast Cinder was. He'd had more than enough time to get off an attack. But he hadn't.

And the only way that made sense was if Cinder hadn't been trying to kill me at all.

What if Cinder hadn't known I was there? *Meredith* had been Rachel's target when she'd sent the construct. Maybe Meredith had been Cinder's target, too. It had been Meredith's flat; even if he'd been expecting anyone else, Cinder would have had no way of knowing it was me. Which would mean he hadn't known I was involved at all.

But the sniper had been targeting me, not Meredith. And the sniper had tried to kill me *before* I'd met Cinder at the flat . . .

A nasty feeling crept up inside me. That meant Rachel and Cinder hadn't sent the sniper—and probably not the bomb-maker, either. Someone else had done it. Which meant that someone else was still out there. And odds were, they still wanted me dead.

But who?

I shook my head in frustration. It didn't make sense. I wanted to blame Belthas. He had the contacts and the resources, as well as Garrick, who I still suspected had been the one shooting at me on the Heath. But I'd been working for Belthas—in fact, I'd just won a battle for him. Why would he want me dead *before* I'd told him where Rachel and Cinder were hiding? And if it was someone else, like Levistus, why would they choose to strike at me now?

I was missing something.

I tried calling Meredith and got her voice mail. I hung up and called Luna, and this time I got through.

Luna took a long time to answer, and when she did, her voice was blurred by the sound of wind. "Hi."

"Luna, it's Alex. Are you free?"

"What was that?" Luna said loudly.

"Where are you?"

There was the sound of voices and I heard the crunch of footsteps. The background noise dropped slightly. "Hi, Alex?" Luna said again. "Sorry, it's hard to hear."

"Where are you?"

"On the Heath."

I blinked. "Why are you on the Heath?"

"Um . . . I was going to see Arachne."

There was something in her voice. "Is Martin with you?"

There was a pause. Luna's not a good liar. I closed my eyes. "Luna, I don't think that's a good idea."

"We were just going to talk to her. To see if she knew about the monkey's paw."

"She said she was leaving."

"But that wasn't going to be for a few days, right? If I asked her . . ."

I sighed inwardly. Luna's one of the very few people whom Arachne's willing to let inside her lair. It was possible; I just didn't like the idea of Martin being there. "Have you seen anything unusual?"

A loud rustling drowned out my words. I heard someone talking and recognised Martin's voice. "Just a minute," Luna called back to him, then spoke into the receiver again. "Sorry, what was that?"

"Forget it," I said. "Just drop by first chance you get, okay? I need to talk to you. Privately."

"Okay," Luna said. "Um, I don't know when Martin and I'll be done. I'll call you afterwards?"

I was really sick of hearing about Martin. "Sure." I heard Martin say something else as Luna cut the connection. I dropped my phone back into my pocket.

I'd been indoors all day. I locked up the shop and started walking. Maybe some exercise would help me think.

The city was bustling in the sunset. I crossed the canal and walked up Kentish Town Road, watching the rush-hour traffic pile up nose to tail. The air was filled with noise and car exhaust.

After a while I realised my feet were leading me towards the Heath. Usually when something's bothering me I go and talk it over with Arachne. But Arachne was either gone or busy with Luna, and I didn't want to deal with Luna and Martin. I changed direction, heading for the southern part of the Heath instead of the deeper regions that hold Arachne's lair.

By the time I reached Parliament Hill, the sun had set and the light was fading. I climbed the hill and sat on one of the benches facing south. It's a beautiful view. Ahead, through the branches of the trees, were the jagged skyscrapers of Liverpool Street; to the right was the looming ugly Tetris block of the Royal Free Hospital. The towers of Canary Wharf were away to the left, small and squat in the distance. The sky was the dusky blue of twilight, and lights were coming on in the windows as I watched.

I noticed my phone was about to ring and pulled it out. I was a bit disappointed to see that it was Sonder but I kept it out anyway and answered on the second ring. "Hey, Sonder."

"Hi." Sonder sounded worried. "I'm glad I got you."

"I found some of those books."

"What?"

"The ones you said you needed. About the monkey's paw."

"About— Oh, oh. Right."

"Okay," I said. "So I'm guessing that's not why you called." Although the Heath was darkening, there were still people scattered across the hill. A spaniel ran past, nose to the ground, stumpy tail wagging. "Something's bothering you."

"Yeah." Sonder seemed to get hold of himself. "Okay. You know the thing we agreed I should check up on?"

"Not the monkey's paw."

"The other thing."

I thought back to the conversation and remembered. "About Martin."

"Yeah."

"Did you talk to Luna?"

"Um . . ." Sonder hesitated. "She said she was busy."

I'll bet. "Okay."

"So, um . . ."

"You went sniffing around anyway," I said. I couldn't honestly say I was surprised. It was the kind of thing I might have done.

"Yeah," Sonder admitted.

It sounded from the echoes as though Sonder was in a corridor. "Are you at Luna's flat?"

". . . Yeah."

"You didn't break in, did you?"

"No! Well . . . not exactly."

"Sonder . . ."

"I didn't go inside! And she'd said she might be around, I was just waiting to see if—"

"Okay, okay." I knew Sonder would get sidetracked if I let him, and I didn't really want to hear the details. "What did you find?"

"Well . . . it was Martin. He made a phone call."

"What, right now?"

"No, on Saturday night."

"Saturday—okay. And you were listening?"

"Yeah, a few minutes ago."

You really need a couple of extra tenses for a conversation about time magic. "Okay," I said. "Who was he talking to?"

"Belthas."

I stopped. "What?"

"I know," Sonder said. "He's not supposed to be working for Belthas, right?"

". . . No. He's not. Working for him?"

"That was what it sounded like. Martin was giving a report and then he said he was on his way to meet him. As in, right then."

I tried to figure out what was going on. I'd missed something, something big. "What was he telling Belthas about?"

"About Luna."

I went still.

"He said he'd spent the evening with her and things were going well." Sonder sounded worried. "Then he said something about two or three days. Then he said he was on his way."

Two or three days from Saturday night would be . . . about now. "Sonder, I've got to go. We've got a problem."

"Why?"

"Because Luna's taking Martin to Arachne's lair right now." I got to my feet and started walking. "See what else you can find but be careful."

"Okay." Sonder paused. "Alex? What do you think Belthas wanted with Martin?"

"I don't know, but I don't think I'm going to like the answer. I'm going to find Luna. I'll check in when I do."

"Okay."

I hung up and speed-dialled Luna's number. I got her voice mail. I tried again—same result. It could mean she was in Arachne's lair. Or it could mean something very bad.

I wanted to run but forced myself to keep to a walk. There was no way this could be a coincidence. Martin and Luna, Meredith and me . . .

An idea stirred, something blank and terrible, the shape of it making me shy away. I tried to think of what Belthas could want with Luna. Luna's curse is powerful in its way, but it doesn't serve anyone but her. If Belthas wanted a chance mage, he could find someone else. Had he done the whole thing to get to me? No, that couldn't be it—Martin had hardly spoken to me.

There must be something Luna had that Belthas wanted. It wasn't her magic and it wasn't her status. Belthas had gotten me involved as well. Maybe it was something to do with both of us. What did Luna and I have in common?

We both knew about the fateweaver. But that didn't fit with what Rachel and Cinder had been doing, and besides, it was old news. We both knew Starbreeze . . . no, I'm the only one with a connection to her.

What about Arachne? We were two of the very few people Arachne trusted enough to let into her lair . . . which was where Luna was taking Martin . . .

I stopped dead.

Arachne. A magical creature.

The technique Rachel and Cinder had been using.

And now Belthas had it too.

"Oh shit," I said quietly. And started to run.

․․․․․․․․․

I t took me ten minutes to cover the distance. I spent less than five putting the pieces together.

Half of that was kicking myself for being stupid. I'd known Belthas was keeping something back. Of course he didn't want Rachel and Cinder getting their hands on something this powerful. He wanted it for himself. And now he had it, he needed a creature to try it out on.

Arachne was too well protected to attack directly. Behind the wards of her lair, she was almost invulnerable. But if you had someone Arachne trusted enough to let in . . . that changed things. And if you had someone like Martin, with the monkey's paw making him immune to Arachne's magic . . . and a small army of men to follow him . . .

Night had fallen by the time I reached Arachne's lair. The Heath was silent but for the sound of distant traffic. I crept forward to the ravine and peered through the trees.

It was dark enough that I had to stare for a few seconds to be sure of what I was seeing but once I did, my heart sank. The entrance to Arachne's lair was open.

Something caught my eye, lying in the grass, and I moved silently to retrieve it. It was a white ribbon, the kind Luna uses to tie her hair. A faint silver mist still clung to it, the residue of Luna's curse.

I should have backed off. It would have been the smart thing to do. The careful thing to do.

I walked down into the ravine. As I came down the slope I heard someone catch their breath just in front of me. The mouth of Arachne's cave was a mass of shadows and I walked towards one of them, straight as an arrow. "Meredith," I said into the darkness, my voice soft in the empty night. "We need to talk."

One of the shadows moved. There was a click and a faint light illuminated Meredith, pale and frightened. "You're not supposed to be here."

I kept walking towards her. "Who's in there, Meredith?"

Meredith backed up. "I—what do you mean?"

"No," I said. "No more games."

"I'm not supposed to—" Meredith stopped.

I nodded. "You're out here to turn people away. While Belthas works." I stepped closer. "I'll make this simple. Where's Luna?"

Meredith hesitated.

I turned towards the entrance. "You're wasting my time."

"No, wait!" Meredith stepped in front of me, hands up.

"Then answer. Where's Luna?"

"She's—" Meredith shook her head. "Just go. Okay?"

I didn't even bother answering. I stepped in. Meredith pressed herself against the earth wall, her eyes going wide.

Suddenly my anger vanished. I'd been splitting my attention, watching for any sign of Belthas's men; now I found myself focusing on Meredith, noticing as if for the first time her softness and beauty. I realised that I didn't want to hurt her, even if it was to . . . What was I doing again? "What's happening?"

Meredith's eyes flicked over my shoulder, then back again. "It's nothing. Alex, you should go. It's dangerous here."

It seemed like a good idea. If Meredith wanted me to leave, I ought to. Except . . . I shook my head. There was something . . .

"Alex? Please."

"Where's Luna?"

Meredith flinched, just for a second. "I . . . don't know. Alex?"

I tried to remember what I was doing. It was hard, like trying to think while asleep. I could feel something fighting me but I resisted it, piecing my thoughts back together one at a time. "She's in there, isn't she?"

Meredith's eyes flicked to one side again. "No. She isn't."

Meredith was lying. It was hard to believe it—I wanted to trust her—but a clearer, stronger part of me was telling me not to. And she kept on looking away, as if . . .

. . . as if she were looking at something behind me.

I tried to turn but my dulled reactions were too slow. Something stung the back of my neck and a wave of dizziness washed over me. It was hard to move, and with a vague feeling of surprise I noticed I was lying on the ground. A man was saying something in a deep voice but I couldn't seem to focus on the words. And then I stopped noticing anything at all.

ı ı ı ı ı ı ı ı ı

Mages have developed a lot of ways to knock someone unconscious. Light mages use them to avoid killing; Dark mages also use them to avoid killing, though for different reasons. I've had more experience with them than I'd like and this had been one of the "softer" ones—I didn't feel any headache or nausea. As I came awake I began to hear the echoing scrape of movement from nearby. I could tell from the sounds that I was in a big room. I opened my eyes.

I was in Arachne's lair, though the layout seemed different. I was lying a rug near the far side. Sofas and chairs had been pushed up against the wall and Luna was sitting on one of them. She was looking down at me. "Hey," I said, still a little blurry. "You okay?"

Luna gave a tiny nod. She was sitting quite still. I couldn't see any injuries on her, though now I took a closer look her clothes looked scuffed. I got to my feet. A brief wave of dizziness hit me and I swayed for a moment before shaking it off.

I had the feeling I was forgetting something. "How did you get here?" I said.

Luna flicked her eyes behind me then back again. It was a very tiny gesture, but something about it sent a chill down my spine.

I turned around.

It's always struck me as a bit unfair that despite being able to see the future, I get so many horrible surprises. You'd think being a diviner I'd be able to avoid them but it seems all that means is that when they finally do catch up with me they're much worse. It's happened so many times that I've learnt to recognise the exact feeling: a sort of hollow, sinking sensation in my gut, like I've just been dropped from very high up.

Belthas was standing thirty feet away, his hands clasped behind his back. He looked relaxed. Of course, he had a lot to be relaxed about.

About ten men from Belthas's private army were standing in a loose semicircle on either side of Belthas, surrounding Luna and me. They were wearing body armour and carried submachine guns. The guns were pointed *almost* at the two of us so that we couldn't quite stare down the barrels but could imagine very easily what it would be like. All of them were looking at us with flat, unreadable expressions. Seeing them up close in the light, they looked tough and competent. They did not look friendly or nice.

Garrick was in the circle too. Unlike the other men, he was standing at ease with his weapon hanging from its sling, though I had the feeling he could probably get a shot off faster than any of them. Unlike the others, he gave me a nod. A few more of Belthas's men were scattered around the lair, including two stationed at the tunnel leading out to the Heath.

Meredith and Martin were there too, a little way behind Belthas. Meredith was sitting on one of the few remaining chairs; she didn't meet my eyes. Martin was standing with arms folded, looking pleased with himself. All told, there were a little under twenty people facing us. None of them looked like they wanted to be our friends.

Arachne's lair had been the site of a short, vicious battle. A few of the sofas and tables had been smashed into firewood, and many more bore the marks of spells or weapons fire. Dresses and coats had been slashed and burnt, then gathered up and piled carelessly in stacks. The centre of the room had been cleared, the clothes and furniture shunted up against the walls.

Arachne was next to the dressing rooms. She was lying motionless on the floor, her vast bulk still, watched over by two guards. Something glinted at the back of her head. At the sight of Arachne, my fear vanished in a wave of anger. I turned to Belthas. "Verus," Belthas said.

I stared at him.

"I trust you're feeling better?"

"You've tried to kill me twice in as many days," I said. "Drop the act."

Belthas raised his eyebrows. "You know," I said, "there's just one thing I'm curious about. How'd you know the monkey's paw would pick Martin?"

Martin stiffened slightly, looking from me to Belthas. "Ah," Belthas said. "That was merely a matter of adapting to circumstances."

"And you just took advantage."

Belthas inclined his head.

"So that's why you ordered those assassination attempts," I said. "You had Meredith and Martin to work on the two of us. But once Martin picked up that item, you didn't need me anymore. He would have phoned you on . . . what, Saturday night?" I saw Martin start. "And by Sunday morning you had Garrick ready to shoot me. You don't waste time, do you?"

"I'm impressed, Verus," Belthas said. "But you've misinterpreted events slightly."

"Why are we even talking to this guy?" Martin said.

"Shush, Martin," I said. "Adults are talking."

"Shut up," Martin said with a sneer. "Me and Luna couldn't stop laughing about you, you know that? Having something like this and being too scared to use it."

"How can you say that?" Luna's voice was shaking. "I thought you cared about me! How could you *do* this?"

Martin turned away with a shrug. "Martin, you're stupid," I said.

"Yeah? Then how come we've got a bunch of guns pointed at you?"

"Doesn't change the fact that you're stupid. For a start, you keep saying 'we.' You're not Belthas's partner, you're his minion. You're stupid enough to use the monkey's paw after I told you the truth about it. And you're stupid enough to keep being Belthas's minion and keep using the monkey's paw even after being told that it'll kill you. In fact, you're so stupid that I can tell you all this to your face and Belthas won't stop me because he knows you're too much of an idiot to know when you're being told the truth. He can just wait for you to get yourself killed without lifting a finger."

Belthas raised an eyebrow but didn't comment. Martin had been listening with his mouth half-open and he started to say something or other but I turned on Meredith before he could finish. "And you. Lying really is a way of life to you, isn't it?"

Meredith stared at me. "Excuse me?"

"That was what Belthas told you to do, wasn't it? Manipulate me."

Meredith's eyes narrowed. "Get over yourself."

"I trusted you!"

"No, you didn't. You never let me in—you don't trust anyone. You're the coldest man I've ever met."

My face twisted in a snarl. "As if you could—" Martin started to shout something and some of the men brought their guns up.

"Quiet, please," Belthas said, his voice cutting across the

noise. He looked from side to side, eyebrows raised, until everyone had fallen silent. "I can understand you have reasons for disagreement but I think it would be best if you resolve your personal issues in your own time."

Martin glowered. Meredith looked away.

"Now," Belthas said once order had resumed. "Verus, I have an offer for you."

"I can't wait."

"There's no need for sarcasm," Belthas said mildly. "As I was saying earlier, while your analysis is impressive, you've gone astray in one or two points. I haven't given any instructions to kill you. In fact, I quite specifically instructed my men to make sure you were unharmed."

"Oh," I said. "So those were the *friendly* kind of assassination attempts."

Belthas sighed. "Verus, you really should . . . how did Meredith put it? Get over yourself. Yes, your value was diminished once Martin reported his success. But do you really think that's enough reason to order your death? I'm not a Dark mage. If I killed everyone who wasn't useful to me, there wouldn't be many people left."

I was silent. "Besides," Belthas continued. "You've been of considerable assistance. It was due to you that we were able to capture Deleo. With her and Cinder on the loose, this would have been impossible."

"Feel free to express your gratitude."

"I'd be happy to. As I said, I have considerable influence with the Council. However, with that influence comes obligations." Belthas gestured to the men around him. "It would hardly have been possible to arrange all this without some assistance. Fortunately, I was able to discover a Council member willing to act as a patron of sorts."

"Great. Who?"

Belthas smiled slightly. "Come now, Verus. I've already explained that I've no wish to kill you. Who do you know on the Council who does?"

I stared for a second—then my heart sank. "Shit."

"Yes," Belthas said dryly. "Did you think he forgot?"

I turned away. "Alex?" Luna said quietly.

"Levistus," I said. Things had just gone from bad to worse. I looked at Belthas. "So what? I was the price for his help?"

"Actually, that's quite an interesting story." Belthas settled himself more comfortably. "I suspected from the start that it was Deleo and Cinder we were looking for, and given your past history, I immediately thought of you as the natural choice to find them. But when I suggested your name to Levistus, he was quite definite that you were not to be involved. Levistus is . . . less tolerant of unpredictability than I am.

"It was the one sticking point in our arrangement. But we had only managed to acquire part of the ritual, and I knew that without Cinder and Deleo I would have no more success than they had had with that barghest. I needed one of them alive to interrogate and I was certain you were our best chance." Belthas smiled again. "You played your role admirably."

I was silent.

"Levistus, unfortunately, did not share my faith in your reliability," Belthas continued. "Enough so that when he discovered your involvement, he ordered your immediate removal." Belthas glanced sideways at Garrick. "Via *someone* whom I had been under the impression was working for me."

Garrick shrugged. "I was."

"I don't believe your contract mentioned anything about freelancing."

"Didn't say I wouldn't, either."

Belthas sighed. "Yes, well. Smoothing that over took quite some work. Levistus assigned a second agent to the same task but fortunately you proved capable of dealing with that matter on your own. At least that unpleasantness at the factory had the advantage of persuading Levistus to reconsider. After some persuasion, he reluctantly agreed to a compromise."

I stood still. "A compromise."

"More a matter of reparation, really. You caused him a certain amount of loss in your last encounter."

"If he wants the fateweaver, he can get it himself."

"Interesting you should mention that," Belthas said. "It was my first assumption too. But it seems that retrieving the fateweaver isn't a priority for Levistus at the moment. Oh, he'd like it some day, but it's not his primary concern. His grudge against you concerns the loss of his agents."

I hadn't been the only one Levistus had sent to get the fateweaver. There had been two others: an earth mage called Griff and a bound elemental named Thirteen. Both had done their best to get rid of me and I hadn't cooperated. "You know," I said, "technically, I didn't kill either of them."

"Ah?" Belthas said politely. "Well, you could raise that point with Levistus if you feel it would help."

I was silent.

"I'm not explaining all this to you because I like the sound of my own voice, Verus. I'm doing it as a sign of good faith. You asked me a moment ago to show my gratitude. I did. I convinced Levistus to stop the attempts on your life, and believe me when I say it took quite some persuasion. What eventually changed his mind was realising that you still had something he wanted."

"Which is?"

Belthas brought his hand from behind his back and tossed something to me, something small that glinted in the light. I caught it reflexively and looked down.

It was a small cylindrical rod, made of glass, the same one I'd brought to the lair tonight. It was the focus I used to call Starbreeze.

"He wants," Belthas said, "a new elemental servant."

||||||||||

looked down at the rod, then up at Belthas.

"I'm sure there's no need to spell it out for you," Belthas said.

"You want Starbreeze."

"Levistus does."

"You want me to call her," I said, my voice flat. "So you can catch her."

"Yes."

"For Levistus?" I said. "You do what he tells you?"

"Do pay attention, Verus," Belthas said. "Levistus is acting as my patron in this matter. He's been quite generous with his assistance. In return, when he asks a favour, he expects me to uphold my end of the bargain."

"What are you going to do with Starbreeze if you get her?"

"That's really none of your concern," Belthas said. "Call the elemental here, and you and your apprentice will be free to go."

I remembered Levistus's servant, the air elemental Thirteen. She'd been like and yet unlike Starbreeze, with all Starbreeze's power yet none of her freedom, enslaved completely to Levistus's will. The only expression I'd ever seen on her face had been surprise, just once, at the moment of her death. If Belthas were able to capture Starbreeze, the same would happen to her.

"What did you do to Arachne?" I said.

"The spider?" Belthas glanced back at her. "Stable, for the moment."

I looked across the room at Arachne. She hadn't moved during the entire conversation, her eyes opaque and still, and I knew she was unconscious. Lying in the corner, with the guards watching over her, she somehow looked much smaller and more vulnerable. Most of the clothes around the room had been ripped or destroyed. The ones that had survived had been thrown carelessly in piles with none of the care that Arachne used.

A wave of fury rose up in me. Arachne had never done any harm to anybody. All she'd ever done had been to sit here and weave her clothes. Her lair had been a peaceful place, a place where things were created. Belthas and his men had smashed their way in here and destroyed it, and now they were trying to do the same to Starbreeze too.

"I hate to rush you," Belthas said when I didn't say anything, "but we have a schedule to keep."

"I'll make you a counteroffer," I said. "Let Arachne go. Then destroy the notes and the focuses you got from Deleo, and make sure nobody ever gets hold of it. Do that and I'll keep working for you. Otherwise, I promise I'll see you dead."

Several of the men laughed. "I'll choose to attribute that remark to your stressful situation and not hold it against you," Belthas said. "The elemental, Verus."

I looked him in the eye. "Go fuck yourself."

Belthas sighed. "Garrick, shoot the girl somewhere painful but nonfatal. No permanent damage from the first bullet, please."

Garrick nodded and raised his weapon, sighting on Luna. Luna's eyes went wide and she scrambled to her feet. "Wait!" I shouted.

"This isn't a game, Verus." Belthas said calmly. "Let me explain what will happen if you refuse. First, I'll have your apprentice shot. It won't kill her, at least not immediately. Then I will offer you another chance. If you still refuse, I will have her shot again. Then I will repeat the process. She will die very slowly and in great pain, and she will be crippled and insane long before her eventual death. At that point we will move on to you. Given your history, I doubt the same treatment will persuade you, but I'll do it anyway, just to be thorough. And if at the end of that you still have chosen not to cooperate, I'll have you killed. And then I'll get hold of the elemental anyway. You will both have died for nothing."

The dispassionate, matter-of-fact way Belthas spoke made my blood run cold. Looking into the future, I knew he wasn't bluffing. I looked between the other people in the room. Martin's smile had vanished and he was looking a little pale. Meredith was still turned away and Garrick was watching me steadily. I knew I didn't have any allies here.

Belthas didn't say anything more, simply watching with his pale eyes. I looked down at the focus, looking into the future. I could call Starbreeze, pretend to cooperate, order her to take us away . . .

It wouldn't work. Not only wouldn't it work, it was exactly what Belthas was expecting. Meredith would have told him how we'd escaped from Cinder. As soon as Starbreeze was inside, he would seal the exits with walls of ice.

The exits . . .

Without turning my head, I looked for a way out. The tunnel entrance leading back onto the Heath was under guard by two of Belthas's men and was at the far end of the room; too far. The passage leading into the storerooms was closer but it was a dead end. Even if I could make it, it would only delay the inevitable.

That just left one way to run. The tunnel at the back of Arachne's lair, leading down into the darkness, uncharted and deep. I didn't know what was down there and I was willing to bet Belthas didn't either. And it was only a few seconds away.

But even a few seconds was too long. I'd be cut down before I got halfway. "Luna," I said.

Luna looked at me. I could tell she was afraid, trying not to show it. I didn't meet her eyes. "Look away," I told her.

"What?"

"Look away."

"Why?"

"Because," I said quietly, "I don't want you to see this."

I felt Luna stiffen. She opened her mouth, staring at me, about to speak, then closed it again. Slowly, she turned to face the wall. Belthas nodded.

I took the glass rod in my hand and stroked it with a finger. I'd had it for a long time. Starbreeze had attuned herself to it, touching it with her magic so that she could always hear my call. Hardly any elementals are willing to give a mage so much power over them. It was a symbol of how much she trusted me.

I wove magic through it, whispering, "Starbreeze, come." Then I tossed it forward. The rod clinked on the stone midway between us, rolling to a stop. All of the men looked down at it.

Belthas raised his eyebrows. "Is that it?"

I closed my eyes.

Focus items are limited things. The glass rod was designed for one purpose only: to carry a message on the wind. But like all focus items, the energy transfer is inefficient. Some of the energy goes into carrying the message, some bleeds off harmlessly, and some—just a little—is left in the item. Each time I'd used it, the energy reserve had increased slightly. It's a tiny amount, so small that you'd have trouble even noticing it, but I'd been using the focus to call Starbreeze for years. Like saving pennies, it adds up.

I can't use offensive magic, not directly. But one thing I'm very good at is manipulating items and anything containing energy can, in theory, be persuaded to release it. It's like throwing a match into a petrol tank. It might not be what it's designed for but you can do it.

The little glass rod disintegrated with a crack of thunder and a brilliant flash, the energy tearing the focus apart in light and sound. Men cried out, and as they did I was already sprinting. "Luna! Run!"

I had one glimpse of the room, filled with chaos as the men fell back, blinded, aiming their weapons at unseen threats. I saw a shield of blue light go up around Belthas, saw Martin collide with a guard and fall. Luna had been turned away from the flash; it hadn't blinded her but her reactions were slower. There were two guards between us and the tunnel. One was blinded; the other, quicker or luckier, was only dazzled and brought up his gun. I saw his intention to club me with the stock, ducked under the swing, put a web-hand strike into his throat that sent him to the ground choking, and ran on without breaking stride.

It couldn't have taken more than five seconds to make the dash to the tunnel entrance but it felt like an hour. I heard the shouts from behind me, saw the blackness of the tunnel mouth growing larger, expecting every minute to hear gunfire. Then just as I made it to the entrance, I heard Luna yell, "Alex!"

Luna had made it about halfway before one of the guards had caught up with her. Either Belthas hadn't told them about Luna's curse or this one was just really stupid because he was grappling with her. I could see the silver mist of Luna's curse flowing into him and as I watched Luna snapped her head around at him. Suddenly the mist wasn't just pouring into him, it was *surging*, and I swear it actually looked gleeful. At the centre of the room, Garrick had recovered. He lined up on me and fired a three-round burst.

As he did, Luna pulled at the guard, struggling to get away. The guard tripped and staggered, swinging between me and Garrick.

The guard saw the danger and tried to dodge, and Garrick was already pulling his aim away, yet somehow the two went in exactly the same direction. All three bullets hit, going through the man's head in a spray of gore. He dragged Luna down with him, dead before he hit the ground.

For an instant everyone stopped, staring at the corpse that a second ago had been a living person. Garrick looked genuinely surprised for the first time I'd seen. Even if you know what Luna's curse is supposed to do, it's another thing to see it.

Then Belthas looked at me. "Kill him."

His hand was coming up, blue light starting to glow around it, and I knew what was coming. I threw myself into the tunnel just as a wall of blue-white ice shimmered into existence, barely missing me and sealing off the tunnel entrance. A heartbeat later I heard the muffled bark of guns, and the ice wall shuddered as impacts spiderwebbed across its other side.

I could hear distant shouting: Belthas giving orders to his men. As I watched, the ice wall shuddered again as more bullets struck it. A fracture went through it from top to bottom with a crack. Luna was on the other side of that barrier, along with Belthas and his men. And in a few seconds more, the barrier would be gone.

I turned and ran, down into the darkness.

chapter 8

I run away a lot. It's something you have to learn if you work alone and have a habit of finding trouble. Against these kind of odds—Belthas, Garrick, Meredith, Martin, and a dozen armed men on one side, and me on the other—staying to fight isn't much different from suicide. I have absolutely no pride when it comes to combat. Running like a squirrel doesn't bother me at all.

But leaving someone behind does. I'd been gambling that Luna and I could both make it out and now we'd been separated everything fell apart. I wanted to go back and help her, but there was nothing I could do against so many. Worse, as soon as Belthas realised I was there, he could threaten to hurt Luna unless I surrendered, and I knew he'd do it.

All I could think was to go deeper into the tunnels. Looking into the future, I could see that some came to dead ends, but others went down and down into darkness. If I was able to get deep enough, and if Belthas sent his men down after me, and if I could hide and let them go by and double back towards the entrance, and if Belthas hadn't left enough men to guard Luna . . .

It was a desperate plan, the biggest flaw being that I didn't have any equipment. I'd left my mist cloak back at my flat, and checking my pockets I found everything else had been taken. Within a few minutes the sounds behind me had died away and I came to a stop, looking into the futures ahead of me and hoping for some luck.

I didn't get it. After only a minute I heard the sounds of movement again, this time in greater numbers. Belthas had gotten organised and he was sending every man he had down into the tunnels, sweeping each passage methodically from end to end. Looking into the future, I saw with a sinking heart that hiding wasn't going to work. All I could do was back away deeper into the darkness.

The tunnels went down and just kept on going. It was pitch-black and sight was useless; only my divination magic kept me from tripping and falling. To begin with I kept trying to find a place to hide, but as Belthas's men pursued me deeper and deeper I realised it would be all I could do to simply get away.

I don't know how long that chase went on. It felt like hours, but deep beneath the earth there was no way to tell. The tunnels were solid rock, worn smooth, and they carried sounds of movement oddly. From time to time I'd hear the sound of Belthas's men but at other times they'd fall ominously silent, and that spurred me on all the more. I didn't let myself think of Luna or Arachne or Belthas or Meredith. All I knew was that to stop was to die.

As time passed the journey began to feel like a nightmare, one of those dreams where you run and run but never get away. Again and again I would stop and wait, hoping I'd lost them, and every time as soon as I stopped I would hear the distant echo of the men on my tail. It grew warmer as we went deeper and the air grew close. I kept staring blindly into the darkness, trying uselessly to see, until at last I shut my eyes and forced myself to rely on my magic. The only sound was my footsteps on the rock and the distant noise of Belthas's men.

By the time I finally lost them, I was too exhausted to notice. The slipping, clambering path down the tunnels had drained my energy to the point where all I could think about was the next tunnel, and the next, and the next. I kept going, one ear open for the sounds of pursuit. Gradually I realised I couldn't hear them anymore.

I stopped at last in a narrow, branching corridor and leant against the wall. My shirt was damp with sweat and I stripped off my jumper, tying it around my waist, before holding my breath and listening for a slow count of sixty. Nothing. I looked into the future and realised no one was coming. I was alone.

I've never liked being underground. Air's more my element, even if I'm not close enough to it to use its magic; I like being high, able to see. Here beneath the earth, I felt tense, on edge. The air felt different: dry and stuffy. I could imagine the thousands of tons of earth and rock above me pressing silently down, and I forced myself to stay calm.

I think the only thing that stopped me from losing it was knowing I could find my way back. I was lost of course—there was no way I could have marked my passage in that flight, and the pitch-black tunnels would have turned me around in seconds. But as long as I have my magic, I can never stay lost. With enough time, I can always find the path.

Except in this case, the path led to about fifteen angry men with guns. I took stock of my position. No food, no water, no equipment, no friends. I had three choices: stay here, go forward, or go back.

In the end I went forward. It wasn't so much a choice as a lack of one. I've been in a lot of really bad situations over the years and one of the small consolations is that you don't have to worry much about consequences anymore.

The upper levels had had open chambers and rooms,

which had narrowed down into twisting passages as I'd descended. Now, as I kept walking, I noticed that the passages were starting to open out again. They'd stopped sloping down, which was some consolation, but I knew I still had to be far beneath the surface. The tunnels would have to climb back up a very long way to reach another exit, which I was frankly starting to believe was pretty unlikely.

After a while—I couldn't say how long—I became vaguely aware that something was different. I was making steady progress but it was getting harder to see what was coming. The corridors and passages were fuzzier, more difficult to tell apart. I felt as though I was walking down a long, straight tunnel but when I looked again I thought I saw a fork. I looked again and saw a T junction. Then I couldn't see any tunnel at all.

I slowed and scanned around me. I was in a large chamber. No, not large—huge. I looked back, disoriented, trying to figure out where I'd left the tunnel, and realised there was no tunnel. There was nothing around me but open space. I stopped and heard my footsteps fade into the distance. They didn't echo.

I was standing in a vast cavern. The walls were ragged and irregular but their edges were smooth. The colour of the stone ranged from grey to brown, and in places I could see the dull glint of crystal. A moment later I realised that I was able to see. There was no light, yet everything was visible.

Slowly I began to walk again, and as I did I noticed that something was wrong with the perspective in this place. Distances didn't seem right, somehow. At first glance I'd thought the cavern was maybe a few hundred yards, but as I walked I realised it was taking far too long to reach the centre. The place was miles and miles wide, the roof so far above I couldn't even see it. At the centre were craggy rock formations, and as I kept walking, they grew larger and larger until I realised that they were the size of hills. There was an entire mountain range at the centre of this place, curled around where I was standing, rising at the centre in a line of jagged peaks and descending on either side to form the shape of a crescent moon. To my left the mountains trailed away to a smooth point, while to my right they ended in a massive rock formation like a mesa.

The mesa rose into the air.

I stopped dead. The mesa was high off the ground, supported at an angle by a titanic pillar of rock. As I watched, it swung in my direction, crossing the miles between us with a kind of lazy grace. The mesa came to rest in front of me, towering over me like a skyscraper while I stood motionless.

Then the mesa opened its eyes.

It wasn't a mesa. It was a head. The pillar of rock was a long, serpentine neck. And what I'd thought was a mountain range was the thing's body. Two enormous eyes, each the size of a castle, focused on where I stood. They looked like rough-cut diamonds, with no pupils I could see.

I stood very still. Piece by piece, I slowly realised what my eyes had seen but my brain had refused to put together. The mountain range was a body, the folded hills beneath them two legs. The line of peaks was the ridge on its back and the trailing edge of mountains to my left was a long, serpentine tail. But it was the head that held my attention. It was long and wedge-shaped, the two eyes set far back before a pair of swept-back horns each the size of a tower, with two nostrils set at the front. Now that it had turned to face me, it was completely still. If I hadn't seen it move, I would have thought it was some impossible rock formation.

The dragon watched me, silent and unblinking.

"Um," I said. "Hi."

It was, looking back on it, a pretty stupid way to introduce myself.

"Um, sorry to bother you," I said. The creature before

me didn't react, and I raised my voice a little. "Didn't mean to intrude."

The dragon stared at me. I don't know much about dragons. Nobody really does. Maybe it couldn't hear me, any more than a human can hear an ant. I began to back off. "I'll just leave you in peace—"

STAY.

The voice went through me as though I were hearing it with my whole body. It felt like an earthquake, thunder through distant caverns. I stopped.

ARACHNE.

I hesitated. "Yes?"

YOU WILL AID HER.

I hesitated again, trying to figure out what to say. It didn't sound like an order. It was more like a statement. "I'm going to," I said at last. "If I can."

The dragon watched me silently. "Okay," I said slowly. "Arachne's above. She's in her lair. She's hurt."

I waited for an answer. Nothing came.

"Can you go to her?" I said at last.

The dragon didn't answer. I didn't know what was going on. "If I brought Arachne here, could you help her?"

YES.

"Is there, uh . . . any way you could help me with that?"

The dragon reared its head back, opening its mouth like a chasm. There were teeth inside, glinting dully. One of its enormous front claws rose up out of the earth and broke off a tooth with a thunderclap. Then the claw descended towards me.

I would have fled then if I could. One brush from that claw would turn me into a bloody smear. I knew I couldn't possibly get away but my instincts shouted at me to run anyway . . . and yet I couldn't move. All I could do was watch that claw descend, bigger and bigger—

The claw was gone. The dragon was back as it had been. Its enormous diamond eyes watched me. *GO.*

ı ı ı ı ı ı ı ı ı

Darkness.

I was lying on stone, face down. It was pitch-black, and the air was warm. I was back in the tunnels.

I sat up, searching around me with my divination magic, watching the futures of myself exploring. I was in a small tunnel with a smooth floor. One end sloped upwards slightly and I had the feeling it led back the way I had come. There was no cavern nearby, and looking into the futures, there was nothing like it within my range. It didn't seem to exist.

I shook my head, disoriented. My memories of the cavern felt hazy, confused, and didn't seem to make sense. Had it been real? Or a dream, my mind playing tricks from exhaustion?

Either way, I'd been down here for hours. The tunnels felt dead, empty. If Belthas's men had been going to search this far, they would have caught up to me by now; they must have given up and gone back. Looking into the future, I couldn't see any sign that the tunnels ahead were going to start sloping back up towards ground level. I turned and began retracing my steps.

It took a long time, but even so the way back was easier. Now I wasn't in a panicked rush, I could see the tunnels weren't as complex as I'd thought. There were only one or two main pathways, with the occasional side passage and dead end. The tunnels followed a single primary route, two or three times my height and much wider.

I kept to a steady pace, narrowing my visions down to only the next few seconds, focusing on my footing and my precognition. As I walked I thought about what I should do. Belthas had to be long gone; I couldn't imagine him setting up camp in Arachne's lair. If I was lucky he'd given up on me and sealed the cave, maybe with a booby trap or two. That would cause problems but I could deal with it. If I was unlucky he'd left guards, in which case . . . well, I'd just have to come up with something.

When the first sliver of light appeared, I almost didn't recognise it; I'd been navigating by sound and touch so long I'd forgotten to use my eyes. As I drew closer I saw it was the reflected glow of the lights in Arachne's lair. There were hollow caves around here, used as rooms; at a quick glance they held bales of thread and cloth. I was only two turnings away from the lair itself and I knew I had to be silent. Quietly, I moved forward to the T junction that led into the lair. My eyes weren't yet accustomed to the light, and even the dim reflections off the rock were enough to dazzle me. I didn't poke my head out; instead I stood with my hand on the rocky wall and looked into the future of me doing so.

It wasn't my lucky day. It wasn't really luck of course; it was that Belthas was so bloody thorough. But it was still hard to take. After everything I'd gone through this night I really needed a break, and I wasn't getting one.

There was good news, bad news, and worse news. The good news, and the biggest surprise, was that Arachne was still in the lair, motionless in the corner, and as far as I could tell she didn't seem to have been touched. I didn't understand why Belthas would leave her here after going to so much trouble to get her but I wasn't going to question it.

The bad news was that four of Belthas's men were there too. They'd gathered the sofas and chairs at the centre of the room, giving themselves some cover and creating a killing ground in front of the entrances. One was watching the tunnels; a second seemed to be napping; the third was back at the mouth of the tunnel leading out onto the Heath, leaning against the wall. He was smoking and I could smell the cigarette from all the way across the room.

The worse news was that the fourth man was Garrick. He was tucked away behind the barricade, almost invisible behind one of the sofas. He looked to be settled comfortably, but even so, his weapon was propped up and levelled at exactly the space I'd need to cross to leave the tunnel. He looked half asleep but I knew he wasn't.

I looked to see what would happen if I moved out. Hopeless. If I didn't get shot down in the first few steps, there were explosives of some kind planted near the tunnel mouth, hidden so I wouldn't see them before they tore me apart. And if I could get past *that*—which frankly, I didn't think I could—I'd be in the middle of an open room with four men shooting at me. Even with my mist cloak I didn't think I could have made it.

I took stock of what I had. My items were gone. About the only advantage I had was surprise—Garrick and his men couldn't know for sure whether I was coming back, and they could have been waiting for hours. There were clothes and materials back in the caves behind me. I couldn't think of any way in which they could help but maybe—

"Coming?" Garrick asked.

The man who'd been napping came awake with a start, and the other two raised their weapons, looking around.

I sighed. *So much for surprise.*

"He's around the corner," Garrick said.

The man who'd been on lookout peered up towards the entrance. "Wait, so—"

"Stay put," Garrick said.

"What's the matter, Garrick?" I said. I felt the men aim their weapons at the tunnel mouth, tracking my voice, and I got ready to run. "Losing your nerve?"

I felt Garrick smile. "What's the rush?"

One of the men, thinking I couldn't see him, started to creep forward, his feet soft against the floor. Garrick looked at him. The man drew back.

"So," I said when they didn't make a move. "Four men with guns, explosives round the door, all just for me."

"Five," Garrick said. "One's posted outside."

"Five," I said. "I'm flattered."

"Belthas thought it was over the top," Garrick said. "I talked him into it."

"Thanks."

"You're welcome. Oh, before you get any ideas, those mines have a remote trigger this time."

I checked and verified what he'd said. Garrick's finger was probably on the trigger right now. "You don't think this is a bit excessive?"

"Consider it a compliment," Garrick said amiably. "You've gotten away from me before."

"Right," I said. It hadn't been by much, either. "You're quite a marksman, by the way."

"I keep my hand in," Garrick said. "Didn't know diviners could dodge like that."

"The ones who can't tend not to live very long."

The men had settled down again, their weapons ready and aimed, listening to the conversation. "So since you aren't having another try," I said, "I'm guessing shooting me isn't your primary goal."

"Nope."

"So you're doing what?" I said. "Playing rear guard?"

"Something like that."

"You know, there's something I'm curious about," I said. "When I first met you, you were doing a job for Talisid. Then you were working for Belthas. *Then* Belthas said you were working for Levistus. Now you're working for Belthas again?"

Garrick waited with an expression of mild inquiry. "So?" I said when he didn't answer.

"So?"

"Who do you actually work for?"

"Depends."

"Depends on what?"

"Who's paying."

"You mean three different people were paying you to do three different things?"

"I'm freelance."

"Wait a second," I said. "You were working with Belthas at the start. So you must have been with Belthas at the factory for that fight with Deleo and Cinder over the barghest. Then Talisid paid you *again* to go back to the *same factory* to kill the *same barghest*?"

"Yep."

"And you didn't think to mention that it was already dead?"

"Client confidentiality."

"No wonder you were so bloody relaxed," I muttered. "So you work for whoever pays you?"

"Hey, fuck this guy," the man who'd wanted to go after me said.

"Shut up, Mick," Garrick said. "Yep."

"Okay. I'll pay you and your men twice what Belthas is paying you to switch sides."

I thought I felt some of the men glance at each other. "Sorry," Garrick said. "Under contract."

"So what? Once you're bought, you stay bought?"

"Yep."

"An *honest* mercenary," I said under my breath. "Great." I raised my voice. "What about the rest of you?"

"Same answer," Garrick said before the other men could speak. "Because they're such loyal, trustworthy people. And because they wouldn't live to spend the money if they said yes."

This time I definitely wasn't imagining the glances. Okay, so that wasn't going to work.

I sat and thought for a minute. "So what's the idea?" I said at last. "You're just going to sit there and wait?"

"Yep."

"You know there are other ways out, right?" I said. I was fairly sure there weren't, but I was also fairly sure Garrick didn't know one way or the other.

"Could be," Garrick agreed.

"And you're not going to stop me finding them?"

"Nope."

"You know, for someone with a five-to-one advantage and all the weapons," I said, "you're very cautious."

"We're not coming after you, Verus," Garrick said. "Don't get me wrong, I could take you. But one thing I've learnt about you, you're really good at running away. Five's not enough to find you. But it's enough to stop you getting out."

"This way."

"This way. But if you'd found another one, I don't think you'd be here chatting."

I was hoping he wouldn't realise that. "So how long are you going to wait?"

"Few days should do it," Garrick said. "These are dry caves. No water. You'll be dead from dehydration by then."

I didn't answer.

"Or you make a break," Garrick said. "Be interesting to see if you can dodge a mine blast." He bent down to check something, then returned to his position. "Or you give yourself up. Your call."

I stayed silent. I couldn't think of a smart answer this time. I'd been sweating and I was already thirsty. There weren't any supplies in the storerooms. I didn't know how long I could last without water. I was pretty sure it was a lot shorter than Garrick was willing to wait.

Divination magic lets you avoid a lot of things. But it's no use against thirst. It doesn't do too well against a firing range filled with land mines, either.

I withdrew back down the tunnel. I knew that Garrick and the men were still waiting, their weapons trained on the entrance. I sat down and tried to think.

I could do what I'd threatened and go back down the tunnel, looking for another way out, but I had the feeling it was a bad idea. It was just possible I'd missed a passage somewhere on the way down, but if I tried a search and failed I might be too weak to do anything else.

Or I could use the supplies in the caves and hope to get past the blockade. I tried to think of some way in which a large pile of clothes could bypass a minefield and several armed men and came up blank.

In the end I did what I usually do. I looked into the future to see what would happen. Maybe Garrick's men would go away or they'd be called off or . . .

. . . Wait, what? What was *he* doing here?

. . . That could work.

I waited a while, then went back up to the tunnel mouth. I didn't try to stay quiet this time and I knew before I got there that all the men were looking at the tunnel, their weapons ready. The man at the tunnel leading back out into the Heath was still smoking. "Hey, Garrick," I said.

"Yep."

"I want you to know I actually kind of respect you. You do a job and you're obviously very good at it. You're more dangerous than most mages."

"That's nice," Garrick said.

"So, out of professional courtesy, I'll give you a warning. You should leave. If you don't, all of your men are going to be killed and you might be too."

"I'll pass," Garrick said.

I shifted my position so I could see down the tunnel. The men were focused on my location; they couldn't see me in the shadows but they could hear the movement. Even the guard at the back was squinting at me. "Okay, one last question. If I told you someone was coming up behind you, and that you ought to stop paying attention to me and aim your guns somewhere else, would you listen?"

"No."

"Good."

There was a red flash and a *whoompf* from the far end of the cavern. Garrick and the other two spun, their weapons coming around.

The guard next to the exit had been holding a lit cigarette.

The cigarette was still lit, along with the rest of him: His body was a blackened corpse, blazing fiercely on the floor. He'd been incinerated so fast he hadn't had a chance to scream. A second later, the fire extinguished itself in a hiss and a cloud of choking smoke. The smoke spread, forming an opaque bank that started swallowing up the far end of the cavern.

The two other guards opened up with their weapons. No controlled bursts this time; I could hear the chattering *ratatatatat* of panic fire, the bullets zipping into the smoke. One of the guards advanced towards the grey cloud, firing as he went. He was about fifteen feet from the edge when a column of flame roared out, washing over him and setting him alight. He went down screaming.

Garrick aimed for where the flame had come from and fired three quick bursts, the shots forming a spread. The guard next to him lost his cool, flicked the selector on his SMG and started blazing away on full auto. Bullets ripped through the smoke, whining and bouncing off the walls, the chatter and roar filling the cavern. He emptied his magazine in only a few seconds and started fumbling for a reload. Garrick slapped his hand down with a snarl. "Stop it! You're giving away—"

Something came flying out of the smoke. I got only a glimpse of it; it looked like a glowing ball of dull red light. Garrick reacted instantly, diving out of the barricade and rolling. The other man stared in confusion as the sphere dropped next to him and exploded with a noise that sounded like a giant cough. Smouldering bits of furniture went flying, along with what was left of the guard.

Garrick came to his feet. He'd discarded his rifle but kept hold of something else. I couldn't see what it was but I knew what it did and as he pushed the button I ducked back. There was a echoing boom as the mines around the tunnel entrances all went off at once. Shrapnel and projectiles flew, snapping and whining off the walls. I heard the sound of running feet, followed by the roar of fire magic. There was another explosion, this one not so loud as the mines but lower pitched, making the stone tremble beneath my feet. A moment later came a groan, followed by the rumbling crash of falling rock.

And then there was silence.

Cautiously, I walked out into the lair. The stone around the tunnel entrance was blackened where the mines had gone off, and shrapnel clinked under my feet. I could make out the shape of Arachne to my right, obscured by the smoke.

The smoke began to clear, revealing a man. Red light flickered around his hands, which faded as I watched. He was as tall as me and heavily built, and until a few minutes ago, he'd been the last person I'd expected to see. He spoke in a rumbling voice. "Debt's paid."

I looked at Cinder thoughtfully. "Yeah," I said. "I guess it is."

Cinder looked from side to side, scanning the chamber. All three guards were dead; two were still burning. Arachne's lair looked like a bomb site, and what was left of the clothes and furniture had been thoroughly trashed. The side tunnel leading to the storerooms had collapsed in a heap of rubble. "Garrick?" I asked.

"Who?"

"The last man."

Cinder tilted his head in the direction of the sealed tunnel. "Might have got him."

I nodded; Garrick must have mined the side tunnels as well, as a last-ditch escape route. I didn't know if he was under that rubble or on the other side but at least we didn't have to deal with him for a while. "How'd you find us?"

In answer, Cinder turned towards the tunnel leading out onto the Heath. "Clear."

We waited for a moment, then through the clearing smoke I saw a small figure emerge from the tunnel. He nearly trod on the remains of the guard, shied away, and circled the body, covering his mouth. By the time he was halfway across the room I recognised who he was.

"Um," Sonder said once he'd reached us. "Hi." He looked from Cinder to me. "I thought you could use some help."

⁣ ⁣ ⁣ ⁣ ⁣ ⁣ ⁣ ⁣ ⁣ ⁣

The explanations took a while.

Sonder told his story first. When I'd failed to check in, Sonder had tried calling me and then Luna. When neither of us answered, he figured something had happened and went to the Heath to find out what. Upon seeing Belthas's guards at Arachne's lair, he did the smart thing and went for reinforcements.

The Council, needless to say, was a washout. First they gave Sonder the runaround, and when he persisted they hinted strongly that he'd be better off minding his own business. Instead of giving up, Sonder looked at the situation logically and decided that since the Light mages weren't being helpful, he might as well try the Dark ones. Cinder had been sort-of-allies with me before, and once again he and I seemed to have a common enemy. So Sonder rang Cinder, and as luck would have it, Cinder answered. Looking back on it, I wonder if I'm setting the kid a bad example.

Sonder skated over the exact details of the conversation, which I have to admit I was morbidly curious about. Once they'd gotten past their mutual mistrust, though, it didn't take them long to strike a deal. Cinder wanted to find Deleo, Sonder wanted to find me and Luna, and there was only one place to start looking. Sonder led Cinder to Arachne's lair and the rest was history.

"There was another guard outside," I remembered.

"Yeah," Sonder said. He looked uncomfortable, and I noticed he was carefully avoiding looking at the bodies. "Cinder . . . dealt with him."

"Well." I looked at Cinder. "I guess I'm not who you were hoping to find, but thanks anyway."

"Where's Del?" Cinder rumbled.

"Belthas has her."

"Where?"

"I don't know." I looked at Cinder. "We team up until Belthas is dealt with or either of us quits. No hostilities until twenty-four hours after that. Deal?"

Cinder nodded. "Deal. How do we find Del?"

"By finding Belthas."

"Is Luna back there?" Sonder asked.

I sighed. "No." I hated having to admit it: Even though there was nothing else I could have done, knowing that I'd left her behind hurt. "Belthas took her." Sonder's face fell.

"So where is he?" Cinder said.

It occurred to me that Cinder was going to be difficult to deal with. He was brutally straightforward and would remain steady only as long as he could see what to do. Now that Belthas's men were dead Cinder had no obvious direction, and if things stayed that way he was going to get frustrated quickly. "They worked for Belthas," I said, looking at the remains. "Maybe they'll have something that'll show us where to go."

Cinder thought about it for a few seconds. "Fine," he said grudgingly. "I'll loot the bodies for you."

Sonder looked at the smoking scorched things that had been Belthas's men and flinched visibly. "You mean . . ."

"Relax, Light-boy," Cinder said, already turning away. "Don't have to get your hands dirty."

"Sonder, I need you to look back at what happened," I said. "Belthas was here, along with Luna and Martin. Find out what they talked about and see if you can track them."

Sonder nodded and turned away, his eyes unfocusing. Reluctantly, I turned towards Arachne. I needed to figure out how to help her before Cinder's patience ran out.

ı ı ı ı ı ı ı ı ı

Odds are you've never tried to give a giant spider a medical checkup. In case you're wondering, it's really hard. It's not like you can take their pulse, and dealing with the fact that they have their skeleton on the *outside* of their bodies is weird enough on its own. After ten minutes' examination, I'd managed to conclude that Arachne was alive, which I'd known already.

Figuring out what Belthas had done was easier. There was a short rod embedded at the back of Arachne's body in her . . . neck? Back? Thorax? Whatever it's called. The thing was about twelve inches long and made out of some iridescent purple metal that caught the light. It was a powerful focus with an active spell working through it. As far as I could tell, it was linked to something else, probably an identical focus with a similarity effect joining them. At the moment the spell was stable. It wasn't draining Arachne's magic or life force but she wasn't getting any better either.

I ran my hand along Arachne's back, feeling the stiff hairs brush against my fingers. There was something terribly depressing about seeing her like this. Ever since I first met her, Arachne's always been one of the few stable points in my world, wise and strong. Having her still and lifeless felt wrong, and I couldn't help wondering if this was my fault. If I'd dealt with Luna better, figured it out earlier . . .

"Hey," Cinder called. I turned to see something flying towards me and caught it one-handed. I'd been standing on a battered sofa to get a better look and had to sway to keep my balance. I took a look and saw that it was a touch-screen phone. "What's up?"

"Password."

The phone had a password lock. I took thirty seconds and cracked it, then skimmed through the call and message history. The phone had belonged to Mick, aka Michael, and had apparently survived the blast that had killed its owner. I put it in my pocket.

"So?" Cinder said.

"Belthas took my phone. I need a new one."

Cinder gave me a look.

"There's nothing there," I said. "Any luck?"

Cinder gestured at the pile of guns at his feet. The five men had been carrying enough weapons to stock an armoury: submachine guns, pistols, grenades, clips and boxes of ammunition, knives, radios, coils of wire, and what looked like plastic explosive. It was enough to fight a small war—unfortunately, at the moment, it was also completely useless.

I looked at the iridescent metal rod. "Know what this is?"

Cinder walked forward and squinted. "Yeah," he said after a moment.

"You and Deleo got them from that mage, didn't you?" I said. "Jadan or whatever his name was. The guy who came up with this bloody ritual."

"Yeah."

"How do they work?"

"Dunno."

"You're kidding."

"Got his materials. Didn't know how to use them."

I sighed. "It's just like last time, isn't it? You guys never understand what you're messing with but you do it anyway."

"Would have been fine if you'd let us kill that enchantress."

"Yeah, well, maybe if you and Deleo had done a bit less collateral damage I wouldn't have gotten involved."

"No."

"No what?"

"Wasn't why you were helping her."

I looked at him. "How would you know?"

"She acted sexy and vulnerable and made you feel good," Cinder said. "So you trusted her. Right?"

I was silent.

Cinder shook his head contemptuously. "Idiot."

The sound of footsteps made us look up to see Sonder emerge from the tunnel out onto the Heath. Cinder walked away. "Sorry," Sonder said as he approached. "He made a gate but I couldn't see through the shroud."

I nodded. "And in here?"

"They left three hours ago," Sonder said. "Belthas, twelve men, Martin, and that woman. They had Luna." He didn't look happy. "Martin was dragging her."

I thought about Luna and how she must be feeling. She'd trusted Martin and thought him a friend, probably in the hope he'd become a lot more, and he'd betrayed her in the worst way possible. Then there was the question of what Belthas would do with her or if she was even still—I shook my head and pushed the thought away. I needed to focus.

"Can you take it out?" Sonder asked.

I looked up to see that Sonder was pointing at the rod in Arachne's back. "Not without killing her," I said. "And even if I could, I don't have the first clue how to fix whatever Belthas did."

"I think it was a paralysis spell," Sonder said. "I only saw bits of it but . . ."

I nodded. Ice mages are good at that sort of thing. Sonder looked at Arachne's motionless body. "Could we get someone to heal her?"

"Maybe," I said doubtfully. I stuck my hands into my pockets. "We'd have to—"

I stopped. There was something in my pocket and I drew it out. It was the fang of some enormous creature, made of some kind of grey stone, heavy and warm and eight inches from base to tip. It was a magical item and a powerful one. I'd never seen it before. I'd checked my pockets just after escaping Belthas and they'd been empty. How had it . . . ?

"Wow," Sonder said. He was staring wide-eyed. "What *is* that?"

"A gate," I said. I realised I knew the command word. And it would take me to . . . "Holy crap," I said quietly. "It was *real*."

"Where does it lead?"

"To someone who *could* fix her." I looked to see what would happen if I used it and saw that the fang would cut through the gate wards easily. For a one-shot item, it was incredibly powerful. "It's designed to take two people," I said. "User and one other . . . Crap." As I looked at the consequences, my heart sank. The spell on Arachne was tied into her life force. Gating her would break the spell and sabotage Belthas's ritual—but it would be fatal for Arachne.

Sonder looked at Arachne. "Can you—?"

I shook my head. "Moving her while that thing's active will kill her." As I thought about it, though, my spirits rose a little. "But now we've got a way to help her. Just got to figure out how."

"Why's it alive?" Cinder said from behind me.

I didn't take my eyes off the fang. "She's not an 'it.' "

"Why's *she* alive?"

"Because Belthas wants to use her for your damn ritual."

"So why's she alive?"

"Because—" I said, then stopped as I realised what Cinder was getting at. The ritual killed its target—I knew that already. So why had Belthas left Arachne here?

Because she couldn't be moved. The spell stopped me from moving her but it would stop Belthas from moving her too. The obvious thing for Belthas to do would have been to have completed the ritual here, already. But he hadn't, which must mean he wasn't ready. Maybe Garrick hadn't been there to stop me from escaping. Maybe Belthas had stationed him there to make sure nobody touched Arachne.

"He's going to do the ritual somewhere else," I said. I turned to Cinder. "Deleo knew bits of it, didn't she?"

Cinder shrugged. "Bits."

I nodded to myself. "That was why Belthas needed her alive. He won't try the ritual until he's absolutely sure it'll work."

Cinder looked at me sharply. "So he still needs Del."

"Yeah. And he'll probably keep hold of Luna too." I saw Sonder perk up.

Cinder nodded. "Okay. We kill it."

"What?"

"Ritual needs a live target." Cinder gestured to Arachne. "Kill it, he has to find another. Gives us more time."

I stepped between Arachne and Cinder, glaring at him. *"No."*

"Going to be dead anyway," Cinder pointed out.

"We are not touching her." I stared Cinder in the eye. "You want Deleo. Fine. I'll help. But you don't touch any of my friends."

Cinder met my gaze. There was a considering look in his eyes and I knew what he was thinking. I'm no match for Cinder. If he decided to kill Arachne, I wouldn't be able to stop him.

Then Cinder shrugged. "Got a plan?"

I thought quickly. "Belthas doesn't know what's happened yet. We track him down and take him by surprise while he's got his hands full with the ritual. Shut it down from the other end. We take Luna and come back here to transport Arachne. You take Deleo and go wherever you like."

Cinder thought about it for a little while. "How long?" he said at last.

"Until what?"

Cinder gestured to Arachne. "Look and see."

It's easy to make the mistake of thinking Cinder's stupid. He's slow and deliberate but he'd seen the obvious point I'd missed: by looking into the future to see when Arachne was going to die, we could learn when Belthas was going to finish the ritual. I looked forward and saw the point at which energy would crackle over Arachne, drawing away her magic and with it her life. I looked away quickly. "Five hours."

Cinder nodded. "You've got four and a half. Then I kill her before he does."

ı ı ı ı ı ı ı ı ı

We left Arachne's lair so Cinder could gate us back. I felt better as soon as I was out in the fresh air, and I saw Sonder taking deep breaths, the colour returning to his face. Burnt flesh has a horrible smell, like charred beef but with a nauseating sweetness, thick and putrid and rich. It smells like nothing on earth and you never forget it. Cinder hadn't shown any reaction. I guess he's used to it.

Cinder gated us to the park near my home and we walked the rest of the way. It was the early hours of the morning, and Camden was as quiet as it ever got. My new phone told me it was two A.M.; it had been seven hours since I'd gotten Sonder's call. It felt like more.

The first thing I did once I got home was take a shower. It cost precious time but I needed to think clearly and having my body caked with sweat was a distraction. As I stood under the falling water, I tried to figure out how to find Belthas and stop him from killing Arachne before Cinder did.

I came out of the shower and dressed in combat trousers, a T-shirt, a jumper, and old dark trainers. I filled my pockets with any items I thought would help, then opened my wardrobe and took out my mist cloak. I stroked it affectionately, feeling the soft cloth ripple under my touch, grateful I hadn't worn it to Arachne's lair—though I doubt it would have obeyed Belthas anyway. Imbued items choose their owners. I pulled it around my shoulders and walked out.

It was very weird to see Cinder in my living room. The armchair he'd picked seemed too small for his bulk, and a cup of tea sat untasted on the coffee table before him. Sonder was pacing the carpet. "Trace the rods," Cinder suggested in his rumbling voice.

Sonder shook his head. "It's a sympathetic link. There's no trail to follow."

"He'll have wards anyway," I said. I crossed the room to stare through the doors onto the balcony. A few lonely lights still shone in the windows of the buildings opposite, but everything else was dark. The night had clouded over, and there was no moon.

"Where would Belthas have taken them?" Sonder asked. He looked on edge, harried.

"A sanctum," I said. I was sure of it. "He won't do something this important except somewhere he feels absolutely safe."

"Get your elemental to find it," Cinder said.

"I can't," I said sadly. "I blew up my caller getting away from Belthas." It hurt more than I'd thought it would. Without that focus I didn't have any way of contacting Starbreeze, and only now she was gone did I realise how much I'd depended on her. Starbreeze had always been my ace in the hole, the one I turned to when everything else failed. Losing that safety net all of a sudden was frightening.

"Okay, look," Sonder said. "*Someone* has to know where Belthas is hiding. Let's call up everyone we know."

I nodded, trying to look confident. It was worth a try, even if I didn't really think it would work.

It didn't. There were only a few mages I trusted enough to call in this situation, and at this hour many didn't answer. Those who did were willing to help but they didn't know anything this specific. With enough time I could dig it up . . . but time was something we didn't have.

Sonder and Cinder didn't have any more success. I saw Cinder glance at the time as he hung up from another call and I checked it as well, unobtrusively. Three hours left. I gritted my teeth. I wasn't going to let it end this way.

"We could try his office . . ." Sonder said again.

I shook my head. "First place I looked. He's not there."

"There might be some leads."

"And a bunch of security systems. We don't have time to get caught up fighting them."

Sonder turned away in frustration. "There has to be *someone*."

I was about to answer when I realised what Sonder had just said. "There is," I said slowly, my mind jumping ahead. "There's someone who'd know. Luna."

Sonder looked at me, puzzled. "But we can't—"

"I can," I said, thinking fast. "Cinder, I need you to gate back to Arachne's lair and get those weapons. Bring as many as you can carry. Then get some of your own. I've got the feeling we're going to need all the firepower we can get."

Cinder tilted his head, shrugged, and walked out.

"Sonder, come with me." I walked into my bedroom, Sonder following. I lowered the lights, then lay down on the my bed, carefully arranging the cloak under me. "Wake me in an hour," I said. "If I don't wake up . . . well, you'll have to improvise."

Sonder looked confused for a second, then his eyes went wide. "Wait, you're going *there*?"

"Shh," I said quietly. It was hard to relax but I knew I had to. Turning my head to one side, I could see the blinking lights of my alarm clock. Two hours fifty minutes. I closed my eyes, willing myself to sleep and beyond. The cloak seemed to help, soft and drowsy. I felt my mind slipping away. My last thought was to hope Cinder had shut the door behind him.

chapter 9

It's not difficult to reach Elsewhere. It doesn't even take magic, though most people think it does. It usually takes newcomers a few tries, but once you've done it, you can always go back. Travelling there the first time seems to set up some kind of bond that lets you always feel it in your thoughts, somewhere in the twilight between waking and dreams.

Leaving Elsewhere . . . well. That can be a little harder.

I've been to Elsewhere but I don't understand it. On past journeys I've done things on instinct and had them work without knowing how or why. One of the few things I'm sure of is that Elsewhere changes depending on who comes to it. When I visit Elsewhere, it always takes the same form: a great, silent city, plazas and colonnades and high walkways bathed in bright white light. Empty but not dead, only sleeping.

But this time would be different. As I looked into the futures of travelling to Elsewhere, I knew Luna was there already; I'd known as soon as I'd looked into the futures of travelling there. The stories say that there's nothing danger- ous in Elsewhere except what you bring with you—but that can be more than enough. The Elsewhere I was about to see would be one shaped by Luna. I didn't know what it would be like but I was about to find out.

I opened my eyes.

I was standing in a maze of crystal passages, all alike. The walls pressed in around me but I wasn't underground; by craning my neck upwards, I could glimpse sky. As I looked around I realised I was in a network of canyons, crooked and twisted. The walls, rocks, and even the ground were translucent crystal. The sky above was overcast and grey, thick clouds blocking out the sun, yet somehow, even down here in the canyons, there was enough light to see clearly. Distant whispers echoed through the passages, seeming to form words just on the edge of hearing.

I turned slowly, studying the landscape around me. I didn't sense any danger, but it wasn't comfortable, either. Somehow I had the feeling I wasn't welcome here. I started walking, my footsteps echoing about the ravines.

The first time I came to Elsewhere I was nearly lost for- ever. Geography doesn't work as it does in our world and not even divination magic can help you if you're led astray. Everything is different in Elsewhere, and what's strong out- side can be weak within. The same sources of strength and power we rely on in our world still function here . . . but somehow they never seem to work the way you want them to. I didn't try to use my magic. I knew where I wanted to go: to Luna. The direction didn't matter.

As I walked I noticed that the crystal of the walls and outcroppings was more varied than I'd thought. It ranged from nearly opaque to clear enough that I could see several feet in, and the colour of the crystal ranged from blue to grey to clear white. One patch caught my eye, coloured a brilliant azure. As I passed I reached out for it . . . and snatched my fingers away just in time. Although it radiated no cold, the crystal had the icy chill of a glacier, enough to freeze flesh. I carried on, keeping a more respectful distance.

The canyon widened as I walked, the glimpses of sky becoming more frequent, until finally the sides curved away, opening up to give me a clear view. Before me was a wide, open bowl, a vast, shallow depression in the ground. The cliffs formed a ring around it and at the centre was a palace of crystal, sharp spires pointing upwards into a brooding sky. A thick canopy of cloud cut off all trace of sun, the layer of grey drifting steadily across the sky from right to left. I altered my course for the palace and kept on going.

The palace was surrounded by acres of broken crystal. The doors were open, leading into a long entrance hall, thick pillars rising up to a vaulted ceiling. It was darker in here and the side passages were covered in shadow. Only when I was in the middle of the room did I realise the whispers had stopped.

I saw movement from the corner of my eye and turned sharply. For an instant I thought I saw a flash of something disappearing behind a pillar, then everything was still. I stood motionless, listening. The hall was silent . . . but something in the silence had changed. It was the silence of something holding its breath.

I thought of going after it but some instinct warned me that would be a bad idea. I waited a moment longer, then when nothing moved I carried on down the hall, slower this time. I half-expected something to jump me, but I reached the doors at the end safely. They opened at a touch.

Luna was inside. The room within was huge and circular, a ring of columns going up and up into the shadows, and Luna was at the very centre upon a wide dais. As I headed for her I noticed at the back of my mind that the whispers had started again.

Luna didn't react as I approached. She was kneeling,

staring into a tall silver mirror that reflected not her image but only a grey mist. She wore a white dress, and as I approached I saw that her lower legs were frozen in crystal. It seemed to have grown up around her, a thin layer spiderwebbing over her ankles and knees, reaching up towards her lower body. The mist in the mirror shifted at the edge of my vision, hinting at something within, inviting me to look. I hesitated, then took hold of Luna's arms and pulled her to her feet.

The crystal shattered, splintering like glass, and Luna stumbled upright, shaking her head as if she'd just come out of a trance. She looked up at me and her eyes lit up.

I grabbed Luna in a bear hug, holding her close. She made a protesting noise, but I didn't care. Elsewhere is the one place Luna's curse is dormant, and as I held her I felt something tense and wound-up inside me ease. Only now did I realise how afraid I'd been for her.

Gradually I realised Luna was trying to talk. I looked down. "Hm?"

"Can't breathe!"

"Right." I relaxed my grip and looked down at her. "Better?"

Luna pulled back. "The caves—you got out?"

"I got out."

Luna sighed in relief and leant her head against my chest. "Thank God."

I stroked Luna's hair. It felt good to hold her. "Were you looking for me?"

Luna nodded. "Like the last time," I said. "Was that where you got the idea?"

"I couldn't find you."

"It's hard to bring someone into Elsewhere if they're awake. Are you okay?"

"I'm fine." Luna pulled back again and looked up at me, her smile gone. "He's going to kill Arachne."

"I know," I said. "We've only got a few hours. Where did he take you?"

"A manor house in the mountains. Belthas brought every-one here. Me, all his guards, that woman . . ." Luna's face darkened. ". . . and Martin."

"Where are you?"

"In the basement. A cell. They locked me in and left me."

"Okay." I took a deep breath. This was the million-dollar question. "Do you know where it is?"

Luna shook her head and my heart sank. "It was too dark," Luna said. "There weren't any lights. It's somewhere deserted, no towns, but . . ."

"But that's not enough." I tried to think of all the deserted, mountainous places Belthas could have set up a base. Hopeless. Even in Britain, there were thousands. Finding it would take days, weeks. "Did you see a landmark? Anything that would give us a location?"

"No. But I think I know who did."

I looked at her in surprise. "Deleo," Luna said. "She's in the cell next to mine."

"Did you talk to her?"

Luna shook her head. "I saw her." A shadow passed across Luna's face. "She looked bad. I think they were . . . getting information from her. For the ritual. She wasn't awake. Asleep, a coma . . . I thought we could talk to her. I don't know how to stop Belthas, but maybe she does."

I thought about it for all of five seconds. I'd never tried bringing more than one person into Elsewhere, and if I had, I wouldn't have picked Rachel . . . and none of that mattered since I didn't see how we had any choice. "Why not," I said. "I'm relying on one psychotic Dark mage, might as well make it two."

Luna gave me an odd look. "What do you—?"

"Tell you later." I started walking again, leading Luna towards the edge of the room. "Um," Luna said. "Where are we going?"

"To Deleo."

"Okay." Luna thought for a second. "Where is she?"

"Up to you."

Luna looked at me. After a second, she realised I was serious.

The pillars ahead turned out to be masking a tunnel into another hallway. "What did you mean about a Dark mage?" Luna said.

"Sonder brought along some muscle."

"Sonder? Really?"

"Surprised?"

"Well, he's a mage. I guess he can get people to do stuff for him, right?"

"Not quite how it happened." I glanced down at Luna. "He's tougher than you think."

"He's a bit nerdy."

"He went looking into this on his own. He's the one who found the link between Martin and Belthas." I shrugged. "Figured it out before I did."

As I said Martin's name Luna's face went blank and she looked down at her feet. We walked in silence for a little while, passing through another columned hall. There were no windows and the shadows were long and deep.

"Want to talk about it?"

"About what?"

"Martin."

"What's the point?"

I didn't answer.

"I was stupid." Luna stared ahead of her, her voice bitter. "I *knew* there were things he wasn't telling me. I thought—I thought it didn't matter. As long as he . . ."

Luna trailed off. "I know this isn't much consolation," I said at last, "but it won't be the last time you make a fool of yourself over a guy. It happens."

Luna kept walking, head down, arms wrapped around herself. "I used to think about it," she said quietly. "I'd see some-one and I'd imagine it. Being with them. But I always knew it was just a dream. This time . . . I thought it was *real*. He said . . ." Luna's voice wavered. "He said he loved me. That everything with the monkey's paw was to help. He said that was why he needed to see Arachne. So we could be together."

I stayed silent, walking by Luna's side; I couldn't see her face, but I knew she was crying. I felt pure hatred towards Martin. I try to give newbies to the magical world a chance, I really do. But Martin had crossed the line.

"There's something else," I said at last. "I know it's not a good time but it's got to be done."

Luna wiped her eyes, her voice muffled. "What?"

"I'm going to get you out of there," I said. "One way or another. But once that's done . . . we're going to have to decide if you'll stay."

Luna looked up, confused. "I've been treating you like a half apprentice," I said. "I've been teaching you but without everything else that goes with it, and it's not working. I realised that yesterday. Belthas was able to get to Arachne through you and I got captured trying to find you. By going with Martin you put all three of us in danger."

"But—" Luna looked stricken. "I didn't—"

I shook my head. "I'm not blaming you for what Belthas and Martin did. But you should have listened when I warned you off. I nearly got killed trying to get you out of there and I can't keep doing that. If I do, sooner or later I'll end up dead, and probably you will too."

Luna and I walked for a little while in silence. "So what am I supposed to do?" Luna said at last.

"You've got a choice," I said. "We can stop the training. No more work, no more late-night outings. We can still be friends. Go on as before."

"Or?"

"Or you become my apprentice—this time for real. I'll teach you what I know, introduce you to my contacts, bring you into mage society. The Light mages have a teaching structure. You'll have classes and tests. You'll meet other apprentices. But there's a price. I'll be your master—not your friend. If I tell you to do something, you'll do it. And I won't be the only one. You'll be under the authority of every other Light mage you meet. You won't get second chances either. Disobey me and you're out. And you won't be able to come back."

Luna stared at me, then opened her mouth to speak. I held up a finger. "Don't answer yet. Once we're out of this, take some time and think about it. Right now, we've got other things to worry about."

Luna kept her eyes on me, searching my face as if looking for something, then finally nodded. "Okay."

"Good." I stopped. "I think we're here."

We'd reached a hallway lined with doors. Shafts of light fell through from small windows high above but the shadows between them were dark and cold. The door Luna had led us to looked no different from the others, yet somehow I felt reluctant to touch it. It was made of black crystal, almost translucent enough to see through but not quite. The whispers had stopped.

As I stood looking at the door I caught the flicker of movement again and snapped my head around. This time I was sure I saw something: a flash of white vanishing back into the hall from which we'd entered. The hallway was silent. I kept my eyes on the entrance but nothing moved.

"Alex?" Luna asked.

I hesitated for a second. Luna might know what it was but this landscape was shaped by thought. Drawing her attention to our pursuer could be a very bad idea. "It's nothing," I said. "Do it."

Luna reached for the door, paused for a second, then put her hand to it. It opened at a touch, the doors swinging silently back.

Beyond was swirling darkness, exactly like a cloud of smoke with every bit of light drained out of it. Tendrils of shadow drifted towards us and Luna stepped back hurriedly.

"Um," Luna said after we'd both stared into the blackness for a few seconds. "What is that?"

"I have no idea," I said honestly.

"I thought this was supposed to be Deleo's dreams?"

"Maybe it is," I said. Something about that darkness scared me. I had the creepy feeling it was just waiting for us to get within reach. I took another step back.

We stared a bit longer. "Do we go in?" Luna said eventually.

"God no."

We stood there. "Well, we have to do something," Luna said.

"I'm thinking," I said. I didn't know if it was my imagination, but it felt as though the cloud of darkness were edging towards us.

Then a voice spoke from the darkness, focused and cold. "What are you doing here?" A second later, its owner stepped into view—and she wasn't alone.

Rachel is average height, with bright blue eyes. When I first knew her she was good-looking, even cute. She's changed a lot since then. It's rare now to see her with her mask off and when I do her face makes me think of sculpted ice, beautiful and cold. The darkness shrank from her, curling about her feet.

Standing on Rachel's right was a girl with dark-red hair. She was smaller and younger than Rachel and felt far more alive, full of vitality and movement. She'd been dead for ten years, but in Elsewhere that doesn't make as much difference as you'd think. She wasn't looking at Rachel and Rachel wasn't looking at her, but they seemed aware of each other somehow, as if they knew exactly where the other was without needing to see.

And on Rachel's left was something that wasn't human at all, faceless and eyeless, made of living shadow. Its body blended with the darkness around, making it almost impossible to pick out its shape, but I had the vague impression of something tall and slender, unnaturally still. Even twenty feet away, I could feel the cold radiating from it.

But it was the redheaded girl who held my attention. "Shireen," I said quietly.

Shireen gave me a wave. "Hey, Alex! Long time no see."

"Shut up," Rachel said in irritation. "You know why he's here."

"We *don't* know why he's here," Shireen pointed out reasonably.

Rachel snarled. "Belthas couldn't get what he wanted while we were awake. Now he's trying dreams."

"You know that's not how this place works. Just because he's here doesn't mean he's there."

"Um," I said.

"You think we should give up?" Rachel said. "Tell him what we know?"

"I didn't say that," Shireen said mildly.

"That's what it means!"

"Excuse me?" I said.

"You know he's probably already got all he needs," Shireen said. "Otherwise he would have been back by now."

"Maybe he *wouldn't* have what he needs if *you* didn't—"

"*HEY!*" I shouted.

Shireen and Rachel turned to me in faint surprise as if they'd forgotten I was there. "Oh, right," Shireen said. "Sorry."

Luna was looking between Shireen and Rachel with the expression of someone who's reconsidering whether this was a good idea. I was just as confused as she was but didn't let myself show it. Why was Shireen in Rachel's dreams? I mean, I knew why she could be in her *dreams*, but—I shook it off. This wasn't the time. "Rachel—"

"That's not my name."

I sighed inwardly. "Deleo. I need to know where you are."

Rachel looked at me. "Is that supposed to be funny?"

I looked back at her.

"You're working for Belthas," Rachel said coldly. "Go ask him."

"Yeah, well, I'm not working for Belthas anymore."

"Good." Rachel took a step back.

"Wait!" I called. "Look, Rachel, I'm trying to help you. If I was working for Belthas, why would I need to know where you are? I'd just ask him!"

Shireen cocked her head at Rachel. She'd kept pace with Rachel, and the darkness was starting to shroud the two of them again. "He's got a point."

"Shut up," Rachel said. "He led them to us! It's a trick!"

"I hate to point this out," Shireen said, "but we're not really in a position to turn down help."

Rachel hesitated, then looked to her left at the shadow and her face hardened. "No."

I knew Rachel was about to step back into the darkness, and once she was in there, she wouldn't come out. "Cinder's with me."

Luna looked at me. Rachel paused. "What?"

"We made a deal," I said. "I'm going there for Luna, he's going there for you, and we've both got a score to settle with Belthas. He's with me back in the real world. We're coming but we need to know where Belthas is."

Rachel hesitated. "Look, what have you got to lose?" I said. "If I'm working for Belthas, it doesn't make any difference to you if I know where his base is. But if I'm telling the truth, this is the best chance you'll get of letting Cinder find you."

I could see Rachel thinking about it. Shireen waited, silent; maybe she knew trying to push Rachel now wouldn't help. The shadow didn't move but I could feel it watching me.

"Scotland," Rachel said at last. "Northern Highlands."

"You saw it?"

"I know it. An old manor on the Black Craeg mountain."

"Does Cinder know where it is?"

"You've got the name."

"Anything else?"

"How would I know? It's a manor. It's got cells. Belthas is there and so are his soldiers."

I nodded. "All right. We'll be there soon."

"Then *if* you're telling the truth," Rachel said, "you might want to hurry up. Belthas has started the ritual. Once it's done he won't need me *or* your precious little apprentice."

I felt Luna flinch but didn't look at her. "Can you help us find a way out?"

Rachel laughed. "In your dreams."

"We die, you die."

"Doesn't mean I'm going with you. You found a way in. You find the way out." She glanced from me to Luna. "Don't come back." Rachel stepped back; the darkness flowed over her and she was gone. Shireen had time for a quick wave before she vanished too. Silently and smoothly, the black crystal door swung closed, shutting with a click. The last wisps of darkness faded and we were alone.

"Well," I said after a moment. "That went about as well as could be expected."

"You're working with Cinder?" Luna asked.

"For now . . . We got what we came for. Time to go."

Luna looked around at the doorways. "So where . . . ?"

I looked down at her, eyebrows raised. Luna sighed. "I get it, I get it. Up to me, right?"

Luna thought for a minute, then crossed the hall, heading for one of the doors. "But word of warning," I said. "Finding someone's dreams in Elsewhere isn't hard. Leaving is."

The door Luna had picked was blue crystal. It opened at a touch to reveal a rounded corridor lit with a pale light. I waited for Luna to step in, then shut the door behind us, taking a quick look around before I did. "You know, if there's anything else you know about this place," Luna said as I caught her up, "now might be a good time to tell me."

"I don't know how Elsewhere works," I said. "Nobody

does. There are books about it but they're not much more than guesses."

"You've been here before, right?" Luna said. "How did you get out?"

I shrugged. "Instinct? Luck? I don't know. There are a few rules that work for me but I don't know if they'll work for you."

"I think I need all the help I can get."

"All right," I said. "Don't stray off the path. Don't strike the first blow. And always look before you leap."

Luna looked at me. "That's not really all that specific."

"Sorry."

We walked for a little while. The corridor was growing lighter and there were slit windows appearing in the side alcoves, bright light streaming through them. "Maybe there's one more thing," I said. "I read a few chapters once out of a much longer book about Elsewhere. The author spent years studying it, getting stories from people who'd been there, and he never found a constant. In the end he decided Elsewhere was shaped by the traveller: What you found there would always link back to you. He found something else as well. How much power a mage had didn't seem to have anything to do with how well he did in Elsewhere. The ones who did best were the ones with the most . . . self-awareness, I guess. The ones most comfortable with who they were."

"Oh," Luna said. She thought about it briefly. "What happens if you . . . *don't* do well in Elsewhere?"

"Nobody knows."

"Why?"

"Because they never wake up."

Luna fell silent. We kept walking.

"Who was she?" Luna asked.

I knew who she meant. "Shireen."

"You know her?"

"Yes."

"And . . . she was in Deleo's dreams, right?"

I didn't answer.

"Is that supposed to happen?"

"No."

"You . . . knew her from before?"

"Luna, I don't want to talk about this," I said. "Not now. Focus on getting us out of here."

Luna looked like she was about to argue, but she didn't. It didn't help me get the same thing out of my head. Why had Shireen been there and what had that shadow been?

The corridor ended in another door. Luna opened it without asking—

And we stepped into a city street. Semidetached houses, yellow brick with hedges and front gardens, formed a line in front of us with hatchbacks and sedans parked by the side of the road. Instead of the unnatural silence of Elsewhere or the whispers of before, I could hear the familiar low buzz of city traffic, though the street itself was still. The sky overhead was still cloudy but lighter, the sun glowing through the white canopy. I looked back to see more houses behind us. The door had vanished.

Looking around, I realised that the city felt like London. It's hard to say exactly what it was—it's not as though city houses look all that different—but I've lived all my life in London and something about the bricks and the trees made me think of a London suburb, though not one I'd ever been to. "Huh."

Luna didn't respond. I looked to see her staring at the house in front of us. It was three storeys high and had a red door with the number 17 on the front. The front yard had a privet hedge and two pot plants.

A flicker of movement made me glance up sharply. "Luna."

Luna started and seemed to come awake. "There's something here," I said quietly. I couldn't see what it was but my instincts were telling me we were being watched.

Luna shrank back against me, staring at the door as though it were going to bite her. I stood tense, trying to watch every direction. I was starting to think that the creature following me *wanted* us to know it was there. The glances I was getting were too deliberate, the disappearances too quick. But this time I couldn't see a thing.

I felt Luna jump and snapped my head around. The door with the number 17 was swinging open and people were coming out.

There were two: a man and a woman. The man looked about fifty with the tanned skin and dark hair of Southern Europe. His hair was greying, but he looked strong and fit. The woman was a little younger and fairer, with Luna's hair and eyes. As she saw Luna her eyes lit up and she ran towards her. "Luna, Luna!"

Luna froze. I tried to step in front of her but somehow they slipped by and a second later the woman was hugging Luna while the man stood by smiling. "Oh, Luna!" the woman said. "It's been so long!"

Luna stared back at the woman and she looked terrified. She tried to pull away. "You're . . . No. I don't . . ."

"Tesoro," the man said with a great smile. "It's so good to see you."

"I—No!" Luna pulled herself away violently. She kept backing away across the road until she came up against a car. "It's not you. It can't be you!"

"It is, love," the woman said. If Luna's reaction bothered her, she didn't show it; her face was compassionate. "Let us help you." She began to walk towards her.

Neither of the pair had reacted to me and they didn't seem unfriendly, but whoever they were, they were freaking Luna out. I stepped between them and Luna, taking care this time to make sure they couldn't get past me. The woman kept walking. "Hey," I said. "Wait a—"

The woman walked right through me. I felt a shock of cold as her body passed through mine, then she was gone.

I turned with a shiver to see her stroke Luna's hair tenderly. "It's all right," she said. "Everything's all right now."

Luna stared at the woman, then at me, then at her, then took a deep breath. She reached up and took the woman's hand from her hair, bringing it down in front of her. "I—I don't understand. How are you here?"

"We came for you, of course," the man said with a smile. "We've been waiting for you."

"But you—" Luna said. "I thought—"

"It's all right," the woman said. She clasped Luna's hand between hers. "It was hard to believe at first, but once we came . . . Well, it's obvious, isn't it?"

"Luna?" I said quietly. I'd stepped to one side. "Are these . . . who I think they are?"

Luna looked between us, then gave a tiny nod. Now I looked closer I could see the resemblance between her and the woman. She didn't take after the man so clearly, but there was something there in how they moved. *"Cara,"* the man said. "Remember what we said?"

The woman nodded. "Yes. Luna, we're sorry. For not believing you, for not listening. You were telling the truth all along and we should have known. We were too scared."

"I—" Luna wavered.

"They're not real," I said quietly.

Luna's head snapped around to look at me. "How do you know?"

I shook my head. "How could they have got here? It doesn't make sense."

"We're really here, Luna," the woman said. She didn't show any sign of hearing me but she answered as if she had. "We found a way into this . . . Elsewhere, that was what it was called? It wasn't easy, but . . ." She smiled and brushed Luna's cheek. "Well. To do this again . . ."

Despite herself, Luna smiled. "Mum, I told you not to do that—"

"They're not real," I said again. "Don't accept it."

Luna looked at me, frustrated. "Give me a second!"

"The longer you let yourself believe they're real, the harder it'll be," I said quietly. "Trust me."

"How are you so sure?"

"Because it's happened to me," I said. "There are *things* in Elsewhere, Luna. No one knows what they are. They can wear the masks of family, friends, people from your past. Do you *seriously* believe your parents found a way into Elsewhere? Both together? Is that the kind of thing they'd do?"

"Luna?" her mother asked. "Who are you talking to?"

Luna drew in a harsh breath. I could see the struggle in her eyes, trying to decide whom to believe. She looked away, her movements jerky, and I knew with a sudden flash of insight that at that moment she hated me. Not for telling the truth, but for making her believe it when the lie would have been so much less painful.

"I have to go," Luna said.

"Go?" her mother asked blankly. "But why?"

Luna didn't meet her mother's eyes.

"Don't you see?" her mother said. "This was why we came. It's safe here. We can be with you without getting hurt." She put her arm around Luna with a smile. "Come inside. There's so much you need to tell us. And I promise you'll never have to run away again."

Luna hesitated, wavering. For a long moment she stared at the house in front of her. Then, gently, she took her mother's arm from around her. "I'm sorry," she said. "There are things I have to do."

I felt my shoulders relax slightly and realised I'd been holding my breath. Just for a second, I wondered if this was what happened to those people who never came back from Elsewhere. I'd always assumed they'd been attacked. But maybe it had been something as simple as this . . .

"Then we're coming with you," Luna's father said.

"You're—?"

"No arguments," her mother said firmly. "After all this time, you think we're going to leave you alone again? It's your choice but we go where you do." She smiled. "We're not going to send you away this time."

Luna looked from her to me, unsure, but I was caught off guard as well. "Okay," Luna said at last. "I'd . . . like that."

"Perfect," the woman said with a smile. "It's settled, then."

"Which way?" Luna asked.

The woman turned Luna towards the end of the street and nodded. "Right there."

Luna looked down the street. Her mother was still holding her arm. She took a step, the scenery seemed to blur and shift—

We stood in the middle of a mountain village. It was after sunset, that time between twilight and darkness where just enough light is left in the sky to see but only by straining one's eyes. The weather was dark and brooding, thick clouds covering the sky with only a tiny sliver of grey showing in the west. A mountain peak loomed over the village, a black shadow in the gloom.

The village looked old, very old, and it wasn't English. The architecture was different, the houses built in a square-edged style with sloped roofs. Some of the houses had walls of brick, others stone and mortar, and all were dark. No lights showed in the windows, and there was no sign of movement. The village was silent, so quiet it was unnatural; there was no sound of wind or life. As I looked around I saw a few open doors, shutters hanging loose. It felt . . . dead. Whoever had lived here, they weren't here any more. As I looked around the silent square, I felt the hairs on the back of my neck rise and I looked unconsciously for lines of retreat.

Luna was a little in front of me, her parents clustered protectively around her. She took a slow look around and something in her eyes made me sure it wasn't the first time she'd seen this place. "Are you all right, dear?" her mother said. "Do you want to go back?"

Luna's gaze settled on the house at the other end of the square. It looked ancient, even older than the other houses, with a ragged roof and crumbling stonework that looked on the verge of falling down. The narrow entrance had no door; there was only a black hole in the wall. Luna raised her arm to point. "There."

"Is that the way out?" I asked. I kept my voice down. I had the feeling something might be listening.

"Yes," Luna said. She sounded absolutely certain.

The doorway was maybe twenty paces away. Luna didn't move towards it and neither did her parents. "What's wrong?" I said quietly.

Luna didn't reply for a second. "You remember when you first brought me into Elsewhere?" Luna's voice was distant and she gazed at the house in front of her, talking as if to herself. "You told me my curse didn't work here."

"Yeah."

"I thought about that, afterwards," Luna said. "I couldn't figure it out. I mean, my curse is part of me. I can't live without it, Arachne told me that. So how can I be here if my curse isn't?"

I looked at Luna but she didn't meet my eyes. "Well, I figured it out," Luna said, staring towards the house. "My curse *is* here. Just not in me."

The darkness behind the house moved and something stepped out of the shadows.

। । । । । । । । ।

I t was beautiful.

Looking back on it, that's the first thing I remember. There was a kind of perfection to it, a purity. It stood taller than a man, its stance hunched with its arms hanging to its knees, but it moved with a smooth, loping grace that hinted at speed and power. It was hairless, its skin bare and pure white, and the fingers were curved in a way that made me think of claws. The head was wolflike, with a lengthened muzzle and two pure white eyes that glowed with a pale light. Despite its size, its movements were almost silent.

The four of us stood dead still. The creature kept moving at a steady pace, keeping its distance from us as it circled counterclockwise, its eyes fixed on us. The only sound was the click of its claws against the stone.

As the creature kept circling, we had to turn to keep it in view. It wasn't making any effort to hide and its pale shape stood out clearly in the gloom. "What's it doing?" I said at last, very quietly.

"I don't know," Luna whispered. She was staring back at the thing. Its eyes had no pupils so I couldn't be sure, but I had the feeling it was looking at her.

The creature had gone a quarter of the way around us. "Cutting us off?" I said, then shook my head. "Doesn't make sense . . ."

"We should go," Luna's mother whispered. She shook Luna gently. "Come on."

Luna didn't move. "It'll get behind us," her father murmured. "Run, *cara*. Quickly."

I shook my head. Somehow I knew this thing was faster than we could ever be.

The creature was almost opposite from where it had started and we'd turned through a hundred and eighty degrees watching it. The doorway was behind us now and we were between it and the creature. We had a clear line of retreat. As if she'd been thinking the same thing, Luna took a step back.

My hand shot out to catch her. "No."

Luna stopped, but she didn't take her eyes off the thing. "It's where we're going," she said.

It was true but my instincts were warning me of danger. This thing had started its circle from next to the door. If it had wanted to block our exit, it could have just stood there. Why had it moved? Unless it *wanted* us to—

A horrible suspicion hit me. I focused, narrowing my eyes, and froze. The creature was leaving a trail of silver-white mist as it walked and the mist wasn't fading, but staying. I looked about and understood. The barrier of mist started in front of the house, blocking the way to the exit, and it was two-thirds of the way around us. The creature was drawing a circle around us. As soon as it finished, we'd be trapped. "Luna!"

I heard Luna inhale sharply as she saw it too. As she did, the mist shimmered into visibility, as though by seeing it we'd broken the spell. The mist looked silvery, harmless . . . just like Luna's curse.

I don't know if Luna's parents knew what the mist was but they knew what it meant. "Luna!" her mother cried.

"We have to go!" her father shouted. He ran towards the quarter of the circle still open.

There was a flicker of movement, almost too fast to see. Luna's father's chest came apart in a gout of blood, droplets spattering onto the stone. The creature loomed above, bright red staining the white skin, and snatched the man up in its claws before fading back into the mist, gone before I could move.

"No!" Luna screamed. *"Dad!"*

"Artur!" Luna's mother screamed. "ARTUR!"

Luna made as if to run into the mist but I grabbed her. "No!"

Luna struggled. "Let go—!"

Something came flying out of the mist. It made a wet thump as it hit the ground and bounced, rolling and leaving a red smear behind it. It came to rest at Luna's mother's feet. She looked down and screamed. Two empty eyes stared up from out of it, glazing.

Luna went rigid, staring in horror. Her mother kept screaming as I looked about wildly. The mist swirled, obscuring the square, and I couldn't see where the thing was. The edges of the mist had almost closed the circle and only a narrow gap was left, leading towards an alley-way.

Luna's mother saw the narrowing gap and ran towards it, still screaming. "Don't!" I shouted.

The creature appeared out of the mist before she'd gone five steps, faster and quieter than anything so big had any right to be. Its claw ripped through the woman's stomach to burst out of her back with a damp snapping noise, and Luna's mother jerked as she was lifted off the ground. The creature held her weight impaled on one arm without difficulty, its empty eyes staring into hers as her mouth worked, trying to speak, then with a lightning motion it snapped its jaws around her throat and ripped it out. Spurts of blood painted red streaks on its skin as it dragged the body off its arm with a horrible scraping, cracking sound before fading back into the mist.

Luna didn't scream this time. She was frozen, stiff and staring. I looked around to see that the mist had closed around us. I couldn't see the exit. "Luna. *Luna.*"

Silence. I moved back to back with Luna, trying to look in every direction at once, my instincts still screaming at me to watch for danger even though my head knew it was useless. The thing was inhumanly fast; if it wanted to snatch me I didn't have a hope of stopping it. "Luna!"

Luna stayed rigid against my back. I took a deep breath and stepped around to look at Luna face to face, leaving my back exposed. Her eyes flicked up to meet mine but they were horrified, blank. "It's not real," I said quietly, putting every bit of belief into my voice that I could. "They're shadows, phantoms. That's how this place works. It strikes at your fears, where you're weak. Your real parents are still alive, out in the world, but if you want to see them again you have to get out of here!"

Luna shivered. Her eyes came back into focus and she stared at me. Then her eyes shifted to focus on a point over my shoulder and slowly, very slowly, she looked up.

A horrible empty feeling opened up inside my stomach. I turned around.

The creature was standing right behind me. The mist had closed in and now we were at the centre of a ring barely twenty feet across. The creature was almost twice my height, the empty white eyes looking down at me, and it smelt of something cold and ancient. Red blood made ghastly spatters on the white skin, but it was already fading and I knew that in only a few minutes the blood of Luna's parents would be gone. Just as mine would be.

The creature moved. I'd like to say I did something brave but I didn't. I shut my eyes.

Nothing happened. One heartbeat, five, ten. I opened my eyes to look.

Luna was standing in front of me, shielding me. Against the backdrop of that monster, she looked tiny, like a child. She was in range of those lethal claws and one strike would have cut her in half, but the creature stood still, its blank eyes looking down at her as Luna stepped forward to meet it. She reached up to place her hand flat against its smooth muscled chest.

There was a single blinding flash and I flinched. Spots swam before my eyes and I scrubbed at them. As my vision returned I realised I could make out the shapes of buildings around me. The mist was gone.

I looked from side to side. There was no trace of the mist, or Luna's parents. The stones of the square were clean, with no blood. Where the creature had stood, only Luna remained . . . and as I looked at her, I saw the silver mist begin to seep from her skin again, strengthening until it formed its aura around her, just as it always did.

Luna didn't look at me. She nodded to the black doorway of the house in front of us. "We can go."

I hesitated. "You first," Luna said. Her voice was distant. "I don't think I'm very safe to be near anymore."

Carefully I circled Luna. She was staring into the

doorway, her face unreadable. A pace short of entering, I stopped. "Are you . . . ?"

"Don't worry," Luna said. "I'll follow." Her eyes met mine. "It's not like I've got anything to stay for, is it?"

I looked at Luna, then nodded slowly and turned to face the doorway. It was lightless, a black void, and I stepped through. Cold froze my bones and I fell into nothingness.

chapter 10

I came awake with a gasp, my heart pounding. Sonder had pulled a chair close to my bed and as I jerked upwards he flinched and nearly went over backwards, his arms flailing before he recovered his balance. "Ah! Alex! You scared me."

"Jesus," I muttered. My heart was thumping against my chest and I was shivering. I could still feel the bone-freezing cold of the gateway. I pulled my cloak around myself, trying to get warm.

"Alex?" Sonder said. Behind his glasses, he looked worried. "You okay?"

"Freaking, goddamn . . ." I glared at Sonder. "If Luna EVER invites you into Elsewhere, say no!"

"Um. Okay?"

I stayed hugging myself a little longer, waiting for my heartbeat to slow and the deadly cold to fade. Just being back in my room helped and I felt my shivering slow as my cloak drew away the chill. "What did I miss?"

"Cinder's back." Sonder hesitated. "I . . . think he's getting impatient."

"Then let's not keep him waiting." I swung my legs off the bed and stood up. I nearly fell straight back down but managed to catch the table and kept hold of it until I'd stopped wobbling.

"Um—" Sonder said.

"She's okay," I said as I headed for the door. "And I know where to find her."

⋯⋯⋯⋯⋯

Cinder was waiting in my living room, not quite pacing. Luckily, I had what he wanted. Five minutes at my computer found us a map of Black Craeg and five minutes more found the only place that fit Rachel's description. We geared up and I led us out the back door, locking it behind me. Once we were in the back alley, Cinder opened a gate to a staging point and we stepped through.

We travelled though a desolate, broken forest, then an abandoned quarry. At the end of the quarry Cinder raised his hand to cast another gate and I held my breath. Gating to an area you've never seen is dangerous. If Cinder messed this up . . .

But he didn't. The black oval flickered briefly, then steadied and opened, revealing a dark slope. I went first and Cinder brought up the rear, letting the gate close.

The first thing I noticed was the cold. In London the autumn weather was only cool, but we were five hundred miles north and two thousand feet up. I've been to Scotland a few times and I've grown to like the clean, fresh scent of the air up here, but it's still bloody freezing. I pulled my cloak tighter to stop myself from shivering and looked around.

There wasn't much to see. I could tell the view would be spectacular by day but it was a cloudy night with no cities or towns and the visibility was only one step above pitch-black.

I could see we were on the side of a hill or mountain and that was it. I closed my eyes.

"Where are we?" Sonder whispered. A chill wind was blowing and I could hear his teeth chattering.

"Wait," I whispered back. Something about the black emptiness made us keep our voices down. "Don't show a light."

I looked through the futures ahead of us, seeing our paths branch out in every direction as we explored outwards, making our way down, up, and across the mountainside. Most of the choices were dark; a handful led to the lights of a building. I followed them closer—

"Perfect," I said. "You dropped us right on target, Cinder."

I felt Sonder looking around. "Um—"

"We couldn't land too close," I said. "Cinder put us a little way around the mountain." I took Sonder's arm and pointed upslope towards the dark mass above us. "Belthas's manor is over that shoulder."

Cinder started walking towards it, and I followed. Sonder looked around at the darkness one last time, muttered something under his breath, and came after.

⁛⁛⁛⁛⁛

Crossing a mountain in the dark isn't fun. I had the easiest time with my divination magic and Cinder toughed it out on brute strength. Sonder found it hardest and before long was lagging behind. But it wasn't a long trip, and after only a little while longer Cinder came over a rise and stopped. I reached his side and we looked down the northeast face of the Black Craeg.

Belthas's manor was most of the way up the mountain, about three hundred feet downslope from our perch. Its windows were lit, turning it into a splash of bright light against the blackness around. I could see two storeys from our angle but as I scanned with my magic I realised there was a lower level, built into the slope. Luna had said her cell was in the basement; she must be below.

Cinder looked at me. "So?"

"Let me scout it," I said.

I'd expected an argument but Cinder only nodded. I crouched down and focused, searching through the futures of us going down into the radius of those lights. Sonder caught up a few minutes later, breathing hard. He looked at me, then down at the manor, and settled down to wait.

Eventually, I stirred. "There are two guards outside. One at the front, one at the back. At least eight or ten more in the building. There's a gate ward over the manor; gate magic is going to be difficult from about fifty feet away and impossible inside the walls. There's an alarm system and attack wards too. Belthas is on the top floor in a shielded room."

Cinder looked at me silently. Sonder looked taken aback. "That's . . . a lot."

"Yeah," I said. I checked my watch.

"How long have we got?" Sonder said.

"Until Belthas finishes the ritual and kills Arachne . . ." I calculated. "One hour, thirty-five minutes."

"When do we go?" Cinder asked.

"We'll want to hit it in about an hour," I said. Looking around, I found a rock to sit on. "Till then, we wait."

Sonder looked at me in surprise. "Why?"

Cinder glanced at me, then leant against a boulder. I knew he understood but didn't want to explain. "Right now Belthas is getting ready to start his ritual," I said. "If we attack he'll be on top of us in two minutes flat. But if we wait until he's started he won't be able to come after us without abandoning the ritual, which will screw it up. The closer he is to the end of the ritual, the less he can afford to be disturbed. He'll leave the battle to his guards and wards and hope he can finish before we can break through."

"But the later we leave it," Sonder pointed out, "the more likely he *will* finish before we break through."

I nodded and Sonder fell silent as he realised what I was

saying. Too early and we'd have to fight Belthas and his guards at once. Too late and Arachne would be dead.

"What's the plan for getting past the guards?" Sonder asked eventually.

I sighed. "We kill however many it takes before the rest run. Somewhere between most of them and all of them."

Sonder stared at me. "But . . ."

I didn't answer. "They're Council security," Sonder said. "Okay, I guess some of them are with Belthas, but . . . they're loyal to the Council. They're just doing their jobs."

"Do you know any spells that'll knock out ten to fifteen armed men?" I said. "Or any way of getting them to surrender and let us through?"

"No, but—"

"Neither do I," I said. "And neither does Cinder. If I was an enchanter or a mind mage I could cloud their senses. If I could use life or death magic I could disrupt their bodies and knock them out. But I'm not and I can't. The only thing I've got that can drop them fast enough to be safe is this gun. If we screw around taking prisoners we're going to get shot." I paused. "Actually, there's a pretty good chance we're going to get shot anyway."

"There's got to be *something* else," Sonder argued. "I don't want anyone to get killed."

Cinder made a disgusted noise. I didn't look at him. "Belthas is down there," I told Sonder. "Along with at least a dozen armed guards in a warded building, and that's not counting Meredith and Martin and whatever else he's got up his sleeve."

"I know," Sonder said. "That doesn't mean we should try to kill them!"

"The point is," I said quietly, "that the odds are against us. Really against us. Even if we don't make any mistakes, there's a good chance that anyone who goes into that manor is going to end up dead. The more restrictions we go under, the bigger that chance gets. When you're playing odds this long, the only way to win is to use every edge you've got."

I could feel Cinder's eyes on me. Sonder looked desperately unhappy. I couldn't really blame him; I knew it felt to him like an impossible situation. But the truth is, it's not about what's possible. It's what you're willing to live with.

But I might as well cut him a break. "Anyway, it's not up to you," I said. "We're going down there, and when we do there's going to be a fight no matter what." I sat down on one of the rocks. "Take a look around but make sure you're not seen."

          ı ı ı ı ı ı ı ı ı

S onder and Cinder moved away and I was left alone in the darkness, which suited me just fine. I scanned through the futures in which I went down there, skipping over the parts where the strands branched into a blur of combat. I didn't try to see how it would go—fights are too chaotic to see more than a few seconds ahead. Instead I searched for openings, doors, alarms, building a mental map of the manor below.

While my mind looked through the futures, my hands moved over the weapon at my side. Most of Belthas's men had been carrying submachine guns of a type I vaguely recognised as MP5s. Garrick had been carrying a model I hadn't seen before, square and blocky with only the tip of the muzzle protruding from the gun, and it was this one I'd taken. It was less than a foot and a half long, made of some black polymer which was surprisingly light, with a retractable stock and laser sight. The bottom of the magazine stuck out from the handle. It held thirty rounds and I had three more full magazines stowed away. One of the men had been carrying a 1911 pistol like mine, with the addition of a silencer, and I'd taken that too. I'd also brought a handful of more dangerous things in my backpack, riding awkwardly under my cloak.

I've never been all that comfortable with guns. Partly it's for practical reasons—they're illegal, for a start, and they don't usually get good reactions from mages—but it's also that I just don't like the things. Carrying a gun makes me uneasy in a way that carrying a knife doesn't, and if I'm going out I'll almost never take one. But I've used them before, and even if I'm not as good a shot as I am with throwing, I can hit a target pretty well. When you can't use offensive magic, guns are a big equaliser, and sometimes you can't afford to be fussy.

I sensed Cinder returning well in advance. Sonder was still back up the slope, struggling with his conscience. I waited for Cinder to get close before glancing up. He was looking down at me, arms folded. "Ice wards."

I nodded.

"Plan?"

"I sneak inside," I said. "I'll try for Deleo and Luna, get as far as I can. When the shooting starts, I'll open up a way in and you do what you do best. We go for the girls first, Belthas second."

Cinder nodded. We both knew he'd follow my orders only as long as they suited him. I took a breath. "One more thing. If I don't make it out, make sure Sonder and Luna get away safe. I'll do the same for Deleo if anything happens to you."

Cinder looked at me. Standing in the darkness, it was hard to make out his expression. An icy wind was blowing, but Cinder let it sweep over him as though he didn't notice. Probably he didn't.

"Why?" Cinder said.

"Why what?"

"Help them."

"Who?"

Cinder just looked at me, as if refusing to answer such a stupid question. "Because I want to," I said.

Cinder studied me for a moment, then nodded in the direction Sonder had gone. "You're not one of them."

I was silent. "Talk, don't fight," Cinder said. "Don't get your hands dirty. How they think. You don't."

"I'm not exactly the fighting type."

"Bullshit," Cinder said. "You act it. Fool some people. Fooled me once. You're a predator. You just hide it."

I raised an eyebrow at Cinder. "Pretty weak for a predator."

"Yeah?" Cinder said. "Last ten years. How many people tried to kill you? Don't mean a skirmish. A proper try."

I shrugged. "Haven't kept count."

Cinder nodded. "How many still alive?"

The question brought me up short. A few people had tried to kill me over the years. Actually, more than a few. Cinder and Rachel didn't really count—they'd always been more interested in getting their piece—but Khazad did. So did Tobruk. Levistus had ordered my death through Griff and Thirteen, and Morden had done the same through Onyx. Then Garrick had tried to shoot me a few days ago, and there had been that bomb-maker at the Deptford factory. There were more—a lot more. As for how many were still alive, the answer was . . .

. . . not that many.

Most of them were dead.

In fact, most of them were dead quite specifically because of me.

I don't often look back over my life. Between paying attention to the present and looking forwards into the future, I don't have much time left to look over my past choices. Now I did and realised what picture they made, and it wasn't all that reassuring.

And I was about to add a whole bunch of new names to the list. If everything went to plan, a lot of people down there were going to die. And as I thought it over, I realised I was going to go through with it. At the end of the day, given a choice between Belthas and his men on one side, and Luna and Arachne on the other, I was going to pick

Luna and Arachne, and if it meant Belthas and his men dead then that was what I'd do. I knew exactly how ugly and vicious the battle was going to be and I was going to do it anyway.

I didn't know what that said about me. Maybe later, I'd think about it. Right now all I cared about was getting the job done. "What do you want, Cinder?" I said. "You want me to back out?"

Cinder shook his head.

"Then what?"

"Del hates you," Cinder said. "Thinks you're weak. I reckon she's wrong. You're ruthless as her. Just hide it better."

"Thanks. I think."

"I'll save your pets if you go down," Cinder said. "But I don't reckon you will. I think end of tonight, you'll be around. And Belthas won't."

I looked back at Cinder, trying to figure out if that should make me feel better.

A sound from behind made me look up in time to see Sonder returning. He was shivering. He really should have taken me up when I offered to lend him a coat. "Belthas started his ritual."

I nodded. "Time to go."

Sonder hesitated. "I—"

I sighed. "For us, not for you. You're not going, Sonder. This isn't your kind of fight." I reached into my backpack and pulled out a radio, a donation from one of Garrick's men. I tossed it to Sonder and he caught it awkwardly. "I want you to stay up here and pull lookout. Tell me if anything changes. I'll call you when I'm in position."

Sonder looked down, then up at me. "Don't beat yourself up over it," I said. "There's a time to play white knight and this isn't it. If everything goes to hell, get out the way we came and follow the valley down. You'll get to a village in about five miles."

Sonder opened his mouth and I saw him thinking about what to say. "Good luck," he said unhappily.

I grinned at him. "Luck's for Luna. See you in an hour or two."

The grin vanished about two seconds after I was out of sight. I put on my mist cloak, pulling down the hood so that it concealed my face. Belthas would know who I was, but there was no point giving the cameras a free show. It was time to get to work.

⁖⁖⁖⁖⁖⁖⁖⁖⁖

Up close, Belthas's manor was solid and imposing. It had been designed to look like a traditional English country house, but there was a blocky quality to it that made me think of a castle or bunker. The lower-level windows looked accessible but I knew they were reinforced and sealed. The only ways in were the front and rear doors.

I'd put the time I'd spent waiting in the darkness above to good use and I had a pretty good idea of the building's weak points. Any kind of security system that can keep out people you don't want can also keep out people you do, and rather than solve the difficult problem of attuning his wards, Belthas had elected to leave two openings over the doors. After some consideration, I'd picked the front one. It was watched over by one guard and a pair of security cameras.

The cameras were easy. There was a slight gap in the coverage and I waited for them to pan away before slipping through to come up against the manor's west wall. I could feel the presence of the defensive spells through the stone: a gate ward and some kind of nasty ice-based attack that would trigger if anyone attempted to force entry. Luckily, I wasn't intending to.

The guard outside the front door was obviously bored and cold. Peering around the corner, I could see him shivering, his hands shoved into his armpits and his MP5 hanging from its strap. There were a few steps leading up to the door and he was standing on top of them, visible in the reflected light of the windows. I walked silently along the edge of the building towards him, pausing from time to time when I got too close to his peripheral vision. The front of the building was bare with no cover, but in my mist cloak I was just one more shadow in the night.

By the time I was up against the steps I was close enough to see the stubble on the guard's face and smell the cigarette smoke on his clothes. Looking into the future, I saw that if I got the guard out of the way and went in now, I'd run into two more in the front hall. All I could do was wait. I stood not ten feet from the guard, listened to his teeth chattering, and checked my watch. Thirty-five minutes until Belthas completed his ritual.

Five minutes passed. I was getting cold but didn't let myself move, tensing and relaxing muscles to stop myself from stiffening up. Ten minutes. Looking into the future, I saw that the guards inside were gone. I pulled a pebble from my pocket, waited for the guard to glance away, and threw it into the darkness.

One of the funny things about divination magic is you can know something will work without having the first clue *why*. The pebble clinked off the rock and the guard snapped his head around as I'd known he would. He stood motionless for ten seconds, then crept down the stairs and slunk left along the wall, trying to blend into the shadows.

Why did he go that way, along the line of the wall, rather than towards the noise? I don't know. I just knew that had been what I needed to do to make him turn his back. I moved quickly up the stairs, opened the door, and slipped inside.

The air inside Belthas's manor was warm, the entrance hall panelled in wood with pictures on the walls. It looked expensive but rarely used. The murmur of voices echoed through the hallway—the doorway to my left led to a front room with four of Belthas's men inside but I knew that for the next few seconds none would be looking at the door. I walked quickly past and up the stairs.

There were cameras inside too, and this time I didn't try to avoid them. In stillness and darkness my mist cloak makes me all but invisible, but moving in the light is another story. Speed was my best chance now. The security station was on the first floor, and as I came up to the top of the stairs I drew my silenced pistol. The door to the security room was open, light glimmering from inside, and I went in with the gun up.

The room was filled with monitors, arranged in an arc around the room's single desk. I could see the approaches to the house, the rooms inside. Pale electronic light bathed the man sitting in the chair. He had a red baseball cap pulled down over his eyes and his arms were clasped over his stomach as he slept. He wasn't holding a weapon.

I aimed the pistol at his head, hesitated, then lowered it again and looked at the camera feeds. I counted at least ten guards plus the one in front of me and the two outside. There were views of a set of four reinforced metal doors in the basement level that looked a lot like cells. No inside view but if Luna and Rachel were here, that was where they'd be. There was a guard down on the basement level too . . . along with a slimmer figure whom I recognised by his hair as Martin. I narrowed my eyes. When I met Martin, he and I were going to have words.

There was a feed showing guards on the stairs leading up but the cameras on the second floor itself were blank. I guessed Belthas didn't want anyone else watching his ritual. I looked under the desk but saw nothing except a bunch of cabling from the monitors feeding into the right wall, and I walked quietly out, keeping my gun ready. The man in the red baseball cap didn't wake up.

The next door to the right opened into a small room full of humming computers. Perfect. I shut the door behind me, slipped off my backpack, and pulled out a block of an off-white, funny-smelling material as well as a pair of detonators.

I really don't know anything about explosives, but being able to see exactly what will and won't cause something to go *boom* makes demolition work a lot less stressful. I stuck the detonators into the block, tucked it behind the computer banks, backed off to the door, and looked into the future to see what would happen if I pressed the button on the detonator. Ouch. Okay, it was working. Mental note: one pound of plastic explosive makes a really big bang.

The next job was to find a way for Cinder to get in. The front door was still too crowded but as I moved to the rear of the building I saw that the back door was deserted except for the solitary guard outside. I stacked my other two blocks of plastic explosive against the door frame, set the detonators, then covered the whole thing with a coat someone had left on a stand. It would take out the door, the guard, the wall, and pretty much anything else.

I could hear voices from the front of the manor; the outside guard had come in and was talking to the ones in the front room. Couldn't go back that way. Getting dangerous now—too many people, too many variables. I couldn't predict everything. There was a back set of stairs and I moved down it away from the explosives, fumbling out my radio as I did so. "Sonder?" I hit the Transmit key. "Sonder!"

There was silence for a moment, then a hiss and Sonder's voice came through, scratchy but audible. "Alex?"

"I'm about to be blown. Tell Cinder to go. I'll open the back door."

"Okay. Are you—?"

I shoved the radio back in my pocket and looked out along a ground-floor corridor. As I did, I heard someone call out, questioning. Damn, he'd heard me. I ducked into what looked like a dining room. The chairs were pulled out but no one was there.

Footsteps in the corridor. A guard was approaching. His

gun wasn't up—he wasn't expecting a fight yet. Looking into the future, I saw that he wasn't going to check this room . . . but he wasn't going to leave the corridor either and in less than sixty seconds a bunch more guards would come down from the first floor. If I hid here I'd be trapped.

Time to give up on stealth. I waited for the guard to walk past, then stepped out into the doorway with my weapon up and sighted on the back of his head. I looked into the future of me pulling the trigger, saw that nothing would happen, flicked the safety off, looked into the future again, saw the burst going up and left, corrected down and right, looked into the future again, saw the burst hit, pulled the trigger. My divination isn't as quick with guns as with thrown items—not as practised, not as intuitive—but it still took barely a second.

Garrick's submachine gun was louder than I expected, a chattering *ba-ba-bang!* that made me flinch, and the second and third rounds went high as the recoil kicked my shoulder, but I saw the red puff as the first bullet went through the guard's head, and that was all she wrote. The body crumpled and as my ears adjusted I heard shouts. The stairs down to the basement were on the west side and I ran for them.

I nearly made it. Would have made it, if three guards hadn't decided to get smart and cut me off. I was less than thirty feet away when they came round the corner.

Most people think combat's about attacks and weapons but it's not. It's about movement and information. Belthas's men were just as skilled as me and just as tough as me but I knew where we'd meet and they didn't. I was already crouching with my gun braced against my shoulder as the first one came around the corner, and I fired before he'd even spotted me. One burst to bring him down, another to finish the job. The other two guards could have rushed me if they'd attacked together but they'd just seen their friend killed in front of them. They backpedalled and started screaming into their radios for backup.

I had an open run to the basement but I'd just be boxing myself in. I could sense more guards closing in and I knew I had about fifteen seconds before they pinned me down. I ducked into the nearest room, pulled out the detonator and braced myself against the wall before pushing the button.

I felt the wall shudder behind me and there was a deep *boom* and a rush of air, followed a second later by a tearing, crashing sound. The lights flickered but most came back on again and the building steadied. I kept going through the room and out the other side into the main hall. Dust and smoke were billowing down the staircase, and I could hear screams from above; some of Belthas's men had been near the second bomb when it went off. I took the right door and headed for the corridor where the two men were hunkered down, coming around from the other side. They'd heard me coming and were waiting with their guns trained on the corner, but it didn't do them any good. I took a grenade from my pack, pulled the pin and let the lever spring free, waited two seconds, then threw it around the corner, bouncing it off the wall to roll next to where I knew the men were crouching. The bang was a lot louder this time. I moved past the torn bodies to the stairs leading down to the basement.

I heard Sonder's voice over the radio as I trotted down the stairs. They were concrete, and narrow. "Alex? Alex!"

I pulled the radio out, listening carefully to the sounds above. There were shouts and orders but it sounded like I'd bought myself a little more time. "Make it quick," I said into the radio.

There was a burst of static. "—did you say?"

The stairs ended in a metal door on the left-hand side. The guard in the basement was on the other side with his weapon trained, ready to fire. I shoved the door open and stepped back as a burst of automatic fire chipped fragments from the wall. "Not the best time, Sonder."

"Cinder's on his way," Sonder said, his voice tense and excited. "Getting to the manor right about . . . now!"

Right on cue, I heard the familiar *whoompf* of a fireball from above followed by an agonised shriek. The guards on the ground floor who'd been heading for me changed direction. "Perfect," I said absently, wedging the radio between ear and shoulder so I could bring up my gun.

"He's burning the whole back wall!" Sonder's voice rose a few notes. "He— Holy crap! That thing just—"

Another burst of fire drilled the wall next to me. I poked the muzzle of my gun around the corner and fired a short burst, the *ba-ba-bang!* deafeningly loud in the corridor, then pulled back fast to avoid the return fire.

"The wards are going off! They're firing back, they're—"

"Sonder, this really isn't a good time," I said absently. "Can I call you back?" Thirty-round magazine, bullets weren't ricocheting . . . too difficult to land a hit. I sent another burst blind around the corner, then shrugged off my pack and rooted through for the last grenade.

The return fire was longer this time, bullets slamming into the wall to my right and embedding themselves in the soft stone, the noise drowning out Sonder's reply. I twisted the pin from the grenade and waited for the guard's magazine to run dry.

Click. The guard dropped, fumbling for a reload, and I leant out. I got a brief view of an open room with an overturned desk, shadows flickering as a light swung from a cord overhead, then I lobbed the grenade to bounce off the far wall and ducked back. There was a brief scream from behind the desk before the explosion cut it off. "Great," I said into the radio. "Keep me posted." I dropped it into my pocket.

The grenade had made a mess of the room and I searched it quickly, trying not to look at what was left of the guard. From above I could hear the roar of fire spells, muffled through the concrete. Cinder wasn't having it all his own way and the chattering bursts of automatic weapon fire were answering him. I couldn't sense any ice attacks, which meant Belthas wasn't joining the battle. If he hadn't come by now, it meant he was close to finishing; we didn't have much time. I spotted a ring of keys beneath a splintered piece of desk and snatched it up, hurrying forward. "Luna!" I shouted.

A faint voice echoed from down the corridor. "Alex! I'm here!"

I was already running towards it, passing a side corridor along the way. Just before the corridor bent to the left were a set of four metal doors, two on each side, solid metal with heavy reinforcement. They didn't have any windows, but each one had a narrow metal hatch at eye level. I flipped the catch and slid the hatch open with a rattle.

Luna was inside and as I saw her I felt a wave of relief that made me weak at the knees. For all that I'd seen her in Elsewhere, for all that I'd known Belthas wouldn't have her killed without a reason, seeing her in the flesh made me feel a hundred times better. Luna looked a little pale, her hair was untidy and her clothes scuffed and torn, but as she saw me she gave one of her rare smiles. "Hey," she said.

"Hey," I said, and I realised I was smiling too. "How's things?"

"Been better," Luna said. "Any chance you could get me out of here?"

"Just waiting for you to ask." The room was a prison cell, crudely furnished, and the door had bolts at top and bottom. I drew them back with a scrape of metal. "Where's Deleo?"

Luna shook her head. "They took her away a couple of hours ago."

I was just about to start going through the keys when something flickered on my precognition. I looked at what was coming and rolled my eyes. "Oh, you have *got* to be kidding me."

Luna sighed. She's been with me long enough to get used to this. "I'm guessing that's not good news."

"Here." I pushed the keys through the open hatch, hearing them clink on the concrete, and stepped away. "Be right back."

Martin was about forty feet down the side corridor when I leant round the corner, my gun lining up to sight on him. "Martin," I said. "Give me a reason not to shoot you."

Martin was wearing a set of black combat gear, probably borrowed from Belthas's men, along with a webbing belt that was slightly too big for him. He looked like an action movie actor trying very hard to pretend he was the real thing. He flinched as he saw the barrel of the gun, then shook it off and grinned. "Oh, hey, *Alex*. Thought it was you."

The laser sight was steady on the black fabric covering Martin's chest and my trigger finger itched. "I've just killed a half dozen people whom I had less reason to want dead than you," I said quietly. "You've got a gun behind your back. Drop it."

Martin's grin widened and he lifted the gun. I fired before he got halfway.

Tendrils of shadow whipped out, thread-thin, and there was the crack of ricocheting bullets. Martin's gun finished coming up and I fired another burst. Still nothing. I emptied the rest of the magazine into him. Black shadows flickered and I saw sparks flash but Martin stayed standing until my gun clicked empty. I stared at Martin. No wounds, no blood. What the hell?

"My turn," Martin said and fired.

Martin was firing an automatic, a fairly powerful one from the sound. Luckily his aim sucked and none of his shots would have hit even if I hadn't ducked behind the corner. I ejected the empty magazine, pulled out a spare, and snapped it into the handle as Martin's shots bounced uselessly round the corridor. While my hands worked automatically, I tried to figure out what was going on. Martin didn't have any magic of his own so how could—

Oh, God damn it.

The *bang bang bang* of fire from around the corner ended, and as the echoes died away I heard Martin laughing. "Figured it out yet?" he called. "You can't touch me!"

"What is *wrong* with you?" I shouted. "Could you *be* any more annoying?"

"You have no idea what this thing can do, do you?" Martin's voice was mocking. "Come on, take a look."

I glanced carefully around the corner. Martin was holding the gun in his right hand and in his left was the monkey's paw. "Second wish," he said, grinning at me. "First one gave me protection from magic. Now I'm protected from everything else." He shook his head at me. "Seriously, man. You had this thing all this time and never used it? How stupid are you?"

I ran through the futures of me emptying a hundred shots at him a hundred different ways. Useless. I didn't know how the monkey's paw was protecting Martin but I couldn't see a way through, and I felt a chill. Drawing away magical attacks was one thing, but bullets? Was there *any* limit to what that thing could do?

But if bullets didn't work, maybe getting in close would. I crouched, ready to spring. Martin could only have a few more bullets in that gun. As soon as he stopped to reload . . .

"Two wishes," Martin said. His grin had gotten wider and there was something manic about it. "Time for number three. I've been waiting for this a long time."

"Let me guess," I said. "You're wishing for your IQ to break double figures."

Martin laughed wildly. "You think I'm a joke, don't you? They all did! You, Belthas, everyone! Because I'm not a mage. Well, now I will be! But you won't!"

"I—" And too late, I saw what Martin was going to do. My eyes went wide. "Oh, crap. No, you nutcase! Don't—"

Martin lifted the monkey's paw above his head. "I wish for all the powers of the mage Alex Verus to be mine!"

I'd been spreading out my magic, trying to watch all the

possibilities. I'd been focusing on Martin, looking to see what he'd do next, looking into the futures of different ways I could attack him and the consequences of each, and finally keeping an eye on potential dangers at the back of my mind with my precognition, all at the same time. As Martin said the last word, I felt a surge of power from the monkey's paw and just that fast, it was gone. The lines of glowing light in the darkness vanished into nothingness and the only sight I had was my eyes. For the first time in ten years, I couldn't see the future. The shock was so great I couldn't move. I stood frozen, staring.

Martin stood with the monkey's paw held high. The corridor was silent but for the distant sounds of battle from above. Martin was gazing past me, that manic grin frozen on his face. As I watched, the grin slid away until he was just staring. His brow furrowed in confusion, his expression changing slowly into a mask of horror. His eyes went wider and wider until they bulged out, turning his good looks into something twisted. His gaze swept over me blindly as he looked around and began shaking his head, slowly at first, then more violently. "No," he muttered. He covered his eyes, staggering sideways into the wall. "No, stop it. No, no. Stop it. Stop it! STOP IT! STOP IT!"

"Alex!" Luna called from behind. I could hear the rattle of keys.

I didn't answer. There's no way to understand what it's like to see the future, know it, rely on it, then have it snatched away. It's not like being blind—it's like being deaf. You can still see, still watch things as they happen—but you don't have the context anymore, the extra information that makes it *mean* something. Someone talks to you and you don't know what they're saying; something could be happening behind you and you wouldn't know what. So much of my life goes into controlling this talent I have, focusing and using and directing it. Now it was gone, an emptiness where there'd been a whole world.

Martin had started screaming, wordless and breathless. He was stumbling blindly back and forth, bashing into the walls; his fingers dug into his forehead as if he were trying to claw his eyes out. I knew I should do something but I couldn't think. Looking into the future was such a reflex that I couldn't stop doing it, even though there was nothing to see. Luna was calling to me but I couldn't hear her over Martin's screams. There were too many things at once and without my magic I couldn't keep track anymore.

The scrape of metal reached my ears over Martin's screaming, and I looked up. The door I'd left ajar back at the entrance to the basement was open, and one of Belthas's guards was standing there, one I'd seen before. He had a submachine gun pointed down at the floor, and he was wearing a red baseball cap. He saw me and the gun came up.

Reflex and survival instinct got me moving when my conscious mind couldn't. I dived past Luna's cell and around the corner as bullets raked the wall beside me. I heard the chatter of fire for another second, then the sound of running feet and silence.

I snatched a glance around the corner, trying to spot where the guard had gone. Nothing. Without my magic I felt slow, stupid. Had he gone left or right? I lifted my gun and aimed awkwardly, leaning out into the corridor.

The guard popped out on the side I wasn't expecting and I threw myself back into cover as another burst of fire struck chips from the wall. My movements were scared, jerky; I was outclassed and I knew it. The fire stopped and I leant out to shoot back.

It was a trap. The guard was waiting with his sights trained on where I'd appear. If I'd been able to see into the future I would have seen it coming . . . but I couldn't and I didn't. Another burst of fire raked the corner and this time I wasn't quick enough. Pain seared my left arm and I fell back with a cry.

The fire stopped. My left arm was numb, in agony, and

couldn't support my gun. I staggered back along the corridor, looking for cover. I could hear the tread of cautious footsteps; the guard knew he'd hit me and was coming to finish me off. I wrenched at the handle of the first door. Locked. The footsteps broke into a jog. Next door . . . locked as well. I ran for the end of the corridor.

Gunfire behind. Something plucked at my shoulder and I knew I'd been hit. I kept running, made it around the corner as another burst slammed into the concrete, trying to get as far as I could before I collapsed. My legs were still working but I didn't know how much longer they'd last.

But I'd run as far as I could. The corridor came to a dead end ahead, and behind me I could hear running feet. I made it to the nearest door and wrenched at the handle.

The handle turned. I scrambled into the darkness, tripped over a bucket, and fell with a crash, gasping in pain as the impact jarred my arm. I tried to get up, hit something else, fell again. No more time. I twisted awkwardly, propping up my gun on my body, lining up on the rectangle of light that marked the doorway.

Silence. The guard must be outside in the corridor but I couldn't see him. I held dead still, trying to quiet my breathing.

A footstep, quiet and stealthy. Another. The guard was advancing down the corridor. Two more steps, then the faint rattle as he tried the first door. He had to know I was in one of the rooms—there was nowhere else to go. It was just a matter of time.

Another footstep, this one closer. I couldn't see where the guard was and I was afraid. I held my breath, trying to block out the pain and the fear, keeping my eyes glued to the light of the doorway, the gun shaking slightly as my right hand held its weight. If he looked around the edge of that doorway I would have a second—no more—in which he was silhouetted against the light. One chance to hit him.

But in that same second, he'd see me. There was a crazy

irony to it. It was the same guy I'd found asleep in front of the monitors. After all the people I'd killed, I was about to die because I'd spared someone . . .

The footsteps stopped and I could hear the guard's breathing just outside the door. I focused on the gun's sight, trying to line it up on the right side of the door frame. One shot—

A flurry of footsteps. I heard the guard turn, then grunt as something hit him. The guard came into view, staggering across the doorway, caught for an instant in my gunsight with Luna's slim body wrapped around him. Then he tripped and both of them fell with a thud out of my line of vision.

"Luna!" I shouted. I tried to roll to my feet, yelped as my arm gave way, gritted my teeth and struggled up anyway. Suddenly I wasn't afraid for myself anymore. I could hear the scrabble of a fight, the guard swearing, boots scraping the concrete. Then there was a cracking noise and a *thump*, and everything went quiet.

By the time I reached the corridor it was all over. Luna had regained her feet and was dusting herself off, still holding the key ring I'd dropped through her door. The guard was lying still, the gun fallen from his hands. A trickle of blood ran down the side of his head and a heavy lump of concrete lay next to it. Looking up, I saw a jagged hole in the ceiling. One of the explosions must have weakened it.

I realised Luna was talking to me. "Alex? *Alex!*"

I looked up. "What?"

"Are you okay?"

"Sure. Fine."

Luna gave me a disbelieving look and pointed at my left arm.

I looked down to see that the sleeve was wet with blood. "Oh. Right." All of a sudden standing up felt really difficult. I slumped against the wall and slid down into a sitting position, wincing slightly.

"Alex!" Luna said.

"'M okay," I said halfheartedly.

"You're not okay. You're *shot*!" Luna made a move towards me and checked, holding back with a noise of frustration. "It's just the arm, right?"

"No," I said vaguely. "Don't think so." Now the frenzy of combat was over, it was so much harder to think. I couldn't remember what I was supposed to be doing.

"Then—can't you look or see how bad it is or—I don't know! Put a bandage on it, or something!"

"Didn't bring one." I laughed; somehow it seemed funny. "Used to. Had a first-aid kit. But so used to getting out of the way . . ."

Luna shook her head. "We can't stay here. Let's go."

"Okay."

Luna took a step back, then waited. "Come on!"

"Where?"

"What do you mean, where? *You* tell *me* where!"

I tried to remember but it was so difficult. My mind kept wanting to go back to looking into the future and every time I did I saw only darkness. But even staring into darkness felt easier than doing anything without my magic to rely on. Maybe if I sat there and kept trying it would come back. "Don't know," I said. "You think of something."

Luna looked at me in disbelief. Then all of a sudden, she exploded. "What—*no*!" She stared down at me, her hands balled up into fists. "I cannot believe this! You're ALWAYS lecturing me, you're ALWAYS telling me what to do, now the ONE TIME I need it you do THIS? What about Arachne? And Belthas? You're the only one who knows what's going on! Now *get up*!"

Somehow I found myself on my feet. I still wasn't sure what I was doing but the names struck a chord in my memory. "Arachne. Right." I tried to remember what the plan was. Stopping Belthas, that was it. I just wasn't sure how.

Luna shook her head. "This isn't working. You're no good like . . ." She chewed her lip. "Alex. *Alex!* What did Martin do?"

"He took my magic." Even saying it hurt. "I mean . . .

no, he couldn't." I tried to concentrate, to focus. "You can't take a mage's power without killing him. It's still . . . there. Everything that lets me use it is still there. The monkey's paw is just taking it. Giving it to him . . ."

Luna was silent. I looked up to see that her brow was furrowed, thinking. "Wait," she said. "You can't take a mage's power without killing him? Is that right?"

"Yeah."

Luna stared into space for a second, then her forehead cleared and she nodded. "I'll be right back."

I turned my head to watch as Luna walked over to the guard lying on the floor. She hesitated, then shook her head and reached down to pull something from the man's belt. It slid from its sheath with a quiet hiss and as I saw the light glint off it I realised it was a knife. Luna rose and came back, holding the blade awkwardly. I watched as she edged around me, keeping her distance so that she wouldn't pass too close. And I kept watching as she walked up the corridor towards where I'd last seen Martin.

Only then did I put it together. "No, Luna, wait!"

Luna looked at me, her expression a mixture of anger and something else. *"What?"*

"You— You don't have to do this."

Luna's voice was tight, on edge. "We've got to do something."

I shook my head. "No." All of a sudden I knew what to do. "There's another way."

ı ı ı ı ı ı ı ı ı

Martin had stopped screaming. He was lying curled up on his side, scratches on the floor where his shoes had scraped. His fingers were clenched, dug into his face, and blood trickled between them in a ghastly mask. He'd lost the gun but was still gripping the monkey's paw, his knuckles white on the lacquered tube. His breath was coming in short gasps and he didn't seem to know we were there.

Luna and I looked down at him for a second. "What happened?" Luna asked.

"He got what he wished for," I said absently. Thousands and millions of futures, pouring into his mind. There's a reason diviners are rare. I spent years building the mental discipline to be able to use my power without going mad. When I look into the future, it's like seeing through a lens: sometimes narrow and focused, sometimes wide and blurred, but always sorting, ordering, picking the futures I need and blocking out the rest. Martin didn't have a lens. He had all my power without any of my skill. He was seeing everything at once.

I knelt next to him. Deep scratches showed on Martin's face from where he'd clawed at his eyes, but his eyes stared blindly into space. "Martin," I said. I could keep talking and thinking as long as I stayed focused, but it was a struggle. I kept wanting to sink back into darkness and I didn't know how long I could keep it up. "The magic's killing you. You've still got the monkey's paw. Wish it back."

No response. Martin's eyes didn't flicker, and his breathing stayed the same, hoarse and ragged.

"Can he hear us?" Luna asked.

I shook my head. Martin had to be most of the way to insane. He probably couldn't even tell the difference between future and present anymore. "So?" Luna said.

I took a breath. "Give me that knife."

Luna set it down on the floor with a clink. I fumbled behind me and missed it twice before looking back around to pick it up, then turned back to Martin. My thoughts were starting to fray at the edges and I knew I didn't have much time. I took a deep breath, and focused. For this to work, I would have to genuinely mean to go through with it.

I forced myself to go back through my memories, thinking of how Martin had betrayed me and Luna. How he'd lied to us from the beginning, tried to use us, taking everything he could and leaving us to our deaths. Then I brought the knife forward in my good arm. The steel blade flashed in the light as I put it to Martin's throat for one quick, measured slash.

My magic senses danger by seeing the futures in which I'm hurt. As I see the futures in which I'm injured or killed, I change the decisions that lead to them. But it's painful. To avoid a future in which I die, I have to experience it. I've learnt to shield myself from the psychic shock of those visions, taking only a hazy glance, enough to know how to avoid that future and no more.

Martin didn't have a shield. In that instant, as I made the decision to kill him, Martin got to experience a million futures of me cutting his throat, a million visions of his own death, every one in perfect detail.

The scream from Martin's throat was like nothing on earth. I jumped back as he spasmed, every muscle in his body flailing, and his voice hurt my ears. *"Take it back!"*

And just that fast, it happened. My magic snapped back into me like a rubber band, the visions flooding back into my mind, glowing lines of light branching out into the darkness. I knew where I'd see Luna if I turned around to look at her. I knew the wound on my arm was painful but not fatal; it would hurt but I'd be able to keep using the arm if I forced myself. And I knew Martin was about to collapse in front of me.

Martin collapsed. I leant against the wall, closing my eyes, feeling my thoughts piecing themselves together again bit by bit. The relief was incredible and I shivered as I remembered the feeling of darkness. I was sure I'd just gotten the material for a whole new set of nightmares.

"Alex?" Luna asked.

"I'm okay," I said. A stray memory nagged at me: Hadn't that guard hit me, with that last burst of fire? I checked and this time my divination magic found an answer: two small holes in my cloak. My mist cloak had saved me, its camouflage blurring my outline just enough to make the shots miss.

I patted it affectionately, then checked my watch. Fifteen minutes. "We'd better go."

Luna was staring down at Martin and when she spoke her voice was toneless. "Are those protections still working?"

Martin was unconscious, lying still on the floor, and as I looked into the futures in which Luna or I moved in to finish him, I saw that nothing would stop us. The monkey's paw had taken back all that it had given. "They're gone."

Luna looked at Martin for a few seconds more and when she finally turned her eyes to me there was something cold in them. "You shouldn't have stopped me."

I looked back at Luna for a few seconds before speaking quietly. "I don't think his life is yours to take."

Luna held my gaze a moment longer, then stepped back around the corner. As I moved past, I felt the futures of her approaching Martin fade away. I headed for the stairs and Luna followed.

chapter 11

By the time we reached the ground floor, the fighting had died down. The manor was a wasteland of smoke and rubble, small fires burning amidst the smoke, but the stone and concrete had weathered the attacks and the structure was stable. I could sense two or three guards still around, but they were keeping their distance.

As we came up the steps, the radio in my pocket crackled. I pulled it out with my good arm. "Sonder."

"Alex! Finally! Did you find Luna?"

I turned the radio's volume up and tossed it to Luna. "It's for you."

Luna caught it awkwardly. " Hi, Sonder."

I could hear the relief in Sonder's voice. "You're okay?"

"I'm fine. What's happening?"

"It's crazy out here," Sonder sounded tense. "I saw the back door explode and Cinder fought his way in but—Alex, are you there? Cinder got driven out. He's fighting on the west slope."

I was analysing a route up to the second floor. "Fighting what?"

"A mantis golem. Belthas got a mantis golem!" I could hear distant sounds of battle over the radio. "It's trying to kill Cinder, Cinder's trying to melt it—"

"Who's winning?"

There was a pause. "Neither, I think."

I checked my watch. We had a little over ten minutes. "We can't wait for Cinder," I decided. "I'm going after Belthas. Luna, Sonder is up the mountainside from here. You can circle around and—"

"*Screw* that." Luna's eyes flashed. "I'm going with you."

I looked back at her for a second, then smiled slightly. "Sonder," I said loudly. "We're going for Belthas's sanctum on the second floor. If you can get a message to Cinder, tell him."

Sonder sounded confused. "Wait—both of you?"

Luna switched the radio off and tossed it to me. We headed upstairs.

We passed several charred bodies on the way up. There were several guards still lurking, but they stayed out of our way. It looked like there'd been some fast natural selection amongst Belthas's security force and the survivors had been the ones who'd figured out that attacking a mage was a very bad idea. As we climbed, burnt flesh, burnt wiring, and smoke mixed together to make a nauseating stench.

The top floor was luxurious but impersonal, like an expensive hotel. A thick carpet lined the central corridor and I could feel the presence of minor magical effects from behind the wooden doors. All was untouched; Cinder must not have gotten this far. I moved down the corridor, watching for an ambush, Luna a few steps behind.

The corridor ended in an anteroom. Two double doors were set into the far wall and I knew they led into Belthas's sanctum. Curtains were drawn over the windows, a wardrobe stood to one side, and several tables held curios.

I stopped in the doorway and waited. The room was silent. There was no sound from outside; the floor had been sound-proofed. Seconds ticked past.

"You might as well come out," I said to the room.

Silence.

I lifted my gun, letting it make a quiet metallic noise. My left arm hurt a little but it was manageable. "How about I shoot those curtains?"

The curtains moved and Meredith stepped out.

For someone in the middle of a battle, Meredith looked far better than she ought to. Somehow she'd found the opportunity to change clothes and was wearing a black figure-hugging outfit that probably would have been distracting if I'd been in any mood to care. It was her eyes I was watching and I could tell from the look in them that she was afraid. She stood, on edge, trying to watch both me and the gun.

"I know why you're here," I said quietly. "Belthas put you out here to slow us down. You said yes because you thought you could stay out of sight till the fighting was over." I nodded back down the corridor. "Run. Now. If you stay, Cinder'll kill you. If you get in my way, I will."

Meredith hesitated, and for a moment I saw the choices branching before her. Then, slowly, she came towards me, keeping her eyes on me. I let her go by. For a moment it looked as though she was about to say something, then she walked away.

Meredith passed Luna without a glance. As she did a tendril of Luna's curse flicked out over Meredith, soaking into her to leave a faint silvery glow. Meredith walked back the way we came and vanished. I looked at Luna and raised an eyebrow.

"What?" Luna said. She sounded a little annoyed. "It won't kill her." She paused. "Probably."

I glanced down the corridor, then turned away. "What if she comes back?" Luna asked.

"She won't."

ı ı ı ı ı ı ı ı ı

The double doors to Belthas's sanctum swung open with a creak.

The room was big: the size of a small dance hall, wider than it was long, with a high ceiling. There were no windows but the roof seemed to be made of some one-way glass, giving a view of the dark sky. Tables and workbenches were scattered around the edge, filled with components and supplies, but aside from that the room was bare: If a fight started I wouldn't have much cover. Another set of double doors in the back corner stood open, and through them I could see shelves.

In front of the doors, set into the floor at the end of the room, was the biggest ritual circle I'd ever seen. It was done in a triple ring design with the outermost ring cast in copper, the middle in silver, and the inner in gold, with runes and sigils inlaid between them. Three lecterns stood in the innermost ring in a triangle, and upon them were laid a wand, a book, and a knife.

Belthas stood at the centre. He'd changed into blue ceremonial robes of the kind used by the Council for formal occasions and he looked every inch the magus in his sanctum. "Verus," Belthas said without looking up. He was tracing lines in the book with his right hand, while holding one of the iridescent purple rods in his left. "I hope you know I'll be taking this damage out of your pay."

"You can call this my two weeks' notice," I said. I had a clear line of sight. I looked into the future of my shooting at Belthas—

—and saw him deflect the bullets effortlessly with an ice shield. "I have to admit," Belthas said, "you've caused me quite an extraordinary amount of trouble."

"Funny. I was about to say the same thing." I could feel the room thrumming with power; the ritual was nearly complete. As I concentrated, I saw that the focus was the rod in

Belthas's hand. It shared a sympathetic link with its twin embedded in Arachne: Once Belthas finished, it would act as the conduit to drain her energy into him. I didn't know what it would do to Belthas, but I knew what it would do to Arachne.

"I have to ask," Belthas said. His tone was mildly curious. "Why *are* you so concerned about these creatures? If you'd just given me the elemental and the spider all this could have been resolved peacefully."

"Belthas," I said, "trust me. You wouldn't understand."

"They're not mages. They're not even human."

"And I still like them more than you. Though that's not saying much."

Luna was hanging back in the corridor, waiting for my lead. I ran through different angles of attack and saw Belthas block them in every future I tried. Most of Belthas's power was going into the ritual but he had more than enough left to protect himself.

But in that case, why wasn't he attacking? I spread my arms. "What's the matter? Don't feel like taking a shot?"

Belthas sighed. "In case it's escaped your attention, I'm somewhat busy. If this is the best you can do, I'd appreciate it if you would come back later."

I took a couple of steps forward. The more I looked into the future, the more certain I was that Belthas couldn't reach me. The ritual circle must be acting as a barrier. He couldn't get offensive spells through it.

But if I walked into the circle . . . I winced at the image. Ow. I wouldn't make it two steps. Ice magic does *really* nasty things to flesh.

"Alex," Luna whispered from the doorway.

I knew she was about to suggest using her magic against him. "Wouldn't work," I whispered back.

"I could get closer—"

"From outside that circle's shielding him," I whispered. "And if you got inside he'd take you apart."

"I must say, I'm a little disappointed," Belthas said, ignoring our conversation. "The more . . . questionable aspects to your background are well known but most mages had been under the impression you were trying to put being a Dark mage behind you. Now you're switching sides? Again?"

"Should have read those reports more carefully," I said. I signalled Luna to stay put and began moving down the length of the room. I kept a wary eye on Belthas as I approached, my precognition alert for danger. "The reason I left was to get away from people like you."

"Which is why you're working for Cinder?" Belthas shook his head. "Honestly, Verus. You break into my home with a Dark cabal and still think you're on the right side? Which one of us has caused more deaths lately?"

"That might be because you keep yourself an army of minions."

"And who made the choice to kill them?" Belthas asked. He hadn't looked up and was still tracing through the ritual in the book. "Those men had families, you know. I do so hate writing condolence letters."

I felt a flare of anger and bit down an answer. I was less than thirty feet from Belthas, just seconds at a run. But then, past Belthas, I caught sight of something in the room beyond. It looked like a bed with someone on it. I moved along to get a better view. It *was* a bed . . . and lying on it was Rachel, wearing what looked like a hospital gown. Her eyes were closed and an IV drip hung from a stand. There was something else next to her. I took another step—

My precognition warned me just in time. I leapt backwards as golden energy slashed the air with a hiss, passing through the spot I'd been in a second ago. I tripped and fell, turned it into a backwards roll, and scrambled away as heavy footfalls sounded from the storeroom. "Oh, didn't I mention?" Belthas said. "Your new friend Cinder drew away that mantis golem . . ."

And a hulking shape appeared in the doorway. ". . . But what made you think I only had one?" Belthas asked, just as the golem fired.

Mantis golems are the personal guards of the Council and only the most well-connected of Light mages have them. They look like seven-foot-tall humanoid praying mantises made of silver and gold, and they're bloody lethal. This one was carrying two blades and an energy projector that spat a rapid-fire stream of bolts. I jumped back as the line of fire walked towards me, dodged *through* the shots in a move I'd never have dared to try if I'd stopped to think about it, kicked one of the benches over, and dropped behind it as the stream of bolts swept back over my head again.

The stream of fire cut off as the golem lost sight of its target, and the heavy footfalls began again as it started to walk around the circle towards me. I popped up and sighted on the thing—although mantis golems are damn near invulnerable to attack magic a lucky hit can damage their joints or sensors—but I only managed to get off one burst before another volley of fire forced me to duck down. This time the golem sent a second volley of fire through the bench where I'd been and I rolled right just in time. I was focusing all my attention on the immediate future, thinking only about surviving the next couple of seconds.

Which was why I didn't realise Luna had stepped out of cover until I caught sight of her in my peripheral vision. She was standing in the open, staring at the golem and concentrating, and I could see a steady stream of silver mist flowing from her to sink into the metal monster. She was within the golem's field of vision but it didn't turn towards her, its simple programming not recognising her as a threat.

But Belthas did. He said something in another language and the golem stopped and turned towards Luna with a hiss of metal. I came up with a shout and fired, knowing the shots wouldn't do any damage but hoping they'd get its attention.

The bullets glanced away and the golem locked onto its new target, oblivious.

The first volley would have killed Luna but for her curse. It's so deadly one can easily forget that its original function was to serve as a protection, drawing luck away from everyone else to bring it to its subject. Normally Luna never trips or falls—the curse protects her from any accident, no matter how small—but as the golem fired she stumbled on the smooth floor and went sprawling, the spread of bolts hissing over her head. The second volley missed too, kicking up splinters as Luna rolled to the left and started to rise, but then the golem planted its feet squarely and I knew the third shot would hit.

It didn't. The golem's movements suddenly slowed, and it took a second, maybe two, to fire. When it did, the energy bolt drifted out of the barrel as if in slow motion, accelerating as it moved away. By the time it hit real speed Luna was on the other side of the room, and the energy did nothing but tear up the floor.

I looked right and saw Sonder in the doorway, his eyes narrowed, concentrating on the golem. As my mage's sight adapted I saw the spell he was holding—it was a slow time field, warping space around the golem so that to us the construct was only a fraction as fast as it should have been. The golem tracked Luna, the barrel of its projector moving as if underwater, but between the delay and Luna's curse there was no way it could hit her now. Stray shots exploded bottles and items on the benches until Luna vanished from sight. Before it could adjust its aim I sighted on the projector, searched through the futures until I found a weak spot, then fired, emptying my magazine. The bullets slowed as they approached the golem until I could almost see them, the impacts sparking along the projector's barrel in slow motion until a lucky hit sent flashes of energy crackling back into the hilt as the weapon short-circuited. The golem started to advance towards Luna, its movements ponderous and slow.

I ran to where Sonder was standing. "Hey," he said through gritted teeth, his eyes locked on the golem. "Need some help?"

I ejected the empty magazine and snapped in a new one. "Good timing." I could see sweat beading on Sonder's forehead; slowing time is not kid stuff. Luna and the golem were playing tag on the other side of the room, Luna still pouring her curse into the golem for all it was worth. With its ranged weapon destroyed and its movement slowed, the golem couldn't catch her . . . for now.

"Can't hold this . . . long," Sonder said. His knuckles were white where he was gripping the door frame.

"You won't have to." I snatched a glance back at Belthas, still standing in the circle. The ambient energy had built higher and I knew we had only minutes before he finished. I looked into the future to see how long—

—and my heart lifted. "Sonder," I said. "Thirty more seconds."

"'Kay," Sonder managed. He was starting to tremble and I knew how much strain he was under. But whether through how difficult it was to counter or just its sheer power, Luna's curse was working better, and I could see the telltale silver glow building up around the golden construct. I waited, counting off the seconds, then shouted out. "Luna, this way! Run!"

Luna gave me one startled glance, then sprinted. The golem turned to follow. Trying to close with Luna, it had come nearly against the wall.

The side of the room blew in with a crack of thunder. The concussion sent me and Sonder staggering and with a groaning, snapping sound, the entire corner of the room fell in, the walls and roof coming down in a roar. The mantis golem disappeared under tons of concrete, the silver and gold of its body buried in rubble. A cloud of choking dust covered the room and a cold breeze swept through, carrying with it the scent of scorched earth. I looked up to see that an entire corner of the sanctum was gone, open to the dark sky.

Cinder landed on the pile of rubble with a crunch. He looked left to see Luna, who was crouching between the debris with wide eyes, all of the falling stone having somehow missed her, and his gaze swept the room before locking onto Belthas. Cinder's hands came up and orange-red fire licked around them, darkening and brightening at the same time until it hurt to look at. The smell of brimstone filled the air.

Belthas looked up just in time to see what was coming, and for an instant his face registered absolute disgust. "Shit."

The fire blast was hot enough to melt metal. If I hadn't closed my eyes it would have blinded me, and it was so bright that even through my eyelids I saw it as a white-hot beam. The circle resisted it for maybe a hundredth of a second before collapsing, and as it did I felt the snap as the ritual broke, the accumulated energy scattering away. A triangulated ice shield flicked up around Belthas just before the beam struck, vaporising the shield in an explosion of steam.

The echoes died away, leaving only the drip of water and the hiss of something evaporating. The sanctum was filled with mist. As it cleared, I made out the forms of Cinder, standing on the rubble, eyes narrowed as he searched for Belthas, with Luna a little way behind. Sonder came to his feet, coughing. "Did he get him?"

Ice slashed out of the mist, three separate strikes of frozen air mixed with razor-edged shards. Cinder's fire shield exploded them into steam but another volley hit a second later, sending him stumbling back as Belthas strode out of the mist. A nimbus of icy blue light glowed around him, the energy forming crystalline shapes, and his eyes glowed

azure. There were scorch marks across his robes but he
didn't look injured. "Cinder." His voice was cold and tightly
controlled. "Verus. Congratulations. You have finally made
me angry."

"Sonder!" I shouted.

Sonder turned in surprise and I shoved him in the chest,
sending him sprawling just as ice shards cut the air where
we'd been standing. It missed me by a foot, but the cold was
intense enough to leave frost on my coat and freeze the blood
on my arm. I dived back just in time to avoid a second strike
and scrambled for cover.

As I saw Belthas, though, I felt a chill. Belthas had nearly
killed me and Sonder without even *paying attention*. He was
facing Cinder, sending lightning-quick slashes of ice and
crystalline blades at him from different directions, sparing
only an occasional flick of a hand to send an attack my way.
Cinder fought back with walls and columns of fire, burning
away Belthas's attacks in flashes of energy, only barely holding his own as the walls and benches ignited and shattered
around them.

I caught sight of Luna, hiding behind a chunk of rubble.
"Get out of here!"

Luna hesitated.

I snarled and raised my voice over the sounds of battle.
"Goddamn it, I gave you an *order*, apprentice! This is way
out of your league, now *run!*"

Luna stared wide-eyed for a second, then jumped up and
ran, just as a strike from Belthas shattered her hiding place.
I didn't have time to make sure she got out. I sprinted down
the length of the room, making myself as hard a target as
possible.

Blades of ice gouged chunks from the walls and searing
fire burnt the stone black. The air was filled with mist and
smoke one minute, burnt to nothingness the next. I sent
three-round bursts at Belthas whenever I could get a shot
but they glanced harmlessly from his shields. I knew now

why Belthas hadn't been scared of Cinder and Deleo. He was holding me off while driving Cinder back and I didn't think he was even going all-out. Cinder had stopped attacking; he was backing away down towards the circle, a silent snarl on his face, all his energies going into the shield of flame around him that was keeping Belthas's strikes from tearing him apart. And then, all of a sudden, the sounds of battle stopped.

I peered out cautiously from a pile of debris that had been a workbench. Cinder was standing in Belthas's circle, the lecterns melted and broken at his feet. I didn't dare stick my head out to get a look at Belthas but I knew he was a little way back.

"You were a fool to come here." Belthas didn't sound out of breath. "You and Deleo couldn't defeat me together. What did you expect to do alone?"

Cinder didn't answer. Flame smouldered around his hands. "I can kill you through that circle," Belthas said calmly. "It'll just take longer." I heard the crunch of rubble as he moved around closer to me. "But I think I'd rather finish this quickly."

Belthas drew level with the doors to the storeroom and I saw what he was going to do. Rachel was still lying unconscious on the bed, visible through the dust and smoke. Belthas lifted a hand towards her and blue light gathered around him.

Cinder got between Belthas and Rachel just as Belthas fired. The ice snuffed out Cinder's shield with a crack and he went spinning to the floor.

But to break Cinder's shield Belthas had needed to draw on his full power, and just for an instant, he wasn't focused on me. I came around the bench at a dead run, my left hand holding the gun, my right reaching into my pocket. Belthas spun, a shield coming up.

A gun's no use against a battle-mage who knows it's there—but it can make a good distraction. The shield was between Belthas and my left side, and as I hit the ice, feeling the deadly cold freeze my body, my right hand came out of my pocket holding the dragon's fang. As Belthas lifted his hand for the spell that would kill me, I spun off the shield and as my fingertips brushed Belthas I shouted the command word.

It was nothing like the gate spells that mages use. A normal gate opens up a similarity between two points in space, forming a portal you can step through. It takes time. This didn't. One minute we were in the shattered remnants of Belthas's sanctum, dust and smoke filling the air, the next we were in an vast cavern.

And there was silence.

Belthas's shield and the dragon's fang had disappeared. I stood toe to toe with Belthas, my fingers still resting against his arm. For an instant we stared into each other's eyes.

Then Belthas hit me with an ice hammer the size of a door.

I twisted to soften the impact but there was no way to dodge this one. If the blow had hit me square on it would have broken my ribs. Instead it only smashed the breath from my lungs, lifted me off my feet, and slammed me down on the rock ten feet away.

Belthas walked forward as I struggled to breathe, stopping with his hand aimed towards me. I looked up to see a deadly blue-white glow hovering on his palm. His voice could have been pleasant, if you didn't meet his eyes. "Explain. Quickly."

I couldn't speak. I fought for breath, trying to make my lungs work. "Verus," Belthas said when I didn't answer. "I have had a long and frustrating day." He sounded calm but I could hear the tightly controlled anger beneath the surface. "Thanks to you, I am going to have to rebuild my plans from the ground up. Now on top of that, you appear to have transported me from my sanctum. So if you do not explain exactly where we are and how you broke through my gate ward, I am going to kill you."

I looked up at Belthas and started to laugh. I couldn't help it. I knew Belthas wasn't kidding, that I was literally seconds away from death. But somehow it was so funny I couldn't stop.

Belthas just waited and I could feel cold hatred radiating from him. He wasn't planning to let me live no matter what I told him. I tried to speak, but between laughing and the pain in my ribs, I couldn't manage it. Only after a few deep breaths was I able to get the words out. "No one . . . ever believes me."

The glow around Belthas's hand brightened and he sighted on my head. "Last chance."

"Doesn't matter . . . how many times." I stopped laughing and met Belthas's eyes. "Look behind you."

I'm pretty good at telling when someone's lying to me. I guess Belthas was the same. Something in my face must have told him I wasn't bluffing.

He turned around.

The dragon was staring down at Belthas. It made me think of a mountain looking down on an insect.

I'll give Belthas credit: He didn't freeze. I saw the blood drain from his face but his reaction was instant. His hands came up to cast a spell.

The dragon flicked Belthas with one claw.

Human bodies are tough. But they've got their limits. When a body is struck by something the size of a city block moving at the speed of a freight train, the results are . . . hard to convey. *Broken*, *torn*, or even *shattered* doesn't describe it. The best word I can come up with is *shredded*.

Drops of blood splashed my face. The dragon and I watched as the bits scattered over a square mile of cavern.

It took about ten seconds for the pieces to finish hitting the ground. Then the dragon turned its massive head, looking down at me with diamond eyes.

"Um," I said once I'd caught my breath. "Any chance I could have another one of those things?"

chapter 12

It was two weeks later.

"How much longer?" I muttered out of the side of my mouth.

"Shh," Sonder whispered.

"Did she stop to do her hair or what?"

"*Shh!*"

We were standing in a high, arched hall, the walls russet and gold. Chandeliers hung from the ceiling and rows of stylised lamps were mounted on the walls, filling every inch of the room with light. About twenty people were scattered around, talking quietly. The acoustics of the hall made them hard to hear, but Sonder and I were up on the stage and anything we said would be amplified.

But I'd been waiting nearly an hour and was getting restless. "Do these things always take this long?" I whispered.

"Alex, can't you please be quiet?" Sonder pleaded. He was wearing brown-and-cream ceremonial robes. "You're not supposed to talk till the ceremony starts."

I thought about asking why but decided it wasn't really fair. At least the outfit Arachne had made for me was as comfortable as ever. She'd gone for a black design with slashes of midnight blue, and while it made me feel like a giant bat, I had to admit it looked good. Off to one side, Talisid was speaking quietly with Ilmarin. Talisid had agreed to preside and find a second, and had arranged the venue too. Before I could open my mouth again, the doors at the far end swung open and two people walked in.

The girl on the right looked twenty or so, with black shoulder-length hair and odd reddish-brown eyes. We'd met only once, though I'd gotten a good feeling from her; she had a gentle manner I found appealing. Sonder had known her through some of his old classes. Her name was Anne.

Luna walked a little behind and to the side. Her robe was done to Council standards but Arachne had somehow made it look better than any apprentice robe ought to. It was pure white with green highlights that set off Luna's pale skin, and the conversation died away as heads turned to watch the girls. Anne led Luna up the steps and the room fell silent as Talisid stepped forward. "Who comes before us?"

Anne and Luna came to a stop. "One who seeks knowledge," Anne said in a soft voice.

"How does she approach?"

"In darkness, unknowing of the Light; in humility, knowing of her ignorance; and in faith, that she might become what she is not."

"Then let her step forward."

Luna did so and Anne moved to one side. "Approach and state your name," Talisid said.

"Luna Mancuso," Luna said. I knew she must be nervous but her voice was steady.

"Luna Mancuso," Talisid said. "Do you swear before this Council to accept the guidance of a master? Do you swear to serve without doubt, to obey without question, and to endure without surrender? And do you swear to serve your

master, and through him the Council and the Light, in all
ways and in all things until such day that you may take your
place among us as a journeyman mage?"

"I do so swear," Luna said. Amazingly, she didn't choke
on the *obey* part.

"Then I ask of this Council," Talisid said. "Is there one
among us willing to take on this charge?"

That was my cue. "I am willing," I said, stepping forward.

"And what do you extend?"

"To teach her in lore and magic; to protect her from others and herself; to aid and sustain her whatever may come;
and to take responsibility for her deeds for good or ill."

"The offer of Mage Verus is accepted," Talisid said. "I
stand witness."

"I stand witness," Ilmarin said.

"Then it is agreed," Talisid said. "This Council is
adjourned."

: : : : : : : : : :

With the ceremony done, the atmosphere in the hall
relaxed. Luna was approached by other mages and
before long she was at the centre of a loose crowd of people.
"I didn't expect this many," I said.

"It shouldn't be too much of a surprise," Talisid said. We
were standing a little way to the side, watching from a distance, each of us holding a glass of wine. "You're acquiring
something of a reputation."

"Really?"

"I didn't say it was a *good* reputation," Talisid said dryly.
"You're now suspected of having a hand in the disappear-
ance of two separate Light mages. With good reason, I
might add."

"I could say they started it."

"Somehow I don't think that would help very much."

Luna was talking with Ilmarin, with Sonder hovering

nearby. The silver mist of Luna's curse was more tightly concentrated than before, surrounding Luna in a radius of one arm's length rather than two. The practice I'd made her put in seemed to have paid off. "They seem more interested in her, anyway."

"Verus," Talisid said. "It's nothing to do with interest. Belthas had a well-deserved reputation as one of the most dangerous battle-mages in the country. That you had a disagreement with him is not a secret. People are expecting him to finish what he started. When he doesn't return . . ."

I watched the crowd, not answering. "Ah, I'm sorry," Talisid said. "Let me correct myself. *If* he doesn't return . . . then a great many people are going to become very interested in you."

"Can't wait."

"I expect some will be quite impressed," Talisid said. "Possibly not for the reasons you'd like. But either way, you're going to be quite famous. And your apprentice as well."

I looked at Talisid sharply. He met my gaze, eyes calm. "You should probably spend some time considering the subject. I suspect that in the next—oh, let's say two months or so—you'll be approached by quite a few people with propositions for you. If I were you, I'd think carefully about how to respond."

"And what about you, Talisid?" I said. "What do you get out of all this?"

Talisid looked back at me for a second, then smiled slightly. "Perhaps some day I'll be able to tell you. Good night, Verus."

I watched Talisid go.

⁙ ⁙ ⁙ ⁙ ⁙

I t took the best part of an hour before Luna and Sonder could disengage themselves and make their way over to me. As Luna got out of range of the other mages, I saw her slump a little. "Whew," Luna said as she reached me. "Alex, can you back off? This is *hard*."

"I saw," I said, keeping a safe distance. As Luna relaxed her control, the silver mist of her curse spread out again to its usual range. "Good job."

"You thought I'd get the lines wrong, didn't you?"

"I was starting to wonder if you'd even show up."

"You'd be slow too if you had to do your clothes and hair without anyone else touching them."

"Was everything okay with Anne?" Sonder asked.

Luna shook her head. "It was fine. She didn't even ask why." She gave me a half smile. "Didn't invite Cinder?"

I laughed. Cinder had been as good as his word back on that night. Despite his injuries he'd brought Sonder and Luna back to London after I'd gone and even dropped them off at my shop. Then he'd taken Rachel with him, still unconscious, and vanished into the darkness. "Is it going to be okay?" Sonder said seriously. "I mean, none of the others are going to be coming after us, right?"

I shook my head. "Belthas is gone. His men don't have any reason to come for us anymore. Same goes for Meredith. She was only in it for herself."

"What about Levistus?" Luna said quietly.

Sonder glanced around, nervous, but no one was within earshot. The gathering was starting to break up, mages strolling towards the doors. "He was the one behind Belthas, right?" Luna said. "I mean, this is twice we've messed up his plans. He's not going to be happy, is he?"

I nodded. "We can't do anything about him. Not directly." I smiled slightly. "But look on the bright side. Every time he's taken a shot at us, it's turned out badly for him. Maybe he'll think twice before trying it again."

Sonder looked around to see that the hall was all but empty. "Should we . . . ?"

"Yeah," I said. "Let's not keep her waiting."

W e travelled across London and onto the darkness of the Heath. A particularly stupid pair of muggers tried to squeeze some money out of us. That didn't work out so well for them. After the brief interlude, we made our way to Arachne's lair.

Walking back into Arachne's cavern felt like coming home. The walls were covered with colours again, hangings and tapestries and rugs making a background of red and green and blue, while the furniture was as piled with clothes as it had ever been. The chairs and couches damaged in the attack had been replaced, and the blast marks on the floor had been cleaned away. Only in the side tunnel to the store-rooms was there any sign of violence: Although the rubble had been cleared, there was a blackened gash in the roof where Garrick's mines had brought it down.

It was the first time I'd been back inside. The dragon *had* given me another tooth—but one that had worked differently. When I used it on Arachne, she'd been transported, but I hadn't. There'd been no way for me to know where she'd gone or if she was even alive. I'd had no choice but to leave, and when I next returned, the entrance to her lair had been sealed. I'd managed to talk to Arachne only once since then and I hadn't seen her. I hoped she was all right.

The three of us moved a little way inside and then stopped. "Arachne?" Luna called. "Are you there?"

There was a moment's silence—and then with a rustle, Arachne appeared from the tunnel, cobalt-blue highlights shining off her black body. "Luna, Alex!" Arachne called. "There you are! And who's this?"

"Um, I'm Sonder." Sonder gave an awkward little bow. "Pleased to meet you."

"Of course, Alex has told me about everything you've done. And Luna, I hear I should be congratulating you?"

We clustered around Arachne and I reached out to stroke

one of her legs. She looked as healthy and well as she'd ever been and I found myself smiling. Somehow, it felt as though everything was right again.

We stayed late that night. Arachne's a charming host once you get over her appearance and it didn't take her any time at all to put Sonder at his ease. It was the first time all of us had been in one place and able to relax and I'd forgotten how nice it felt. Luna was the focus of the evening, wanting to know everything she could about what being an apprentice would be like, and both Sonder and Arachne had a lot to tell her. Arachne's seen whole generations of apprentices grow up and Sonder himself had only been a journeyman for less than a year. Oddly, I had almost as much to learn as Luna. I'd never seen much of the Light mage's apprenticeship system—and the apprenticeship system I *had* seen was one that I was absolutely not going to inflict upon her. Luna wasn't the only one who was going to need to learn some new tricks.

It was after midnight when Sonder started yawning, with Luna following a little way behind. After the third set of yawns I spoke up. "All right, kids. Time for bed."

"Really?" Sonder said. He sounded disappointed; he'd been in the middle of quizzing Arachne about some obscure historical period I'd barely heard of.

"In a bit," Luna said.

"No," I said firmly. "We're meeting Talisid to pick up your materials tomorrow morning. Off with you."

Luna gave me a quick look, then got to her feet. "Thanks, Arachne."

"You're welcome, dear. Congratulations again."

"Alex?" Sonder said. "You're not coming?"

"I've got a few things to finish up. You and Luna go back together, okay?"

"Okay!"

"Good-bye," Luna said to Arachne. "Night, Alex."

The two of them walked away down the corridor. I leant

back on the couch, listening to their footsteps as they faded away, waiting until I heard the distant rumble of the entrance opening and then closing again.

"She acts more like it now," Arachne said.

I smiled. "Glad to hear it."

"It's good you worked things out."

I glanced around the walls. "You did a good job cleaning the place up." My eyes wandered to the jagged roof of the side tunnel. "How many bodies were there?"

"Three." Arachne's tone of voice suggested it was an ordinary question.

"You didn't find a fourth?" I nodded at the tunnel. "Under the rubble down there?"

"No. Why?"

"Just wondering." So no trace of Garrick, and if Arachne hadn't found his body, I was pretty sure he wasn't dead. Probably he'd set up an escape route ahead of time. He'd always struck me as the type to plan ahead. "You're okay?"

"Perfectly fine. It took me a little while to recover but that focus didn't do any permanent damage." Arachne paused. "Of course, if the ritual had been completed . . ."

"I know."

"Thank you."

I looked up in surprise. Arachne was looming over me, her legs on either side of the couch. Her presence was at odds with the sound of her voice. "I know how much danger you put yourself in for me."

"Uh . . . that's okay." I couldn't help but feel that the whole thing had been partly my fault. After all, the way Belthas had managed to break in had been through Luna and Martin . . .

"No," Arachne looked down at me with her eight eyes. "Alex, I've lived a long time. A very long time. I've seen many mages and there have been some I could trust as much as you. But not many. I've never known why some mages are loyal to creatures like me when other mages see us as monsters, but I've learnt to know it when I see it. I see it in you and I'm grateful. If you ever need my help, you'll have it."

I didn't know what to say. "Thank you," I said at last, and rested a hand on one of Arachne's legs. I can't really read Arachne's expressions but I think if she could, she would have smiled.

We talked a while, about old times and new, remembering past stories and wondering about what was yet to come. Finally I looked into the future and sighed. "Well, I'd better go take care of something."

Arachne gave me her equivalent of a nod. "I understand."

I rose and stretched, then paused. "Arachne? I know you don't like talking about yourself—but I'd like to know. Why did that dragon help us?"

Arachne was quiet for a little while before speaking. "A creator can be as a mother."

I looked at her, puzzled.

"You would recognise her name." Oddly, Arachne sounded as if she were smiling. "I expect you'll work it out some day."

I thought about it as I made the journey back up the tunnel, and as I did, something else occurred to me. When the dragon had given me the tooth, I'd assumed it was meant for Arachne. I'd thought that by using it against Belthas I was going against the dragon's plan, and I'd wondered if the dragon might not be very happy about it.

But now I thought about it, the dragon had never actually *said* who I was supposed to use it on.

I stepped out into the cool night air and walked up the slope of the ravine as the entrance closed behind me with a faint rumble. There's an old tree trunk near the ravine, one that fell many years ago. The park rangers cleaned it up and tidied away the dead branches but left the log where it was, and I sat down on it and looked up at the sky. It was a clear night, and the autumn stars shone down through the fuzz of the city lights, the Square of Pegasus high to the southwest while Orion rose in the east. It wasn't silent—even on the Heath, London's never really silent—but it was as quiet as it gets. The only sounds were the faint murmur of nighttime traffic and the wind in the leaves.

I waited.

I heard him before I saw him: dragging footsteps mixed with the crunch of undergrowth. He fell once on his way up the hill, lying still for a moment before pulling himself to his feet. I waited for him to get close enough, then when he was within twenty feet I switched on my torch, keeping it pointed down and away.

The figure standing before me was a wreck. The clothes were ripped, dirty, and threadbare. The once-blond hair had been rained on and dirtied until it was a brownish mess, and the eyes blinked, squinting in the light. He looked like he'd walked the whole way from Scotland. Maybe he had.

It took a good few seconds before a light of recognition came on in those eyes. "You."

I looked back at him steadily. "Hello, Martin."

Martin just stared at me.

"I was expecting you sooner," I said when Martin didn't speak. "I guess you didn't have anyone to give you a lift."

"You," Martin said again. His voice shook. "You've got it. Why? I've seen it, all of them, all of it, should be killing you, you're just *there*, you're sitting there, you're . . ."

"You can't learn to be a mage in a day, Martin."

"Couldn't be, I saw it, I had it." Martin shook his head, distracted. "Wrong. Shouldn't be dark, should . . ." He trailed off, muttering to himself.

"You know," I said after a moment, "I spent a long time trying to figure out what to do when you made it here. And the funny thing? I realised I didn't actually want you dead. Kind of weird. I mean, you nearly got us all killed and it's not like I'm all that great at being forgiving."

Martin glanced at me, then shook his head and looked away, muttering "not that, not that" under his breath. "I don't know," I said. "I guess I could say you can't do us much damage anymore but that's not really true, is it? Maybe it's because of Luna. I think she actually loved you. God knows that was a bad enough mistake but I don't really like the idea of her first relationship in however long ending like this." I let out a breath. "Or maybe it's just that I've seen enough people die lately."

Martin didn't react at Luna's name. "So I'll tell you the truth," I said. "Just like that day you came into my shop. Stop using the monkey's paw. Drop it, leave it, whatever. If you do, I promise you'll live. I don't know how much of your mind you'll get back, but you'll have a chance."

Martin stared through me, then laughed, a high sound that made my hairs rise. "Tricking, tricking . . ." His eyes narrowed and he snarled. "Liar! Liar, liar, liar! *You* did it, it was you! Should have worked, all of it, your fault, *your* fault!" Martin raised his right hand. His fingers were grubby and caked with dirt but the monkey's paw was untouched, pale in the dim light. "One more wish, you know, don't you? Been waiting, waiting . . ."

"Martin," I said. "Trust me. You don't want to do that."

Martin laughed again, his voice wild. "Coward liar, coward liar . . . I know what it does, you couldn't, too scared! Why not, hm? All this, anyone would use it, crazy not to use it . . ." A fine tremor was going up his arm as he held the monkey's paw, levelled at me like a knife. "*I* know. *You* couldn't see."

I sighed. "You know something, Martin? People like you—Belthas, Meredith, all of you—you make it *really* hard to be a good person. I just attacked a Light sanctum and killed pretty near everyone inside. I worked with one Dark mage and rescued another." I stared into the darkness. "All those years ago, I ran away from Richard . . . but if he could see me now, would he really be all that upset?" I looked at

Martin. "And then I look at you. And I wonder how big a deal it would really be if I went the rest of the way."

"You're scared, I know you are." The glow of the torch shone back from Martin's manic eyes. "No more. All of it, I lost it, you too." He aimed the monkey's paw straight at me. "I wish. I wish for you to die!"

I looked back at Martin in silence.

Martin held my gaze for a moment, then puzzlement crossed his face. He looked at the monkey's paw, shook it. "Die. Supposed to be dead, what's wrong, why not?"

I rose, stepped to one side, not taking my eyes off Martin. He brandished the monkey's paw at me. "Die. Die!" He snarled in rage. "Why not? *Why isn't it working?*"

"It's working," I said quietly. I could feel a surge of magic building from inside the item, slow but inexorable, like a rolling wave. I began backing away along the ridge. Martin didn't seem to notice; he stood in the edge of the cone of light from the torch, shaking the monkey's paw. "No, no, no. Not now, not now. Work! Have to work!" He stared down at it. "You promised. Do it. Come and do it." The monkey's paw sat silently and Martin's voice rose to a scream. "Come out! COME OUT!"

Something came out.

I can't remember what it looked like. It's not that I didn't see it; I did. But when I try to remember, all I get is a blank. I don't think it was the light. I think my mind got one glimpse and shut out the rest, like tripping a circuit breaker. I don't know why and I don't want to. Even my curiosity has its limits.

I ran. Behind me I heard Martin start to shriek, a high, horrible sound with no trace of sanity. I ran down the slope as fast as I could, every trace of my attention on the two or three seconds of footsteps ahead of me as the shrieking continued. Cool air whistled around me, the grass swishing under my feet. The shrieks rose in pitch and intensity, then abruptly cut off. The echoes rolled out over the Heath, fading into silence.

I kept running and didn't look back. I reached the edge of the Heath before collapsing against a tree, my lungs on fire and my legs shaking. Only then did I dare to look behind me. The Heath stretched out into the night, dark and empty.

I sucked in a deep breath and started running again.

ı ı ı ı ı ı ı ı ı

It was after three A.M. when I got home. The new window gleamed orange in the streetlights as I unlocked my front door with shaking hands. Once I was inside with the door closed behind me, I felt a little better. I went upstairs, stripped off my clothes, and took a shower.

I stayed under the hot water for a long time, letting the water wash away the sweat and the cold. Once I was warm again I towelled myself dry and went to my bedroom. I got halfway across the room and stopped.

The monkey's paw was resting on my bed. The cylinder was open just a crack, the inner tube pulled out half an inch but not quite enough to reveal what might be inside. I stood looking at it for a long time. "So you've come back," I said at last.

The monkey's paw sat quietly. Carefully I picked it up, and carefully I walked out of my bedroom, being very sure not to jar the cylinder and slide it open. I opened the door to my safe room and placed the monkey's paw on an empty space of table, well away from everything else. I looked down at it, then walked out, switching off the light.

Behind me, in the darkness, the monkey's paw snapped shut with a faint click.

Read on for an exciting excerpt from
Benedict Jacka's next Alex Verus novel

taken

Coming September 2012 from Ace Books

The Starbucks in Angel is on the corner of the busy inter-section of Pentonville Road and Upper Street, set deep into the offices around it but with a glass front that lets in the light. The counter's at ground level, but climbing to the first floor gives a view down onto the high street and the crowds streaming in and out of Angel station. Opposite the Starbucks is Angel Square, a huge, sprawling, weirdly designed office building checkered in orange and yellow and topped with a clock tower. The clock tower looks down onto City Road, a long downhill highway linking Kings Cross and the city. It was eleven A.M. and the morning rush was long past, but the roads and pavements were still crowded, the steady growl of engines muffled through the glass.

Inside, the shop was peaceful. Two women in professional-looking outfits chatted over their lattes and muffins, while a stolid-looking man with greying hair hid behind his *Times*. A student sat absorbed in his laptop, and three men in business suits were bent over a tableful of spreadsheets, their drinks forgotten. Music played quietly over the speakers, and the clatter of cups and coffee machines drifted up from the floor below. And near the window, my chair turned so that I could watch both the street and anyone coming in, was me.

I like the Angel Starbucks for meetings. It's easy to reach, there's a nice view, and it's just the right balance between public and private. It's quiet except at lunchtime, since most of the trendy people go to the cafes north along Upper Street, but it's not so quiet as to give anyone ideas. I'd probably like it even more if I drank coffee. Then again, given how much people like to complain about Starbucks's coffee, maybe I wouldn't.

I'd already checked out the surroundings and the other customers, so when the woman walked into the shop downstairs I was free to focus on her. There are two ways of getting a look at someone with divination magic: You can look into the futures of you approaching them, or you can look into the futures of them approaching you. The first is better if you want to study them; the second is better if you want advance warning of what they're going to do. I chose the first, and by the time the woman stepped onto the first floor, I'd been watching her for nearly a minute.

She was good-looking—*really* good-looking, with gold hair and sculpted features that made me think of old English aristocracy. She wore a cream-coloured suit that probably cost more than my entire wardrobe, and everyone in the room turned to look as she passed. The three men forgot about their spreadsheets, and the two women put their chatter on hold, watching her with narrowed eyes. Her heels clicked to a stop as she looked down at me. "Alex Verus?"

"That's me," I said.

She sat opposite, legs together. I felt the eyes of everyone in the room switch to me, comparing the woman's outfit with my rumpled trousers and sweater. Now that she was on the same level I could see that it wasn't just the heels, she really was tall, almost as tall as me. She carried nothing but a small handbag. "Coffee?"

She glanced at a slim gold watch. "I only have half an hour."

"Suits me." I leant back on the chair. "Why don't you tell me what you're after?"

"I need—"

I held up my hand. "I was hoping you might introduce yourself first."

There was a brief flash of irritation in her eyes, but it vanished quickly. "I'm Crystal."

I already knew her name. In fact, I'd gone out of my way to find out quite a bit about Crystal in the two days since she'd contacted me to request a meeting. I knew she was a Light mage, one of the "nobility" with lots of connections. I knew she wasn't a player in Council politics but had friends there. I knew the type of magic she could use, where in England she was based, and even roughly how old she was. What I didn't know was what she wanted me for—but I was about to find out. "So what can I do for you?"

"I expect you know about the White Stone?"

"The tournament?"

Crystal nodded. "Isn't it due to start soon?" I said.

"The opening ceremony will be this Friday," Crystal said. "At Fountain Reach."

"Okay."

"Fountain Reach is my family home."

My eyebrows went up at that. "Okay."

"I want you to help manage the event," Crystal said. "It's very important that everything goes smoothly."

"Manage how?"

"Providing additional protection. A diviner would be perfect for that."

"Right," I said. I've run into this a lot lately. People hear about my background and assume I must be a battle-mage. Now, it's true that I'm a mage, and it's true that I've fought battles, and it's even true that I've fought battle-mages, but that doesn't make me a battle-mage myself. "I'm not really a bodyguard."

"I'm not expecting you to serve as a battle-mage," Crystal said. "You'd be more of a . . . security consultant. Your job would be to warn me of any problems."

"What sort of problems?"

"We're expecting at least fifty mages for the tournament. Initiates and journeymen, possibly even Dark representatives as well." Crystal clasped her hands. "There'll be competition. It's possible some of the participants will carry grudges off the piste."

It sounded like a recipe for trouble. "And stopping them will be . . ."

"There'll be Council battle-mages present. We're well aware of the potential for trouble. There will be sufficient security. We just need to make sure the security is in the right place at the right time."

"You haven't received any warnings, or threats?"

"Nothing like that. There's been no suggestion of trouble so far, and we'd like your help to make sure it stays that way."

I thought about it. I've usually steered clear of Light tournaments in the past; Helikaon thought they were a waste of time, and I agreed with him. But if there were initiates there, that changed my feelings a bit. Trying to protect adult mages is a thankless task, but apprentices are another story. "What exactly would you be expecting me to do?"

"Just to keep an eye on the guests. Possibly some investigation if anything comes up. We're particularly concerned about keeping the younger apprentices safe, so we'd been hoping you could help with that."

I started to nod—and then stopped.

Crystal looked at me. "Is something wrong?"

I kept still for a second, then smiled at her. "No. Not at all. You mentioned investigation work?"

"Obviously, some mages are more likely to make trouble than others. We don't have anybody we're especially suspicious of, but it's likely things will crop up to turn our attention to someone. When they do, it would be very helpful if you could find a few things out for us."

"I assume the place is staffed?"

"Oh yes, the servants will handle all that. You'd be considered one of the guests."

"And you said the opening ceremony was on Friday. The guests will be arriving by what, Thursday?"

"Exactly." Crystal was relaxed now; the interview was going well. "We're expecting the first guests by the afternoon before, although of course the sooner you can arrive the better."

"And regarding payment?" I thought about cash, as soon as possible.

"Future service, as usual. Though if you'd prefer something more tangible, that's perfectly acceptable."

"When could you arrange payment by?"

"Immediately, of course."

"Well." I smiled at Crystal. "That settles that."

"Excellent. Then you'll be able to come?"

"No."

The smile vanished from Crystal's face. "I'm sorry?"

"Well, I'm afraid there are a couple of problems." I leant forward casually, folding one hand over the other. "The first issue is that I've had a lot of approaches like yours over the past few months. And while they all looked good on the surface, the last couple of times I've said yes they've turned out to be . . . well, let's just say I don't feel like a repeat performance."

"If you have a prior engagement, I'm sure we—"

"No, we couldn't. Because the second problem is that you've been reading my thoughts ever since you sat down."

Crystal went very still. "I'm afraid I don't follow," she said at last.

"Oh, you're very subtle," I said. "I'd guess most mages wouldn't even notice."

Crystal didn't move, and I saw the futures whirl. Flight, combat, threats. "Relax," I said. "If I was going to start a fight I wouldn't have told you about it."

The futures kept shifting for a moment longer—then settled, stable. "I'm sorry," Crystal said. She brushed back her hair, looking remorseful. "I shouldn't, I know. I was just so worried you'd say no." She met my eyes, entreating. "We need someone as skilled as you. Please, won't you help?"

I looked back at Crystal for a long second. "No," I said at last. "I won't. Good-bye, Crystal."

Again the smile vanished from Crystal's face, and this time it didn't come back. She watched me expressionlessly for a long second, then rose in a single motion and stalked away, heels clicking on the floor.

I'd known Crystal was a mind mage, but even so I hadn't noticed her spell. Active mind magic like suggestion is easy to spot if you know what to look for, but a mage who's good with passive senses, reading the thoughts that others broadcast, is much harder to catch. The only thing that had tipped me off was that Crystal had been too neat. In a real conversation no one tells you *exactly* what you want to hear.

That last reaction had made me wonder, too. Between her magic and her looks, it occurred to me that Crystal probably wasn't very used to not getting her own way. I'd better be careful around her if we met again.

I realised suddenly that everyone else in the shop was watching me. For a moment I wondered why, then smiled to myself as I understood what it must have looked like. I left my drink on the table and ran the gauntlet of stares as I walked down to the ground floor and out into the London streets.

| | | | | | | | | |

never used to get offers like these. This time last year, I could go weeks at a time without seeing another mage. In mage society I was an unknown, and all in all, that was how I liked it.

It's hard to say what changed. I used to think it was because of that business with the fateweaver, but now, looking back, I get the feeling it was more to do with me. Maybe I was just tired of being alone. Whatever it was, I had gotten involved in the magical world again, and had started getting myself a reputation.

Although not necessarily a *good* reputation. I got the fateweaver against some stiff competition, making a couple of very powerful enemies in the process, one of which came back to bite me six months later. A Light battle-mage named Belthas was trying to get sole ownership of a very nasty ritual, and when I tried to stop him, it came down to a fight. When the dust settled, Belthas was gone.

That was the point at which other mages started to take notice. Belthas had been good—*really* good, one of the most dangerous battle-mages around. All of a sudden, a lot of people were paying attention to me. After all, if I'd been able to defeat someone like Belthas, I'd be a useful tool to have on their side. And if I *wasn't* on their side . . . well, then they might have to consider doing something about that, too.

All of a sudden, I had to play politics. Take a job, and I'd be associated with whoever I agreed to work for. Turn one down, and I'd risk causing offence. Not all the job offers were nice, either. More than one Dark mage figured that since I'd knocked off one Light mage, I might be willing to do a few more, and let me tell you, those kinds of people do *not* take rejection well.

But I'm not completely new to politics, either. My

apprenticeship was to a Dark mage named Richard Drakh, in a mansion where trust was suicide and competition was quite literally a matter of life and death. It's left me with some major issues with relationships, but as a primer on power and manipulation, it's hard to beat. Crystal hadn't been the first to try to take advantage of me—and she hadn't been the first to get a surprise.

But right now, I didn't feel like dealing with that. I put Crystal out of my mind and went to go find my apprentice.

ıııııııı

M ages don't have a single base of operations—there's no central headquarters or anything like that. Instead, the Council owns a wide selection of properties around England, and they make use of them on a rotating basis. This one was an old gym in Islington, a blocky building of fading red bricks tucked away down a back street. The man at the front desk glanced up as I walked in and gave me a nod. "Hey Mr. Verus. Looking for the students?"

"Yep. And the guy waiting for me."

"Oh. Uh . . . I'm not supposed to talk about . . ."

"Yeah, I know. Thanks." I opened the door, closed it behind me, and looked at the man leaning against the side of the corridor. "You know, for someone who's not a diviner, you seem to know an awful lot about where to find me."

Talisid is middle-aged with a receding hairline, and every time I see him he always seems to be wearing the same nondescript suit. If you added a pair of glasses he'd look like a maths teacher, or maybe an accountant. He doesn't look like much at first glance, but there's something in his eyes that suggests he might be more than he seems.

I've never known exactly what to make of Talisid. He's involved with a high-up faction of the Council, but what game they're playing I don't know. "Verus," Talisid said with a nod. "Do you have a minute?"

I began walking towards the doors at the end of the hall. Talisid fell in beside me. "So," I said. "Since you're here, I'm guessing I'm either in trouble or about to get that way."

Talisid shook his head. "Has anybody ever told you you're a remarkably cynical person?"

"I like to think of it as learning from experience."

"I've never forced you to accept a job," Talisid pointed out.

"Yeah. I know."

The doors opened into a stairwell. Narrow rays of sun were streaming down through slit windows of frosted glass, catching motes of dust floating in the air. They lit up Talisid and me as we climbed, placing us in alternating light and shadow. "Okay," I said. "Hit me."

"The task I'd like your help with is likely to be difficult and dangerous," Talisid said. "It's also covered by strict Council secrecy. You may not tell anyone the details, or even that you're working for us."

I looked over my shoulder with a frown. "Why all the secrecy?"

"You'll understand once you hear the details. Whether to take the assignment is up to you, but confidentiality is not."

I thought for a second. "What about Luna?"

"The Council would prefer to limit the number of people in the know as far as possible," Talisid said. "However . . . due to the nature of the problem, I believe your apprentice might be of some help." Talisid paused. "She would also be in greater danger. The decision is yours."

We reached the top floor and stopped at the doors to the hall. "I'll be waiting down the corridor," Talisid said. "Once you've decided, come speak to me."

"Not coming in?"

"The fewer people that know of my involvement, the better," Talisid said. "I'll see you in twenty minutes."

I watched Talisid go with a frown. I've done jobs for Talisid before, and while they'd generally been successful, they hadn't been safe. In fact, most had been decidedly unsafe. If he was calling the job "difficult and dangerous" . . . I shook my head and pushed the doors open.

The top hall had once been a boxing gym. Chains hung from the ceiling, but the heavy bags had been removed, as had the ring at the centre. Mats covered the floor and light trickled in from windows high above. Two blocky ceramic constructions were set up at either end of the hall, ten feet tall and looking exactly like a pair of giant tuning forks.

Inside the room were five students and one teacher. Three of the students were against the far wall: a small, round-faced Asian girl, a blond-haired boy with glasses, and another boy with dark Indian skin and the turban of a Sikh who was keeping an noticeable distance from the first two. All looked about twenty or so. I didn't know their names but had seen them around enough times to recognise them as seniors in the apprenticeship program.

The next girl I knew a little better. She was tall and slim, with black hair that brushed her shoulders, and her name was Anne. And standing close to her (but not too close) was Luna, my apprentice.

The last person in the room was the teacher. He was twenty-eight, with short dark hair and olive-tinted skin, well-dressed and affluent-looking, and he stopped what he'd been saying as I walked in. Five sets of interested eyes turned in my direction, following the teacher's gaze.

"Hi, Lyle," I said. "Didn't know you'd taken up teaching."

Lyle hesitated. "Er—"

I waved a hand. "Don't let me interrupt. Go right ahead." I found a spot on the wall and leant against it.

"Um." Lyle looked from me to the students. "Er. The thing—Well, as I—Yes." He floundered, obviously off his groove. Lyle's never been good with surprises. I watched with eyebrows raised and an expression of mild inquiry. I didn't feel like making it easy for him.

Lyle was one of the first Light mages I met when Richard Drakh introduced me into magical society. We'd both been teenagers then, but Lyle had a few years of experience on me: His talent had developed earlier than mine, and he'd had time to learn the ins and outs of the social game. I'd been a Dark apprentice, and there'd never been any question that Lyle would try for the Council, but all the same, we became friends. We were both the type to rely on cleverness rather than strength, and our types of magic complemented each other nicely. Our goals, unfortunately, turned out to be much less compatible.

At the time I was still feeling my way, unsure of what I wanted to be. Lyle, on the other hand, knew exactly what he wanted: status, advancement, prestige, a position in the Council bureaucracy from which he could work his way upwards. And when I lost Richard's favour and with it any standing I might have had, Lyle had to choose between me and his ambitions. Supporting me would have cost him. So when I showed up six months later, alone and desperate, Lyle's response was to pretend I wasn't there. Under mage law, the master-apprentice relationship is sacred. An apprentice is their master's responsibility, no one else's. I'd defied Richard, fled from him, and it was Richard's right to do with me as he pleased. So the Light mages shut me out. They knew Richard would come to collect his runaway, and they waited for him to finish things.

But something happened then that the Light and the Dark mages did not expect. When Richard sent Tobruk—the cruellest and most powerful of his four apprentices—to kill me, it was Tobruk who died. And in the aftermath, instead of coming to take vengeance, Richard vanished, along with his last two apprentices, Rachel and Shireen. I was left alive, safe . . . and alone.

Technically, under mage law, I hadn't done anything wrong. It's not illegal for an apprentice to successfully defend himself against his master; it's just so bloody rare no one's ever bothered to pass a law against it. But I'd broken tradition older than law. An apprentice is supposed to obey his master, for good or ill, and no other mage would take me on—after all, if I'd rebelled against one master, I might rebel against another. Besides, no one was quite sure what had happened to Richard. He might be gone for good—or he might reappear, in which case nobody wanted to be anywhere near me when he did. So once again, other mages distanced themselves from me, and waited.

They waited and waited, and kept waiting so long they forgot all about me, by which time I was glad to let them do it. I started to make a new life for myself. I travelled, had some adventures. As a result of one of them I inherited a shop, a little business in the side streets of Camden Town. I'd only been planning to run it a few months, but as the months turned into years I realised I enjoyed what it brought me. The shop and the flat above it became my residence, then my home. I made new friends. Gradually, I began to remember what it was like to be happy again.

And then one day Lyle walked into my shop, and brought me back into the mage world with its politics and its alliances and its dangers. This time, I was prepared. And this time, to my surprise, I found I liked it.

I snapped out of my reverie. Lyle was talking, and seemed to have regained his confidence, though it was obvious that he'd prefer I wasn't here. "Remember that in a duel, you're representing both your master and the Council," Lyle was saying. "Now, I know some of you have done this before, but it's very important that your form is exactly right. Let's go through the basic salutes and flourishes one more time . . . Yes?"

The one who had raised her hand was Luna. "Um," Luna said. "Could you explain how these duels work?"

Lyle blinked at her. "What do you mean?"

Luna looked around to see that everyone else was

watching her. "Well . . ." She seemed to choose her words carefully. "You've explained about the selection process. And the rituals and the salutes, and the withdrawal at the end. What about the part in the middle?"

"What part?"

"Um . . . the actual duel."

From

BENEDICT JACKA

fated

An Alex Verus Novel

Alex Verus is part of a world hidden in plain sight. He runs a magic shop in London, and while Alex's own powers aren't showy, he does have the advantage of foreseeing the possible future—allowing him to pull off operations that have a million-to-one chance of success.

But when Alex is approached by multiple factions to crack open a relic from a long-ago mage war, he knows that whatever's inside must be beyond powerful—and Alex predicts that by taking the job, his odds of survival are about to go from slim to none . . .

"Harry Dresden would like Alex Verus tremendously—
and be a little nervous around him.
I just added Benedict Jacka to my must-read list."
—JIM BUTCHER

facebook.com/AceRocBooks
penguin.com

M1037T0112

DEAD WATERS

With Manhattan's Department of Extraordinary Affairs in disarray (forget vampires and zombies—it's the budget cuts that can kill you), Simon Canderous is still expected to stamp out any crime that adds the "para" to "normal." And his newest case is no exception . . .

A university professor has been found murdered in his apartment. His lungs show signs of death by drowning. But his skin and clothes? Bone-dry. Now Simon has to rely on his own powers plus a little help from his ghost-whispering partner and technomancer girlfriend—to solve a mystery that has the NYPD stumped and the D.E.A. shaken and stirred.

THE ULTIMATE WRITERS OF
SCIENCE FICTION

John Barnes	Jack McDevitt
William C. Dietz	Alastair Reynolds
Simon R. Green	Allen Steele
Joe Haldeman	S. M. Stirling
Robert Heinlein	Charles Stross
Frank Herbert	Harry Turtledove
E. E. Knight	John Varley

penguin.com/scififantasy

ACE RoC